I0641946

Fernando **Pessoa**

THE TRANSFORMATION BOOK

The Transformation Book

Edition
Notes
Introduction

Nuno
Ribeiro
& Cláudia
Souza

Selected Other Works by

Fernando Pessoa

Alexander Search *Charles James Search* *Jean Seul de Méluret* *Pantaleão*

sFORMATION Book
ook of Tasks, edited by
iro *&* Cláudia Souza

E LA TRANSFORMATION
des Tâches, édité par
iro *&* Cláudia Souza

Contra Mundum Press   New York · Berlin

A TRANSFORMAÇÃO
das Tarefas, editado por
iro *&* Cláudia Souza

Fernando
Pessoa

The Transformation Book

THE TRANSFORMATI
— or the Book of Tas
Nuno Ribeiro & Clá

LE LIVRE DE LA TRA
— ou Livre des Tâche
Nuno Ribeiro & Clá

O LIVRO DA TRANSF
— ou Livro das Taref
pela Nuno Ribeiro &

Library of Congress
Cataloguing-in-Publication Data

Pessoa, Fernando, 1888–1935

[The Transformation Book.
English. French. Portuguese.]

The Transformation Book or
Book of Tasks / Fernando Pessoa

—1st Contra Mundum Press
Edition
512 pp., 5×8 in.

ISBN 9781940625041

   I. Pessoa, Fernando.
  II. Title.
 III. Ribeiro, Nuno.
 IV. Souza, Cláudia.
  V. Introduction.
 VI. Segalini, Alessandro.
VII. Book design.

2014932358

Table of Contents

INTRODUCTION

0.1 — The Project of
The Transformation Book

This edition of Fernando Pessoa's *The Transformation Book — or Book of Tasks* is a transcription and collocation of a series of fragments that were never published during Pessoa's lifetime and are held at The Pessoa Archive in the Biblioteca Nacional de Portugal. *The Transformation Book* provides significant insight into the construction of Pessoa's plural literary universe and is, in many senses, a plural book. Its fragments are written in three languages (English, Portuguese, & French) & move between a number of literary forms (and even include translations by Pessoa): poetry, fiction, & satire accompany essays on politics, philosophy, & psychiatry. One element that makes *The Transformation Book* particularly unique is that it is not per se written by Pessoa himself but is attributed to four of his "pre-heteronyms": Alexander Search, Pantaleão, Jean Seul de Méluret, & Charles James Search.

Pessoa's pre-heteronyms are literary personalities created prior to his full-blown "heteronyms," each of which has his own authorial personality, biography, œuvre, vision of the world, and so on. In his "Bibliographical Notice," published in 1928 in the Portuguese literary review *Presença*, Pessoa introduced Alberto Caeiro, Ricardo Reis, & Álvaro de Campos as his only heteronyms. The first public appearance of one of these heteronyms occurred in the modernist Portuguese review *Orpheu*, when Pessoa published the "Opiary" and the "Triumphal Ode" of Álvaro de Campos — but by that time he had already written under the names of dozens of pre-heteronyms.[1] *The Transformation Book* belongs to this so-called pre-heteronymic period, and Alexander Search, Pantaleão, Jean Seul de Méluret, & Charles James Search can be counted among Pessoa's pre-heteronyms. These four figures already constitute a plural literary microcosm — a world that Pessoa makes, but that is occupied by a multiplicity of authors — and clearly anticipate the emergence of Pessoa's heteronyms.

---

1. The number of Pessoa's literary personalities and, therefore, pre-heteronyms (as a kind of literary personality), remains a matter of dispute. In the book *Pessoa por Conhecer*, Teresa Rita Lopes counts 72 literary personalities, most of which are produced in the pre-heteronymic period (that is, before 1915). Recent studies have radically revised that number, claiming there are over 100 literary personalities. Regarding this subject, see also: Fernando Pessoa, *Teoria da Heteronímia*, ed. by Richard Zenith & Fernando Cabral Martins (Lisbon: Assírio & Alvim, 2013); José Paulo Cavalcanti Filho, *Fernando Pessoa: uma quase autobiografia* (Rio de Janeiro / São Paulo: Ediora Record, 2011); Fernando Pessoa, *Eu sou uma antologia: 136 autores fictícios*, ed. by Jeronimo Pizarro & Patricio Ferrari (Lisbon: Tinta da China, 2013).

The Transformation Book was conceived by Pessoa in 1908, a year of great social & cultural transformation in Portugal — on February 1st of that year, King Carlos & his heir, Luís Filipe, the Royal Prince, were both assassinated. This double-assassination set off a series of political convulsions that led to the rapid dissolution of the Portuguese monarchy after the revolution of October 5, 1910 — and thereafter, to the ratification of the Constitution of the First Portuguese Republic. The projects and text-fragments Pessoa created for *The Transformation Book* were written, for the most part, in the period that begins with the Portuguese regicide & ends with the fall of the Portuguese monarchy. Animated by the revolutionary spirit following the regicide, *The Transformation Book* was designed to reflect and advance social and cultural transformation in Portugal — and even beyond its borders. This work, then, is the singular result of an intersection of Pessoa's personal intellectual trajectory with his hopes for fomenting cultural transformation.

Although Portuguese by nationality, Pessoa spent most of his childhood and early youth in South Africa, where his stepfather, João Miguel Rosa, began to serve as Portuguese consul in 1886. As a result, Pessoa had an English education & immersed himself in English poetry & prose, which deeply affected the development of his work.[2] In 1905, Pessoa returned to Portugal to study at the Curso Superior de Letras (Superior Course of Letters) at the University of Lisbon, between 1905 and 1907. In this period, Pessoa read books by and about numerous figures and movements in the philosophical tradition, from the pre-Socratics to early twentieth-century philosophers such as Henri Bergson.[3] In addition, probably as a result of his proximity to his grandmother Dionísia — who suffered from mental disorders — Pessoa also began to study human psychism (phrenology & psychiatry), reading the texts of psychiatrists such as Cesare Lombroso, Charles Feré, Charles Binet-Sanglé, Max Nordau and Théodule-Armand Ribot, among others.[4] Coupled with the social & cultural changes that followed the Portuguese regicide, the English education Pessoa had received in

2. For further information regarding Pessoa's English education, see the "Introduction" to: Fernando Pessoa, *Philosophical Essays: A Critical Edition*, ed. by Nuno Ribeiro (New York: Contra Mundum Press, 2012).

3. For other analyses of Pessoa's interest in philosophy, cf. Nuno Ribeiro, *Tradição e Pluralismo nos Escritos Filosóficos de Fernando Pessoa / Escritos Filosóficos de Fernando Pessoa* (Lisbon: Faculdade de Ciências Sociais e Humanas da Universidade Nova de Lisboa, 2012); Fernando Pessoa, *Philosophical Essays*, ibid; António de Pina Coelho, *Os Fundamentos Filosóficos da Obra de Fernando Pessoa, Vols I e II* (Lisbon: Editorial Verbo, 1971); Pablo Javier Pérez Lopez, *Poesía, Ontología y Tragedia en Fernando Pessoa* (Madrid: Editorial Manuscritos, 2012).

South Africa — as well as his interest in philosophy and the sciences of human psychism — would deeply affect the construction of *The Transformation Book*. Pessoa outlines biographies for each of the four pre-heteronyms involved in that project — with the exception of Pantaleão, whose identity Pessoa purposefully conceals — while he also enumerates the literary tasks assigned to each of them. The complex history of these four pre-heteronyms necessitates a brief review of their characters, œuvres, & inter-relationships.

0.1.1 — Alexander Search

The first pre-heteronym one encounters in *The Transformation Book* is Alexander Search, and Pessoa's creation of him has a very intricate structure and history. He appears at the crossroads of the definition of other literary pre-heteronyms — and even, of Pessoa himself. According to the biographical data in *The Transformation Book*, Alexander Search was "Born [on] June 13th 1888,

---

4. For a detailed discussion of Pessoa's readings related to human psychism, cf. Cláudia Souza, *Ciências do Psiquismo Humano, Política e Criação Literária no Espólio de Fernando Pessoa (1905–1914)* (Belo Horizonte: PUC — Minas Gerais, 2011); Kenneth Krabbenhoft, *Fernando Pessoa e as Doenças do fim de Século* (Lisbon: Imprensa Nacional-Casa da Moeda, 2011); Jerónimo Pizarro, *Fernando Pessoa: entre génio e loucura* (Lisbon: Imprensa-Nacional Casa da Moeda, 2007).

at Lisbon,"[5] and his task is "not the province of the other three," that is, it does not pertain to the other three pre-heteronyms of this book. In addition, Pessoa assigns five different literary tasks to Search: first, a political essay ("The Portuguese Regicide and the Political Situation in Portugal"); second, an essay on philosophy ("The Philosophy of Rationalism"); third, an essay on psychiatry ("The Mental Disorder(s) of Jesus"); and finally, two collections of poems ("Delirium" and "Agony").

The resemblance between the biographical data of Alexander Search and Pessoa is immediately apparent. Alexander Search is born (we are told) in the same city & on the same date as Pessoa. Pessoa attached so much importance to this pre-heteronym that he even created a business card for him and received letters addressed to Alexander Search, which reveals the proximity between Pessoa & the interests he delegated to Alexander Search.

5. BNP/E3, 48C — 2.

LISBON   Rua da Bella Vista (Lapa), 17, 1.º

[BNP/E3, 26 — 65ᵛ]

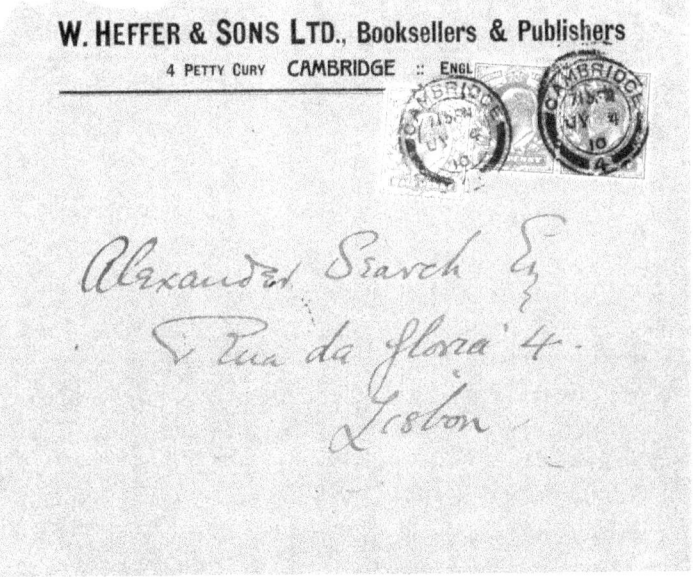

[BNP/E3, 35 — 25ᵛ]

But the problems related to the definition of this pre-heteronym are far more convoluted than this obvious proximity to Pessoa's own biography might suggest, for Pessoa also establishes the proximity — &, in a certain period, the identity — between Alexander Search and another of his pre-heteronyms: Charles Robert Anon.[6] In fact, at the end of a humorous English poem entitled "Elegy," one reads this enigmatic signature:

C. R. Anon

id est Alexander Search.

[BNP/E3, 78B — 55ʳ]

6. We have explored in detail the problems related to the Anon–Search relation elsewhere: Nuno Ribeiro, Cláudia Souza, "Charles Robert Anon & Alexander Search: filosofia e psiquiatria," in *Revista Filosófica de Coimbra*, Vol. 21, Nº 42 (Coimbra: Instituto de Estudos Filosóficos da Faculdade de Letras da Universidade de Coimbra, 2012) 541–556.

This signature may suggest that Pessoa intended, in a certain period of his literary production, to establish a parity between Charles Robert Anon and Alexander Search. These two pre-heteronyms do share a number of works found in The Pessoa Archive. Although it is true that there are marked resemblances between these two pre-heteronyms & their respective outputs, there are dissimilarities between them too. They have different biographies & were created at different periods. Charles Robert Anon appears in the 1903 notebooks, while Alexander Search's earliest poems date from the beginning of 1904 — though Search inherits, in many cases, Anon's works. This is probably why Pessoa decided, at least for a time, to establish the "identity" of these pre-heteronyms.

Moreover, Pessoa casts Alexander Search as the character in his theatrical play *Ultimus Joculatorum*, under the name of Cæsar Seek. In the cast of this play, one reads the following:

Ultimus Joculatorum.

Persons:

Cæsar Seek (= Alexander Search) whose character is without laughter, moving from deep thought & torturing to bitterness (bitterly joking sometimes ? ? ?)

Dr. Nabos: whose character goes from bitterness to open mirth

Ferdinand Sumwan (= Fernando Pessoa, since Sum-
wan = Some one = Person = Pessoa) A normal,
useless, lazy, careless, weak, individual.

[BNP/E3, 48C – 18]

In this cast, corresponding to some of the characters
of a play that Pessoa intended to write but never com-
pleted, Alexander Search is described as Caesar Seek, a
character who is "without laughter, moving from deep
thought and torturing to bitterness." This description of
Caesar Seek catches the spirit of Alexander Search's po-
etry quite well. Curiously, Pessoa himself appears as one
of the characters of *Ultimus Joculatorum* — Ferdinand
Sumwan. Pessoa provides an intriguing explanation for
the surname Sumwan, since "Sumwan" is not — as it
might appear — a pseudo-Japanese name, but rather a
phonetic mask for "some one," thus for "Person," the Eng-
lish word for "Pessoa." Regarding Pessoa's description of
Alexander Search (i.e., Cæsar Seek), it also rather pre-
cisely fits an autobiographical text signed by Search:

> No soul more loving or tender than mine has
> ever existed, no soul so full of kindness, of pity,
> of all the things of tenderness *&* of love. Yet no
> soul is so lonely as mine — not lonely, be it noted,
> from exterior, but from interior circumstances. I
> mean this: together with my great tenderness *&*

kindness an element of an entirely opposite kind enters into my character, an element of sadness, of self-centeredness, of selfishness therefore, whose effect is two-fold: to warp and hinder the development and full *internal* play of those other qualities, and to hinder, by affecting the will depressingly, their full *external* play, their manifestation.

[BNP/E3, 20 – 1ʳ]

0.1.2 — Pantaleão

The second pre-heteronym of *The Transformation Book* is Pantaleão. Pessoa purposefully omits Pantaleão's biographical data, saying only this: "(if necessary give true name)."[7] Pessoa attributes four literary texts to this pre-heteronym: first, an essay that includes a psychiatric analysis of the Portuguese social context, "A Psychose Adeantativa" (The Advancing Psychosis); second, a satirical text in oracular style, "As Visões do Sñr. Pantaleão" (The Visions of Mr. Pantaleão); third, a seemingly banal political essay, "A Nossa Administração Colonial" (Our Colonial Administration); and fourth, a collection of verses, "Versos do Sñr. Pantaleão" (The Verses of Mr. Pantaleão).

---

7. BNP/E3, 48C – 3ʳ.

The fact that Pessoa omits all biographical data for Pantaleão seems to indicate that this pre-heteronym is in fact a pseudonym of one of his *other* pre-heteronyms. Indeed, Pessoa's practice of giving pseudonyms to his pre-heteronyms dates to one of the earliest literary journals of his youth, written between 1902 & 1905, *O Palrador* (*The Twitter*). The series of journals titled *O Palrador* — together with the single, even earlier journal *A Palavra* (*The Word*) — preserves Pessoa's earliest stage of experimentation. In this series of journals, one finds a group of literary personalities who cooperate with each other. Adolph Moscow is entrusted with the task of writing a romance, *Os Rapazes de Barrowby* (*The Boys of Barrowby*); Marvell Kisch is the author of a romance titled *Os Milhões de um Doido* (*The Millions of a Crazy Man*); and Eduardo Lança is a Brazilian poet, to whom Pessoa attributes the authorship of several books of poems. These are just a handful of the pre-heteronyms dating from Pessoa's first pre-heteronymic period. One of the *O Palrador* manuscripts, dated July 1903, already includes pseudonyms of Pessoa's pre-heteronyms: Pad-Zé, for instance, a pseudonym of Roberto Kóla; & Dr. Pancrácio, a pseudonym of Francisco Páu. Similarly, we may assume that Pantaleão is the pseudonym of one of Pessoa's more mature pre-heteronyms.[8]

Pessoa's choice of the name Pantaleão is itself illuminating, considering the task of social criticism this pre-heteronym is given: *Pantaleão* is Portuguese for "Pantaloon," a stock character in the Italian *Commedia dell'arte.*

"Pantaloon" was a critical character, usually a greedy merchant (and advisor) from Venice — and both criticism and instruction are elements that define Pantaleão,[9] who is characterized as a pessimistic pre-heteronym. He maintains a critical attitude towards life and his own epoch, as can be seen in an aphorism attributed to him:

Pantaleão.
Life is an evil worthy of being enjoyed.
[A vida é um mal digno de ser gosado.]

[BNP/E3, 27³H — 29ʳ]

───────────

8. Pseudonyms were one of the commonest means employed by Pessoa's contemporaries when they feared persecution by the government, and it seems reasonable to assume that Pessoa created Pantaleão as the pseudonym of a pre-heteronym who was politically engaged in current events and a caustic critic of the Portuguese monarchy.

9. For discussions on the relation between the creation of Pantaleão & its roots in the character of Pantaloon of the *Commedia dell'arte*, cf. Cláudia Souza, *Ciências do Psiquismo Humano, Política e Criação Literária no espólio de Fernando Pessoa (1905–1914)* (Belo Horizonte: PUC — Minas Gerais, 2011); Aníbal Frias, "Pessoa à Coimbra et Coimbra dans Pessoa," *Biblos, VII* (Coimbra: Faculdade de Letras da Universidade de Coimbra, 2009) 363–387.

0.1.3 — Jean Seul de Méluret

The third pre-heteronym of *The Transformation Book* is Jean Seul de Méluret, who was "supposed to [have] be[en] born in 1885 on the 1ˢᵗ. [of] August, [and is] one year older than Charles Search and three [years] older than Alexander."[10] Pessoa specifies that Méluret's task is to write "in French — poetry *&* satire or scientific works with a satirical or moral purpose."[11] Pessoa explicitly attributes the authorship of three scientific and satirical fictions to this pre-heteronym, all of which are created with a moral purpose: first, "Des Cas d'Exhibitionnisme" (The Cases of Exhibitionism); second, "La France en 1950" (France in 1950); and third, "Messieurs les Souteneurs" (Gentlemen Pimps). Animated by Pessoa's readings on psychiatry, Méluret was meant to deliver a critique of the French society of Pessoa's day: Méluret regarded early twentieth-century France as a decadent *&* degenerate society.[12] The following fragment, originally written in

10. BNP/E3, 48C — 4ʳ.

11. Ibid.

12. On the relation between Jean Seul de Méluret and the critique of French society, cf. Cláudia Souza, *Ciências do Psiquismo Humano, Política e Criação Literária no espólio de Fernando Pessoa (1905–1914)* (Belo Horizonte: PUC — Minas Gerais, 2011); Teresa Rita Lopes, *Pessoa por Conhecer, Vol. I* (Lisbon: Editorial Estampa, 1990); Fernando Pessoa, *Obras de Jean Seul de Méluret*, ed. by Rita Patrício and Jerónimo Pizarro (Lisbon: Imprensa Nacional-Casa da Moeda, 2006).

French, is representative of Méluret's critique of French society:

> The case of France is sad in an entirely different way. Despite its enormous vitality, it is already in a state of decadence — decadence of such order that its vitality can't hide it — and be that cause either social or political, the hope of □ is much weaker and without basis.
>
> [BNP/E3, 92E — 43ʳ]

Though Pessoa says in *The Transformation Book* that Méluret has the task of writing poetry in French — along with scientific *&* satirical fictions — one doesn't find any explicit reference to poems in the enumeration of Méluret's works to be included in the project. Pessoa presumably thought it better to leave them out, but in The Pessoa Archive one finds this example of the poetic activity of Méluret (also originally written in French):

> Seul
>
> Nothing is; everything passes
> Everything is its own flow,
> The day gives up
> On being day.
> The tears that roll
> Already fall

The eyes that □
The times — vulture.
Roll then ball
    "   " roll,
Always, always.

[BNP/E3, 50A¹ — 14ʳ: detail of the fragment below]

0.1.4 — Charles James Search

The fourth pre-heteronym of *The Transformation Book* is Charles James Search, the elder brother of Alexander, who is "supposed to [have been] born in 1886 and therefore to be two years older than Alexander."[13] His task is an accessory one: "solely that of translation." But Pessoa explains further that Search may "write the prefaces to his translations if these do not involve analysis, etc., when they will be written by Alexander."[14] Charles Search is assigned a list of nine translations: one from the Spanish Romantic poet, José de Espronceda, & eight from various Portuguese sources:

1. Espronceda's "Student of Salamanca."

2. Anthero de Quental's "Complete Sonnets." (together with pessimistic pieces — ? —).

3. Couto Guerreiro's "Epigrams."

4. Sonnets (chosen) of Camoens.

5. Guerra Junqueiro — Choice.

6. Eça de Queiroz's "The Mandarin."

7. "Some Sonnets from Portugal." (excluding those separately translated).

---

13. BNP/E3, 48C — 5ʳ. Charles's precise date of birth, indicated by Pessoa, is "18ᵗʰ April 1886."

14. Ibid.

8. Henrique Rosa's Poems (some).

9. Almeida Garret — Choice.[15]

[BNP/E3, 48C — 5^r]

Considering that Pessoa worked as a translator through-out his life, handling commercial letters for several companies, the creation of a pre-heteronym exclusively devoted to the task of translation is especially significant. The task of translation assigned to Charles Search anticipates, in many respects, the kind of task that will later be delegated to other personalities created for the purpose of translating and disseminating Portuguese authors. In the heteronymic period, for instance, Pessoa fabricated Thomas Crosse with the purpose of translating Portuguese works — among them Alberto Caeiro's (one of Pessoa's heteronyms) *The Keeper of Sheep* — and in many cases, of writing prefaces to these translations. A comparison of the above list of Charles James Search's translations and the following list of Thomas Crosse's translations clarifies the importance of Charles Search for Pessoa's future personalities:

15. José de Espronceda (1808–1842); Anthero de Quental (1842–1891); Miguel do Couto Guerreiro (ca. 1720–1793); Luís de Camões (1524–1580); Abílio Guerra Junqueiro (1850–1923); Eça de Queirós (1845–1900); Henrique dos Santos Rosa (1850–1924); João Baptista de Almeida Garrett (1799–1854).

Thomas Crosse: Some Portuguese Poets [↓Writers]

I have chosen rather lesser known, *&* unjustly unknown, poets:

1. The Poetry of the Song-Books.

2. Chriſtovam Falcão *&* Bernardim Ribeiro.

3. José Anaſtacio da Cunha.

4. Anthero de Quental.

5. Guerra Junqueiro.

6. Cesario Verde.

7. Decadents *&* Pessimiſts.

8. The "Sensationiſts."[16]

The liſt attributed to Thomas Crosse is not an exaĉt replica of Charles' liſt. Since Charles Search's liſt was written around 1908 *&* Thomas Crosse's around 1915, they reveal the evolution of Pessoa's literary intereſts.

---

16. Cristovão Falcão (1512–1557); Bernardim Ribeiro (1482–1552); José Anaſtácio da Cunha (1744–1787); Cesário Verde (1855–1886).

143-5

Thomas Crosse: Some Portuguese Poets
writers

I have chosen rather lesser know, & unjustly
unknown, poets:

1. The Poetry of the Sing. Birds.

2. Christovam Falcão & Bernardim
Ribeiro.

3. José Anastacio da Cunha.

4. Anthero de Quental.

5. Guerra Junqueiro.

6. Cesario Verde.

7. Decadents and Pessimists.

8. The "Sensationists".

[BNP/E3, 143-5^r]

0.2 — The Genesis of Pessoa's "Drama in People"

The Transformation Book marks one of the fundamental stages in Pessoa's elaboration of a new conception of literary space, one that he came to express as a "drama in people." With his creation of heteronyms and his labors in a plurality of literary genres and styles, Pessoa constructs a heterogeneous image of literary space, dramatically inhabited by a plurality of figures. Thus, in a text titled "Aspects," which Pessoa wrote as an introduction to a collection of works by his heteronyms that he intended to publish (but never did), we read this:

> The Complete Work is essentially dramatic, though it takes different forms — prose passages in this first volume, poems & philosophies in the other volumes. It's the product of the temperament I've been blessed or cursed with — I'm not sure which. All I know is that the author of these lines (I'm not sure if also of these books) has never had just one personality, & has never thought or felt except dramatically — that is, through invented persons, or personalities, who are more capable than he of feeling what's to be felt.

There are authors who write plays *&* novels, and they often endow the characters of their plays and novels with feelings and ideas that they insist are not their own. Here the substance is the same, though the form is different. [17]

This excerpt from a fragment of "Aspects" indicates how Pessoa sees his "drama in people." The notion of drama — of dramatic play — is the point of departure for Pessoa's constitution of a new literary space. Dramatic play is the *substance* of his literary production, although he alters its typical structures or *forms*. In Pessoa's "Essay about Drama," he elaborates on this:

The drama, as an objective whole, is organically composed of three parts — the people or characters; the interaction of those people; and the action or fable, by which *&* through which that interaction occurs and those people appear. [18]

What here specifically characterizes drama is the fact that the characters, their interactions, and the 'fable'

17. Fernando Pessoa, *Selected Prose of Fernando Pessoa*, ed. *&* tr. by Richard Zenith (New York: Grove Press, 2001) 1.
18. Fernando Pessoa, *Obra Poética e em Prosa, Vol. III* (Porto: Lello *&* Irmãos — Editores, 1986) 106. We are responsible for the translations, in which we quote directly from the Portuguese.

through which their interactions occur, are all gathered into a unique text that constitutes the play's organic form. With the creation of the heteronyms, Pessoa changes that form. He not only develops a multiplicity of styles but roots each style in a certain personality that bears its own name and biography, authors its own texts, expresses distinctive ideas, and espouses literary & philosophical points of view. In the "Bibliographical Notice" Pessoa published in 1928 in *Presença*, he outlines these ideas in part:

> The heteronymic works of Fernando Pessoa were produced, until now, by three people — Alberto Caeiro, Ricardo Reis, & Álvaro de Campos. These three individuals must be considered as distinct from their author. Each one forms a kind of drama; & all together they form another drama.[19]

In the sequence of the text Pessoa adds:

> The works of these three poets form, as said, a dramatic set; and the intellectual interactions among these personalities, as well as their own personal relations, are studied in detail. All this will contain biographies to be made, together,

19. Fernando Pessoa, "Tábua Bibliográfica," *Presença* Nº 17 (1928) 10.

when published, with horoscopes and, maybe, with photos. It is a drama in people, instead of a drama in acts.[20]

In this way, Pessoa fractures dramatic form. His construction of a heteronymic literary space as a "drama in people" is created through a progressive establishment of differences among the various heteronyms. Similarly, among the biographies created by Pessoa for the various pre-heteronyms in *The Transformation Book*, one finds several 'dramatic' cross-references. In Alexander Search's biography, for instance, Pessoa delimits his work as being "*not* the province of the other three." Then, in Pessoa's description of Charles James Search, one reads that he "may write prefaces to his translation if these do not involve analysis, etc., when they will be written by Alexander."

The Transformation Book can then be seen as the genesis of Pessoa's elaborate "drama in people." Pessoa's pre-heteronyms are defined — much as in his later, heteronymic "drama in people" — in this book by progressive differentiations among their lives, styles, and concerns. In this way, *The Transformation Book* is a crucial text for understanding Pessoa's gradual creation of the heteronyms.

---

20. Ibid.

0.3 — *The Transformation Book*: Previous Announcements & Publications

Although some of the texts conceived as part of *The Transformation Book* have previously been published in isolation or as fragments, this is the first complete and critical edition of *The Transformation Book*, and most of the texts in this edition are published here for the first time.

The first and, perhaps, most important announcement of *The Transformation Book* occurs in Teresa Rita Lopes' *Pessoa por Conhecer*. In the context of enumerating several of Pessoa's literary personalities (heteronyms, semi-heteronyms, pre-heteronyms, etc.), Lopes presents the biographies of various pre-heteronyms contained in *The Transformation Book* and refers to some of the fragments that Pessoa regarded as forming a part of it. [21]

---

21. Other recent studies provide further important data regarding the personalities contained in the project of *The Transformation Book*. Cf. Cláudia Souza, *Ciências do Psiquismo Humano, Política e Criação Literária no Espólio de Fernando Pessoa (1905–1914)* (Belo Horizonte: PUC — Minas Gerais, 2011); Nuno Ribeiro, *Tradição e Pluralismo nos Escritos Filosóficos de Fernando Pessoa / Escritos Filosóficos de Fernando Pessoa* (Lisbon: Faculdade de Ciências Sociais e Humanas da Universidade Nova de Lisboa, 2012); Nuno Ribeiro, *Fernando Pessoa e Nietzsche: O pensamento da pluralidade* (Lisbon: Verbo Editora, 2011); Fernando Pessoa, *Teoria da Heteronímia*, ed. by Richard Zenith and Fernando

Other publications contain some of the titles of texts meant to be included in *The Transformation Book*, but none of them present the book as a whole. And even where there have been previous publications of texts from the project, the presentation of these texts differs considerably. Not only does our critical edition include both "Part I" and "Part II — Addenda" (containing previously unknown fragments),[22] but here, wherever possible, texts are arranged according to the indications Pessoa left in his papers (which are not always accurately reflected in previous editions). Moreover, in a number of places, our edition includes corrections of previous transcriptions, hopefully making for a more accurate if not definitive version.

Poemas Ingleses, an edition of Pessoa's English poetry attributed to Alexander Search,[23] includes poems that

Cabral Martins (Lisbon: Assírio & Alvim, 2013); José Paulo Cavalcanti Filho, *Fernando Pessoa: uma quase auto-biografia* (Rio de Janeiro/São Paulo: Ediora Record, 2011); Fernando Pessoa, *Eu sou uma antologia: 136 autores fictícios*, ed. by Jeronimo Pizarro & Patricio Ferrari (Lisbon: Tinta da China, 2013).

22. It is impossible to state exactly the precise number of unpublished texts considering the amount of articles and books concerning new aspects of The Pessoa Archive that have been and are currently being published. Many editions risk asserting the amount of unpublished fragments they are offering and afterwards discover that some of them had already been published. As a guide, we refer to the main editions of Pessoa's works.

23. See: Fernando Pessoa, *Poemas Ingleses — Poemas de Alexander*

Pessoa designed for his projects "Delirium" & "Agony."
That edition collocates Pessoa's texts according to the
lists of poems that he left with the titles just listed, but
in our view, this criterion is unreliable. Pessoa left several
lists for the same group of poems, many of which have
only an experimental character and are, in a number of
places, inconsistent among themselves (i.e., giving differ-
ent numbers and titles). A clear example of this appears
in the lists that Pessoa left for "Delirium," as is evident
by looking at the lists transcribed in the addenda to our
edition (Part II, 1.2). In Pessoa's list for "Agony" (Part II,
1.3), problems arise again, since it only indicates the title
of a single poem, while The Pessoa Archive houses many
more poems signed by Search that evidently belong to
the same project. Consequently, we have decided to in-
clude here all of the documents containing poems signed
by Search & explicitly assigned to "Delirium" & "Agony."

Escritos sobre Génio e Lourcura, which appeared in
2006, reproduces some of Pessoa's fragments on "The
Mental Disorder of Jesus."[24] In our edition (Part I, 1.3),
however, these fragments are ordered according to the
numerous indications left by Pessoa in his manuscripts

Search, Tomo II, Vol. V, ed. by João Dionísio (Lisbon: Imprensa
Nacional-Casa da Moeda, 1997).

24. See: Fernando Pessoa, *Escritos sobre Génio e Loucura, Vols I and
II*, ed. by Jerónimo Pizarro (Lisbon: Imprensa Nacional-Casa
da Moeda, 2006).

— indications not always honored in *Escritos*. Also in-cluded here are texts related to the subject of "The Mental Disorder of Jesus" but which are absent in *Escritos*, among which one, titled "Character of Christ," specifically deals with the problem of Christ's degenerative stigmata.

The fragments included in our edition under the title "The Philosophy of Rationalism" also appeared in our 2012 critical edition of Pessoa's *Philosophical Essays*.[25] This is the only instance of a re-publication from that book.

Pantaleão is perhaps the least known of the pre-heter-onyms encountered in *The Transformation Book*, which is likely due to the fact that his texts — namely, the "Visões" (Visions) (Part I, 2.2) — can be counted among the most difficult to transcribe in The Pessoa Archive. In Teresa Rita Lopes's *Pessoa por Conhecer*, one finds a transcription of only one segment of the preface to "Visões," and part of Pessoa's project for that work.[26] Moreover, in *Escritos*, one finds a transcription of the few remaining fragments of Pantaleão's text, "A Psychose Adeantativa" (The Advancing Psychosis), which are also published in our edition.[27]

---

25. Fernando Pessoa, *Philosophical Essays*, ibid.
26. Teresa Rita Lopes, *Pessoa por Conhecer*, Vol. II (Lisbon: Editorial Estampa, 1990) 211.
27. Cf: Fernando Pessoa, *Escritos sobre Génio e Loucura*, Vol. I, 237–241. In this case, there was not much to change regarding the structure presented in *Escritos*, since the remaining fragments are very brief and appear, in The Pessoa Archive, in almost the exact order they should be published.

Jean Seul de Méluret is the subject of *Obras de Jean Seul de Méluret* (2006),[28] which includes a detailed collocation of the French texts attributed or attributable to that pre-heteronym. Our edition differs from *Obras* in terms of the organization of Méluret's texts, as well as — in some cases — their transcription. As announced in the introduction to *Obras*, the editors risked a "conjectural" organization of certain fragments that do not bear any indications regarding their placement. In our edition, Méluret's French fragments are collocated according to Pessoa's own indications, while fragments that provide no indication regarding their placement, or are only conjecturally attributed to one of Méluret's French texts, are placed in the "Addenda."

Finally, Charles James Search is — alongside Pantaleão — one of the lesser-known pre-heteronyms in *The Transformation Book*. The fact that Charles Search is only given the task of translation resulted in Pessoa scholars' cool indifference towards this pre-heteronym. However, recent studies about Pessoa's role as translator have prompted scholars to reevaluate the role of Charles James Search. *Pessoa Inédito*,[29] for instance, includes a

28. See: Fernando Pessoa, *Obras de Jean Seul de Méluret*, ed. by Rita Patrício and Jerónimo Pizarro, (Lisbon: Imprensa Nacional-Casa da Moeda, 2006).

29. Maria Rosa Baptista, "2.3. ...e fez traduções..." in Teresa Rita Lopes (org.), *Pessoa Inédito* (Lisbon: Livros Horizonte, 1993) 76–80; Maria Rosa Baptista, "2.5. *Tradutor*" in Teresa Rita Lopes (org.), *Pessoa Inédito* (Lisbon: Livros Horizonte, 1993) 212–225.

chapter devoted to Pessoa's role as translator, including many examples of his planned translation projects — among them, a translation of Anthero de Quental's poetry.[30] Although Ferrari's *Os Sonetos Completos de Anthero de Quental* contains a transcription of Pessoa's translation fragments for "Anthero de Quental's 'Complete Sonnets,'"[31] our edition includes a complete transcription of all of the genetical elements in Pessoa's original document (Part I, 4.1). There are also transcriptional differences between Ferrari's edition & ours.

In conclusion, our complete edition of Pessoa's *The Transformation Book* marks a significant effort to better understand and more accurately represent a crucial period in Pessoa's development as a writer.

0.4 — The Collocation of the Present Edition & the Fragments of *The Transformation Book*

The present edition is divided into two parts. Part I contains all of the fragments of *The Transformation Book* — or *Book of Tasks* that we were able to identify as such

30. See: Teresa Rita Lopes (org.), *Pessoa Inédito* (Lisbon: Livros Horizonte, 1993).

31. See the Appendix to Anthero de Quental, *Os sonetos Completos de Anthero de Quental*, ed. by Patricio Ferrari (Lisbon: Guimarães, 2010) 171–250.

in The Pessoa Archive. These fragments are organized according to the plans that Pessoa left for that project, in manuscript, to these pre-heteronyms: Alexander Search, Pantaleão, Jean Seul de Méluret, and Charles James Search. The sequences of texts by each pre-heteronym are preceded by a transcription of their respective biographies, along with Pessoa's enumeration of the literary tasks to be undertaken by each one. Part II includes other biographical texts and fragments variously related to the literary output of these four pre-heteronyms.

This edition opens with the texts attributed to Alexander Search, whose biography & literary tasks follow in Part I, section 1.0. Part II, section 1.0, contains other biographical texts that enable one to understand the construction of Alexander Search's literary character.

The first text by Alexander Search is "The Portuguese Regicide & the Political Situation in Portugal."[32] This work was conceived as a political essay about the national and institutional decay of Portuguese society, and is written with the purpose of triggering a revolution in Portugal. As a matter of fact, in a biographical text signed by Alexander Search & transcribed herein (Part II, 1.0), this intent is stated explicitly:

---

32. The Pessoa Archive holds a series of documents, numbered from 1 to 24, containing the beginning of that work, transcribed in this edition as Part I, section 1.1.

> Besides my patriotic projects — writing of "Por-
> tuguese Regicide" — to provoke a revolution here,
> writing of Portuguese pamphlets, editing of older
> national literary works, creation of a magazine,
> of a scientific review, etc.
>
> [BNP/E3, 20 — 5ʳ]

The remaining fragments of "The Portuguese Regicide"
begin with a comparison of the human organism and
the social or political organism, drawing special atten-
tion to the notions of "forces of integration" & "forces
of disintegration" in organic entities. The notions of
individual and collective organisms debated through-
out this essay are very similar to those discussed by
Friedrich Nietzsche regarding the self as a multiplicity
& the structure of the political body.[33] It is impossible
not to recall Nietzsche's assertions concerning the plu-
ral structure of the self when one reads the following
excerpt from "The Portuguese Regicide":

> But it should be remembered that the organism
> is fundamentally *many* (that is, composite) and
> not *one*. [...] Because the essence of the organism

---

33. For an exploration of this subject, see: Nuno Ribeiro, "O Corpo
Político e a Política do Corpo em Nietzsche e Pessoa," in Paulo
Borges (org.), *Olhares Europeus sobre Pessoa* (Lisbon: Centro
de Filosofia da Universidade de Lisboa, 2010) 231–238.

is not unity but multiplicity (though it exists by being a unity), which is easily seen when we, considering its dual nature of one and multiple, examine whether it can be described as "unity made multiplicity" or better as "multiplicity made unity."

[BNP/E3, 79A — 75a-74a]

The second text attributed to Alexander Search in our edition is "The Philosophy of Rationalism" (Part I, 1.2), a philosophical essay that corresponds to the third stage of the "Essay on the Nature & Meaning of Rationalism" in Pessoa's *Philosophical Essays*.[34] Pessoa left this text in his archive of projects and gave several titles to the series of English fragments on rationalism, including the title "Essay on the Nature & Meaning of Rationalism."[35] The second[36] & third[37] stages of this work contain only the indication "rationalism," without any clue as to the complete title of the series of documents produced during those stages. In The Pessoa Archive, one finds at least two other titles: first, "The Meaning of Rationalism,"[38]

---

34. For further details regarding this subject, see: Fernando Pessoa, *Philosophical Essays*, XXXII–XLIV.

35. BNP/E3, 15⁵ — 78-79.

36. BNP/E3, 15³ — 37-45; 133F, 64-64a.

37. BNP/E3, 15² — 62-70; 55G — 24ʳ; 15¹ — 45-47; 15⁵-19.

38. BNP/E3, 48C¹— 48ʳ.

with a parenthetical earmark "(for Rationalist Press Asso-
ciation)"; & second, "The Philosophy of Rationalism,"[39]
a title attributed to Search in the plan of works designed
for him in *The Transformation Book*. "The Philosophy
of Rationalism" was the last title conceived by Pessoa for
that project of Alexander's. If we assume that the title
"The Meaning of Rationalism" corresponds to the second
stage of the writings about rationalism, and that "The
Philosophy of Rationalism" corresponds to the third
& last stage, we have reasons to publish the third stage
of that group of writings under the name of Alexander
Search.

The third text attributed to Alexander Search in *The
Transformation Book* and included in our edition is
the "Mental Disorder of Jesus" (Part I, 1.3), a psychiatric
essay concerned with the possible madness of Jesus of
Nazareth. As registered in the project transcribed above,
this essay is a commentary on and a critique of Charles
Binet-Sanglé's four-volume work, *La folie de Jésus* (1908–
1915), a copy of which is held in Pessoa's Private Library.[40]
Search's text is an attempt to demonstrate, through a
symptomatic analysis of the character of Christ, that
Jesus was a madman. The basic structure of Search's
argument may be gleaned from the following fragment:

39. BNP/E3, 48C — 2ʳ.
40. CFP, 1–9.

1. Jesus was either God, or man, or both God & man.

2. Being man, Jesus was an abnormal man.

3. Being an abnormal man, he was either a genius, or a madman, or a criminal.

4. He was not a genius, nor a criminal.

5. Therefore he was a madman.

[BNP/E3, 26A — 53ʳ]

Pessoa left several fragments for this work; in order to collocate it, we followed Pessoa's own indications as they appear in those documents. We have transcribed them in the body of the texts (as "I," "II," "III," etc.) so that the reader may clearly understand their positioning. All of the fragments that lack indications are placed in the Addenda (Part II, 1.1), along with other psychiatric materials that relate to the insanity of Jesus. In this we differ, as already mentioned, from the recent edition *Escritos*, which omits from its main text any indications left by Pessoa, & which misplaces many of the surviving fragments.

The fourth and fifth texts attributed to Search in *The Transformation Book* are "Delirium" (Part I, 1.4) & "Agony" (Part I, 1.5). These titles designate two collections of poems signed by Alexander Search. The poetical production attributed to Alexander results from Pessoa's engagement with English literature during his stay in South Africa. Characterized by an atmosphere of dream

& anxiety, these collections introduce many of the topics that will mark Pessoa's later, heteronymic poetical production. At the same time, they disclose the way in which Pessoa uses elements from other areas of knowledge — here, the psychiatric problem of madness — to produce literature. Pessoa attached so much importance to the poetical creation of Alexander Search that he thought of publishing some of his poems under Search's name, in England and in the United States:

> Poems.
>
> Make a careful choice of English poems and see to what extent they can be published in England or the United States.
> Consider, no less, the possibility of publishing the strange (and imperfect) early and non-early poems under the name of Alexander Search or some like name.

[BNP/E3, 48D — 18ʳ: detail of the image]

For the collocation of the "Delirium" & "Agony" poems, we've followed the explicit indications left by Pessoa in the poems themselves, and not those in his various lists. As already stated, Pessoa's lists of poems are frequently inconsistent, not only among themselves (as when Pessoa includes the same title in very different lists), but also with other indications in the manuscript documents of the various poems. The lists of poems have only an experimental character: most of the time they are abandoned for other, future projects or later lists. Thus, since

Pessoa left the explicit marker "Delirium" or "Agony" on many of the documents with poems signed by Alexander Search, we consider this to be the more reliable criterion for assembling the poetry drafted by Pessoa with these collections in mind. Within each of these collections, we have arranged the poems chronologically, from earliest to latest, with the exception of those poems whose parts were written at different times, such as the poem "Flashes of Madness." In this case, the date of the first segment of the poem was followed.

In the addenda to these poems, the following texts are also included: (1) projects and lists of poems concerning "Delirium" (Part II, 1.2); (2) fragments and other poems related to "Delirium" (Part II, 1.2.1); (3) a list concerning "Agony" (Part II, 1.3); & (4) a note from a diary, which specifically refers to "Delirium" (Part II, 1.4).

In our edition, the texts of Pantaleão are preceded by an enumeration of the literary tasks attributed to this pre-heteronym and related to *The Transformation Book* (Part I, 2.0). We also include other biographical documents that can elucidate the biography, definition of personality, and literary character of this pre-heteronym (Part II, 2.0), & therefore, can be read in connection with Pantaleão's role in *The Transformation Book*.

The first text attributed to Pantaleão in *The Transformation Book* is "A Psychose Adeantativa" (The Advancing Psychosis) (Part I, 2.1), which corresponds to an essay that develops a psychiatric analysis of the Portuguese social context around the year 1908, and was created with the intent of criticizing certain political and economic measures that were in effect during the last years of the Portuguese monarchy. These economic measures, specifically, were cash "advances" made by the Portuguese government to the Portuguese royal house. They created a general social instability and can be seen as one of the causes that led to the fall of the Portuguese monarchy in 1910. In order to criticize these measures, Pantaleão invents a new kind of clinical diagnosis, the "Advancing Psychosis," which is a pun on the cash advances then being made to Portugal's royal family.

In the Pessoa Archive, there are other variant titles for this work, including: "A Nevrose Adeantativa" ("The Advancing Neurosis"),[41] which shows that Pessoa — or rather Pantaleão — hesitated in making a specific diagnosis of this disease. But what should be emphasized in the creation of this work is the way in which Pessoa uses his studies of psychiatry to deal with the social and economic issues of his day. This text also recommends a curious therapy for those afflicted by "the advancing psychosis" (or "neurosis"): nostalgia. According to Pessoa, those who suffer from advancing psychosis acquire their disease by failing to love their own country. The only way to cure them of this disease, then, is to enable them to love their country. What makes this possible

---

41. BNP/E3, 48-24ʳ.

is nostalgia, & Pessoa's (ironical) therapy for producing nostalgia is banishing the sick from their native country. Curiously, the text of "A Psychose Adeantativa" is presented as an inaugural thesis written by Usquebaugh V. Bangem — is this the true name of Pantaleão, omitted in the biography? Or does it rather correspond to another of Pessoa's pre-heteronyms? It may be a merely satirical name — like the "University of Nowhere," or the translations *into* Portuguese, by Fernando Pessoa.

The second text attributed to Pantaleão in *The Transformation Book* is "As Visões do Sñr. Pantaleão" (The Visions of Mr. Pantaleão) (Part II, 2.2). Pessoa also recorded a variant title for this project: "As Visões Politicas do Sñr. Pantaleão"[42] (The Political Visions of Mr. Pantaleão) (see Part II, 2.1), a project that would have entailed writing one hundred such visions, but was never realized. The remaining fragments of these "Visões," which are often lacunar, consist of short satirical & symbolic texts, written in an oracular style with the intent to criticize — directly or through symbolic allusions — several of the monarchic personalities that were active in Portuguese public and political life between 1908 & 1910. The extant fragments of the preface to "Visões" say outright that their aim is to attack the Portuguese monarchy. The majority of the "Visões" are contained in a notebook[43]

42. BNP/E3, 48A — 44–47.
43. BNP/E3, 144A².

that begins with "Visão do Rei Lear" (Vision of King Lear), probably a symbolic allusion to King Carlos of Portugal.

This notebook also contains other writings that have no direct bearing on either Pantaleão or *The Transformation Book*. Thus, we have transcribed only the texts directly related to the "Visões." The fragments of Pantaleão's "Preface," though they appear after many of the "Visões" developed in that notebook, have been placed before the "Visões." We have also been able to identify another group of "Visões," written on separate loose sheets,[44] which are published here along with the sequence of "Visões" written in Pessoa's notebook.

The third text attributed to Pantaleão and included in this edition is "A Nossa Administação Colonial" (Our Colonial Administration) (Part I, 2.3). This is a political essay criticizing the way Portuguese colonies were managing their funds. The remaining fragments of this essay outline, in a pamphleteering manner, the beginning of Pantaleão's critique of the colonies' financial management and its disastrous consequences. We were able to identify a series of five documents in The Pessoa Archive that correspond to the beginning of this essay.[45] And in the Addenda (Part II, 2.2), we also include other fragments related to it. *The Transformation Book* also refers to the

44. BNP/E3, 92X — 86, 88–96.
45. BNP/E3, 92H — 22–26.

"Versos do Sñr. Pantaleão" (Verses of Mr. Pantaleão), but we were unable to identify any such verses in The Pessoa Archive.

The biography of Jean Seul de Méluret & a description of his literary tasks are included in Part I, section 3.0. Other biographical texts regarding this pre-heteronym are included in the Addenda (Part II, 3.0).

The first text of Méluret included in this edition is "Des Cas d'Exhibitionnisme" (The Cases of Exhibitionism) (Part I, 3.1). The text published here is arranged, when possible, according to the indications left by Pessoa in his original documents. All of the other documents that are conjecturally attributed to this project, or which do not contain any reference regarding their placement, are included in the Addenda to that text (Part II, 3.1).

"Des Cas d'Exhibitionnisme" is a moral fiction written with the intent of castigating the phenomenon of nudity in French music-halls as a manifestation of the clinically diagnosed symptom of "exhibitionism." Psychiatrically speaking, exhibitionism is characterized by a tendency to exhibit intimate parts of the body, such as the genitals, to strangers, typically in public places. According to Méluret, the fact that a similar phenomenon can be observed in the music halls of France (circa 1908), and is spreading throughout the nation, is a sign of civilizational degeneracy.

The second text attributed to Méluret and included herein is "La France en 1950" (France in 1950). The Pessoa Archive contains a variant title for this project, namely, "La France à l'an 2000" (France in the Year 2000).[46] But all of the fragments we have identified for this project use the first title.

"La France en 1950" is a futuristic moral and satirical fiction. The fragments of this project, which are mostly lacunar, depict an apocalyptic future for France, a society that is pervaded by an atmosphere of sexual perversion. People engage in intercourse with several others at the same time in a public setting. Mothers sleep with their sons, and fathers with their daughters — if not, they would be legally punished. The fragments of this fiction are marked by Sadean motifs, & refer explicitly to Sade. The intent of this satire is to warn against the possible future degeneration of French mores, that is, to show what France would look like if it continued to develop in the direction it had taken in Pessoa's own time.

To arrange the fragments of this text, the following criteria have been used: we have included in the first part of the edition (Part I, 3.2) those texts that contain the explicit indication "France en 1950" (or other similar references indicating that the fragment belongs to the

---

46. BNP/E3, 144D² — 41ᵛ.

project) according to the reference in The Pessoa Archive, since most of these fragments do not have any indication regarding their ordering or placement, with the exception of the last fragment of the work,[47] which contains the explicit indication "End" (in English), and therefore is placed as the last fragment of "La France en 1950." All of the other fragments related or relatable to this project are included in Part II, section 3.2.

The third text assigned to Méluret is "Messieurs les Souteneurs" (Gentlemen Pimps) (Part I, 3.3). This fiction satirizes French literature at the beginning of the twentieth century, characterized in Méluret's fragments as a literature of pimps who prostitute their own books. In fact, in a list of works marked "Titre des Satires" (Title of Satires),[48] one reads the following alternative title for this text: "La Littérature des Souteneurs" (The Literature of Pimps). This seems to suggest, at first sight, that "La Littérature des Souteneurs" is an alternate title; what is more, many of the French fragments conceived as part of the work are preceded by this indication: "La Littérature des Souteneurs." On the verso of the document containing Pessoa's "Titre des Satires," however, one finds the following clue regarding the latter title:

---

47. BNP/E3, 138A — 1.
48. BNP/E3, 144J — 29ʳ.

Non-satires.

Appel aux socialistes.

———————

Les Insignifiants — appendix à le "Dégénérescence"
de Max Nordau.

———————

Or one book beginning with one Chapter Littérature
des Souteneurs.

[BNP/E3, 144J — 29ᵛ]

According to this indication, the title "La Littérature des
Souteneurs" can be considered as a chapter title at the
front of a planned book, & that book can only be titled
"Messieurs les Souteneurs." Thus, taking all of these ele-
ments into consideration, we have organized the text
of "Messieurs les Souteneurs" in the following manner:

1) first, a sequence of three documents [BNP/E3, 27²²T⁴
   — 1–3] corresponding to the introduction to that text;

2) second, a series of eleven documents [BNP/E3, 14³
   — 86–96] preceded by the indication "La Littéra-
   ture des Souteneurs," & therefore to be considered
   as the fragments of the first chapter of that book;

3) third, two documents [BNP/E3, 133F — 39 and 133F
   — 46], both with the indication "Fin" (End), and
   therefore to be considered as the final fragments of
   "Messieurs les Souteneurs."

In Part II, section 3.3, we include further French fragments related to the topics developed in "Messieurs les Souteneurs."

Part I, section 4.0, contains the biography & literary tasks of the pre-heteronym Charles James Search. This is the only biographical text that we have been able to identify in The Pessoa Archive. Despite the fact that Pessoa attributes the translation of ten titles to this pre-heteronym, The Pessoa Archive contains evidence that only some of the titles on that list were actually translated, while in the case of the first text on Charles Search's list of translations — "The Student of Salamanca" — the exclusive attribution of that translation to Charles is problematic. In fact, the translation project of Espronceda's "The Student of Salamanca" has a complex history. The task of translating this work belonged to different projects and personalities at different times. The pre-heteronym Charles James Search was only one of the personalities entrusted with the task of translating Espronceda. Nevertheless, in the extant fragments of Pessoa's translation of "The Student of Salamanca," the only signature we were able to identify was Alexander Search's — not Charles Search's. Since the translation of the beginning of "The Student of Salamanca" has the indication "translated by Alexander Search" (Part II, section 4.1), we thought it more correct to place it in the Addenda.

The first translation included in Part I of this edition is thus the one containing fragments of Anthero de

Quental's "Complete Sonnets" (Part I, 4.1), which correspond to the second title in the list of translations to be undertaken by Charles Search. The Pessoa Archive preserves a series of thirty-two documents containing the fragmentary translations of Quental's *Complete Sonnets*.[49] The fragments of these translations are arranged in the exact order in which they appear in The Pessoa Archive. Regarding the first document,[50] titled "*Soulful* sight of Unknown things / (Translation [of] Anthero de Quental)," previous editors have taken this line to be a misplaced, alternate rendering of a line from the sonnet, "Lacrimæ Rerum." And "*Soulful* sight of Unknown things" is indeed a translation of one of the verses in "Lacrimae Rerum." Nevertheless, that verse was probably placed in such a prominent position, not by mistake, but because it was meant to serve as the title for the future publication of Quental's *Complete Sonnets*. This is why Pessoa then 'signs' "Translation [of] Anthero de Quental" immediately below that verse.

Anthero de Quental (1842–1891) was a poet who could be described as Pessoa described himself: "I was a poet animated by philosophy."[51] And this is probably why Pessoa was particularly interested in Anthero's work. Anthero also wrote philosophical & political essays, &

---

49. BNP/E3, 74 — 24-55.

50. BNP/E3, 74 — 24ʳ.

51. BNP/E3, 20 — 11ʳ.

was one of the advocates of Hegel's philosophy in Portugal. Indeed, a clue that Pessoa's interest in Quental was focused on the link between philosophy and poetry is provided by Portuguese philosopher António Sérgio's *Notas Sobre os Sonetos e as Tendências Geraes da Philosophia de Anthero de Quental*,[52] a book Pessoa owned & read. This work is devoted to an analysis of Anthero's *Sonnets* & one of his philosophical essays, and Pessoa's copy is preserved in the Pessoa Archive. The attribution of the translation of Quental's *Complete Sonnets* to Charles James Search is thus of particular importance: it closely associates Search with Pessoa's attempts to define himself as both a poet and a thinker.

Charles Search's second translation in our edition is "Sonnets (chosen) of Camoens" (Part I, 4.2). Camões (1524–1580) is the most influential & renowned classical Portuguese poet. He is the author of *Os Lusíadas* (*The Lusiads*), a verse epic poem — modeled on ancient Greek & Roman epic poems — narrating the Portuguese discovery of a sea-route to India. Camões was, naturally, very important to Pessoa. In a 1912 series of articles on new Portuguese poetry published in the literary journal *A Águia*, Pessoa prophesies, through an elaborate historical analysis of the evolution of several literary traditions, that the coming of a "supra-Camões" was about to occur in Portugal: a poet who could supersede even the

---

52. CFP, 8–502.

monumental literary achievement of Camões. Pessoa was himself on the verge of becoming that poet, yet the reference to Camões shows the stature that Pessoa recognized in him: overcoming Camões was to mark the inauguration of a new epoch in Portuguese literature. Charles James Search's translations of a selection of Camões' sonnets similarly express Pessoa's reverence for that author.

In this edition, we include the following translations of Camões' sonnets, all of which are held in The Pessoa Archive: (1) three versions of the sonnet "O gentle spirit mine that didst depart"[53] ("Alma minha gentil, que te partiste"); (2) one version of the sonnet "Everyone conceives me to be lost"[54] ("Julga-me a gente toda por perdido"); & (3) one version of the poem "Those lovely eyes that □ to weep"[55] ("Aqueles claros olhos que chorando").

The third translation by Charles Search included in this edition corresponds to the title "Guerra Junqueiro — Choice." Guerra Junqueiro (1850–1923) was a pamphleteering nationalist poet whose poetry breathed the revolutionary spirit that led to the fall of the Portuguese monarchy in 1910. The title "Guerra Junqueiro — Choice" indicates that Pessoa, through his pre-heteronym Charles James Search, intended to translate a selection of excerpts from Junqueiro's works. We were

---

53. BNP/E3, 74B — 74; 74B — 87 & 87ᵛ.

54. BNP/E3, 74B — 86.

55. BNP/E3, 74B — 79.

able to identify in The Pessoa Archive three documents containing translations of Junqueiro's poems: (1) a document with the translation of a segment of "Morte de D. João"[56] (Death of Don Juan); (2) a document translating part of "Canção Perdida"[57] (Lost Song); (3) a document translating "Luz Negra"[58] (Black Light).

0.5 — Criteria of Publication & Provenance of the Texts

The texts transcribed in this edition correspond to the remaining fragments of the works Pessoa conceived as parts of his project, *The Transformation Book, &* are all held in the Fernando Pessoa Archive (E3) at the Biblioteca Nacional de Portugal (BNP). In transcribing the material, we have always kept the first version of a word or sentence wherever there are variants. We have adopted this criterion since Pessoa left, in many cases, more than one variant for a word or sentence without indicating his preference, for he never made a final and complete version of these particular texts. Pessoa would write a first word or sentence & then insert variants that could be included in place of the first. But considering the optional and open character of these variants, we have

56. BNP/E3, 74B — 36.
57. BNP/E3, 74B — 77.
58. BNP/E3, 74B — 82.

taken his first version as a criterion. Finally, all textual variants, as well as genetic notes, are given in footnotes that also contain any elements that were crossed out, and any other changes Pessoa made to his original text. This will give the interested reader a sense of the compositional process behind these texts, and will provide Pessoa scholars with a valuable critical apparatus. In the case of "The Portuguese Regicide and the Political Situation in Portugal" (Part I, 1.1), signed by Alexander Search, there are two long sections that are crossed out — with long diagonal lines — in the original documents [BNP/E3, 79A — 73-75^r; 79A — 80^r-77a^r], indicating that those segments signed by Search would probably have been subject to revision. We decided to leave these crossed out segments in the main text, as in Pessoa's original draft, since the elimination or displacement of these segments would disturb the sequence and comprehensibility of the text. We have followed the same principle, for the same reasons, in presenting the list of poems related to "Delirium" (Part II, 1.2).

For the transcription of these texts, the following symbols have been used: [59]

---

59. Some of the symbols used for the transcription of the texts included in this edition can be found in the following bibliographical reference: Nuno Venturinha, *Lógica, Ética e Gramática — Wittgenstein e o Método da Filosofia* (Lisbon: Imprensa

~~X X X X X X~~ struck-out segment

X X X X X X ↑ˣˣˣˣˣˣ segment inserted above

X X X X X X ↓ˣˣˣˣˣˣ segment inserted below

X X X X X X →ˣˣˣˣˣˣ segment inserted on the right side

X X X X X X ←ˣˣˣˣˣˣ segment inserted on the left side

X X X X X X ⁄ˣˣˣˣˣˣ\ variant segment

X X X X X X underlined segment

| X X X X | segment doubted by the author

† illegible word

□ empty space left by the author

[x|y] substitution by superposition, in the relation
[~~substituted~~ | substitute]

|*X X X X| conjectural reading

[X X X X] segment added by the editor

[...] absence of material support [damaged segment
in the original material]

Nacional-Casa da Moeda, 2010). Others were adapted or
created for the purpose & specificity of a general edition of
Pessoa's writings — these symbols will be used in future
editions of Pessoa's fragments.

Acknowledgements

We are very grateful to Bento Prado Neto (Federal University of São Carlos) and Márcio Suzuki (University of São Paulo) for so warmly receiving our proposals for two research projects concerning The Pessoa Archive. Their interest & support were essential in the development of our research concerning The Archive, & thus, in the development of this critical edition of Pessoa's texts. We are also grateful to the Fundação de Amparo à Pesquisa do Estado de São Paulo (FAPESP), which provided material conditions for the development of those two projects (BP.PD – 12 / 12102-0; BP.PD – 13 / 05665-0). We are grateful, as well, to Alexandre Souza, who helped us to assess the last stage of the introduction. Finally, we want to express our gratitude to the two anonymous readers enlisted by Contra Mundum Press, who helped us to significantly refine the introduction.

IMAGES

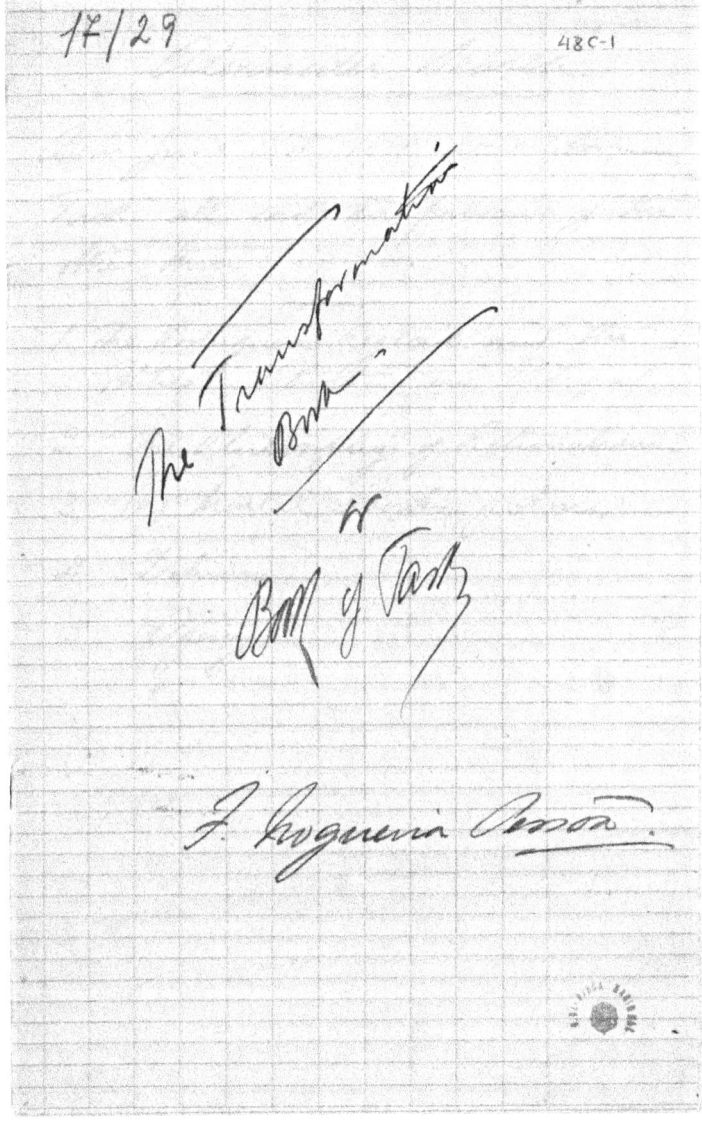

17/29

The Transformation Book ―

"

Book of Tasks

F. Nogueira Arson.

17/30

Alexander Search.

Born June 13th. 1888, at Lisbon.

Task: all not the province of the other three.

1. "The Portuguese Regicide and the Political Situation in Portugal."

2. " The Philosophy of Rationalism."

3. "The Mental Disorder(s) of Jesus."

4. "Delirium."

5. "Agony."

17/31

48C-3

Pantaleão.

(if necessary give true name).

1. "A Psychose Assentativa".
2. "As Visões do Snr. Pantaleão".
3. "A Nossa Administração Colonial".
4. "Versos do Snr. Pantaleão".

17/32 Jean Seul.

Full name supposed to be:
Jean Seul de Méluret.
Supposed to be born in 1885
on the 1st. of August, one
year older than Charles Aarch
and three older than Alexander.

Task: writing in French — poetry
and satire or scientific works
with a satirical or moral
purpose.

1. "Des Cas d' Exhibitionnisme."
2. "La France en 1950". – Satire.
3. "Messieurs les Souteneurs" – Satire.

17/33   48C-5

Charles James Search.

in l.: Charles Search.

supposed to be born in 1886 and ∴ to
be two years older than Alexander.
To be precise, born on the 8ᵗʰ April 1886.

Task: solely that of translation.
May write the prefaces to his
translations if these do not in-
volve analysis, etc.; when they
will be written by Alexander.

Translations to be undertaken:

1. Espronceda's "Student of Salamanca."
2. A. de Oliveira's "Complete Sonnets."
   (together with preservation price -?-).
3. Conti Guarini's "Epigram."
4. Sonnets (chosen) of Camoens.
5. G. junqueiro - Choice.
6. E. de Querig's "The Mandarin."
7. Some Sonnets from Portugal
   (excluding them separately translated).
8. A. Rosa's Poems (Some).
9. Almeida - Garrett - Choice.

— THE TRANSFORMATION BOOK OR BOOK OF TASKS

$$\left[48C - 1^r\right]^1$$

The Transformation
Book —

OR

Book of Tasks

F. Nogueira *Pessôa*.

1. The numbers in square brackets preceding the transcription of
each section correspond to the original numbers identifying those
documents in The Pessoa Archive (E3), kept at the Biblioteca
Nacional de Portugal (BNP). The numbers always precede the
transcriptions they belong to.

1.0 — Alexander Search

$$[48C - 2^r]$$

Alexander Search.

Born June 13[th.] 1888, at Lisbon.
Task: all not the province of the other three.

1. "The Portuguese Regicide and the Political Situation in Portugal."
2. "The Philosophy of Rationalism."
3. "The Mental Disorder(s) of Jesus."
4. "Delirium."
5. "Agony."

1.1 — The Portuguese Regicide and the Political Situation in Portugal

[79A — 71–82]

The Portuguese Regicide
and the Political Situation
in Portugal.

Alexander Search.

[72$^\text{r}$]

Introduction.

National & Institutional
Decay.

[73$^\text{r}$]

Introduction.

National & Institutional Decay.

I.[2]

Bichât[3] defined life as the sum-total of functions which resist death. The definition — all admit — is correct though it has not the comprehensive clearness[4] that is required in a definition. But it is pregnant.[5] What is necessary is to define, or, at least, to outline a definition[6] of death. In itself death is nothing, that is, cannot be defined so as to be understood; absolute extinction, unless it be the absolute extinction of form, the notion of which[7]

---

2. The segments from 79A–73 (Introduction. / National and Institutional Decay. ...) to 75ʳ (... what is called vitality.) & from the end of 80ʳ (IV / From the considerations...) to 77aʳ (... by sloth and carelessness.) are struck-out in the original documents, which seems to indicate that Pessoa intended to reformulate those segments signed by Search. But, since the stricken segments enable one to understand the sequence of the argument developed in "The Portuguese Regicide & the Political Situation in Portugal," we've decided to leave those sections in the main text, according to the way they are presented in the original documents.

3. Marie François Xavier Bichat (1771–1802) was a French anatomist and physiologist, known for being the first person to introduce the notion of "tissue" in anatomical descriptions of bodies and in the study of how diseases attack the organs.

4. it is ↑has not explicit nor has the ↑ comprehensive clearness

5. pregnant / ↑ suggestive \

6. necessary / ↑ supernecessary \ / it renders necessary \ is to define, or, at least, to give a shadow of ↑outline a definition

7. ↑the notion of which

we derive directly from experience, cannot enter into our comprehension. From a material standpoint, death can almost be defined as decay. When an organism decays, it tends to die. Death is more: it consists in *absolute* decay. Decay means disintegration. Death means absolute, pure disintegration, *disintegration unintegrated.*

We are now in a position to understand what the French medical philosopher meant by his definition: this, that life is the sum-total of functions that resist total disintegration. If for "life" we put "vitality," wishing to define this, the definition is, naturally, not simply disintegration, because,[8] as we shall see, this is a condition of life little changed: Vitality is the sum-total of functions [74ʳ] that resist disintegration — not now total disintegration, but disintegration itself, any disintegration at all. "Disintegration," of course, can be translated by "decay."

It is necessary to understand in what sense this is meant. Disintegration is a condition of life; the life of organisms is a perpetual disintegration, a perpetual change, a perpetual decay.[9] But life is more than disintegration: it includes integration also. All must change except (for a time, of course — till death) the unity that we call the organism. This is what is called life. The elements must pass — it is the law — but the mould, the form,

8. ∴ [because]
9. ~~tendency to~~ decay.

8

that there may be life, must remain. We arrive then at a simple definition of life: Life is disintegration integrated. We do not deny the extreme conciseness of this definition. But we do not intend to give a complete and comprehensive definition. For our purpose — to give an exact one — it[10] is sufficient.

We have not yet abandoned that phrase of Bichât. The suggestiveness of it, its pregnancy, consists in its peculiar tune. All life — it indicates — is a battle; the words "resist-death" are most often true & conclusive.[11] That definition of ours — "disintegration integrated" — is correct but not representatively comprehensive;[12] it evokes no vivid[13] and large idea. The French philosopher's[14] phrase does; it betrays a comprehension of the perpetual organic effort, of the perpetual struggle of the organism for its own conservation.

All life consists indeed in *resisting* disintegration, in the *combat* against dispersion and loss of the organic unity. All things tend to disintegrate the organism and the organism's whole attempt is to resist that

[75ʳ]

---

10. t̶h̶ it

11. m̶o̶r̶e̶ ̶t̶h̶a̶n̶ ↑most often true, m̶o̶r̶e̶ ̶t̶h̶a̶n̶ ̶a̶p̶t̶ ̶s̶o̶m̶e̶ ̶t̶h̶a̶n̶ ↑and conclusive.

12. ↑representatively comprehensive;

13. s̶u̶c̶h̶ vivid

14. philo-[75ʳ]sopher's, *in the original. In general, and most especially if a document reference splits a word, we have placed such references in the margins for the sake of elegance & greater reading fluidity.*

disintegration. The *power* of resisting disintegration is what is called vitality.

Let us carry our analysis further. If the organism be, as it is, capable of integration and of disintegration, it is evident that it must contain a force that makes or tends to make it, to keep it *one*, as well as another force that tends to make it many, that is, to disintegrate it, to kill it. Now it is easy, relatively easy, to determine what these are.

The organism is indeed *one*, but it is not simple, indivisible as the "soul," according to the spiritualist notion of it in philosophy. The organism is composed of a great number of elements — cells, finally, within[15] biology. Now all multiplicity, all lack of proper unity involves disintegration. This is why theologians argue that the "soul" being one and simple, it is immortal; they, from their standpoint, are right: if the soul be admitted to be one *&* simple, it cannot but be allowed to be immortal, since it contains not the element of decay, of [75a] death, of disintegration, and that element is *composition*, multiplicity in its unity. This the organism has: hence the force of disintegration.

The force of integration is more mysterious; in it lies the problem. It is not that unity is mysterious; it is *unification* that is. The organism is indeed composed

───────────

15. h̶o̶n̶ t̶h̶e̶ within

of many elements. But it is not a *sum*, it is a synthesis. To borrow chemical language, the organism is a combination, not a mixture. The combination of the elements in the organism produces something more [16] than is contained in the elements, though the nature of that we ignore, as fully indeed as we ignore the nature of the chemical change. Whatever that "something more" is, *&* all we know of it is that it rises out of the union of the elements and is dependent on them, we are sure that it is in it that the integrating force of the organism lies. The peculiar synthesis that is life, that is the organism, indicates the integration, and the force, whatever it is, that makes the organism a synthesis of its elements *&* not a sum of them, is the integrating force. We cannot go further because no science can take us.

Thus, to put things in a fitting manner, the organism is liable to disintegration because it is *many* (that is, composed of elements) and capable of integration because it is *one*, that is, because those elements are unified.

But it should be remembered that the organism [74a] is fundamentally *many* (that is, composite) and not *one*. This melancholy truth must be learned of life (and it is this that gives such exactness to the definition of Bichât): the essence of it is disintegration, tendency to decay. Because the essence of the organism is

---

16.   ↑ some things more

not unity but multiplicity (though it exists by being a unity), which is easily seen when we, considering its dual nature of one and multiple, examine whether it can be described as "unity made multiplicity" or better as "multiplicity made unity." Obviously the latter is the better phrase. Hence [17] the preponderance of the disintegrating over the integrating tendency. Hence the tendency of all things to decay, hence the decay of all things that live, hence, in a word, the sad law of death. That paradoxical definition — "life is death" — remains the best.

II.

These simple facts, being true of life in itself, are susceptible of application to all lives & forms of life, not only to organisms proper, but also to those other species of organisms — societies and nations.

If we concern ourselves with the state, with a nation, seeing that it is an organism, we are bound to find it obey the law of organisms, of life: it must contain a force that integrates and a disintegrating force.

Let us apply to the organism called the state the general law of life. Which are the elements (compos- [73a] ing the cells) of this organism? Obviously the people,

17. |*↑ Unto| Hence

that is, the individuals composing the nation. Which is then, in the state, the force that integrates, which the force that disintegrates? There is an exact analogy — how could there not be, since both are living "bodies"? — with the individual organism. Thus, in the state, obviously, the disintegrating force is that which makes the people *many* — their *number* — and the integrating force is that which makes them *one*, a people — the unification[18] of sentiments, of character brought about by identity of race, of climate, of history, etc. The disintegrating force is in the fact that the people are *many*; the integrating force in the fact that they have a collective opinion and will, better, a collective sentiment.[19]

Since all vitality consists in the power of resisting decay, the vital energy of all states consists in avoiding individualization of opinion, and this individualization has two forms: one by faction, and the other by carelessness and sloth, one by extreme division of opinions, the other by growing lack of interest in the duties of a citizen.[20] All government — at least, all good government — supposes a more or less great consciousness of opinion, that is, a thing that can be called a popular will.

---

18. ~~whole~~ unification

19. will, ↑, better, a collective sentiment.

20. sloth, ↑one by ↑extreme division of opinions, ~~or~~ ↑the other by growing lack of interest in the duties of a citizens.

What is [21] said, more limitedly, of opinion, can be said, more □ of sentiment, all nationality supposes an active collective [22] character, collective sentiment, when this grows proportionate, the individual begins to totter.

The expression of the popular will is the government: that is the highest manifestation of the integrating tendency (just as the brain is the highest integration of the organism). The individual, *qua individual*, is, in the state, the expression of the disintegration tendency.

The government representing the will of the people (we have been speaking, of course, of an internally free [23] country) and the "will of the people" representing the integrating tendency in the state, that which gives it, though composed of a large number of elements, its unity; if the government (in the exact sense of the governing, not of the *governors*) be consistently incapable, [24] troubled, incoherent, the conclusion to be drawn is that the activity of disintegration is becoming greater in the state than [25] the contrary force of activity, and that the country is in decay. The death of the state — it is hardly necessary to add — were where everyone should do as

[72a]

---

21. ~~All nationality supposes~~ What is
22. ↑active collective
23. ↑internally free
24. ↑exact sense of the governing, not of the *governors*) be ↑consistently incapable,
25. ↑in the state than

14

he liked, following his will to its end. Why? Because this were the abolition of the collective will and substitution of the individual one: hence complete disintegration.

All this we have said of the decay of the states may mean or not the decay brought about merely in their governing powers. If we deal with a free state,[26] obviously the decay in the governing powers means a decay in the whole nation; if in a nation not free, the decay of governing powers, of powers proper, does not of necessity involve national decay, but certainly the decay of the institutions, of the groups that command, and whose state does not of necessity represent the state of the people. We will now proceed to study institutional, as contrasted with national, decadence.

[71a]

III.

Power has three forms — force, authority and opinion. All the evolution of nations & of societies is fundamentally an ascension on the scale of those, from the first to the last. First came the state of violence, rising slowly out of its pure form in the savage tribes and groups.

---

26. ~~nation~~ ↑ state,

Then comes the rule of authority, begotten of force. And all tends to, or is at,[27] the sway of opinion, this word meaning, of course, "popular will," "democracy." (The persistence of monarchy, authority's best □, is proof that our □)

All this evolution represents the gradual approach to the government of the nation by the nation. It begins virtually at an anarchical or semi-anarchical state of things: it is the empire of force, the government of the weak by the strong & of the strong by the stronger. The state of society is then one of |*intermissive| strife (if this word may here be used), one of |latent| or every-day war. Then gradual integration begins; first it is partial. The selection of the fittest begins to split the tribe or nation (no matter how it is called) into two parts. Monarchy and aristocracy are born. This means that |force| is transformed with authority. "Transformed" — be the word noted, for it must not be forgotten — and this is of sovereign importance — that the original basis of authority is force; nor would there be any other basis,[28] any other origin to authority; authority would not *become* authority in any other way.

The chief or leader of savage tribes is not always [76ʳ] (being often considerably less in possession of power, because authority is not yet sufficiently evolved from force)

27. a̶s̶ ↑is at,
28. ↑other basis,

an earlier type[29] of the absolute monarch, but he contains the † essence of him. The presence of a chief indicates [the] existence of the element [of] "authority" in the tribe. Time works the further transformation and force is gradually changed into authority. Superstition becomes religion. The king is "god-ordained."

The essence of the idea of monarchy is, we see, *authority*. But authority involves other ideas. Monarchy is[30] but one manifestation of it. The authoritarian or conservative spirit has three forms: it is monarchical, it is religious, and it is militarist.

The superstitious veneration or respect for the chief in lower tribes becomes the monarchical spirit, and the superstition remains, the sacred nature of the king remains, he being considered ordained, given his rights, by God. With a religion like that of ancient Rome he may be considered a god,[31] or of the family of the gods, or an embryo deity. Hence the close union, the inseparable nature of monarchy & of religion.

We have seen that the spirit of authority rises out of the spirit of force by a superficial transformation, deepening more or less afterwards, not at all by anything resembling an elimination or a substitution of its

[77ʳ]

---

29. ↑earlier type

30. (includ is

31. religion like like that of ancient Rome he may be considered a god god,

characteristics. The savage superstitious veneration for a chief had become the less savage but quite as [32] superstitious respect for a monarch conceived as ordained by God. Similarly the oppressive and ferocious spirit of the earlier age is turned down with the *spirit of conquest*, that is, of *external violence*. But the basis of both forms of aggressiveness is the same; they are both aggressiveness, and this contains all.

Authority introduces into force, or, rather, into the instincts and passions that characterize the period of force, the factor "order." Authority is but force made, not orderly, but *ordered*. We believe these words impart something of the significance we mean them to convey. But the essence of authority is still force. Hence what goes is the "externals" of savagery, the incoherent superstitious instinct that, in one of its two forms, almost [33] makes an idol of the chief, [34] the open fierceness and constant pugnacity of the age of force; all these, which bear the brand of disorder, became by the introduction of order, the religious, monarchical, militant instinct. We can now see how the psychology of conservation, of authority, involves in its very essence these three instincts, really but three forms of itself, entirely inseparable from it, entirely

---

32. ~~more~~ ↑ quite as
33. ↑ in one of its two forms, almost
34. ~~king~~ chief,

constitutive of it: monarchy, militarism, religion. And the laſt is not the leaſt.

[78ʳ] Then comes the degeneration of authority and the formation of the rule of opinion. Hiſtory tells us that this is always obtained by a revolution of the same kind. Let us graſp the process of degeneration of which we have ſpoken.

The result of the syſtem of authority is to eſtablish and to eradicate a monarchy and ariſtocracy, a religion and a militariſt and warlike ſpirit, for authority reſts ſtill fundamentally on force, showing thus its origin. The syſtem of authority finds it easy to exiſt so long as it im-poses itself — morally, not by force, for when it needs force it is not its end. To impose itself morally it needs two things: dignity on its side *&* ignorance, "superſti-tion" as that of the peoples,[35] the second more necessary than the firſt. Now as the fate of all things is to decay, it happens always that the syſtem of authority degenerates. But at the same time the people, by gradual education and natural development, rise out of their ignorance and *fetichism*. The less dignity authority has, the more ſtrength opinion obtains. The decadence of the one aids the evolution of the other. It[36] becomes evident that one will eliminate or subſtitute the other; and it is easy to see that it is opinion that will eliminate authority.

35. ↑ "superstition" on that ↑ of the peoples
36. ↑ The decadence of the one aids the evolution of the other. It

By their degeneration monarchy & aristocracy become imbecile, base and cruel. The system of authority begins to totter. Corruption & oppression then come into the scene. The army, which had been used for war (that is, for external violence) becomes (unless it shortens matters by placing itself on the people's side) used for internal violence. Corruption[37] normally accompanies [79ʳ] violence. The reason why is clear. There is an excellent reason for it. The system of authority begins to loose its grip on the popular mind, but as that mind is not raised yet to large civic consciousness, the system of authority hangs over those it can, those yet unconscious of the baseness of being bought. And at the same time as it buys those or corrupts them in the innumerable ways there are of corrupting (some of them so honest!), the system of authority falls upon the others, those that cannot be bought, the clear-righted of the rising "middle" or "lower" classes. Corruption for some, violence for others — oppression for all. The revolutionary spirit is the immediate product.

The story ends differently in different countries, it is even radically different in various nations, owing to the other influences, but a revolution or an attempt at one is sure to come; what follows it is also, of course, not the same in all cases.

---

37. Corrup-[79ʳ]tion, *in the original.*

The last phrase leads us naturally to closing this section with an explanation as owed the reader. Of course the *collaborating* causes of the institutional decay or regeneration of a country are many, complex and interactive — the race, the character of the people, etc.,[38] or accidental circumstances. The natural decay of institutions is but the central fact, but it may be controlled by causes which differ in various countries, just as the primary origin of that institutional decay may not be a different one in each country, for though the fate of the system of[39] authority is to degenerate (as is the fate of all things) yet the efficient cause of that degeneration is not one in all instances.

[80ʳ]

We have been considering *independently* of all these other elements, the *pure* action, the *general* nature of the decay of the system of authority. We do not assert — we repeat — that the degeneration of institutions takes that road in all nations; we know well that the revolutionary movement is not always republican, but may be but[40] liberal within a monarchy. But we feel justified in presenting a picture of institutional decay as we have done, seeing that our purpose was[41] to present it ab-

---

38. ~~the climate,~~ the character of the people, "~~au~~ etc.,
39. ~~the~~ a different one in each country, for though the fate of ~~monarchy and~~ ↑the system of
40. ↑be but
41. was /↑is\

ſtracting from all the influences *&* counterinfluences of race,[42] character, etc., that may haſten, check, or turn in another direction the decadence of the ſyſtem of authority. The *fundamental* characteristics of such decay will[43] be found to be those we have shown. As we have been concerning ourselves purely with inſtitutions, we have abſtained from considering other causes of decay: that were to depart from the subject and from our purpose in making these preliminary observations. But we give this explanation leſt the reader should object to a dogmatic ſtatement of a generality.

IV.

From the considerations we have made the reader will already[44] have[45] drawn a fair idea of what is national, [80aʳ] what inſtitutional decay. We have not yet however sufficiently indicated their points of similarity and their differences.

In the firſt place since both are decay they muſt have a resemblance. In what does that consiſt?

42. ~~climate~~ ↑ race,
43. ↑ of such decay will
44. al-[80aʳ]ready, *in the original.*
45. ~~IV / From the considerations we have made the reader will al-~~ [80aʳ]ready have

All decay in question is direct political decay — we are at present concerned with no other. Now the sentiments that are legitimate in the sphere of government are, on the part of the citizen, a feeling of citizenship, of responsibility as [a] member of a state, part indeed of his personal dignity and, fundamentally, a branch of his instinct of preservation of life & of happiness, depending much [46] on the preservation of the state; hence the duty every citizen feels of defending his country and of having interest & taking part in its government by his vote. On the part of the man who governs the legitimate, the same state of mind consists in the sentiment of public good, of responsibility towards the nation, mingled with the half-selfish desire of winning approbation thereby.

Now we have shown that all political degeneration consists in an *individualization* (so we will call it, for want of a more expressive word), & this means absorption of the sentiments of the *citizen* in those of the *man*, substitution of these for those. Thus in the citizen, carelessness of public matters takes the place of interest, & so on. And another thing may occur, really as [79aʳ] expressive of national decadence, but in an opposite way. The former is more characteristic of the higher classes (we are speaking of free nations, and therefore "higher classes" here means the bourgeois); the other, of which

46. ~~on~~ much

we shall treat, of the lower. For since the higher or middle classes, having degenerated, become careless of public good and consequently tyrannical & contemptuous of those below them, disdainful of them and of their rights, usurpers of their work, of their health, of their lives; this weeds in the lower class sentiments of revolt which, seized by [the] degenerative spirit of the country, finds vent in extravagant and dangerous ideas of utopical reform, based partly on a legitimate hatred, thoughts of subverting the whole social nature and order, instead of attacking the immediate[47] and eradicable order of things. We say this *may* happen; if it do[es] there is yet a certain hope of regeneration in the county, for a revolutionary instinct (however strange and distorted) is still a sign of a certain amount of vitality. In extreme and complete national decadence, there is no protest (that is, no protest worthy of note) anywhere, no strength, no dignity, no vitality for such a protest.

Thus, in nation decay, in the citizens, in the higher & lower classes, selfishness takes the place of the "collective feeling," of the feeling of citizenship, producing, in those whose life is easy, carelessness, sloth & unconcern, and in those whose life is hard, either, in the better case, fierceness, revolt or revengeful hatred, or, in the worse, an incurable apathy & depression.

---

47. the the immediate, *in the original.*

[78aʳ] We turn now to public men, to those who govern, for we have been dealing but with those who are governed, with the body of the nation. In times of social health the politician finds two sentiments more or less balanced in his mind: the desire of public good and the desire to distinguish himself, his personality by contributing to it. No sooner does decadence begin, however, than in the politician the first sentiment is overthrown by the second: the public man becomes merely ambitious, unscrupulous, aiming at interest or at effect, accordingly as he represents one or the other section of the degenerate people. The conservative politician nourishes feelings of oppression, of harsh ambition of power; the more liberal politician tends rather to dishonesty, to care in personal aggrandisement alone, and the popular representative, the revolutionary, aims at mere verbal attraction of the masses, careless of all results of his speaking, unthinking[48] in □ & in expression.

Thus, the citizen sunk everywhere in the man, in the two forms of this — faction and inaction — the whole community sinks in a wave of disorder.

This is national decay.[1] [NOTE.[1] This, the reader will understand, is to be taken with an explanation identical to that given by us at the end of the third section of this Introduction.]

---

48. un~~rep~~ ↑ thinking

From these observations it might seem that only free nations are liable to national decadence. No: extremes meet. It may take place also in a nation under absolutism. For when in a country under absolute government [77aʳ] the people are either so base as in their great majority to submit, to abdicate from their natural rights, or so weak as to be unable to overthrow or resist the oppressors, it is just as if they consented in the government, as if they gave it their aid, making their common cause with it. "He who is not for me is against me" seems[49] an old phrase, here it is "he who is not against me is for me." There is a Portuguese proverb that says — "He who says nothing gives his consent"; it is applicable here. Between this kind of national decay & the other there is, as will be better understood further on, a radical[50] difference: the first is pure national decay; the second is institutional decay become national decadence.

Analysing the matter well, we find that the true and complete national decay is this last, for that taking place in free nations is more want to be manifested[51] by faction rather than by sloth & carelessness.

49. ~~says~~ ↑ seems
50. ~~one~~ ↑ a radical
51. ~~among~~ manifested

IV.

We are now in a position to compare and distinguish national and institutional decay. The essential distinction between them is easy to make and easier to understand. In the second section we studied the decay of states in its general features: in the third we showed how institutions enter into decadence. What we call national decay remains then to be examined.

The distinction, we have said, is not difficult. National decay is essentially and initially *social* decay; institutional decay is essential and initially *political* decadence. In these words lies the whole distinction. In the term "social decay" we embody of course the decadence of all activities that upkeep a society — industrial, moral, etc. The decadence of government in free countries *is produced by* the social decay. In countries not free yet in decay or going thither, the decadence of government *produces* the other forms of decay that we have called social decadence.

[76aʳ]

|It is obvious, we believe|, that the expression [52] "national decay" conveys the idea of an *origin* & not of a *condition*; that is to say, what we call "national decadence" does not mean that the decay is complete or incomplete,

---

52. |It is obvious, ~~next~~ ↑ we believe|, that ↑ the expression

advanced or not — it means merely that such decay has a *national* (or, social), as opposed to *institutional* origin, be it noted.

This genetic classification of decadences made, we have to consider the classification according to [an] *extension* of decay, and this is simpler yet, the divisions being naturally decay complete and incomplete. To this we might add — why, will soon be seen a "semi"-complete decadence.

Complete is distinguished from incomplete decay by the presence (in the latter) of sufficient elements of regeneration, elements tending to integration.

Two roads lead to complete decadence. One — the direct and national one [53] — is that of national decay; the other is by institutional. The reason is simple. Institutional decadence involves slightly a national decadence, because to be possible it needs that the people be not perfectly healthy *&* conscious, and this contains [54] the genus of national decay. If the system of [81ʳ] authority seemed [to be] either in crushing a public resistance or in having none at all, it will contaminate the whole people *&* the decay of the institutions will thus become [the] decay of the whole nation. This is the case of the Roman Empire.

---

53. direct ↑ and national one
54. con-[81ʳ]tains, *in the original.*

Incomplete decay is purely institutional; it never can be national. It is always less serious. When the institutions of a country are in decadence and there is an opposite and strong current of opinion, coherent & sane, there is incomplete decay, for the forces of regeneration exist and the first step to regeneration is simple — the overthrow of the monarchy. [55]

Semi-complete decay is not so easy to explain. It may be national or institutional in origin. When originating in institutional decadence its meaning is this: the decay of the monarchy has produced that of the people and these are turned passive, but nevertheless there exists, within the monarchy, a man or men, capable of regenerating the country. When national in origin, semi-complete decay has this meaning: these are indeed in the nation forces of regeneration, but their *end*, their *program*, is impracticable, utopical; whence ultimately violence, which violence, though it cannot, of course, result in the carrying out of ideas essentially impracticable, yet shakes the nation and wakes it from its passiveness. This may also happen in cases of prolonged institutional (but always combined with some national) decay, as, in the best known examples, in the case of the French Revolution.

[82ʳ] There is this difference to be noticed in the characteristics of regenerating forces in incomplete & semi-

55. monarchy /↑ institution\.

29

complete decay: that in the first the regeneration (almost always sure) comes from the *purpose* of those forces — their correct, positive, in[di]vidual program; while [in] the second the regeneration (not always sure sometimes [of] a hastening of decadence) comes from the *action* of those forces and *not* at all from their *purpose*, which purpose, utopical *&* ill-conceived,[56] bears in itself traces of the national decadence whence it arises.

V.

We believe to have here indicated, in as |clear yet| succinct a way as possible, the general laws, or lines [57] of the decay of states. The precise examination of them, of their apparent exceptions, of their complications with other conditions, were matter, of itself, for a book and not for an introduction to one. Our end in opening this work with the present chapter is merely to guide the uninitiated reader in the comprehension of the situation of Portugal, a country, as will be seen, in [58] institutional, incomplete decay, in which the forces of regeneration are in daily growth. This however is here out of place.

56. ~~unthought~~ ↑ ill-conceived,
57. or, ~~rather,~~ lines
58. ~~with~~ in

1.2 — The Philosophy of Rationalism

$$[15^2 - 62\text{-}70]$$

Rationalism.

Rationalism holds that the only things that can be affirmed as facts are those [59] which reduce experience by reason to the coordination called science. [60] Rationalism holds that all things outside this are simply unknown, [61] or as yet unknown; but it does not affirm either that they are unknowable and still less that they are false. For what cannot be proved cannot also be disproved. The affirmation that Christ is God, for example, cannot be rejected by a Rationalist because it cannot be affirmed by him. It may be an error; it may be the vision of a higher sight — the Rationalist cannot determine which it is, because he does not know a thing to be wrong unless he can subject it to reason, and he cannot affirm a sense to be non-existent simply because he himself has not got it.

---

59. tho[e|s]e
60. to ↑the coordination called science
61. ~~as yet~~ unknown

For this reason atheism is not rationalism at all, and no atheist can describe himself as a rationalist unless he ignores[62] the meaning of rationalism, of atheism, or of both. The truth is that atheism is not a form[63] of disbelief, but of belief. It is commonly supposed that an atheist is a man who does not believe in the existence of God. This is wrong, for he is not so negative. He is a man who believes in the existence of not-God. Hence his positiveness, his happiness, & that[64] buoyant faith of a militant unchristian.

Rationalism is knowledge bounded by ignorance.[65] It is no more than this. Where atheism is intolerant or contemptuously tolerant, rationalism is fully tolerant. The pity is that it is not an attitude that can be popular, and this is one of the reasons why real rationalists are seldom, if ever, democratic.[66] It is also one of the reasons why they are so ready to deal kindly with what the staunch atheist would regard as gross and immoral superstition. Where they do not know, they ignore.[67]

---

62. i[i|g]nores
63. f[l|o]rm
64. ↓ and th[e|a]t
65. knowledge /↑ science\ bounded by ignorance /↑ agnosticism\
66. ~~very~~ seldom, ↑ if ever democratic
67. superstition. ← Where they do not know, they ignore.
68. ~~tested~~ it

The atheist knows that palmistry is wrong. If he has not tested it, or cannot test it,[68] the rationalist says nothing.

Neither can it be said that rationalism[69] & agnosticism are the same thing. Agnosticism directly implies the[70] affirmation that the unknown is unknowable. Rationalism cannot say of the unknown that it is so far known as to be known to be unknowable. A wider[71] agnosticism may affirm that even the known is unknowable — a far more tenable & rational proposition. In this case it[72] may be called Absolute Rationalism — the belief that nothing can be believed unless it is brought[73] under reason, with the addition of the belief that nothing can be brought under reason.

[63ʳ]

Some agnostics distinguish between the unknown of science and the unknown of metaphysics — the lesser & the greater unknowns, Ursa Minor & Ursa Major[74] of an inexistent sky.

---

69. ~~agn~~ rationalism
70. th[a|e]
71. wider ^/↑ sadder\
72. ↑ [w|H]ere agnosticism In this case it
73. b[e|r]ought
74. Ma[n|j]or

Scepticism may also be confounded with rationalism. But the sceptic, if he really be one, has no belief at all; the rationalist does believe in reason. To a certain extent, as far as reason, the rationalist is a believer. As a matter of fact, he is wholly a believer. It is because the sceptic is not a believer that he destroys himself: scepticism, as in Pascal, was ever the fore-prey of mysticism.

The half-sceptic speaks like Socrates, I know only that I know nothing. The whole sceptic speaks like Francisco Sanches, [75] *Haud scio me' nihil scire*, I do not even know if I know nothing.

(My countryman is said to have preceded Descartes, probably because he came before him. But that is mere chronology. I do not believe he influenced Descartes (vide/Stark). [76] Metaphysical speculation is not one of the violent pastimes of the Portuguese; even Spinoza had to be also a Jew and a Dutchman to find a private universe. The most any Portuguese ancestor of his could have done was to help to find the present earth at the [77] opposite end.)

□ the transcendental atheism of the Buddhists.

───────────────

75. Francisco Sanches (1550–1622) was a Portuguese philosopher. His book *Quod nihil scitur* (*That nothing is known*) is said to have influenced Descartes' method of doubt.

76. Descartes → (vide/Stark)

77. the ↓ some

Modern scientific speculation has brought the old atheists to their lack of senses & has given them a finite world, robbing them of the now unfashionable infinity which they had taken from God to give it to the blackness of mute space and the emptiness of dull time.

□ that negative omnipresent God of the Indian mystics who rises down to himself through the black Jacob's ladder of an increasingly [78] depersonalized autolatry.

[64ʳ]

Rationalism.

For [79] human experience includes very little that is rational. That is the primary fact the rationalists must undergo.

□ the terrible intellectual phenomenon of these |*being| such a thing is vain, which is a part of the just spiritual phenomenon of these being anything at all. [80]

Those strange aesthetes of the lesser mind, who can understand the paradoxical beauty of a genius clothed among fools with obscurity, [81] but not the paradoxical

---

78. a̶ ↓ an increasingly

79. |For|

80. ↑ the terrible p̶h̶e̶n̶ intellectual phenomenon of these |*being| such a thing is vain, which is a part of the just h̶i̶g̶h̶e̶r̶ spiritual phenomenon of these being anything at all.

81. clothed / ↑ celled \ ← among fools with / ↑ in \ obscurity,

splendour of the God crucified among thieves. [82]

Rationalism gathers in very little, because reason has exact[ly] very little scope in[83] which to operate. When we leave the figures which denote the coefficient of expansion of iron, we have only the mystery of iron left over.

The strength of rationalism is in its narrowness for all strength is a narrowness. [84] It leaves us ever humble [85] before the infinite remainder.

It may be thought that this is why great Christians, like St. Thomas Aquinas, were rationalists. But the point is the other way. St. Thomas was neither a Christian nor a rationalist. He was only a Catholic and a reasoner. The rationalist inverts the position which he put. He made, as the old phrase has it, philosophy the handmaid of theology. But the rationalist, who has no use for theology, which is the affectation of mysticism, considers philosophy as no more than[86] the poetry of thinking.

All I want to give is an expression to a new mood in the withdrawal from speculating.

The materialist is sure. The rationalist is aware.

□ & man who would not forget to † a knight with "God" will note St. Paul worth the Saint; for this is [87] no etiquette □

---

82. ↓ᵃ God crucified among ~~the~~ thieves.

83. has ←exact very little scope [o̶|i]n

84. for all strength is a narrow↑ness.

85. ↓ever humble

86. ~~makes theology~~ ↓ considers philosophy as no more than

87. for ↑this is

[65ʳ]

Rationalism.

If this slight book be read by any rationalist who had Paine for governess, he will, when this point is reached, have pleasure in finding me out. But, like Mr. Jingle,[88] I would rather have that than that he found me in.

For this is only a notion of reality. Reality is not only stones and plants, with a moving sprinkling[89] of animals. It is also the dreams, the visions, the mystical experiences, of the substance & passing of mankind. Christ may not be real as reality, but has been real as an ideality. For the realist, who is the rationalist, that is as enough as the stars. The ideal men have loved is as real as the woman men have loved, for love is the one actual thing.

The end of reason is a weariness of thinking. Yet reason is so strong that even its weariness is a part of its strength and we dream rationally if we have learnt reason. ....

| The rumour[90] is abroad that the Gods are dead. But the Gods, being immortal, are very lively. |

---

88. Alfred Jingle is a fictional character created by Charles Dickens and presented, in the novel *The Pickwick Papers*, as a charlatan.

89. a ↑moving sprinkling

90. rumours

|We may conceive the total of mankind as the passengers and crew of a ship of fools, left helmless on an uncharted ocean. They will make games laſt while life endures, and have death for a certainty, with some expectation of being saved, for there may be a better map for a ship coming[91] on their way.|

[66ʳ]

Rationalism.

… dreary as a languid gorgeousness, like that of [the] *Faerie Queene*, which not even Edmund Spenser ever dared to read through in all the entirety there is of it.

---

91. [w|c]oming

92. of ↑the wrong rationalism,

93. John Mackinnon Robertson (1856–1933) was a member of the English rationalist movement that emerged in the United Kingdom between the end of the XIX and the beginning of the XX century. In Pessoa's Private Library, there are twenty-three of Robertson's books: *Pioneer Humanists* [CFP, 1–129]; *Pagan Christs* [CFP, 2–54]; *Browning and Tennyson as Teachers* [CFP, 8–475]; *A Short History of Freethought* [CFP, 1–130]; *Christianity and Mythology* [CFP, 2–49]; *Essays on Sociology* [CFP, 3–67]; *Criticisms* [CFP, 8–476]; *Essays in Ethics* [CFP, 1–128]; *Modern Humanists* [CFP, 3–68]; *A Short History of Christianity* [CFP, 2–55]; *Explorations* [CFP, 2–51]; *The*

□ the old bourgeoisie of the wrong rationalism, [92] from poor old Thomas Paine, who □ to Mr. J. M. Robertson, [93] who dispossessed [94] God of infinity in favour of that universal interval called space.

It is brilliant to [the] point of nauseousness…

But the rationalist makes no conflict with any man's opinions. He admits the possibility of the existence of God & the possibility of that God being the wood idol of the African wilds. Like Baudelaire, he would say to the disgusted sailor who wanted to throw that idol into a corner, [95] *"Et si c'était le vrai Dieu?"*

Religion is an emotional need of mankind. The rationalist may not want it, but he has to admit that other people may. It is emotional but it is also a need. [96]

Genuine in Shakespeare [CFP, 8–472]; *The Baconian Heresy* [CFP, 8–471]; *Charles Bradlaugh* [CFP, 9–61]; *The Dynamics of Religion* [CFP, 2–50]; *The Saxon and the Celt* [CFP, 3–69]; *The Problem of "Hamlet"* [CFP, 8–474]; *"Hamlet" Once More* [CFP, 8–473]; *Jesus and Judas* [CFP, 2–53]; *The Evolution of States* [CFP, 3–66]; *The Historical Jesus* [CFP, 2–52]; *William Archer as Rationalist* [CFP, 8–31], a collection of writings edited by Robertson; *The Philosophical Works of Francis Bacon*, ed. with an introduction by Robertson [CFP, 1–3].

94. disposses[s]ed

95. Baude[al|la]ire, he would say to the ↑ disgusted sailor who wanted to throw that idol into a corner, in disgust,

96. It is an emotional need It

There are conflicts between the pure and the practical reason. The rationalist admits Catholicism but he cannot admit the application of that intolerance which is the legitimate right of the Catholic within himself. The tolerant man draws the line at the intolerance of others. He preaches peace & must kill in self-defence.

Kant's great distinction between pure and practical reason...... He was the greatest rationalist the world has ever had thinking upon it. He worked out his own salvation of all reason in that quiet Koenigsberg, alone with moral law and the stars. He had that little Koenigsberg where to stand & thence he could move the earth.

I pay the tribute of thankfulness to that full and exact learning which has been deprived of its due recognition. But, if I honour Mr. Robertson for the learning which he has, I cannot respect him for the rationalism which he has forgotten to have. He is the irrationalist pure and simple; there[97] is no third of reason in his believing soul. He even believes in the infinity of space and the eternity of time, and I wonder what science or experience has taught him that those incommensurables exist.[98]

---

97. ~~thre~~ there
98. wonder what ← science or experience has ↓ ~~confirm~~ / ↓ can have \ taught him that those |incommensurables| ~~es~~ exist

[67^r]

Rationalism.

All science is, substantially, an attempt at science.[99] Even if reason itself did not warn us against the conferring of too much truth upon our generalizations, which[100] are necessarily always hasty, & upon our observations,[101] which are necessarily always imperfect, the historical experience of scientific theories would give our conjectures[102] that advice. The history of science and of knowledge has seen so many truths sink into mere speculations or into provisional dreams,[103] that the historian of our minor, as that of our major, philosophy may put a constant query to the end of any & every paragraph[104] he indict. Even the dearest littlenesses of science may to-morrow be subverted by great cyclones of mind. We may have to abandon the coefficient of expansion of iron. We may have to controvert Boyle's Law. It is not impossible to formulate, in a sort of tired dream, the negation of the choicest principles of our external

---

99. an attempt ↑ at science / ↑ seeing \.

100. , ~~whei~~ which

101. ↑ upon our observations,

102. ~~speculation~~ ↑ conjectures

103. ~~truth sink like~~ so many truths sink into ↑ mere speculations or ↑ into provisional dreams,

104. ↑ constant query to the end of ↑ any and every paragraph

sureties.[105] Even two and two may one day cease to be four, to a brighter[106] understanding of the surface and femininity of things.

Yet, since we have no better assurance than reason for the objectivity of certainty, to take a thing as true because it can be proved is yet an excusable[107] shift of our unknowing. In common with all men, each of us has[108] no more than the objective universe, which we may test together,[109] and the principles of reason, by which we can communicate without our souls. Truth is unattainable, but logic is intelligible. Ghosts may be things, but things are things, even if they be ghosts. We must keep to the world that has been given us, and to the manner of test that we have been allowed, or, at the least,[110] have not been deprived of. If a God has made us, it is a sort of blasphemy to doubt the world he made us in and with, and the reason which he gave us as the means for the understanding of that world. If deeper things in our souls reveal objective truths deeper than visible things, and if subtler[111] operations of our minds yield more certain

---

105. sureties /(assurances)\ /(certainties)\.
106. brighter /↑ deeper and ~~fren~~ ↓ stranger \
107. excusab~~b~~le
108. ~~we have~~ ↑ each of us has
109. ~~in common~~ ↑ together
110. ~~at any rate~~ ↑ at the least
111. ↑ objective truths deeper than visible things, and [o|i]f subtler

results than reason, we have no power to distinguish, having[112] nothing clearer than our senses, or to criticize, having nothing more coherent than our logic. Perhaps God[113] makes a mockery of the things he has himself given us, and plays hide-and-seek with his own self. For all we know, this may be possible. But, as wise men, we will take the gift we see and use [the] tools we have received; the rest we shall leave to the action of Fate and to the hidden purpose if these be one of the unknown substance[114] of things.

[68ᶜ]

Rationalism.

The scientific spirit means three things: (1) the holding as actually (or, at least, provisionally) true only those laws or facts which have been subjected to an objective test, which anyone, given the culture, the instruments *&* the opportunity, may equally well apply; (2) the holding as actually (or, at least, provisionally) false of the[115] doctrines or pseudo-facts which directly contradict such laws or

---

112. to distingui[g|s]h, hav[e|i]ng

113. ← Perhaps God

114. ↓ to the hidden purpose ↓ if these he own of the unknown /↓ verted \ substance

115. } of the

facts and are either insusceptible not by nature, but by statement,[116] of objective proof or, being susceptible of it, are not or have not been brought to it; (3) the holding as unknown as to their truth those theories or ideas which, being[117] of a nature wholly incommensurable with the laws and facts which can be verified objectively, are, by that very nature, insusceptible of objective proof.

This means, to exemplify, that we can hold by coefficient of expansion of iron as being a certain proportional figure;[118] we will not hold by a mystic theory which,[119] without a counter-proof equally objective, may affirm that the coefficient in point is another one; we will neither hold nor not hold by such mystic doctrine independent of that application. The proof that the literal interpretation of the statements of Genesis as to the creation of the world is wrong does not affect the metaphysical principles of the religions based on that Genesis. It affects solely the doctrine of physical creation, in so far as it is thus understood.

When a man of "science" says that, as a man of science, he does not[120] accept the doctrine of the Trinity,

---

116. insusceptible / ↑ irreducible \ not by nature, but by statement,
117. ~~doctrines or~~ theories or ideas which, ~~are either~~ being
118. ~~figure proportional to the length of the~~ proportional figure;
119. ~~wheih~~ which,
120. sciencie, he ~~disbeliev~~ does not

he is talking like anything except a man of science. All that he can say, as a man of science, is that he not only has not, but cannot have, any opinion on the doctrine of the Trinity. He may also say, as a man — not of science but of mankind —, that he does not believe in the doctrine of the Trinity; in the same capacity, he may say that he does believe in it. He is entitled to either affirmation of faith; but, be it negative or positive, it is always an affirmation of faith. The moment he makes it he has ceased to be a man of science at all. He has become merely a man.[121]

This seems very simple, but human perverseness seems to make it as difficult as all final simplicities are. If, however, a mystic[122] putting forth that physical doctrine, affirm[s] that it is linked with the essence of his spiritual[123] doctrine and that it is a true type & figurement of it, he should not complain[124] if, his own statement being taken as he has given it, the general[125] theory be held wrong on the score of the particular application[126] being proved wrong.

---

121. merely a man. ← justly also, which may be more or less, sufficient: he has become just a man

122. mystic /↑ religiousist \

123. affirms that it is linked with the ~~sess~~ essence of his spi[t|r]itual

124. compl[ia|ai]n

125. ~~essential~~ ↑ general

126. the ↓ particular application

[69ʳ]

Rationalism.

Rationalism. Theoretic Rationalism. Practical Rationalism.

Sociology is simply a baser metaphysics. It is so far metaphysics that it seems to be a substitute for it, metaphysical & sociological speculation being generally in the inverse quantity at the same time.

It is easy to defend law and order [127] as necessary to civilization. But Athens was never orderly and the Italian Republics of the Middle Age[s] and of the Renascence had very little order & very little law; yet if the creation of art and culture which distinguished them be not civilization or one of its distinctive characteristics, then civilization is its own opposite. It is easy to contend that a unified nation is essential to its own life; yet Greece, which created the mind of the civilized world, was never the whole of itself, & Italy was best scattered than united, in so far as results to mankind in general are a valid test. It is easy to defend any sociological theory. As in everything, except the bare useless facts, [128] the theory is worth what the theorist is worth, & all is made up, in the ultimate, of aspects of truth. [129]

---

127. ~~order and~~ law and order
128. ~~the theo~~ except the bare useless ↑|*chosmic| facts.
129. aspects of untruth. /↓ the possibility of truth.\
130. ↑we ~~were~~ all

The legal profession is an immoral and absurd one, but we all[130] counsel of our beliefs, & the better sophist wins — fortunately only temporarily — the futile case he has put himself into.[131]

Some, like Kant, make their philosophies out of themselves. Others, like Nietzsche, make their philosophies out of the negation of themselves. The placid man is placid in his philosophy. The sick man is the philosopher of strength □

Slavery is perfectly defensible. We cannot defend it because Christian morality excludes slavery, and Christian morality is one of the bases of our civilization. The death penalty can be defended, but it will not pass the emotional test. The Inquisition can be defended, and it has been defended. But it will not pass the cultural test — it is rebutted, not by any valid argument which cannot be emptied of force, but by the rationalistic individualism which the Greeks have given us for the soul of our mind.

$$[70^{r}]$$

Rationalism.

The Christian ethics may be, as Nietzsche puts it, the ethics of slaves. It is, however, our ethics. We have not to say that we do not want that ethics; we can but say that

---

131. put ↓ ~~high~~ / ↓ higher \ himself into

we are slaves. (We may accept Nietzsche's assertion, but we must accept the ethics. It is possible that that ethics is indeed the ethics of slaves; if it be so, then we are slaves and that is our ethics.)

When any man defends cruelty or lust or treason, he may do so with the full armoury of an intellectual arsenal he was born with for a soul; but he speaks to sticks[132] and stones when he would persuade more of us than the surface of our possible reasons to agree with him. We may be cruel, lustful or treasonable by our passions; we cannot be so by our emotions. The door[133] of those theories is definitely blocked in our civilization: it is blocked by the Cross.

The rationalist does not assert that Greek Culture is the best culture: he asserts that, good or not, it is the culture we have. The rationalist does not assert that Roman Order is the best type of order: he asserts that, for better or for worse,[134] it has been wedded to the substance of ourselves. The rationalist does not assert that Christian Ethics is the best possible ethics: he asserts that it is the only one possible to our emotions.

---

132. *In the original document Pessoa writes "stocks" instead of "sticks," presumably by mistake. We've corrected this word since the original idiom in English is "sticks and stones."*

133. ~~The shadow of the cross~~ The door

134. ~~best or worst,~~ for better or for worse,

The rationalist does not assert that the internationalist civilization created by the Portuguese discoveries & the |*Greek| democratization[135] of learning is the best type of civilization: he asserts that it is ours. For whether it should be there or not, (he asserts that) it is here. There is no more ease in shaking[136] off Greek Culture, Roman Order, or Christian Ethics than there is in, by the use of some transcendental extension of Mr. Well's Time-Machine, reversing the film of history and disiscovering[137] and reunpeopling[138] the transoceanic world.

As we cannot repudiate our parents or divorce our ancestors, or divorce our mother to be an ex-mother,[139] we cannot make a secure statement that we owe nothing to the fathers or will henceforward have owed them nothing. We may pay or not our[140] debts, we may right or not have debts — we cannot say they were something which is not particularly done.[141]

---

135. ↑ |*Greek| democratization / ↑ hellenization \

136. ~~shak~~ shaking

137. *As is in the original:* "disiscovering" *means here the contrary of* "discovering."

138. ~~carrying~~ reversing the film of history and ~~un~~ ↑ dis iscovering & ~~unpeopl~~ reunpeopling

139. our parents ← or divorce our ancestors, or divorce our ~~father~~ ↑ mother to be an ex-~~father~~ ↑ mother

140. ↑ or not our

141. ↑ or not have debts — we cannot say they were something w[hich] is not ↓ particularly done.

[55G — 24^r]

There are two rationalisms. There is a lower, or fetichistic, rationalism which is that of rationalists [142] commonly so called, and commonly so calling themselves; and there is a higher rationalism. Both believe — at bottom this is, like the bottom of everything else, an unverifiable [143] belief — that reason is all that we have, or the best we have, [144] to investigate truth. The two differ as to what they consider the truth that can be investigated. The lower rationalism is still captive of the old metaphysical myth — that reason can reach metaphysical conclusions. The higher rationalism, basing on the premise that all knowledge comes from the senses, & that reason is not a sense, cannot admit the possibility of reason more than sifting the data of the senses; and as there are no known senses (unless the mystics are right, which we cannot verify to universal satisfaction) which supply metaphysical data, reason is powerless to arrive at any conclusion as to the fundamentals of being. All faiths, however absurd they may seem, or contradictory, are therefore possible; they cannot be denounced as false; they must simply be let live

---

142. of ~~the~~ rationalists
143. inverifiable, *in the original. Possible authorial lapse.*
144. we have, ~~and the most that~~ or the best we have

as probabilities that never can be verified. This leads to tolerance without an effort.

The attitude of higher rationalism receives its symbol in that celebrated anecdote, which is related of Baudelaire. A naval officer, a friend of his, who had just returned from a long colonial voyage, was showing him a fetish he had brought back; he showed him with disgust that wooden object, the astonishing idol of a human race. And, as he, after having shown it, was going to throw it in disgust into a corner, Baudelaire laid sudden hands upon his arm. "Stop!" he said, "What if it were the true God?" — *Et si c'etait le vrai Dieu?* — This[145] is the higher rationalism, both in essence and in tone.

The two rationalisms split, again, over the sociological problem. It is almost invariable that the lower rationalist should be a democrat, a believer in that myth called "the people." As he is generally an atheist — that is to say, a believer with a minus sign — he carries the typical attitude of belief into a concrete sphere, as all believers do. Where one believes in the Pentateuch, another believes in Democracy.

$$\left[15^1 - 45^r\right]$$

The monism of Force-matter has become, as you know, old; it has been superseded by the Force-Monism of

145. T[j|h]is

Gustave Le Bon.[146] The blind, stupid, unscrupulous philosophy (for so it is called) of Hæckel[147] has grown old in[148] its metaphysical aspect.

The lack[149] of criticism of reason, by which your system is dogmatic, is the cause of this. What affirms the right of reason to pursue the infinite? Scientific prejudice, convention — ultimately in some cases intellectual dishonesty.[150] Common sense is the worst enemy of philosophy.

----

146. Gustave Le Bon (1841–1931) was a psychologist, sociologist, and amateur physicist. His work concerned the psychology of the masses and the evolution of social forces. In the field of physics, he developed many theories concerning the evolution of matter. In Pessoa's Private Library, there are three of Le Bon's books: *L'évolution da la matière* [CFP, 1–81]; *L'évolution des forces* [CFP, 1–82]; and *La psychologie politique et la défense sociale* [CFP, 1–83].

147. Ernst Hæckel (1834–1919) was a German naturalist and one of the great figures of positivism. He is known to be one of the most important divulgers of Darwin's works. In Pessoa's Private Library, there are four French translations of Hæckel's books: *Les merveilles de la vie* [CFP, 1–65]; *Origine de l'homme* [CFP, 5–17]; *Histoire de la création des êtres organisés d'après les lois naturelles* [CFP, 5–16]; *Les énigmes de l'univers* [CFP, 1–64].

148. grown ↑ old in

149. ~~Thus for instance infinity of matter~~ The lack

150. cases ↑ intellectual dishonesty

53

$$[15^1 - 46^r]$$

The second reason for differing from your system is the[151] numerous inconsequences of scientific thought. Any really profound thinker, rationalist or not, will grasp at the joining of the ideas of matter *&* of eternity, not to speak of those of eternity and infinity and of evolution. Scientific inquiry and observation blunt the reasoning[152] powers; there is no sure way of training the mind in dialectics than reasoning independent of observation.[153]

Rationalism is dogmatic, *&* it is not a system of philosophy. Telescopes[154] search the sky and, as they find no limit, they declare matter infinite. But such is no scientific method. Such is a pure assumption, which is the outcome of your idea of Rationalism. How do you know that reason has the power to affirm infinite multiplication.

$$[15^1 - 47^r]$$

The foundations of morals are triple: instinct, which produces civics; obedience, which produces inhibition; reason, which produces harmony in action.

---

151. ~~is that~~ is the
152. blunts ↑ the reasoning
153. ~~other~~ sure way of training the mind in ~~reasoning~~ ↑ dialectics than reasoning independ[a|↑e]nt of observation
154. ~~How~~ Telescopes

Reason, by itself, is not moral, because there is no moral to come out from reason. Reason does not create; it merely limits.

A true rationalist is incapable of altruism, because he cannot see, by reason, any reason for altruism. Morality is irrational. But life is irrational, and morality is fundamental as being such.

[15⁵ — 19]

Liberal Rationalism
1. Chapter on: *Fallacies*

There are two errors that may be committed in this respect. One is to make metaphysics a science, the other to make science a metaphysics. The first any theist commits; the second is committed for instance by [155] Professor Hæckel in his "Riddles of the Universe."

Let us abandon, indeed, metaphysics for science, but, doing so, let us remember that science does not *substitute* metaphysics; its province is another. If a man attempt[s] to fly and fail[s], we may laugh and abandon the idea of flying, by walking; but we must say that we are flying. It is into this error that many scientists fall, materialists or deists, Sir Andrew Lang [156] or Hæckel or Brüchner. [157]

---

155. committed ↑ for instance by

[19ᵛ]

Christianity, anthropomorphism can be attacked — at least attacked by science. Pure Deism never — its form is another. Quite outside (if not above) Science.

156. Andrew Lang (1844–1912) was a Scottish poet, novelist, literary critic, and translator. He became known for his collection of fairy tales and folk stories, as well as for his translation (in collaboration with others) of Homer's *Iliad & Odyssey*. He also developed work in the field of the psychical sciences, & later became president of the Society for Psychical Research.

157. Ludwig Brüchner (1824–1899) was a German physicist and philosopher and is known as a partisan of materialism. In Pessoa's Private Library, there are two of his works in French translation: *Force et matière* [CFP, 1–15]; *L'homme selon la science* [CFP, 1–16].

1.3 — The Mental Disorder of Jesus

$$[134B - 26^r]$$

Preface *Teschou*[158]

We had always thought that the most terrible adversary of the Christian Religion[159] would be, when it grew to its strength, medical psychology.

$$[26B - 29^r]$$

This[160] pamphlet aims at being no more then an explanatory criticism of Dr. Binet-Sanglé's[161] astonishing book[162]

---

158. Effects of an insane man's preaching on *the people*

   No normality.
   Man a hysteric animal.
                    etc. _____
   Preface ~~Ch~~ *Teschou*

159. Christ[ian] Rel[igion]

160. ~~The ☐ of~~ This

161. Charles Binet-Sanglé (1868–1941) was a French psychiatrist and doctor. He became known, in his time, by his book *La folie de Jésus*. Pessoa's Private Library contains volume II & volume III of *La folie de Jésus* [CFP, 1–9].

162. Dr. B[inet]-S[anglé]'s astonishing book

— the first volume of a complete □ — on the insanity of Jesus. An explanatory commentary and a reasoning one this aims at being — this and no more.

English readers are little[163] acquainted, we believe, with the modern psychiatric account, especially in its applications to the psychology of criminals, of men of genius & of madmen.

[26A — 50–51]

I.

Man is a hysteric animal. That is to say, man is an animal far more impressionable than the others in thought[164] (that is, comprehending more), in feeling (□) & in will (□) — we meaning here by impressionable excitable, irritable.[165]

Animals differ less from one another than man from man; indeed, enormous differences[166] part some men from others.

Thus what we call normality, which does not exist even in[167] the animal & about which all oscillates, still

---

163. ~~have been~~ ↑ are little
164. ~~both~~ in thought
165. ~~will to~~ irritable
166. diff[eren]ces
167. ↑ even in

less exists in man. What we call normal men are those that oscillate near to a certain hyper-real type[168] — not an ideal type, but a type of perfect man, according to nature, of a man with faculties perfectly balanced.

Our commonest experience of life, what we call intuition[,] teach[es] us that there are no degrees of normality in men, but only degrees of abnormality, that the normal is only the less abnormal.

[50ᵛ]

All this is comparatively true.

Man is an animal more full of abnormality.

No where is that *abnormality* (as we have called it) more evident than in the psychological life. The perpetual change, oscillation □ is specially great in those facts which are studied by psychology.

Now one side[169] of "abnormality" is "*susceptibility*" to *external influences*. The more *Abnormal* the body, the more diseases it is open to.

Similarly with the mind, the more oscillating □ it is, the more it lends itself to □. Illness need[s] that there be a predisposition, a condition of the body or mind making it possible. This is obvious.

---

168. ~~unreal~~ ↑ hyper-real ~~superior~~ type
169. ~~phase ph face~~ side

[51ʳ]

In proportion to "abnormality,"[170] "oscillation" is great, so is susceptibility to disease or aberration great.

Now as the mind is more "abnormal" than the body, the mind is more prone to aberration, nay, *more prone to disease.*

We are now aware of the reason why madmen and abnormal people can so easily dominate crowds.

&c.

Mankind [is] easily led (1) by emotions (2) by recently *fond* sent[imen]ts, more prone to irritability (Ribot),[171] such as the religious sense.

(later sentiments are *less* easy to awake[n] — the religious (e.g.) than the sexual sense.)

But more liable to instability?

---

170. as ~~suggestibility~~ "abnormality,"
171. Théodule-Armand Ribot (1839–1916) was a materialist French psychologist *&* thinker. His psychiatric work was devoted to the study of inherited elements in the constitution of mental life, ignoring all spiritual explanations.
172. *B[inet]-Sanglé*

[134B — 23-25]

Binet-Sanglé — Comment. [172]

II — (?)

Since some time & especially since Lombroso [173] pub-
lished his "Man of Genius" and Max Nordau [174] his

---

173. Cesare Lombroso (1835–1909) was an Italian psychiatrist, in-
fluenced by the study of phrenology. He wrote several books
on criminology, madness, and other related subjects, defending
the idea that an analysis of the somatic characteristics of a per-
son would enable one to foresee criminal tendencies in them.
In Alexander Search's reading notebook [BNP/E3, 144 – 20],
one finds references to six of Lombroso's books: *L'Homme
criminel*; *La femme criminelle et la prostituée*, written by Lom-
broso and Ferrero; *Le crime politique et les revolutions*, written
by Lombroso and Laschi; *L'Anthropologie criminelle et ses ré-
cents progrès*; *Nouvelles recherches d'anthropologie criminelle et
de psychiatrie*; *Applications de l'anthropologie criminelle*.

174. Max Nordau (1849–1923) was a physician and social critic, as
well as the co-founder of the World Zionist Organization. His
most relevant work is *Entartung*. In this work, Nordau estab-
lishes an analysis of the literature and art of the *fin de siècle*,
revealing, through the application of a psychiatric method, that
the artistic & literary productions of this period were symp-
toms of 'degeneration.' In Alexander Search's reading note-
book, one finds references to four of Nordau's books, three
in French and one in English: *Psycho-physiologie du genie et
du talent*; *Dégénérescence*; *Vus du déhors*; *Conventional Lies of
Our Civilization*.

"Degeneration" — admirable[175] in □, but more admirable still in the impulse it gave — a conviction has been drawing, conviction not yet quite clearly expressed, that the importance of nervous mental diseases[176] in history has been great. As a matter of fact, the history of mankind,[177] in part the biography of great men, in part [23ᵛ] (little being left beside) a history[178] of great deeds and of great decadences is no more than the history of several neuroses, |neuropathies|. The history of literature seems[179] a history of Decadence. (Here partly enumerate — □ Nordau.)[180]

(cite)

The French revolution is a public neuropathy, where no form of degeneration — from genius to criminality — is lacking. Napoleon was not sane.

[24ʳ]

Thus history is but the chronicle of a succession of neurotic □ — public or personal — those of great men or

---

175. since ↑ Lombroso published his "Man of Genius" ⅋ Max Nordau ~~published~~ his ~~admirable~~ "Degeneration" — admirable

176. ↑ mental diseases

177. ↑ the history ↑ of mankind‚

178. history /↑ relate \

179. literature /↑ literary biography \ seems

180. N[ordau]

those of nations. Not the least interesting study is that of the |propagation| or the propaganda of neurosis — the influence of great madmen in people and nations, the public irradiation of a personal neuropathy.

$$[24^v]$$

That history should be so is evident. To be great, to be important something — personal or public — must be not the usual, not[181] of the normal.

But history is[182] not the chronicle of greatness properly, but of *abnormalness*. Nero was not great, he was abnormal.[183]

$$[25^r]$$

———

Theory that men are all abnormal *&* that the religious unbalance is natural.

———

The unnatural is also natural; else it would not exist. All that exists is natural, because it[184] exists — no more

———

181. ~~be~~ not
182. ~~Because a~~ ↑But history is
183. ~~unless in~~ ↑he was abnormal.
184. ∴ [because] it

proof is needed. Parricide is unnatural, but bec[ause] un-
natural was abnormal. But it is quite natural, in the tem-
perament[185] that produced it, else it would not have been.

$$[26B - 14-15]$$
$$— II\ (b).$$

The fact is that Dr. Binet-Sanglé,[186] having found a fine
case of madness in the 4 gospels, is as desirous of retain-
ing them and of being able to believe these authentic
as any Christian believer. But[187] — it may be at once
remarked — are not to him the 4 gospels obviously
proved[188] true by their *biologic truth*? Is it not certain
that the 3 synoptics & the gospel according to Johanan
(or John) are correct, exact[ly] because[189] they are mu-
tually psychiatrically confirmative? Dr. Binet-Sanglé[190]
himself says that the evangelists invented, they must
have been neurologists, to be able to invent a case of in-
sanity[191] with all its symptoms. Does not this seem exact?
Is it not obvious that another species of proof of the

---

185. temp[eramen]t
186. Dr. B[inet]-S[angl]é
187. ~~To him~~ But
188. are not to him obviously the 4 Gospels proved, *in the original.*
189. ∵ [because]
190. B[inet]-S[anglé]
191. insanity / ↑ madness \

authenticity of the gospels must be admitted — the   [14ᵛ]
"biologic proof," as Prof. Binet-Sanglé[192] calls it — in
the fact that they constitute a *living* case, a *whole* case
of madness? Surely this is self-evident?

No; it is self-evident[193] only to those unacquainted
with the real nature of the question.

In the 1ˢᵗ place, if it were proved that this or that
passage of this or that gospel |were| inauthentic, no
professor[194] of psychiatry could call it back to authentici-
ty with the |magnet|[195] of "psychiatric necessity." Confirm
what it might confirm — if inauthentic, it must remain so.

The only alteration that the consideration of such
a passage presenting a symptom □ could induce us to
make was to be slower in admitting the inauthenticity of
the passage, at most to put[196] "psychiatric necessity" into
the balance as an aid to an argument for genuineness.[197]
This *&* no more.

[15ʳ]

But this is not all, nor is this anything but a preliminary
consideration. We came to the principal question. Jesus

---

192. B[inet]-S[anglé]
193. ~~not~~ self-evident
194. ~~psy~~ ↑ professor
195. |magnet| /↑iman\
196. inauthenticity ~~but~~ of the passage, ↑at most to ~~p~~ put
197. ~~authenticity to~~ genuineness.

is, according to Dr. Binet-Sanglé[198] — no matter here the diagnosis he is aiming at — a "mental degenerate." Now modern theories of medicine do not permit us to admit a *mental* degeneracy without some concomitant *physical* degeneracy. Degeneracy however, mental or physical, is known by what we called[199] ſtigmata, physical or mental, of it. "Stigmata" means much the same as symptoms, but is applied to degeneration only. Now the liſt of physical *&* mental ſtigmata of degeneration has been made so large by modern psychiatric science that every man acquainted with them can manage, if he wishes it, to discover degeneration in anybody. This is no jeſt, no criminal ſtatement — for this is not the place for jeſts or crimes. This is absolutely true. Not only is there no evident limit to the number — even,[200] it seems, to the hitherto discovered number — of ſtigmata, psychical and mental, of degeneration, but the objective idea[201] of a degenerate *&* the description of one in any medical work — and mental degenerates more than physical — is extremely vague. We say "objective idea" because[202] all psychiatricians and many other people also have[203]

[15ᵛ]

---

198. Dr. B[inet-]S[anglé]

199. ~~is~~ ↑we called

200. even ~~to,~~

201. ↑ objective idea

202. ∵ [because]

203. ↑ and many other people also have

more or less an intuition of what a degenerate is —
physically & mentally — but no adequate description,
nor any description approaching to adequate has ever
been given — that we know — of the type or types. That
drawn by Gilbert Ballet, in □ (quoted by Dr. Binet-
Sanglé, and therefore, considering his knowledge, a[204]
good one if not the best) is conspicuously vague and
insufficient![205] The very word "degenerate," in[206] its psy-
chiatric mental sense, of course, has not yet been pro-
perly defined. Insufficiencies and incorroborations we
do not hold to be all or part of a lucid definition.[207]

The greatest □ of all physical stigmata is Prof. Lom-
broso, that[208] eminent and erratic man of science, full of
marvellous intuitions and of absurd generalisations □
& confusedly great. Modern science owes much to him,
both in impulse & help, but this cannot make us forget
that by his method of finding stigmata □

What Lombroso has done for the physical stigmata,
Nordau has done for the mental. The appalling number
of neurotics, madmen that crop up under Nordau's □

204. B[inet]-S[anglé], & therefore, considering the ↑ his knowledge, of a
205. Dr. Galloffer in his luminous preface to □ has ↑ gives, by far, to be
    in my opinion, by far the best idea of what degeneration is &
    degenerates are. [Author note.]
206. we in
207. a lucid / ↑ what can be called a \ definition.
208. that we that

[26A — 70–72]

The meaning of this semi-digression is that the type of the mental degenerate is as yet vaguely established, that mental stigmata are superabundant, that consequently it is not hard to degeneratize any creature provided any exterior data are supplied[209] about him, where some stigma[ta] or another is sure to be found. Now narratives involving supernatural events, *although invented,* are[210] generally full of facts that lend themselves splendidly to the net of the psychiatrician.

Suppose we interpolate[211] in one of the gospels saying[s] like these, with[212] the end of making Christ preach lines insane:

"I am the son of the Lord *&* the Lord also is great" *&*c.

The conclusion is "megalomania." But really there is nothing of the kind; there is only an invention, an interpolation.

[70ᵛ]

Words purporting supernatural things can generally if not always be made[213] to enter into some species of delirium — whereas they may be mere[214] fabrications.

---

209. ~~provid~~ supplied
210. ~~tend to~~ are
211. ↑ we ~~invent~~ interpolate
212. ~~what~~ with
213. ~~put into the mouth of an individual~~ can generally ↑ if not always be
214. ~~invent~~ ↑ mere   [made

We are perfectly convinced that if any man sat down and wrote from his imagination a gospel of some Christ of his invention, that a □ of [215] psychiatry could easily prove that a madman is in question.

What are [216] the deductions from this? The 1ˢᵗ one is that all expressions naturally invented to represent supernatural things or missions *resemble delirium.* The conclusion is too obvious. That any man's belief in a supernatural mission is proof of his insanity.

But this can be denied. We have no right it may be said — to deny *revelation* because [217] it resembles insanity. If any ideal representation of revelation in supernaturalism appears naturally one of insanity, the conclusion is simply that both are abnormal — no other is legitimate. Because if revelation exists, if there be supernaturalism, it must be its own proof. [218]

[71ʳ]

It would be natural, for instance, for a man *inventing* (this is the purest hypothesis) a sort of gospel: [219]

---

215. ~~the~~ a ~~scientist~~ □ of

216. ~~is~~ ↑ ᵃʳᵉ

217. ∵ [because]

218. if ← revelation exists, if there be supernaturalism, it must be its own proof.

219. a ↑ ˢᵒʳᵗ ᵒᶠ gospel: ~~to~~

(1) To indicate the hearty character of a Teacher by
     making a division between him & his family —
     as, for instance, treating his mother as "woman."

(2) To □

Believers might then ask us, since we prove all insanity, to include the resurrection, for instance, in delirious phenomena.

[71ᵛ]

We are entirely ignorant of any reply made to Dr. Binet-Sanglé's [220] book. We know there have been contradictors of it, but we have not read anything — either in favour or against — nothing, as a matter of fact, regarding the book, except advertisements & the book itself. We do not know therefore if this — the only possible apologetic retort — has been made. We have deduced it ourselves. We will ourselves destroy it.

We shall destroy it absolutely and relatively — absolutely in regard to any case at all; relatively with regard to the special case of Jesus.

---

220. Dr. B[inet]-S[anglé]'s

$$[72^r]$$

All gospels — all as our hypothesis contain 3 elements:

   (1) Supernatural phenomena — miracles. [221]

   (2) Abnormal [222] phenomena — speeches, [223] acts of
      the Teacher that are not natural.

   (3) Normal facts of his life — as of any life — voyages &c.

We are not concerned with the normal of course.
Let us take 1ˢᵗ the abnormal, then. Consider it together
with the supernormal.

Any madman is abnormal — not supernatural at all.

What, for instance, is a vision? This, apparently super-
normal, is undoubtedly normal. Not only is it common, □

Now what is the type of the supernormal? A miracle.

$$[72^v]$$

The 1ˢᵗ thing in a miracle is its evidence, □

The supernatural is only the *collective abnormal*, the *social
abnormal*.

---

221. a̶s̶ miracles.
222. A̶b̶n̶o̶r̶m̶a̶l̶ ↑Abnormal
223. a̶s̶ speeches

A miracle[224] is either a collective error or a collective hallucination.

––––––––––

The only difference[225] between miracles and visions is the fact that vision[s] come to one, miracles to many.

If it can be proved that miracles, □ one characteristic of □ [226]

[26B — 22]

— II —

Jesus being insane what[227] is his historic part?

A madman cannot create.

Properly speaking no man can. But a man of genius.

A madman may create[228] discordant things — things incapable of practice. — But religion is one of these.

––––––––––

A genius is no more than a *sane madman*, or *a clear madness*.

––––––––––

––––––––––

224. A miracle
225. diff[eren]ce
226. ~~proved~~ ↑proved that miracles, □ one characteristic of ~~various~~
227. J[esus] being insane ~~he a~~ what
228. ↑may create

But, it will be asked, how can a man not a genius fill such a plan in history? Can any analogous case of epoch-making insanity[229] be found?

[26A — 84–86]

II.

The idea that |Christ| was insane, far from being a thing incapable of being obtained[230] except under scientific examination, can, on the contrary, be deduced in a manner that can be classified as *a priori*.

Critics having determined — Strauss, Renan, etc. — the error of *Christ* being the son of God, the following argument naturally follows such a determination:

|Christ| once conceived as a man and not as the son of God, few seemed to see what conclusion was to be drawn from this mere fact.

Christ, son of God, was conceived, of course, as a perfect[231] man, as a being of sovereign and unequal benevolence and goodness. Being conceived as a man, it is strange how none could make this simple reflection: being a man, a human being, obviously he could not have been, because no man can be a perfectly good, a perfectly perfect creature.

---

229. of ↑ ~~making~~ epoch-making insanity
230. ~~con~~ obtained
231. ~~man~~ perfect

[85ʳ]

In the midst of our rationalism we still considered Jesus
— by an |atavism| and □ subjective — as a man whose
life was the perfection of goodness. We did not see,
we repeat, that this perfection of goodness pertained,
could pertain to no one but a being higher than man,
a god, a son of God. Strauss, Renan, all other biblical
critics fall into this error.

We were Christs ever; [232] we remained worshippers
of Christ. It was owing to this that so many rationalists,
atheists and free-thinkers had moments of return or
almost return — mental[ly], unspoken at least — to a
belief of the divinity of Christ. Considering him as a
perfect man in goodness and love of mankind, the mind
unconsciously reasoned — and it reasoned well — that
such goodness and perfection or love of man could be
only the characteristic of a God. The unconscious [233]
reasoning of those rationalists, atheists & free-thinkers
was better than the conscious one.

In a few words, the critics having determined that
Jesus was no god, that he was a man, it becomes impos-
sible to hold the theory that he was that perfect being
[85ᵛ] we believe. He must have had faults, however few, he
must have had defects.

But the deductions do not stop here. There is more.

232. ~~in the~~ ever
233. ~~unconscious~~ ↑ unconscious

Christ considered as a man and therefore as a being that must have some defects, — Christ conceived (of) as a being of this earth, the theory he exposed, the conceptions he had — which seemed indeed natural in a being [234] not of this earth, in one not of the stuff of men, being thus another thing inducing the side of his godship — assume, considered as a man's, a manifest character of intense abnormality & extravagance.

It becomes impossible to conceive these ideas as other thing than delirium, so little natural are they to mankind, except to morbid and certain pathologic conditions of mind.

The very incompatibility of such a system [235] of ethics with that natural to men, of its flushed coldness of morality to our other |*violated| social warmth gives a verdict, [236] which Christ was to be a god, if his divinity [237] becomes, he [was] known as a man, an abnormal [238] and inhuman, non-human-code.

[86ʳ]

Thus from the mere conception of Christ as a man & not as a god, we have drawn, purely by reasoning, the following conclusions: that he must manifestly have been

234. ~~were~~ ↑seemed indeed natural in a ~~human~~ being
235. ~~morality~~ system
236. ~~an idea~~ verdict
237. ~~divinity~~ divinity
238. ~~a~~ abnormal

an abnormal, a very abnormal man, secondly, that that being the case, his code of ethics is an abnormal, a very abnormal code & must become subject to examination ere some think of it as a thing to be put into practice.

Mental abnormality is either insanity or what Grasset[239] calls half-insanity (demifolie) and Trelat "lucid insanity" (folie lucide), both[240] meaning a degree of mental abnormality that did not absolutely exclude a more or less normal life among men.

$$[26C - 29]$$

$$J.C.$$

III —

No man[241] is "normal" in an absolute sense. There is no dividing line between the normal and the abnormal, or between sickness and[242] health. Those expressions are relative & our interpretation of them, as we are about

---

239. Joseph Grasset (1849–1918) was a French psychiatrist who developed his work in the fields of neurology & parapsychology. In Pessoa's Private Library, there are two of Grasset's books: *L'occultisme hier et aujourd'hui* & *Morale scientifique et morale évangélique devant la sociologie.*

240. ~~and~~ both

241. ~~There~~ No man

242. sickness / ↑illness \ and

to use them, is wide and obviously plain intuition[243] rather than exact. The nearest we can go to a positive definition is observing[244] that men are abnormal physically and mentally, in proportion as they are easily led into disease, as in them the manner of cellular activity called health can[245] easily be turned into the manner of organic activity called illness.

There is no man, for instance, who cannot be made insane. The question is one of more or less difficulty in doing it, of more *&* more out-of-the-way methods having to be employed to produce insanity.[246] The man lives not who cannot be tortured — this way or that — into madness.   [29ᵛ]

———

We have to enter into a consideration of the psychology of ignorance.

An ignorant man is generally emotional, *&*, in a sense, imaginative — intensely emotional and imaginative.

———

243. ~~widely~~ relative *&* our interpretation of them, as we are about to use them, is ↑ wide and obviously plain intuition

244. ~~We~~ The nearest we can go to a positive definition is ~~saying~~ observing

245. as ↑ in them the manner of cellular /↑ organic\ activity called health ~~is then~~ can

246. ~~it~~ insanity

[26 A — 69]

— end —

Men of the west, practical dreamers, □

You have lifted temples to Christ.

Men of the west — for 20 centuries you have adored a *madman!*

1.4 — Delirium

Delirium
To a Hand.

Give me thy hand. With my wounded eyes
I would see what this hand contains. —
Ah, what a world of hopes here lies!
What a world of feelings and doubts & pains!
Oh to think that this hand in itself contains
The mystery of mysteries.

This hand has a meaning thou dost not know,
A meaning deeper than human fears;
This hand perchance in times long ago
Wiped off strange and unnatural tears;
Perhaps its gesture was full of sneers,
Perchance its clenching was full of woe.

There is that in thy hand my soul doth dream
And the shades that haunt my mind;
The howl of the wind & the flow of the stream,
The flow of the stream & the howl of the wind,
All that is horrible and undefined
Of things that are in the things that seem.

As I look at thy hand my mind is rife
Of thoughts and memories deeper than rhyme;
Thy hand is a part of my soul's deep life,

[2ʳ] And I knew thy hand ere the birth of time,
And in ages paſt it led me to crime,
In dim praying |ages| of [dark] |caſtled| ſtrife ²⁴⁷
A world of woes and of fears *&* sighs
And love that better had been hate,
And crimes and wars and victories,
And the painful fall of many a ſtate —
All these *&* more that the heart abate
My rowing soul in thy hand descries.

No painter mad, not a fetichiſt
O'er thy hand would be thus held blind.
At mere blank I thought of its being kissed
By my lips I thrill with a fear none find
In the waking thoughts of a human mind
Save when reason by its own self is miss'd. ²⁴⁸

Thy hand has a meaning thou doſt not know,
A meaning deeper than human fears;
It has aught of the sea and of the sun's glow
And the seasons too and the months *&* years,
And the colour hidden in human tears
And the form and number in human woe.

[3ʳ]

Thy hand was a lofty and empty home,
A collar of pearls and a castle keep;
Thy hand knows well all the thoughts that roam;
Thy hand is the music eternal and deep
That long ere birth held my soul asleep
In a palace quaint with a curious dome.

How finely made is this hand of thine
With its fingers tapering and white,
Soft and palely warm and fine;
There is something in it of day & night.
Ah, dearest child, could I read aright
The text before me deep and divine.

There's a kind of Fact that persists and hangs[249]
O'er thy hand, as on a scratched scroll;
'Tis as if some thought had buried its fangs
In an unknown part of my soul.
In a land far in me a bell doth toll,
And my heart aches wild as it shrinks or clangs.

---

247. ~~And in ages dark it led me to~~ ↓ In ~~an obscure~~ dim praying |ages| of [dark]
|castled| ~~civil~~ strife

248. ~~finds~~ ↑by its

249. ← + There's

There is aught of new and wild and unreal
In thy hand where my look is pained:
'Tis as if thy hand in itself could see all —
Horrible thought, where fear is gained
By a drollness mad and dimly sustained
As of some wide hint out of the Ideal.

There is aught of Personal, of It, of Such
In thy hand and o'er me there steals
A sense of dread like a |murderer's| clutch;²⁵⁰
I know not how, my hand in thine feels
An eternal thing and my mad brain reels
As if eternity we could touch.

I see that hand not a hand, but whence
This horrible Fact that creeps in me?
|Ah, I have thy hand the seeing intense|
But aught more than hand in that place I see
That abrupt elision did make to be
Between thought of things & what we call sense.

My thought doth look at thy hand direct
Without eyes or sense or aught of this,
And my reason at such a thing is wrecked
Into such a fear that both pain and bliss
Are plunged in conscious unconsciousness
For that is no hand that my dreams detect.

[4ʳ]

---

250. a |murderer's| /↑ an unseen \

[5^r]

And I gaze yet more and I shake from me
The dream of time and the dream of ſpace,
And as a drowner who sinks in the sea
I dream of the wonders of all we trace
In everything and I plunge full-face
In the sense of what more than seems to be.

There is aught of lovely, wild $\mathcal{C}$ unbrute
In thy hand, and I lose it well;

For fearing more than firm thoughts of hell
By a sudden portal in the Visible
I have a glimpse of the Absolute.

The sight of thy hand of a horrible heaven
The portals mute throws open again

Thy hand is like music, in it I gain
Passing a wild fear $\mathcal{C}$ a bitter pain
Weird things more weird than the sense of Seven.[251]

All things ſtare myſtery at my mind,
But thy hand moſt, to oblivion conn'd;
Thrilled with a mute life not all defined,
What is thy hand in itself beyond   [6^r]
The scope of sense where the heart is fond,
The realm of thought where the soul is blind?

251. $^{\leftarrow\times}$ Weird

Where is the soul that thy hand reveals
In its own *there* — self till its thought affrights?
What bells are those that say HAND in peals
That traverse impossible infinites?
What fills with lightnings of hands the nights [252]
Where the sense of dread into thoughts congeals?

Take thy hand away; for I now shall dream
Of strange and grotesque and unnatural lands
Watered by many a painful stream
Whose waves are hands, whose banks are hands,
Of gardens with trees whose leaves are hands [253]
And a white stiff hand covering the sun's gleam. [254]

And troops of hands all in sight scent and sound
In their touch but felt to the visual mind
Dance and howl and mix interwound
In mere visual wise [255]
Yet never shut, always stiff, defined
Howe'er fast they move in their tragic round.

252. of ~~words~~ ↑hands the
253. ~~who~~ whose
254. ↑stiff hand
255. ←+ And troops of hands ↑all in sight scent & sound /↑—no sound—\
      ←+ In their touch & ~~(horror) their soul and~~ ↑but felt to /in\ the visual
      Dance and howl and mix interwound   mind
      In ~~my fearful dreams~~ ↑mere visual wise

85

[7ʳ]

Then, oh horror worſt, they begin to live
With a vital life, and to graſp and clutch,
And to twitch *&* squirm till my thoughts unweave,
& like worms *&* snails that my throat should touch
My soul qualms and retches at horror such
At fear's transcendent superlative.

And what more doth follow I cannot say,
But it seems that madly I traverse, lone,
Traċts of hells where a hand doth *stay*
In such a manner that if a groan
Of a madman could in its soul be known
It would be to it as night is to day.

And my thoughts drag on in their weary ſtrain;
Wild and grotesque, or quick or slow,
Uncouth and unseemly they reel in my brain,
Startingly mad as they go,
As a sudden laugh in the midſt of woe
Or a clown in a funeral train.

January, 1906.

Alexander *Search.*

86

[78 — 14–15]

Delirium
Comedy.

I.

Once in a theatre comic
'Tween acts I pondered to see
On a column sculptured, wide *&* comic,
The grinning mask of Comedy;
And broad and wild in satyr-glee,
The grinning face of Comedy.

II.

"Ah," said I, "face merry and comic,
There is happiness in thee,
Few faces like thine, wide-mouth'd *&* comic,
Oh, grinning face of Comedy;
Boisterously wrinkled, ugly and free,
The grinning mask of Comedy."

III.

But as I gazed at the face that smiled,
With mine eyes half-dreamfully,
"Ah," said I, "it is forced and wild,
Untrue smile of pitiless glee;
Forcedly wrinkled, unreal, unfree,
Hard-grinning mask of Comedy."

$[15^r]$

IV.

And I trembled — now it no longer smiled,
It had forcedly smiled — now not even so.
Oh, fearful face, terribly wild,
Terribly silent face or woe;
Worn, hysterical, mad, unfree,
Woe-twisted face of Comedy.

Alexander *Search*.

January, 1906

[78 — 16–22]

Documents of Mental Decadence.

Delirium[256]

Flashes of Madness.

I.

Thy hand with its lovely fingers
And the heavy rings on them!
How my soul over them lingers!
Each finger with a heavy gem,
Each ring like a small diadem!

When thou and I are alone,
One only wish my soul ſtings —
Holding thy hand in my own,
All night, while the night-bird sings,
To take off and replace thy rings.

Alexander *Search*

January *1906.*

---

256. *Del*[*irium*]

[17ʳ]

Delirium[257]

Flashes of Madness.

II.

When thou seeëst me spend hours
Holding in a feverish glance[258]
Thy mouth or teeth, or thy hand,
And notest how my soul devours
With a sleepness like to trance
The commonest things that stand,

And askest what in them I see
That into each my spirit delves
As if each had a mystery,[259]
Thou err'st in thy conjecturings,
For what ever obsesses me
Is not things in their weary selves
But the being there of things.[260]

Alexander *Search*

February 1906.

---

257. *Del*[*irium*]
258. feverish /↑ too-local \ glance
259. As if i̶t̶ ↑ each had a mystery,
260. Is not things in their weary /↑many \ selves
 A̶n̶d̶ ↑But the c̶o̶m̶m̶o̶n̶ ̶s̶o̶u̶l̶ ↑b̶e̶i̶n̶g̶ ̶h̶e̶r̶e̶ /↓being there\ / such \ of things

[18ʳ]

Delirium

Flashes of Madness.

III.

Eyes are strange things.
Meaning in them becomes life,
    Life in them has wings.

Look at me thus. Thy glance is mad and rare.
Thine eyes show deep and wild an inner strife.
    How they are more than Horror fair!

Alexander *Search.*

1908.

$[19^r]$

Flashes of Madness

IV.

1.

When thou didſt ſpeak but now I felt [261]
      A terror mad and ſtrange.
Conceive it thou. I could have knelt
To thy lips, to their curve, to its change.
      The talking curve of thy lips
      And thy teeth but slightly shown
Were my delirium's waking whips.
      I felt my reason o'erthrown.

A super-sensual fetichism
      Haunts my deep-raving brain.
Greater than ever grows the abysm
Of my reason's and feeling's schism,
      Cut with the pickaxe of pain. [262]

More than they show all things contain.

---

261. ~~laugh~~ ↑ speak
262. pickaxe /↓ earth maker\

2.

Something not of this world doth lie
In thy smile, in thy lips live turn;
A figure, a form I know not why
That wakes in me — without a sigh
But with terror I cannot ſpurn
With terror wild and mute —

Is it remembrances, is it
Desires so vague half-known they flit
And not in thought nor sentiment take root?

My mind grows madder and more fit
In everything to catch and find
Meanings, resemblances defined
By not a form that thought can hit.

Smile not. Thou canſt not comprehend!
What is this? What truth doth sleep
In these ravings without end
And beyond notion deep?
Laugh not. Know'ſt thou what madness is?
Wonder not. All is myſteries.
Ask not. For who can reply?
Weep for me, child, but do not love me
Who have in me too much that is above me, [263]
Too much I cannot call "I."

263. ~~Who~~ have

$$[21^r]$$

Weep for the ruin of my mind
Weep rather, child, that things so deep should move me
To lose the clear thoughts that could prove me
One worthy of mankind.

Alexander *Search*

July 5th. 1908.

$[22^r]$

Delirium[264]

Flashes of Madness.

V.

My child, I see thine eyes upon
A shadow, as cast by the wings
When a swift bird passes close by
The castle-window before the sun:
So through thy glance the shadows fly...

The souls of things dead *&* bygone
Haunt the appearances of living things.

Alexander *Search*

December — 1905.

---

264. *Del* [*irium*]

$$[78 - 27\text{-}28]$$

Delirium

Nirvâna.

A non-existence deeply within Being,
A sentient nothingness ethereal,
A more than real Ideality, agreeing
Of subject and of object, all in all.

Nor Life, nor Death, nor sense nor senselessness,
But a deep feeling of not feeling aught;
A calm how deep! — much deeper than distress,
Haply as thinking is without the thought.

Beauty and ugliness, and love and hate,
Virtue and vice — all these nowise will be;
That peace all quiet shall eliminate
Our everlasting life — uncertainty.

A quietness of all our human hopes,
An end as of a feverish, tired breath...
For fit expressions vainly the soul gropes;
It is beyond the logic of our faith.

An opposite of joy's stir, of the deep

Disconsolation that our life doth give,
A waking to the slumber that we sleep,
A sleeping to the living that we live.

All difference unto the life we have,
All other to the thoughts that through us roam;
It is a home if our life be a grave,
It is a grave if our life be a home.

All that we weep, all to which we aspire
Is there, and like an infant on the breast,
We shall e'er be with more than we desire²⁶⁵
And our accursed souls at last shall rest.

Alexander *Search*

1906.

---

265. We shall e'er be with more than we desire / ↑ transcend the little we
desire \ / ↓ the plans of our desire \ / the cripple we desire \

$[78 - 27-28]$

Delirium

Doubt.

Tell me, tell me who dreams most —
He who sees the world aright
Or the man in dreaming lost?

What is true? What is't that seems —
The lie that's in reality [266]
Or the lie that is in dreams?

Who is unto truth less near —
He who sees all truth a shadow
Or he who sees dreams all clear?

He who is a good guest, or he [267]
Who feels alien at the feast?

Alexander *Search*

June 19ᵗʰ 1907

---

266. ~~That~~ ↑ The lie
267. ↑ good guest, or his

[78 — 42]

Documents of Mental Decadence.

Delirium

Mania of Doubt.

All things unto me are queries
That from normalness depart,
And their ceaseless asking wearies
    My heart.
Things are and seem, and nothing bears
The secret of the life it wears.

All things' presence e'er is asking
Questions of disturbing pain
With dreadful hesitation tasking
    My brain
How false is truth? How much doth seem
Since dreams are all and all's a dream.

Before mystery my will faileth
Torn with war within the mind,
And Reason like a coward quaileth
    To find
More than themselves all things reveal
Yet that they with themselves conceal.

               Alexander *Search*
June 19th. 1907.

$$[78 - 49]$$

Delirium

The world.

The world, as far's I understand,[268]
Which is no further than the blind
Of colour and of shade can find
In that obscurity of theirs,
This world sunlit and grand,
Of which we are the heirs
With a proud unconsciousness,
Is worth as much as all our rhymes,
As all our things, its gilded slimes —
Nothing, and that's the most I'll say
Ere on the bed of nothingness
I turn myself the other way.

Alexander *Search*

July 1907.

---

268. far's /↑ as\ I

[78 — 51–52]

Delirium.

The Story of Solomon Waste.

This is *all* the story of Solomon Waste.

Always hurrying yet never in haste,
He fussed and worked *&* toiled all frothing
And at the end of all did nothing.
This is *all* the story of Solomon Waste.

He lived in wishing and in striving,
And nothing came of all his living;
He worked and toiled in pain and sweat,
And nothing came out of all that.
This is *all* the story of Solomon Waste.

He thought much and had no conviction,
His feeling was at best affliction;
Though tender he and hating evil
He might have gained the name of devil.
His every wish and resolution
Even in his mind was but confusion.
This is *all* the story of Solomon Waste.

And things begun and never ended,
And much undone and much intended,   [52ʳ]
And all things wrong yet never mended:
This is *all* the story of Solomon Waste.

Each day new projects did betray,
Yet each day was like every day.
He was born *&* died and between these [269]
He worried himself to tease.
He bustled, worried, moved and cried
But in his life no more's descried
Than two clear facts: he lived and died.
This is *all* the story of Solomon Waste.

Alexander *Search.*

August 11ᵗʰ. 1907.

---

269. He ↑he l̶i̶v̶e̶d̶ ↑was born and

[78 — 58]
Documents of Mental Decadence.
Delirium
The Curtain.

A curtain hides the mystery
That in the world is known to be,
Mute-horrid as impending thunder,
From eyes unsensual that would see
Behind it things for more than wonder —
A curtain past whose *living* folds
His court of shadow Horror holds.

And he that curtain who shall part
But in his mind, will feel the heart
Grow weak before the irony
That Nothingness pains more the heart
Than things that are or seem to be,
That Nothingness can give a fear,
A sorrow nothing can give here.

Alexander *Search.*

August 26th 1907.

$[78 - 59]$

Documents of Mental Decadence.
Delirium
The Picture.

In a saloon |that is a sleep|
Mine eyes did a picture meet,
And wondrously wise and woefully deep [270]
And horribly complete.
A profound meaning more than tears
Are seen to give, and human fears,
And human madness and woe,
Come as a scent from that picture weird.

The name of the painter is ignored
And his purpose none do know.

Alexander *Search*.

August 1907.

270. And /↓One\

[78 — 60]

Documents of Mental Decadence.

Delirium.

A Temple.

I have built my temple — wall and face —
Outside the idea of space,
Complex — built as a full-rigged ship;
I made its walls of my fears,
Its turrets many of weird thoughts *&* tears —
And that strange temple thus unfurled
Like a death's-head flag, that like a whip
Stinging around my soul is curled,
Is far more real than the world.

Alexander *Search*.

August 1907.

[78 — 63–64]
Delirium
The Sepulchre.

Mystery, mystery is here
That brings a joy with a fear.

Oh, that Death should greater be
Than Time & Space and all we see,
That Change should deeper be than thought
And Time, like a portentous tomb,
Should feel corruption in its womb
      Yet itself crumble like its rot!

For e'en the sepulchre's cold stones
Shall have a death like the dead bones
They shut in.
      (What coffer can lock
Corruption out? or rottenness
What wit with cell & bolt can mock?)

Ay, even marble shall like bodies die
A death, shall have an end. The passer-by
Shall tread the dust of the stone
That on the grave did lie,
In dust now like each bone.
For to Corruption all must go,   [64ʳ]
The difference in this alone:
That some things rot quick & some slow.

Ay, the hard stone will wear away
Making the day when it was rock
Unreal as a distant day.

Only a Shadow none do know,
By the lock'd door of Time and Space, [271]
With obscure & peculiar grace
Keeps watch never to go.

Alexander *Search*.

September 18th. *1907*.

271. ← × By

[78 — 68–70]

Delirium.

Horror.

In the darkness of my soul,
Just as dark as the souls of men,
By the blessing of their eternal curse,
     Flashes like a bodiless ghoul, [272]
In its rare fulness above all ken,
The sense of the sense of the universe.

And such a cowardice of thought,
Absorbing all my life and all
I have in me, more gall than gall,
Takes me, that I fear to open my eyes
And my mind to a most horrid surprise,
And I feel my being near to suppression
In a horror past Fancy's confession.

More than the cowardest of beasts
Before a gaping flash overhead,
More than the drunkard in his unrests
Who sees visions of more than dread,
More than all that fear can conceive,
More than madness can make to believe,

---

272. By the blessing of their eternal curse, →×
    Flashes like a bodiless ghoul, →×?

More than cannot be imagined,
The sense of the mystery of all,
When it flashes on me full as can be,
Doth my maddened soul appal.

[69ʳ]

Speak it not — nor can it be spoken, —
No, not the shadow of the sensation,
Of the chord of sanity that is broken
In me by that moment's distress
And intensity of negation;
Think it not, thought is powerless
This horror less than to express.

The meanest thing grows terrible
And the basest thought sublime —
All in a world more horrible
Than the sense of the soul of time,
Than the fear of the depth of death,
Than the remorse of more than crime.

'Tis half as if its solution it brought,
That mystery |that foul is as rot|.
Yet if it did so bring
Dead were my thought
And my whole self dead as any thing:
'Tis this that coarsely men can name,
Looking on the face of God.
And that feeling, that sense can more than maim

[70ʳ]

The Spirit, more than make it a clod;

It would kill outright — straight, outright,
With a shock of which hell is no mirror,
More than is known in terror,
More than is dreamt of fright.

Alexander *Search*

17th. October 1907.

[78A — 14–17]

Delirium[273]

Little Bird.

Poet.

Little bird, sing me a sweet song deep
    Of what is not to-day;
Be it not the future that yet doth sleep
In the hall where Time his hours doth keep,
    More than far away.

Sing me a song of the things thou knew'st
    And desirest e'er,
Be it a song to which but is used
The heart that has to love refused
    What is merely fair.

Bird

Young, too young, hither I was brought
    From the dells and trees;
Weep with me — I remember them not
Save with a vague and a pining thought:
    Can I sing of these?

---

273. D[elirium]

$$\left[15^{\text{r}}\right]$$

Poet

Sing, little bird, sing me that song —
　　None can be more dear —
Come of the ſpirit that doth long
Not for the paſt with a sadness ſtrong,
　　But for what was never here.

Sing me, sing me that song, little bird;
　　I would also sing
Of sounds I remember yet never heard,
Of wishes by which my soul is ſtirred [274]
　　Till then bliss doth ſting.

Bird

To breathe that singing I have no might;
　　Sing it deeply thou!
I sing when the day is clear and bright
And when the moon is so much in night
　　That thy tears do flow.

---

274. Of sounds I remembered yet never heard,
　　Of voices ↑ wishes by which my soul is stirred

[16ʳ]

But thou, thou sing'st in woe, in ill,
  And thy voice is fit
To speak of what the wish doth fill
With pinings indescribable,
  Shadows vague of it.

Poet

Ay, little bird, let us sing in all weather
  A song, of to-day,
Come of the sense we feel together
That nothing that doth die and wither
  Truly goes away.

Alexander *Search*

January 10ᵗʰ. 1908.

[78A — 18^r]

Delirium [275]

The World Offended.

I said unto the world one day:
    "I suspect thee of existence!"
And the world showed a smiled resistance [276]
    To what I did say.
"Let us go to court," he replied; "go we
Before a Court both wise and rare.
Let *Reason* one judge of our cause be;
Imagination be also there
And *Feeling* the judges our cause to hear."
We went before the Court, and *Reason*
Said to me: "*Thy* crime is half-treason!
The World's acquitted of what thou say'st:
    Of existence 'tis guilty not.
This by the written code of Thought
    In the pages of Unrest." [277]

Alexander Search.

January. 10th. 1908.

---

275. Del[irium]
276. ~~strange~~ $^\uparrow$ smiled
277.   In the pages of Unrest.
  ~~I was but in the costs condemned~~
     ~~Of the suit I lost as play;~~
  ~~But those, they leave me poor and yet~~
     ~~Are more than I can pay.~~

[78A — 19^r]

Delirium.

A Question.

"Tell me," one day to a poet said
  A deep, brutal man, [278]
"If you had to choose between seeing dead — [279]
 Your wife whom you do love so well —
 And the loss complete, irreparable,
  Of your verses all, instead —
 Which loss would you rather feel?"

 The poet glanced with sudden woe
 And deep distress at him who so
 Broke with a question ill-foreseen
 His inner silence half-serene,
 And he did not answer; & the other
 Smiled, as elder to younger brother:
 The tortured glance of startled sense
 And sudden self-knowledge intense
 And newness of self-consciousness
 Was bitter, as ev'n he could guess.
 More than a smile were violence.

       Alexander *Search*
January 10th. 1908.

---

278. ← ^{x} A ~~cru~~ deep,
279. ~~your wife~~ ↑^{seeing}

[78A — 21–23]

Delirium

The Bells.

Ring, bells, ring — ring out clear!
Perhaps by the vague sentiment that you raise —
I know not why — you remind me of my infancy.
    Ring, bells, ring! Your soul is a tear.
    What does it matter? My childhood's glee —
    You cannot call it back to me.

    Ring, bells, ring out your song!
You remind me of some happiness
    (Perhaps one that I never felt),
Of what has been, of what lasts not long,
Of what was not but seems now a bliss.
Something of sorrow, something of despair
    Is in me by your melody.
Sing, sing of the past which was fair —
    You cannot call it back to me.

    Though you sing but your set melody,
    Yet ring out wildly, wildly, bells!
Ring out the song that tears out the heart,
    Speaking of what I know not, sing
    To and fro till the soul's deep smart
Calms itself by too much, too deep in the heart.   [22ʳ]

In the wordless ſpeech of your own
    Ring out, wild bells, ring out!
Ye have something of souls left alone;
Ye give me a sorrow, a deep ache of doubt,
    Ununderſtood sentiment sad…
Do you sing of my childhood that thus you[280] should moan?
    Then I was unconscious; now I am mad.

Ring out bells! Your sadness that ſtings
    Has a sob as an inner sound.
    I have in me |colossal| things.
Ring on! in your music I am drowned.
All in the world has a limit and bound.
    Ring on, deſperate & free!
Can ye not of skies and of wings
    Speak loud to my misery?
Speak an ye will; except sorrow & pain
    Ye bring not anything to me.

    Ring out, wild bells, clearly, deep!
Whatever the pain ye sing of may be —
What does it matter? Life, death are one sleep
    Full of dreams of agony.
    All is unreal and we blind.
Ring out your song! I desire to weep
    For all that my life might be.
All that you call or recall to my mind
You cannot bring nor bring back to me.[281]

[23ʳ]

Alexander Search

January 16th. 1908.

---

280. ↑ thus you

[78A — 30–31]

Delirium.

A Day of Sun.

I love the things that children love
  Yet with a comprehension deep
That lifts my pining soul above
  Those in which life as yet doth sleep.

All things that simple are and bright,
  Unnoticed unto keen-worn wit,
With a child's natural delight
  That makes me proudly weep at it.

I love the sun with personal glee,
  The air as if I could embrace
Its wideness with my soul and be
  A drunkard by expense of gaze. [282]

I love the heavens with a joy
  That makes me wonder at my soul,
It is a pleasure nought can cloy,
  A thrilling I cannot control.

---

281. For all that ↑my life might be.
  All that you ~~bring~~ ↑call or ~~bring back~~ ↑recall to my mind
  You cannot ~~call~~ ↑bring nor ~~recall~~ ↑bring back to me.

282. expense /↓excess\

118

So stretched out here let me lie
　　Before the sun that soaks me up,
And let me gloriously die

　　Drinking too deep of living's cup; ²⁸³

Be swallowed of the sun & spread
　　Over the infinite expanse,
Dissolved, like a drop of dew dead
　　Lost in a super-normal trance;

Lost in impersonal consciousness
　　And mingling in all life become
A selfless part of Force and Stress
　　And have a universal home;

And in a strange way undefined
　　Lose in the one & living Whole
|The limit that I call my mind,
　　The bounded thing I call my soul. |²⁸⁴

Alexander *Search*

March 17ᵗʰ. 1908.

───────────────

283. Drinking too deep of living's cup; / ↑ Deep drinking of mere living's cup \
284. The limit that I call / ↑ am to my \ my mind,
　　　The bounded / ↓ place where \ thing I call my soul. | / ↓ The place wherefrom I draw my soul. \

[78A — 35]
Documents of Mental Decadence.
Delirium.
Familiar Conversation.

Disappointment, my old friend,
I had forgot thou wert with me.
Forgive me. I did half pretend,
Deceiving ill my misery,
That thou hadst gone. Forgive me thou.
Thou old true friend, thou'rt with me now!

Despair, my old companion sure,
Thou too — though not forgotten quite —
Yet for a moment I had fewer
Thoughts of thee — | somewhat of | respite.
Entirely to forget thee were
Impossible. Friend, thou art here!

And thou, old comrade, Solitude,
Bare of affection and of hope,
Thou twin with me — I were quite rude [285]
Were I to omit by thee to stop
And play the game of cares & fears? ...
Why come ye to shame me, oh tears? [286]

Alexander Search.

August 26th 1907.

---

285. were quite / ↑ were I not \ rude
286. ye to shame me / ↓ no more I have no terms.\ ,

[78A — 36]

Documents of Mental Decadence.
Delirium.
The Accursed Poet.

Here the accursed poet lies,
Hid far from the pure blue skies; [287]
Mixed with mud filth he lies
At the bottom of the stream.
He dreamed many a strange dream.
He loved mankind but he did nought
For mankind's good. Vain was his thought.
He would be loved and he was not.
The sun in morn or evening glow
Can reach him not where deep he lies
With mud and filth far from the skies.
He ached to feel, he ached to know.
He did aspire to what should last
Beyond the time that did it show.
Full of the giant city's waste
The river over him doth flow.
Dark over him flows the river.
Down to him no light can go.
     Damn'd be he for ever! [288]

Alexander *Search*

August 6 — 1908.

_____

287. the pure,
288. by be

[78A — 37]
Documents of Mental Decadence.
Delirium.
Pity? No!

Pity? No! I wish not pity.
That were but a bitterer scorn,
Disdain ruthlessly made witty
With a serious look to strain
Its awful joke. No; let me mourn
In peace. Pity me not again!

Pity? No! Let more scorn come,
More indifference, more disdain:
These are the comforts of my home.
To change their look to pity were too far
To make me feel a direr pain.
Pretend not good: it cannot be.
Let evils all seem as they are.
To mask them were a mockery [289]
Heartless *&* evilly rare.

Alexander *Search*

August 6 — 1908.

───────────

289. Let evils be ↑all seem as they are.
     To mask them is ↑were a mockery

[78A — 44]
Delirium.
On the Road.

In a cart.

Here we go while morning life burns [290]
In the sunlight's golden ocean,
And upon our faces a freshness comes,
A freshness whose soul is motion.

Up the hills, up! Down to the vales!
Now in the plains more slow!
Now in swift turns the shaken cart reels.
Soundless in sand now we go!

But we must come to some village or town, [291]
And our eyes show sorrow at it.
Could we for ever and ever go on
In the sun and air that we hit;

On an infinite road, at a |mighty| pace, [292]
With endless and free commotion,
With the sun e'er round us and on our face
A freshness whose soul is motion!

Alexander *Search*.
Oct. 26 — 1908.

290. Here we go while ~~the~~ morning [↑life] burns
291. ~~to~~[↑must] come
292. On an infinite road, at a |mighty| [/↑unthought\ /unknown\] pace,

1.5 — Agony

$[77 - 76\text{-}77]$

Agony [293]

Beginning.

Darkness and storm outside make inward gloom,
Quiet *&* home within and useless pain
weight down upon me as a wasted life,
      Save where from the vile tomb
Of day there comes a semblance of a strife
Through the blown varying of the pallid rain.

The mansion's form no thunder-busting shake
A blankly-smiling day unfirms our eyne,
And there is here a ghastness and a gale
      That make the frail form quake; [294]

---

293. Ag[ony]

294. ← × Darkness and storm outside make inward gloom,
   ← × Quiet and home within and useless pain
     weight down upon me as a wasted life,
   ← ×   Save where from the vile /↑pale\ tomb
   ← × Of day there comes a semblance of a strife
     Though the blown varying of the pallid rain
   ← × The mansion's form no thunder-busting shake /↑Before the thunder shall the mansion shake\
   ← × A ~~no~~ blankly-smiling day unfirms our /↑the\ /my\ eyne,
   ← × ~~But~~ ↑And there is here a ghastness and a gale
     That make the /↑my\ frail form quake;

And strange to me who think all things must quail,
A voice is raised in joy — alas! not mine.

Why cannot youth be joyous, full of love?
Why am I made [a] corpse that woes & fears
And problems grim and world-enigmas die
   Should like a body wove
|Close to my nature, in which is a fire
The fervorous source of lying pains and tears?|

[10ʳ]

Blow hard, thou mind; look pale, thou awful day! [295]
Ye cannot in your dread and horror match
The thing that I bear in me and is me,
   These idle thoughts that stray
Subordinate to the deep agony
Of him who hears the gate of reason's latch [296]
Fall with a sound termination,
As of a thing locked past and for e'er done.

         Alexander *Search*
March 1905.

―――――――――――

295. ⌐ˣ Blow hard, thou mind; look pale, thou awful day!
296. ~~of~~ who

[77 — 78]
Agony [297]
Resolution.

Why do I waste in dreams fruitless *&* vain
The substance of my youth in idle tears?
Why do I count with feverish eye the years
And number with sad heart the ways of pain?

Why should I weep thus, since there is no gain
To me, to men from sighings and from fears?
Since from afar at me the future sneers,
[All] the while the past with me cannot remain.

High Heaven, that errs not *&* that wills not wrong
To each on earth doth give a work to do,
A distant recompense and rest remote;

I'll to my work then, so God make me strong
To bring the Demons of mine own self to
Their knees, and take the Devil by the throat.

Alexander *Search.*

7th May 1905.

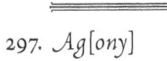

297. *Ag*[*ony*]

[78B — 46–48]
Agony [298]
Soul-Symbols.

My soul — what is my soul? But symbols mute
Its horror and confusion can |give| out: [299]
A desert |out of| space where absolute
Reigns expectation full of horrid doubt.

It gives the sense that giveth, strange and dark,
Some unknown river weird, hauntingly lone,
In some old picture storiless, sole work [300]
Of some great painter horribly unknown.

It is an island out of human track,
Mysterious, old within the sea and full
Of caves and grottoes unexplored & black,
Pregnant with many horrors possible.

It is an olden inn with corridors
Woven in a labyrinth and scarce of light,
Where through the night the sound of shutting doors,
Vague in its cause and place, fills us with fright.

It is a mountain region wild and free,
Precipiced, hid and silent, never seen,
Where we dare not think of what might have been
[47ʳ]   Nor wish idea of what things may be.

298. Ag[ony]
299. Its horror and confusion can |give| / ↑ speak \ out
300. some / ↑ an \

If ever mystery, romance & fear
Have shown their heart on canvas and on scroll,
It must assuredly to men appear
As to mine inner sense appears my soul.

It is a vision-desert full of rocks
Where all than reason is both more & less,
'Tis a lone coast where the sea's endless shocks
Fill with an empty sound its lifelessness.

Something of lost, forgotten, vague and dead,
Yet waking, as a slumberer mystical
Seems to perceive, for who looks knows with dread [301]
That something he doth see to make appal.

All this my soul is in its weak despair,
Full of sense unto pain, of thought to tears, [302]
Having for meed of reason a mute care,
For company to feeling — woes & fears.

So to my glance, as if with opium wide,
My very self is grown a mystery;
In inextatic fear Life doth abide
And madness like my breath is within me. [303]   [48ʳ]

Alexander *Search*
February 1906.

---

301. ~~Where they who watch perceive with troubled dread~~ ↑In who eyes Seems to perceive, for who looks knows with dread
302. Full of ~~life~~ ↑sense unto pain, of thought to /↑past\ tears,
303. And ~~m~~↑madness like my breath /↓lip\ /a heart\ is within me.

[78 — 36–37]
Agony [304]
Regret.

I would that I were again a child
    And a child you sweet and pure,
That we might be free and wild
    In our consciousness obscure;
That we might play fantastic games
    Under trees silent and shady,
That we might have fairy-book names,
    I be a lord, you a lady.

And all were a strong ignorance
    And a healthy want of thought,
And many a prank, many a dance
    Our unresting feet had wrought;
And I would act well a clown's part
    To your childish laughter winning, [305]
And I would call you my sweetheart
    And the name would have no meaning.

---

304. Ag[ony]
305. To / ↑ Towards \ your childish laughter winning / ↑ learning \,

Or sitting close we each other would move
    With tales that now gone are sad;
We would have no sex, would feel no love,
    Good without fighting the bad.
And a flower would be our life's delight   [37ʳ]
    And a nutshell boat our treasure:
We would lock it in a cupboard at night
    As in memory a pleasure.

We would ſpend hours and days like a wealth
    Of goodness too great to cloy,
We would deep enjoy innocence & health
    Knowing not we did enjoy…
Ah, what bitterest is is that alone [306]
    Now one feeling in me I trace —
That knowledge of what from us hath gone
    And of what it left in its place.

Alexander *Search*

May 29ᵗʰ· 1907.

---

306. is ↑ is

[78 — 38]
Agony [307]
Death in Life.

Another day is past, and while it past,
What have I pondered or conceived or read?
Nothing! Another day has gone to waste.
Nothing! Each hour as it is born is dead.

I have done nothing. Time from me has fled,
And unto Beauty not a statue raised!
By thought's firm power no creed nor lie debased
By this young soul useless and wearied.

Is it my lot then ever to remain
Like a grain of sand upon the beach,
A thing at will of wind, at will of sea?

Alas, that aught that wishes *&* has pain, [308]
Because e'er fall'n from what its power should reach
Less than a thing inanimate should be!

Alexander *Search*

May 30th 1907.

---

307. *Ag*[ony]
308. Alas, that o↑ᵃ ught that ~~suffers~~↑ wishes and has pain,

[78 — 39]
Agony[309]
Woe Supreme.

A friend said once to me: "All that thou writeſt,
Surely 'tis fancy, and pretence, & feigned;
Surely the moaning wherewith thou affrighteſt
The healthy mind is preconceived and ſtrained!

"In all the songs and tales that thou indicteſt
Why's there no word that is not hard or pained?
Why in good things & true thou not delighteſt,
But even in youth by thee joys are disdained?"

Because, dear friend, though to be mad is sweet
Sometimes, and though at others nameless woe,
Yet never human pain the pain can meet

Of the mad brain that doth its madness know;
Because my science learn'd has made complete
The knowledge of an ill that cannot go.

                              Alexander *Search*

8th June 1907.

309. *Ag*[*ony*]

[78 — 46–48]
Agony [310]
Epitaph.

Here lies who thought himself the best
Of poets in the world's extent;
In life he had nor joy nor rest.

He filled with madness many a song,
And at whatever age he died
Thus many days he lived too long.

He lived in powerless egotism,
His soul tumultuous and disordered
By thought and feeling's endless schism.

In everything he had a foe
And without courage bore his part
In life's interminable woe.

He was a slave to grief and fear
And incoherent thoughts he had
And wishes unto madness near.

Those whom he loved, by arts of ill
He treated worse than foes; but he
His own worst enemy was still.

310. *Ag*[ony]

[47ʳ]

He of himself ever did sing,
Incapable of modesty,
Lock'd in his wild imagining.

Useless was all his toilless trouble
Empty of sense his fears and pains
And many of them were ignoble.

Vile thus and worthless his distress;
His words, though bitterer far than hate,
His bitter soul could not express.

Thus was he miserable & bad,
Who yet could sob in tenderness —
And none was found to know him mad.

Let not a healthy mind pollute
His grave, but fitly there will pass
The traitor and the prostitute;

The drunkard and the wencher there
May pass, but quick, lest they should ponder,
Perchance, that pleasure is but air.

Each weak and execrable mind
Which plagued man with its rottenness
[48ʳ]   Its conscious master here will find, [311]

Conscious, for in him he could tell
Madness and ill were what they were,
But neither did he will to quell.

Pass by therefore ye who can weep;
Let rottenness work in neglect,
While the rough winds the dead leaves sweep.

His slumbering brother to the sod
Not even in imagining
Disturb not with the name of God.

But let him lie at peace for ever
Far from the eyes and mouths of men
And from what him from them did sever.

He was a thing that God had wrought
And to the sin of having lived
He joined the crime of having thought.

Alexander *Search*

July 1907

$$[78 - 65]$$
Agony [312]
Inaction.

A thousand hearts are labouring for the good
Of poor mankind ill-civilized and chill;
A thousand minds are making war to ill [313]
With thought or feeling ponderate or rude.

And I alone, as if not understood
By me the suffering that the sense doth fill,
Am sunk in an abeyance deep of will
In a wild, crazy somnolence of mood.

Thus show I mute and cold to misery
Yet not suspected thoughts like dim clouds float,
The presages of horrors, in my mind.

Thus am I miserable and my soul in me,
A skilful helmsman in a helmless boat,
Is like one loving beauty yet born blind.

Alexander *Search*

23ʳᵈ September 1907.

312. *Ag*[*ony*]
313. to /↑on\

[78 — 66–67]
Agony [314]

Never have I so deeply felt my exclusion from
    mankind.

To one side the sane, to the other side the
    lame and the halt & the blind;

To one side the healthy, the good, the strong,
    those in life's prime,

To the other side the slaves of genius, of mad-
    ness, of crime.

Build prisons and hospitals and Bedlams.
    To one side the glad,

To the other side the sickly, the stupid, the
    ill and the mad.

At no time have I felt so deep the gulf between
    me & men.

Is it idiocy, madness or crime, or genius — or
    what is this pain?

I have felt it to-day with full truth & have felt
    to remember it well:

I am one thrown aside — a torturer and tor-
    tured in my being's hell;

Yet I asked not to live, nor had choice of my
    living's rotten worth,

I had no power on my life, nor am I guilty
    of my birth.

---

314. *Ag*[ony]

So I shall sing my song without hope, cheer-
 less & forlorn,

That men may learn — at least they may
 laugh — to what some hearts are born;

Song all mystery, all symbols, contradictions
 in ignoble dance,

But that this is madness complete not the
 smallest ignorance;

Song all of tortures of soul, of a being's human
 abysm

And never a doubt but this is but raving
 egotism;

Song of evil, song of hate, song of revolt, song
 of love

Of Nature, of Mother Nature, the earth at
 my feet and the sky above;

Song of the hatred of customs, of creeds, of
 conventions, of institutions

Song of madness unpondering to human pro-
 stitutions;

Song of one that better were dead, song of
 one set aside, [315]

Song of one that hell and earth conspired &
 combined to deride.

Peace! let the sane be set on that side & the
 ill on this side. [316]

           Alexander *Search*
October 16th 1907.

[67ʳ]

315. ~~the~~ one
316. ill /↑ mad \

138

[78 — 74-77]

Agony [317]

Song of the Leper.

He was a nauseous leper
Who in the ruins was;
There ever and anon
The hollow wind did pass,
And wild and feeble & yellow all [318]
    Was the grass.

And the leper sang this song:

"The leper is excluded from his race,
    The leper is driven out,
    The leper is thrust out
    From hall and street and way;
    He must not show his face
    Where human beings may.
    For him there are whips & stones;
    He cannot even stay
    Where mongrels fight for bones
    And are allowed to play.

---

317. Ag[ony]
318. ~~aged~~ ↑ wild

$$[75^r]$$

"No beast as the poor leper is
Worms and snakes have greater bliss.
　　　But the leper is accurst
　　　And he knows that well accurst [319]
Is he because a nauseous leper,
Of evil things the worst.

　　"The toad, the newt, the viper
　　Are tolerate and borne,
　　But the vile and nauseous leper
　　Makes vomit in deep scorn;
　　Repugnance is for him
　　Inevitably born.

　　"Sometimes he hears the laughter
　　Of human feast to come,
　　And music | followed after |
　　By sounds of peace and of home.
　　　　Upon the wind they stray,
　　　　The wind bears them away,
　　And the nauseous leper, he remains,
　　Through night, through day,
　　Alone with his sores, with his pains.

---

319. accursed ↑ t

[76ʳ]

"And bands of strollers pass,
　Taking the road afar,
　For in the ruins they know well
　The leper's sores there are.
　And if perchance they see
　The leper from their way,
　He sees their finger point
　And he knows that they say:

"He is the nauseous leper
　Who in the ruins doth sit;
　He is viler than the plague,
　More loathsome far than it;
　If near to him we dared do come
　Upon him we would spit."

"Poor leper who is a man,
　Poor leper who is alive,
　Under his being's ban,
　Whose torture's chain unearned
　No pity comes to rive.

"A Hand of Might created

[76ʳ]

　| The newt, the toad, the viper,
　But gave them not its worst;
　Kept them from loneliness,
　Gave them their kindred's bliss.

But that hand made the leper
And it made the leper leper:
And that Hand Almighty is
 Of all things the most curst." | [320]

Alexander *Search*

October 25th 1907. —

And when I hear the leper
Sing his song to the wind
I ask — this nauseous leper
What Law of the □ kind
Makes necessary to make smart
Why is this leper a part
Of the system of the World

God's damned hand.

---

320. curst. ["] |

Marginalia

(2.)

Too bitter for pure song,
My life has marred my verse
And made poet in me wrong
And the critic in me worse.

———————————

My life has wasted been
Not even in poetry [321]
Grew it beautiful or serene…
My life was bounded to be

———————————

The same in every way
Born spoilt, God's blended a spite…
Thus □ has been my day
I hope naught of the night… [322]

———————————

321. to ↑in
322. of /↓from\

$$[78 - 78-84]$$
Agony[323]

In the Street.

—But I, *mein Werther*, sit above all; I am
alone with the stars.
Sartor Resartus.

I pass before the windows lit
    With inward, curtained light,
And in the houses I see flit
Now *&* again shadows that hit
    The curtain's yellowed white.
Others a little gleam but show:
Inside, the people chat, I know.

And I feel cold and feel alone,
    |Not that I no one have,|
But — ah that dreams should ne'er be done! —
That among many I am one,
As among flowers a grave;
One, and more lonely than can be
Imagined conceivably.

───────────────

323. *Ag*[ony]

If I were born not to aspire
    Beyond the life that lead
These people whom life cannot tire,
Who chat and slumber by the fire
    Contentedly indeed,
Behind those curtains, by that light
That to the street is somewhat bright;

[79ʳ]   Could I no more aspire than these,
    Were all my wishes bound
In family or social ease,
In worldly, usual jollities [324]
    Or children playing round,
Happy were I but to have then
The usual life of usual men.

But oh! I have within my heart [325]
    Things that cannot keep still —
A |mystic| and delirious smart
That doth a restlessness impart,
    An ache, a woe, an ill;
I wearied Sysyphus I groan
Against |the world's ironic| stone.

---

324. ⁺ˣ In worldly, usual jollities
325. — oh! —

I, the eternally excluded
    From socialness and mirth,
The aching heart whose mind has brooded
Till thought turned raving wild hath flooded
    The soul that gave it birth —
I weep to know I have in me
Aught at once joy & misery.

[80ʳ]

And cold before the normal, cold
    And fear-struck I remain,
As one old, formidably old, [326]
Who doth portentous secrets hold
    That he cannot explain
But which the world's show doth suggest
Unto his mind that knows not rest.

How good after dinner to chat
    And sit in half a sleep,
Without a duty-sense to strike flat
All ease, all cosiness to abate
    An aspiration deep;
To have an ease no pains do throng
Nor felt as an ease that is wrong.

---

326. ~~these~~ formidably

A home, a rest, a child, a wife —
    None of these are for me
Who wish for aught |beyond this| life [327]
With an incessant inner strife
    That knows not victory.
Ay me! & none to comprehend
This wish that doth all things transcend.

[81ʳ] |Some in some theatre are away
    Or other place of joy|
And keep, for ever glad and gay,
The hounds of thought and care at bay
    That cannot laugh or toy:
These are awaited in some homes,
A faint light from their windows comes.

A cosiness these homes must steep
    In something like a slumber,
And in that surface-living deep
'Tis hard to know that hearts do keep.
    Yet these are normal; I that sigh
And dread their living — what am I?

---

327. |beyond this| /↑ not this |in|\ life
328. |more than| /↑ aught like\
329. |not stupid| /↑ senseless\

Oh joy! oh height of happiness!
　　　To wish no more than life,
To feel of pleasure, of diſtress,
A normal more, a normal less,
　　　By friend or child or wife!
None of these for my soul can be
For |more than| madness is in me. [328]

[82ʳ]

I weep |sad tears| — oh, not to live
　　　As these in human joy!
Oh, that I could as much believe
As sense & cuſtom joint can give
　　　Which living cannot cloy!
Man's happiness is poor, I know,
But true — a thing all unlike woe.

Sometimes I dream that I might sit
　　　By my own fire, and quiet
Might see my wife & children flit
Half in a sleep and not a whit
　　　In one of dreamy riot;
And I might noble be and pure
In mind, |not ſtupid| nor obscure. [329]

Sometimes I dream one of these homes
     Secluded socially
One for the many thousand |tomes|
Of life might keep my heart that roams
     Weak, desolate & free;
That quiet haply might console
My aching heart, my pining soul.

[83^r]

But at the thought of such a glad
     Existence simple here,
As if the thing a venom had
I shiver, tremble & grow sad
     As with a mystic fear;
I dread to think my life might pass
Like that of men, as is and was.

I dread to think of a life |sweet|
     By family and friends.
|Mine eyes the finite that they meet
Abhor — the houses and the street.
     And all things that have ends.|
I know not to what I aspire,
Yet know *this* I cannot desire.

So always incompatible
    And by the usual cold,
I go about, my own deep hell,
Hearing to toll in me the bell
    That tells me I grow old,
Yet this in such an accent strange
It bears the mystery of Change.

[84ʳ]

And so — alas! must e'er I be
    A stranger everywhere;
The leper in his leprosy
In his exclusion nears not me
    Who cannot living bear:
The world my home, my brother men
Are prisons, chains that bind & pen.

I pass. The windows are behind,
    And I forget their peace,
But tremble yet at what my mind
Conceives and feels; and in the wind
    |I wander without cease,|
Glad yet sad in me to perceive
Something none other can conceive.

Alexander *Search*

November 12ᵗʰ. 1907.

150

[78 — 85–86]

Agony[330]

Song of the Leper.

I feel a rage — ay, a rage!
At time that passes, passes away,
A thirst of life nought can assuage,
An anger that nothing can stay.
And every hour that passes by
And merges into night a day
Makes, when I think, my soul to cry:
"Torture eternal, torture without end!
All days pass and not a deed!
A desire strong as a greed
By an ill of will — oh, misery! —
To be a dream of pain condemned!"

I feel a rage! 'tis to feel
Mystery and sadness at one time,[331]
Till the maddened brain doth reel,
Looking on that bodiless curse.
The passing of the world, as one
Paralytic at a deed of blood
Which he hath no power to avert.
I feel a stranger before the sun,
 A weeper before field *&* flood,
[86ʳ] A cynic before dirt,
 A revolt before God.

Alexander *Search*

December 3ʳᵈ. 1907.

Agony [332]
My Life.

I.

Duty calls on me; I muſt fight againſt
That which 'tis duty unto all to fight.
Therefore, oh, illness of my will that ſtain'ſt
My mind — oh, leave me free to seek the right!

Take me from the vile sleep of purpose cold,
Give me an impulse to do good, to make
A ſtruggle for the new againſt the old
Ere time my useless life away may take.

Keen is my feeling of the suffering
Of men and nations, keen into deſpair;
But not a will to ſpeak it doth it bring,
Moveless I reſt, not like a thing too fair,

But like a ſtagnant water full of filth,
A bog of will, inactive & alone,
Unopen unto Learning's fresh and tilth
And locked from doing good as men have done.

---

330. *Ag*[*ony*]
331. m̶ ↑ˢadness
332. *Ag*[*ony*]

[8ʳ]

Pain ever, pain for ever! pain, oh pain!
Pain filling all my life like time or change.
Woe that goes from an inner waking strain
Unto the sleepiness of fears most strange.

Despair & horror, madness lone that feels
Its own too bitter taste until it quails,
The horror of a mind that fails and reels
And knows full well how far it reels and fails.

I sorrow for the past and at the future,
On that which never was I weep and pine,
Upon the things that never were in Nature,
On those that are and never shall be mine.

The sadness of the pleasure that has been,
The sorrow of the pain that once we had,
The ache of that which in dim visions seen
Leaves but an echo to make itself sad.

The knowledge that a dream is nothing more,
The science that our life is less than this:
It passes as it, & the bliss it wore
Was at its best the shadow of a bliss. [333]

---

333. ~~Is~~ ↓Was

[9ʳ]

I ponder on the fates of men and things,
Thereat my soul grows dark and feeble grows,
To find Thought's body weighing on the wings
Which Fancy opens over fields and snows.

I ponder upon evil and on good
And both in life irrational I see,
One because it exists not, yet it should,
The other since it is and should not be.

|Nothing is clear unto me; all is dark,
All is confusion to my Thought's o'er-much;
Alas for him who thinks in life to work
Having cast far away Convention's crutch.

He finds that Custom, the least thing of all,
Is king & queen and law and creed and faith,
That Custom goes not further than our pall,
That Custom is with us past our own death.|

I mourn that there are thrones, prisons & tombs,
And yet to see all ill I am half glad:
That there are deaths, decays and rots & dooms,
A gladness whose eyes sparkle, because mad.

[10ʳ]

I weep all times the limits close that muſt
Deep souls ununderſtood in living pen,
But weeping deeply wake to the disguſt
That I weep for myself in other men.

My tears are for myself; so that they teach
To know men's ineradicable woe,
What matter what high point of pain they reach?
Haply their birth one day they'll cease to know.

And that I shall forget this pain of mine
Forget myself — ah, would that it could be!
Forgotten like the drunkard in his wine
Or like the pauper in his misery.

'Twere madness, but sweet madness, better than
The waking, fully living consciousness
That unto a full unity doth ſpan
The many woes & throes of my diſtress.
'Twere madness but 'twere better than to know
That evil is the source of life & thought,
For to feel madness is the greateſt woe
That upon human consciousness is wrought.

$[11^r]$

To feel excluded, miserable, lone,
 A leper deep at heart, having for sore
 His being, is a misery past moan
'Tis better all to rave & to ignore.

'Tis better? — nay, who knows? the mystery
 Of consciousness and knowledge who can find?
 In madness and in thought what things may be?
 How far is horror deep within the mind?

II.

This is my life; what will the future be?
With horror I grow sick past sighs and tears,
To think how life is torture unto me,
 How Thought is father of strange cares and fears.

Yesterday one spoke to me of my youth.
Youth? Life? Twelve years I had of happiness;
The seven since then have been without ruth —
Twelve years of sleep and seven of distress.

Time, I grow sick of thee! Sounds, motions, things,
I feel a tiredness before your eyes…
 Give me, oh, Dream of mine! thy purest wings
That I may take from solitude my cries,

[12ʳ]

That I may seek the Heaven of this life —
Death, mother of all things that seem to be.
Die thus the hand that could not serve for strife,
The brain that strained and toiled with misery!

III.

Life — what is Life? Death — what is Death? My brain
Reels as I think on this, as one that reads
Far into dusk lifts up his eyes with pain,
Aching and dim; & my heart slowly bleeds.

IV.

To work? I cannot. To be gay? I've lost
Long, long ago all laughter save a base
Mirth where Despair with Apathy is crost,
That has the scent of rots and of decays.

To do good? all desire tends unto it
But all my will is feeble before all:
I am become a bust for my Thought's wit [334]
Which is no wit but Consciousness all gall.

---

334. ‡‡ ↑ my Thought's

And what avails it e'er to toil or trouble,
To make my torture of my life and thought? [335]
Is not all life the slender-fair soap-bubble
That by a child in empty mind is wrought?   [13ʳ]

And what avails all verse, all art and song,
All that doth make a body for itself?
My heart is keen to feel all human wrong,
I careless, as one born to ease & pelf.

And what avails it ever to grow pale
Over the mute and endless lore of old
Until the wearied senses strain and fail
And the worn heart is passionless & cold?

Avails it anything? It avails not.
Let me sleep then: give me a grave for bed
In the earth's heart where I not life nor thought
But rottenness & peace may have instead.

                                        Alexander *Search*

January 9ᵗʰ. 1908. [336]

---

335. To ↑ make my
336. 190[7|8].

$$[78A - 24\text{-}27]$$

Agony [337]

Prayer.

Oh God, if Thou be'st anything
Hear this frail prayer that I fling
Like a flame leaping past control
From out the hell that is my soul:

Oh God, let me not fall insane!
I know that half-mad I am now;
I feel behind my |youthful| brow
Horrors it sickens to contain,
Ideas that my sense deride
And inhibition cast aside;
I feel |each day, every| day
At least in one deep moment's hell
My consciousness completely stay
|My reason like a vision reel.|

Let me not be insane, my God,
Torture me in all ways beside,
But let me keep, otherwise trod
Under the foot of Time, & tried
In all the horrors that men know,

---

337. Ag[ony]

A little portion of the sense [338]
Of things that full is normal men's.
Seclude me not completely, no,   [25^r]
From men in an unconscious woe.

I suffer much, yet let me not,
Though thus I suffered not at all,
Pass into emptiness of thought,
To madness deep which is a gall
Filling the soul till bitterness,
Becoming part of us, doth ſteep
The whole soul in unconsciousness.
A little sense, oh, let me keep!

Pour down on me all woes, all ills
All else that the ſtrain'd ſpirit fills.
With horror and with terror mute;
But madness, madness absolute,
Keep from my trembling mind away.
The pain that withers and that kills,
The love that tears to shreds the heart,
The cares that horror and that may
Give death with an ignoble smart —
All these may come, but oh, let me
From madness true keep ever free.

---

338. A̶l̶l̶ little

No more — who knows but as I write
Madness in me is not complete?
Who knows, who can see things aright?
Where is the true |unerring| sight [339]
Its own deep ills to meet?
Who knows but I am mad e'en now?
Oh, torture horrible to know!
Who knows but when unconscious I
Or thinking that I dream pass by,
People say not: "there goes the youth
That is a madman" all in truth?

Who tells me that while now I think
That genius I possess and have,
That inspiration I do drink
Of all before, beyond the grave,
I do not rave, entirely rave?

Who knows, who anything can tell? —
My brain is reeling as I write —
Void am I & anxious of light —
That I am not in madness quite…
Oh doubt, oh agony, |soul-hell!| [340]

339. |unerring| /↑ and direct \
340. |h↑ soul-hell!|

No more, no more; let me believe
That I am sane, and, oh God, hear
Whate'er thou beëst, my true prayer   [27ʳ]
Shaken from my soul's giant fear …

Torture me in all ways that are,
Let me be scorned and crushed *&* trod,
Plunged in full conscious agony,
Let me become a fear, a care,
But madness, madness, oh my God,
Do not let madness come to me!

Alexander *Search*

January 18ᵗʰ. 1908.

[78A — 34]

Documents of Mental Decadence.

Agony.[341]

Towards the end.

To-day I sought to write, and found I had
With expectation my worn mind abused,
Yet deemed I not so choked & so confused
My thoughts already should be. I grow mad.

Bare of ideas, lame in my o'er-used
Uselessly tired reason, feeling bad
Before the light sun, I stand lone & sad,
Friendship and kinship by mankind refused.

I labour but to think. I cannot think.
My thinking raves or sickens into dream
As I of some deep-witchêd brew did drink.

That did strange horrors in my soul reveal.
A storm approaches. All grows dark. I feel
My reason leave me like a last sunbeam.

Alexander *Search*

July 2nd. 1908.

341. *Ag*[ony]

[78A — 45]

Documents of Mental Decadence.

Agony.[342]

To my Dearest Friend.

Then I am dead you'll write — I know you will —
A thoughtful sonnet on my early death,
In which, stating that life but wearieth,
You'll notice how I lie pale, cold, and still.

This in the quatrains, which likewise you'll fill
With some reflections on how soon goes breath
And how the cold & heavy earth beneath
There is an end to living, good or ill.

After this, in the tercets, you will say
That death's a mystery, that nought doth stay,
Perhaps that immortality is true.

Then you will sign & put your name to it.[343]
And, having read again the sonnet, you
Will be content, seeing it is well writ.

Alexander Search.

February 25th 1909. [344]

---

342. *Ag*[ony]
343. your name ^{/ ↑ the date \}
344. 2nd ↑ 25th

[78A — 46]

Documents of Mental Decadence'.
Agony.[345]
Approaching…

With dragging steps severe, like creeping hate,
Through the black silence of my conscious brain
I hear madness advance, and feel with pain
The ground it treads on writhe & palpitate.

How to avoid its coming soon or late?
How not to feel the mind's grand vainly strain,
But rooted lie awaiting its dread reign,
That cometh inopposable as Fate?

If only madness came as lightning doth —
Suddenly — that were the least greatest ill…
But oh! to feel with consciousness's clear sight

Reason's day go to twilight in swift growth,
And the twilight of reason, pale and chill,
Darken towards impenetrable night.

Alexander *Search.*

March 28th 1909.

---

345. *Ag*[ony]

2.0 — Pantaleão

$$[48C - 3^r]$$

Pantaleão.

(if necessary give true name).

———————

1. "A Psychose Adeantativa."

2. "As Visões do Sñr. Pantaleão."

3. "A Nossa Administração Colonial."

4. "Versos do Sñr. Pantaleão." [?]

2.1 — A Psychose Adeantativa

[92H — 16]

A Psychose Adeantativa.

These inaugural para ser apresentada na universidade de
Nowhere pelo candidato[346]

Usquebaugh V. Bangem

vertida para portuguez, com a autorização do autor por

F. Nogueira Pessoa.

[92H — 17–18]

A Psychose Adeantativa

I.

Os ultimos acontecimentos, as ultimas revelações que em
Portugal se teem dado e feito fazem constar a presença
de uma nova psychose notavelmente parecida com a du-
vidosa especie nosológica chamada "loucura moral."[347]

---

346. ~~estudante~~ ↑ candidato
347. "loucura moral" ~~, "neurasthenia moral," etc~~

De facto as sessões parlamentares ha um tempo para cá que deixam perceber, em muito □, um[348] notavel estado mental que se não encontra descripto na symptomatologia de qualquer psychose ou nevrose conhecida.[349] Offerece — é certo — alguma[350] analogia com a epilepsia larvada *&*, mais certamente, com o peculiar estado psychico dos criminosos que se tem pretendido — com razão[351] ou sem ella — identificar áquella nevrose.

[17ᵛ]

Analizando cuidadosamente □ permitte-nos essa analogia chegar ao resultado seguinte, que expomos na esperança de que algum alienista possa resolver o problema apresentado — quér confirmando ser esta uma especie nosologica até agora desconhecida — nem mesmo entrevista —, quer filiando-a, com seus symptomas, em qualquér psychose ou nevrose já estudada.

Até que isso se faça, porém, (tão especiaes[352] nos parecem os symptomas da referida doença mental) persistiremos em a considerar como uma especie nosologica

---

348. uma̶

349. ↑ou nevrose conhecida.

350. a̶l̶ alguma

351. a̶ ↑o peculiar estado psychico dos criminosos que se tem pretendido — s̶e̶r̶á̶ ̶o̶u̶ ̶n̶ã̶o̶ — com razão

352. d̶e̶s̶e̶n̶c̶o̶n̶t̶r̶a̶d̶o̶s̶ ↑especiaes

— & a reclamar para nós a honra de a ter descoberto como[353] tal.

Dito isto, passamos a enumerar os symptomas.

[18ᵛ]

Denominamos[354] "psychose adeantativa" esta forma de alienação mental (se é o que é) porque o seu symptoma principal, caracterisante consiste no que se chama "adeantar," "pagar" ou "receber adeantamentos."[355]

Desde já convém notar que o proprio termo "adeantamento" é invenção (empregado neste sentido)[356] de um dos observados. É bom notar desde já que este termo |cheira| a degenerescencia, com aquelle "fin-de-siècle" de que falla Nordau. Assim como do nome de Sacher Masoch se formou a palavra *masochismo*, como do nome de M. de Sade se tirou o termo[357] "sadismo," assim, cremos, se poderá formar um termo scientifico,[358] não do nome, mas do termo usado por um que soffre d'esta psychose.

---

353. reclamar ~~pedir~~ para nós a honra de a ter descoberto ~~por~~ como

354. ~~Chamamos~~
     Denominamos

355. adeantamentos["].

356. ↑empregado neste sentido

357. ~~fez~~ ↑formou a palavra *masochismo*, como do nome de M. de Sade se ~~fez~~ ↑tirou [a|o] termo

358. ~~nome com~~ ↑termo scientifico,

[18ᵛ]

O leitor conhece o que Nordau disse do termo "fin-de-siècle," sabe o que de mórbido se encontra[359] em termos especiaes que os psychopathas frequentemente empregam. Por isto já a propria doença de "adeantamento" é grave indicio de alienação mental em quem o produziu.

Posto isto, passemos aos symptomas:

Kleptomania. A kleptomania[360] é o symptoma mais characteristico da psychose adeantativa. Com[361] insufficiente consciencia d'este acto os doentes[362] classificam-n'o de adeanto e costumam explical-o por varios modos. Todos estes, porém, dão em falso. É evidente tambem, n'isto, o que depois tratam — a ausencia de senso moral[363] dos observados.

[92H — 15]

A therapeutica naturalmente indicada para a psychose adeantativa é a que consta do seguinte[364] mui simples raciocinio:

---

359. e teratologico se encontra
360. A klep- kleptomania
361. E- Com
362. observados ↑doentes
363. por tambem, n'isto, o que depois tratam — a ausencia de moral senso moral
364. consta do /↑ se obtém pelo\ seguinte

O que falta aos que soffrem d'esta psychose e que faz com que os seus principaes symptomas — kleptomania,[365] apatia, etc. — |éclatem| é o amôr á pátria. Visto ser isto que lhes falta parece ser racional a therapeutica que o produza. Ora para cerebros tão doentes ha só um modo de fazer isto: produzir o mais forte [15ᵛ] sentimento que póde por sua vez produzir[366] o amôr á patria. Ora este sobretudo é a *nostalgia*.

Impõe-se pois, como unica therapeutica para os "adeantados," para todos os que soffrem da psychose adeantativa, o tratamento pela ausencia perpetua de terra natal.

---

365. ~~psy~~ ↑kleptomania,
366. póde ↑por sua vez produzir

2.2 — As Visões do Sñr. Pantaleão

$$[144a^2 - 25^v\text{-}26^r]$$

Prefacio ás Visões.

FIM

Nem venha ninguem dizer que este livro é aspero [367] &
brutal.

N'esta □ de amnesia,[368] quando os adeantadores não
se lembram se adeantaram nem os adeantados se recebe-
ram, não faço eu excepção, esquecendo-me absolutamen-
te da veneração que comporta aos Sñrs. Assassinos[369]
e do respeito que é devido aos Sñrs. Ladrões.

———————
———————

Propriamente[370] fallando, eu não combato a monarchia;
combato a monarchia portugueza. Não admitto nem
que a monarchia seja profunda, nem que ella seja egual
em valôr[371] á republica em parte alguma. Mas n'este caso,
repito, não é a monarchia que combato. É a monarchia
portugueza.

———————

367. ~~pouco delicado~~ aspero
368. ~~epo~~ □ de amnesia,
369. d[o|a] ~~respeito~~ ↑veneração que ~~é devida~~ ↑comporta aos Sñrs.
[a|A]ssassinos
370. ~~Eu,~~ [p|P]ropriamente
371. egual ↑em valôr

A monarchia tem-se tornado em alguns paizes compativel com a maior civilização, deixando de ser o menos possivel monarchia. Quanto menos monarchia é, melhor sahe. A mornarchia portugueza não está n'este caso. Não é preciso provar. A monarchia portugueza ahi está. [26ʳ] Basta olhar para ella. Não há melhor argumento.

Não combato, digo-o outra vez, a monarchia. |Combato a monarchia portugueza. Combato-a symbolisada nos partidos rotativos, cumulo do Nada em Portugal, & nos partidos jesuiticos — o nacionalista e o outro.

A monarchia em Portugal é hoje isto: |interiormente| o Sñr. D. Manuel, o Sñr. José Lima e o Padre José Lorenço de Mattos; a incapacidade, a *intrujice* e a maldade; o Cocó, Ranheta, Facada *da comedia* dos adeantamentos, no seu |acto actual|. E, exteriormamente, a monarchia portugueza é isto [372] hoje: o general Gouveia, o chefe Amorim e o Sñr. Abilio Magno; a incapacidade, a intrujice e a maldade.|

[144A² — 1-6]

Visão de Rei lear.

O rei Lear gritou na planicie, expulso do palácio de sua filha, onde a outra filha imposta assentou abrigo. Chorava o velho rei.

---

372. ~~hoje~~ isto

[2ʳ]

Ouvi então soar dois tiros, subitos, rápidos, nitidos, com um som extranhamente falso;³⁷³|*cortante|. E depois, com um baque pesado e obsceno que dava a ideia da queda d'um corpo gordo e *obeso*, ouvi cahir nos³⁷⁴ degraus de uma escada um corpo d'homem. Senti-o principiar a cahir pela escada abaixo. Ouvi-o cahir. E até senti a pelle arrepiar-se-me, os olhos sahirem-me das orbitas com um terror |enorme|. Ao rolar aquelle corpo fez um barulho extranho, *cheio*, marulhento, meio metallico. Alfim comprehendi: o corpo estava³⁷⁵ cheio d'ouro.

E então como se empolgado fora por uma hallucinação maior, eu ouvi o pesado chocalho do ouro no obeso [2ᵛ] corpo invisivel sem mudar mudar-se, sem alterar teor, mais ao longe já na queda pela □ escadaria, um som novo, que contudo parecia o menos ouvido por ouvidos mais certos, mais *entendedores*; era um som vago, indeterminado mas era um som terivel: † de gritos, soluços, uivos longuinquos indicações da miséria d'um povo, apagados indicios da decadencia d'uma nação.

---

373. soar ↑dois tiros, subitos, rápidos, ‡ ↑nitidos, com um som ~~falso~~ extranhamente falso;

374. ~~com~~ nos

375. ↑o corpo estava

[3ʳ]

Visão de Futuras Contas.

Ministerio das Obras Publicas.

|Reparos| no balouço de Sua Majestade El-Rei[376] D. Manuel II RS. 15.585 $324.

Construção de um assobio na parte de traz da caneta com que Sua Majestade El-Rei assigna os decretos para Sua Majestade assobiar[377] ou um trapezio † 7.238 $500

Reparações no museu dos biberons de Sua Majestade 23.855 $326.

Um nó no chicote de Sua Majestade[378] 124.302 $404.

Um outro nó, mais na ponta do dito chicote 88.204 $305.

[4ʳ]

Visão d'um Museu Monarchico

— Uma nevralgia do Sñr. João Franco.

— Um relogio sempre adeantado que pertence ao Sñr. D. Carlos.

---

376. |Reparos|/ ↑ ações \ no balouço de S[ua] M[ajestade] El-R[ei]

377. ↑ com que S[ua] M[ajestade] El-[Rei] assigna os decretos para S[ua] M[ajestade] assobiar

378. S[ua] M[ajestade]

— Um sobrescripto.

— O mata-borrão em que se limpa o decreto de 30 de Agosto de 1907. Está queimado em varios logares por cinza de charuto.[379]

— Um exemplar do *Dernier Jour d'un Condamné* por Lamartine[380] que pertence ao Sñr. Pereira dos Santos.

— Um cadaver vivo. (Está em bom estado de conservação).

— Uma amostra de vinhos potaveis.

— Um burro.

— Outro burro.

— Mais burros ainda.

[4ᵛ]

Secção[381] de curiosidades obscenas

— O padre José Lourenço de Mattos.

— Uma conta de comida que não foi paga por peregrino em Janeiro.

---

379. ~~ei~~ charuto.

380. In this text, Pessoa attributes to Lamartine the work *Dernier jour d'un Condamné*, which was written by Victor Hugo. This is either deliberate, with the intent to create an ironical or satirical effect, or a mistake.

381. ~~Uma~~ *Secção*

178

|— Um revolver ³⁸² de barro. Está descripto como "bomba de dynamite." |

— Um exemplar do "D. Carlos, o Martyrizado" do Sñr. Ramalho Ortigão.

— O "Suave Milagre" do Sñr. Conde D'Amaro.

— O art.º 5º. ³⁸³

— A lei 13 de Fevereiro. Junto está um caixote com processos para a abolir.

— O porteiro do Ministerio da Fazenda, com ouro.

— Uma "ausencia" do Sñr. José Luciano.

— Varias amnesias.

— Uma colher que tem escripto ³⁸⁴ "ignobil porcaria"; está lambida de todos os lados.

— Uma capa muito grande.

[5ʳ]

Excavações em Portugal Morto.

— Um bocado de jornal que mostra as lettras PORT… & em um canto □ Mattos.

---

382. ←? — Um revolver

383. ? — ~~O Sñr. Carlos Malheiro Dias.~~
    — O art.º [V̶|5º]. ~~do projecto de~~

384. Uma ↑ colher que tem escripto

Não está em casa

A mão portugueza que bate á porta dos políticos con-
stitucionæs.

[6ʳ]

Senti-me, sim, senti-me, pois não sei que³⁸⁵ nome dar
ao sentido que d'aquillo me deu a intuição, em uma
terra extranha e mysteriosa, cheia de terror e de indi-
siveis males,³⁸⁶ uma planicie indefinidamente extensa,
erma, negra, caliginosa — uma planicie erma como a
fome sob o céu escuro³⁸⁷ como um odio. Era uma □ vi-
sual³⁸⁸ do tudo que se encontra nas palavras *horror, ter-
ror, mysterio,* □ vi de repente — vi? Não sei se foi visto
aquillo que □ — que essa planicie tinha uma estrada e
que á beira d'essa estrada immensa havia corpos, cadave-
res cahidos. Estes eram brancos, brancos-brancos, de³⁸⁹
uma brancura extranha, que não entra nas concepções
d'este mundo. Sim, não havia luar, não havia luz alguma,
mas esses corpos eram brancos, nitidos, côr de leite, [6ᵛ]
mais³⁹⁰ brancos ainda. Eram brancos de uma brancura

---

385. q̶u̶a̶l̶ que
386. indisiveis e̶ ↑males,
387. escuro /↑negro\
388. visual /↑no espaço\
389. p̶o̶r̶ de
390. m̶a̶i̶s̶ mais

sua, parecia que um luar extranho sobre elles incidia.[391] Mas o luar vinha d'elles mesmos.

Tremendo, meio louco de horror, approximei-me d'elles pela estrada da planicie. Vi então o que elles eram. Os corpos cahidos á beira da estrada eram as nações mortas, os povos perdidos.

Estava alli a Grecia, que tão grande fôra; Roma, que tanto dominou; Carthago, Assyria, †, Egypto, jaziam[392] todos em attitudes extranhas de morte á beira da curiosa estrada. Nos olhos d'alguns boiavam danças, □, outros como que trahiam a visão de torres e □

[144A² — 9–13]

Visão.

— Sonhei que era artista, que era caricaturista.

— E que visão teve você do trabalho que fazia?

— Esta. Que tinha que desenhar a monarchia absoluta, a monarchia constitucional,[393] a monarchia demo-cratica.

— E como as desenhou você?

— Como não desenho, como não[394] tenho o instincto do

---

391. ↑ sobre elles incidia

392. ~~amont~~ jaziam

393. monarchia ~~total~~ ↑constitucional,

394. ↑como não

risco, imaginei que a minha □ era apenas no escrever das palavras.[395] M. A. escrevi as palavras em lettras de sangue. M. C. — escrevi estas em lettras d'ouro, de moedas. M. L. escrevi estas em lettras de fumo.

Tudo em fundo[396] preto.

― ― ―

Visão

Sonhei que contava contos a creancinhas.

Um velhinho — visionei — ia de vez em quando de sua casa para casa de Sñr. Povo.[397] Ia, ficava lá e voltava. Quando ia, notei, ia, coitadinho, muito direitinho. Quando voltava, coitadinho, voltava todo cahidinho para o[398] lado. Sempre que ia, ia direitinho; sempre que vinha, lá vinha elle, cahidinho p'ro lado do muro que ia entre sua casa e a casa do Sñr. Povo.

Porque será, dizia eu. Muito trabalho ha-de ter, coitadinho, aquelle velho que vai tão direitinho e vem tão dobradinho para o lado da parede.

― ― ―

395. minha ~~ea~~ □ era apenas no escrever das palavra /↑que desenha a escripta das palavras\.

396. em /↑sobre\ /↓com\ fundo

397. ~~Um dia~~ [u|U]m velhinho — visionei /↑~~sonh~~ diria eu\ /↓vi-o em visão\ — ia ~~todos~~ de vez em quando de sua casa para casa de Sñr. ~~Estado~~ Povo.

398. ~~p'ro~~ ↑para o

182

[9ᵛ]

Então um garoto vê-o zangar e o velhinho baixou-se *&*
quis bater no garoto. Ai, meus meninos, então se viu por-
que é que o velhinho ia tão dobradinho para o lado da
parede. É que quando ia não levava nada nas algibeiras
e quando vinha trazia cheia d'ouro a algibeira do lado[399]
da parede.

— E o velhinho, Sñr. Pantaleão, não se zangou com o
garoto?

— Zangou, sim. Disse "Então você fez-me virar *o meu
lado politico* a toda a gente? Felizmente o meu lado
pessoal posso eu moſtrar."

— Eu sei um conto mais bonito Sñr. Pantaleão.

— Conta lá.

— Era um velhinho que ia muito direitinho de sua casa
para tal casa de [que] falla o Sñr. Pantaleão, e volta-
va tambem muito direitinho. Era o mesmo velho de
que fallava o Sñr. Pantaleão, mas iſto era depois.

— Ah, então emendou-se?

— Não foi, Sñr. Pantaleão, não se emendou.

— Então?

— Tinha ambos os bolsos egualmente cheios.[400]

───────

399. ~~levav~~ trazia cheia d'ouro a algibeira ~~vindo~~ do lado
400. ~~— E o garoto não o provocou.~~
    ~~— Provocou, sim, Sñr Pantaleão, mas elle anda pouco direi-~~
    ~~tinho.~~

183

[10ʳ]

Visão.

Vi-o passar — sonhei; ia [401] de casaco claro.

— Bons dias, Snr. Conselheiro, disse.

Depois d'ahi a tempo, vi-o outra vez. O casaco claro estava cheio de nodoas. Fiquei pasmado.

— Bons dias, [402] Sñr. Conselheiro, disse.

D'ahi a tempo tornou a passar. Trazia um casaco mais escuro.

— Bons dias, Sñr. Conselheiro, sondei. [403]

— Agora, disse eu para um amigo, agora está decente.

— Decente? Aquillo não é senão a nodoa que se esten-deu ao casaco todo.

––––––––––––

[10ᵛ]

Visão.

Vou contar a minha visão do crucificado. [404]

Foi osculado, & pelo osculo [405] trahido por quem se dizia seu amigo.

––––––––––––

401. —Vi-o Vi-o passar — subir; pa ia
402. Toda a gente notava
    — Bons dias
403. disse ↑ sondei.
404. d[e|o] um crucificado.
405. beijado ↑ osculado, & pelo beijo osculo

Cuspiram-lhe, humilharam-no,[406] pregaram-lhe uma coroa d'espinhos.

Crucificaram-n'o.

Notei a sua physiognomia e vi com[407] espanto que não era Christo, que não fôra a minha nova visão do filho de José.

Reparei para aquelle que o trahira, osculando-o. Tra-zia uma coroa e lia uma carta. Olhei para aquelles que o cuspiram e que o fustigaram;[408] não eram soldados, eram homens de sobrecasaca & chapeu alto. Mirei os que[409] lhe pregaram a coroa d'espinhos. Eram homens idiotas; pois os que o crucificaram eram semelhantes.[410]

Pareceu-me então ter um fim de visão extranho. A cruz quebrara de repente e ella & o crucificado cahiram em cima dos algozes.

[11ʳ]

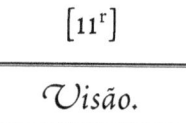

Visão.

O chefe[411] dos bombeiros almoçava.

Chegou um[412] bombeiro á pressa.

— O edifício está em chamas.

— Não para mim que estou a almoçar.

---

406. ~~fustigaram~~ ↑humilharam-no,

407. ~~Morreu.~~
    Notei a sua physiognomia e vi ~~qu~~ com

408. ↑lia uma carta. Olhei para aquelles que o ↑cuspiram e que o fustigaram;

409. ~~Puz os olhos em~~ ↑Mirei os que

410. ~~os mes~~ semelhantes

[11ᵛ]

Attentei enfim com extranha commoção a um velho que jazia um pouco fôra da estrada. Tinha[413] um aſpecto nobre e cavalheiresco, um ar, morto embora, de ousadia. Via-se-lhe nas linhas do roſto sangues de grandes feitos, como que fitei-o — por extranha e incommensuravel associação de sentimentos e ideias se viu ao longe naus, galeras, eſtandartes, exércitos de victorias,[414] arrancos d'ousadia.

O velho não[415] tinha na mão a eſpada; a lamina via-se vagamente a diſtancia. Uma manta d'ouro que trazia havia-lhe sido arrancada. Na sua queda parecia que quebrara, mas quebrada talvez já eſtivesse, uma cruz de pedra sob a qual jazia; como que começou[416] a cahir: era um padrão.

Attentei então no olhar do velho e eſtemeci. Não tinha no olhar nada que nos outros se leia. Não tinha o ultimo fulgor da □, o relampejo último[417] do vivo, o derradeiro □

411. chefe / ↑leader \
412. o̶ um
413. A̶ Tinha
414. s̶u̶c̶c̶ de victorias
415. j̶a̶ não
416. U̶m̶a̶ c̶r̶u̶z̶ d̶'o̶i̶r̶o̶ q̶u̶e̶ Na sua queda parecia que quebrara, mas quebrada ↑talvez já e̶ſ̶t̶a̶v̶a̶ ↑eſtivesse, uma cruz de pedra q̶u̶e̶ sob a qual jazia; o̶r̶a̶,̶ e̶r̶r̶a̶m̶ ↑como que começou

186

do termo. Não. Nem n'aquelle olhar se via uma sombra de □, de □ A sua expressão não era essa: era a expressão d'aquelles que sentem[418] uma morte ignobil. Ruína □ — muito[419] muda, indignação, □ tudo isto alli estava. Era, sim, a expressão d'aquelles que morrem de mortes ignobeis — da mulher que se vende,[420] para obter pão para o filho, da aldeã violada por um soldado de um selvagem exercito ariano, do velho guerreiro esbofeteado cuja mão já não pode com a espada. Um soluço de indignada angustia havia naquele olhar.

Ah, que agonia muda, que muda contenda d'indignação e de dôr, que ódio do seu fim, que asco alli[421] se via, que repulsa, que □!

[12ʳ]

— Velho prodigioso, disse, velho em cujo morto olhar[422] não sinto nem uma saudade, apagada que foi toda a lembrança de um passado grandiozo, pelo asco e pela indignação de uma morte ignóbil. Que morte foi essa, velho extranho e symbolico? Quem te matou?

---

417. ~~Olhei~~ ↑Attentei então ~~para~~ no olhar do velho e estemeci. Não tinha no ↑rosto olhar ~~nada~~ que nos outros se leia. Não tinha o ultimo fulgor da ~~va~~ □, o ~~ardor~~ ↑relampejo último

418. ~~se~~ sentem

419. m[ui]to

420. ~~sente~~ ↑morrem de mortes ignobeis — ~~da aldeã violada~~ ↑da mulher que se vende /↑morre\,

421. ~~asco~~ ↑asco alli

422. ↑morto olhar

187

Quedei silencioso.[423]

— Não[424] foi o vicio, grande velho, exclamei, não o vicio que te matou. Não foi a guerra, não foi o mal que vem ☐, nem o[425] ☐. Alguma cousa mais esses teus olhos indicam, alguma cousa mais significam. Morte mais ignobil soffreste, velho prodigioso! Diz-me quem te matou?

Pareceu-me então que a visão toda desapparecia, que se rompia, que se rasgava, que um sol subito fazia desapparecer aquella planicie extranha, aquelle velho symbolico. Mas pareceu-me tambem que uma voz tremenda & accusadora[426] — quão tremenda não o posso dizer — rompia d'aquella bocca já morta, que n'aquella[427] longa planicie, d'aquelles tristes labios frios rompia a vida d'um morto que lançava no espaço, um grito ermo de asquerosa[428] ira, de indignada dor:

Quem me matou fôram os ladrões!

———

423. ~~Fez-se um silencio~~ Quedei silencioso.

424. [Ө|N]ão

425. o ~~q~~

426. ~~tremenda~~ ↑ tremenda & accusadora

427. [d|n]'aquella

428. ~~as~~ asquerosa

[13ʳ]

Visão.

Foi uma visão rapida, incompleta, pouco nitida — visão d'uma taboleta.

O que vi foi apenas isto: *Sociedade Protectora dos Ladrões* — [429]

E isto, por baixo: Secretario Ferreira do Amaral.

— Quem será o presidente? pensei.

———————————

[144A² — 20-22]

Visão

Vou contar a minha horrenda visão do crucificado. Uma já contei. Esta que vou contar é mais horrenda [430] ainda.

Elle era um pobre trabalhador, fraco e doente. Aquelles que d'elle deviam tomar cuidado tinham-no deixado assim ficar, chegar áquelle ponto do mal. O seu pobre terreno, não fecundo, estava pouco cultivado porque falhavam [431] as forças e a saude ao |abandonado| lavradôr.

———————————

429. *L*[adrões] —

430. é outra ↑que vou contar é mais ~~longa, mais triste, mais~~ horrenda

431. ~~lhe~~ falhavam

Um dia foram buscal-o para o crucificarem.[432] Antes
fustigaram-no e elle estorceu-se e gemeu. Umas vezes
gritou com dor e estorceu-se. Mas não gritou muito nem
muito se estorceu. Bem sabiam os que o torturavam que
elle só gemer [433] podia.

Mas não gostaram do [434] seu grito de dôr. Cuspiram-
lhe na cara e chamaram outros de fóra para o fazer. "Cus-
pam-lhe" disseram. "Já nada pode fazer. [435] Nós tivemos
cuidado em que elle ficasse assim." Cuspiram-lhe e elle
deu um grito de raiva e de dôr que se conhecia impo-
tente. [436] Um dos que d'elle haveria [437] de curar bateu-lhe
então na bocca e elle calou-se. "Vencemos" disseram *elles*.

A victima tremia, de raiva talvez, talvez de frio ou
de fome.

[21ʳ]

Visão

Ouvi soar uma voz que se dirigia ao povo portuguez;
era a voz dos politicos da monarchia.

Diziam elles: "Povo, ou a monarchia (*que' o rouba*) ou
a victoria estrangeira (que lhe tira a existencia)." Ora a

---

432. buscal-o ~~o~~ ↑ para o crucificarem ~~no~~

433. elle ↑ ~~an nem~~ só gemer

434. não ↑ gostaram do

435. fazer."

436. ↑ que se conhecia impotente

437. ~~hav~~ haveria

monarchia é o roubo; a victora estrangeira o assassinato do paiz. [438]

Ouviram bem. E ouvi. E lembrai. Há uma phrase extranhamente, completamente idota. É esta: [439]

"A bolsa ou a vida."

É ou não é? [440]

Quem diz esta phrase costumam ser os ladrões. Analysem, procurem: a analogia é completa.

Visão

Tive a visão de uma planicie immensa, muito esteril, muito arida. Está muito cravada por fortes signaes de ferraduras.

— Que planicie [441] é esta? perguntei ao cicerone espectral das minhas visões.

— É a planicie do thesouro publico. [442]

— Ah. E [443] estas marcas — estas profundíssimas mar-

---

438. a carteira)." ↓Ora a m[onarchia] é o roubo; a victora estrangeira o assassinato do paiz.

439. É esta: / ↓Ve-se pois na m[onarchia] que o verdadeiro sentido das palavras dos politicos é este: \

440. É ou não é? / →ou (Não é a melhor das provas mas já não é mau) \

441. ~~Que pla~~
    — Que planicie

442. publico. ~~Se pensar~~

443. É, *in the original. Probably by mistake.*

cas — de ferraduras — que⁴⁴⁴ grandes beſtas que as deixaram cá?

— Os politicos.

— Ah sim, sim. São beſtas, são. Mas o seu caminho eſtá indicado pelas marcas que aqui deixaram.

Visão.

Tive uma visão de uma camisaria (eſþiritual. Parece asneira, mas não é.)

Se a vergonha⁴⁴⁵ fôsse uma gravata, a maior parte dos homens publicos portuguezes não usaria gravata.

E ha muitos d'elles que nem collarinho teriam⁴⁴⁶ para a pôr.

Visão

Tive outra visão.

— Quem dera, dizia um individuo que n'ella apparecia, que se pudesse fazer do passado de Portugal umas cousas para barracas de feira. Dava dinheiro...

---

444. marcas d̶e̶ — estas profundíssimas marcas — de ferraduras — q̶u̶a̶l̶ que

445. A̶ ̶v̶e̶r̶g̶o̶n̶h̶a̶ ̶e̶r̶a̶ ̶s̶i̶m̶b̶o̶l̶i̶z̶a̶d̶a̶ ̶p̶o̶r̶ ̶u̶m̶a̶ ̶g̶r̶a̶v̶a̶t̶a̶.̶
Se a vergonha

446. teriam / ↑tinham \

192

— Faça você isso, faça, disse um outro.

— Porque pensa? [447]

— Faça, faça, que eu |*assim| garanto-lhe os rendimentos...

[22ʳ]

Visão

Esta é a visão dos canalhas.

As fadas e os deuses tinham o poder de se transformar em varios bichos e cousas.

Hoje não há fadas ou deuses, mas vivem uns outros entes que têm o mesmo condão: [448] são os canalhas.

Enquanto o corpo está vivo tornam-se sanguessugas. Quando o corpo está morto tornam-se vermes. Lá de comer não deixam elles.

Visão

Vi em visão uma cobra dar uma dentada no seu proprio rabo. [449] Ha cobras que fazem isto.

Mas isto acontece só ás cobras. É pena. [450]

Não poderem os politicos portuguezes adeantarem-se do seu proprio dinheiro!

Visão.

Quem espera sempre alcança.

É verdade. Estes homens de sobrecasaca e chapeu alto que vejo na minha visão… em *novos*, eram *esperados*,[451] agora são *alcançados*.

$[22^v]$

Visão.

Não é extranho, perguntou-me um phantasma em uma visão, que um dos paizes mais atrazados seja aquelle em que ha mais politicos adeantados.

---

447. ~~este tal~~ pensa?
448. ~~pod~~ condão
449. no seu proprio rabo ^/↑ em si mesma\
450. ~~Isto foi numa visão; só~~ /↑ Mas isto\ acontce ↑só ás cobras. ~~Quando mortas aquellas ellas não gostam.~~ É pena
~~Inda um~~
~~Os politicas nem se adeantam~~
451. em *novos*, /↑(na †)\ eram *esperados* (~~na †~~),

[144A² — 26ᵛ–29]

Visão.

O homem da má cara teceu com cuidado uma corda suja *&* grossa que usaria depois [452] sorridente. Depois, ajudado d'outros, pegou no homem meio desfallecido que alli havia e atou-o fortemente a uma arvore. [453]

D'ahi a pouco a victima [454] tomou mais força, mas não poude romper |o laço| que em seu desfallecimento fôra atado.

Passa-se [455] algum tempo, a victima ora gemia, ora se indignava, ora quasi desfallecia atada á arvore, e houve desavença entre um dos chefes dos outros homens e o homem [456] da má cara.

Então, rindo interiormente, o tal chefe arranjou outro bocado de corda egualmente sujo e grosso, e junto-o [457] ao outro, pegou no homem da má cara pelo pescoço *&* atou-o á arvore tambem.

---

452. ~~teceu~~ ↑ ᵗᵉᶜᵉᵘ com cuidado uma corda suja *&* grossa que usaria depois ~~entre~~

453. uma ~~estrado~~ arvore

454. [o|a] ~~homem~~ victima

455. ~~D~~ Passa-se

456. ↑ ~~tal~~ homem

457. ~~que juntou~~ ↑ ᵉ ʲᵘⁿᵗᵒ⁻ᵒ

[27ʳ]

O homem da má cara não gostou. Olhou para a corda & percebeu que era grossa, rija e suja.

— Que ignóbil porcaria, disse.

"Oh meu camarada d'arvore, disse então ao outro o homem da má cara, oh [meu comarada d']arvore, ar-rependo-me de tudo quanto te fiz, arrependo-me sim, arrependo-me. O meu coração chora decerto em mim. Se d'aqui sahir hei de tirar esta corda (apre, que doe!), hei de te tirar d'aqui e tambem livrar de ti."

O triste infeliz acreditou, mas ás vezes pensava.

"Só ⁴⁵⁸ não se livra elle & se vier alguem soltal-o não é com a condição de o ⁴⁵⁹ deixar soltar-me a mim."

Passou mais tempo e veio uma mão gorda que desatou a corda que prendia o homem da má cara. Este vendo o pedaço de corda livre, foi, rindo ⁴⁶⁰ interiormente, e, para que elle se não perdesse deu duas voltas a ella á roda do corpo do antigo companheiro d'arvore, que olhava para elle indignado e pasmado.

D'ahi a pouco appareceu o homem ⁴⁶¹ da má cara. Trazia mais corda ☐

---

458. D̶e̶ Só
459. de m̶e̶-o
460. < † > ↑ᶠᵒⁱ, rindo
461. [u̶m̶|o] homem

[27ᵛ]

— Vou-te prender — disse elle poeticamente com um raio de luz.

Atou-o com uma outra corda.

De vez [em] quando vinha e trazia mais corda e ata-va-o mais. As vezes vinha e cuſpia na cara do outro.[462]

E dizia-lhe: "o homem da mão gorda também te manda um escarro."[463]

E quando o cuſpia ou quando o atava olhava para uma janella que havia proxima e d'onde o Eduardo, o Affonso, o Victor alli eſtavam e dizia, piscado os olhos: "Cuſpo, o homem da mão gorda coſpe, ato — e elle quietinho que é um goſto. Vários não vem elle que eſtá quieto é porque acha que é bom."

O homem da má cara cuſpiu outra vez, e outra vez trazia cuſpo do homem[464] da mão gorda.

A victima eſtorceu-se horrorosamente. Viu em si os olhares visiveis de uma multidão que o cercava, olhava para as janellas e via o riso e o scarnio dos outros. Olhava para o chão e via o traço de escarro[465] que lhe haviam cuſpido.

---

462. outro. ~~Mas á medida que apertava ia-se esque~~.
463. escarro." / ↑ manda um tanto \
464. cuspiu ↑ outra vez, e ↑ outra vez trazia cuspo do ~~out~~ homem
465. ~~cuspo~~ escarro

Tanto tivera, tanto a soar de indignação que quasi desfez os nós das cordas.

Tudo de reſto o homem da má cara viu assim de longe. Disse ao homem da mão gorda: iſto preso assim é uma corrente.

"Hum" dizia o outro, † em deante.

[28ʳ]

Olhe, alertou [466] o homem da má cara, vá o senhor adeante com a corrente & prenda-lh'a. A mim doe-me no pé.

Lá fôra e o homem da mão gorda, a sorrir, atou [467] a corrente varias vezes á roda da victima. Não acabou de o fazer, parou, quando aconteceu [468] uma cousa. Atando muito a victima pelo corpo, as cordas á roda das pernas ficaram mais livres. Na sua alta indignação, a victima conseguiu soltar-se levemente.

Atraz do homem da mão gorda eſpantava, a sorrir, o homem da má cara.

De repente o pé da victima levantou-se e arremessou no homem da mão gorda um formidavel pontapé. O homem da mão gorda apanhou-o em cheio e cahiu morto.

---

466. de repente ↑ alertou
467. at atou
468. ext aconteceu

A corrente que prendera, ainda não fechada[,] de-
senrolou-se *&* cahiu.

O homem da má cara desatou[469] a fugir, engolindo
mais cuſþo.

Mas tão depressa ia fugir que a corrente não se lhe
enrolava[470] n'um pé, arraſtando ele consigo.

O homem da arvore lá cortou o atado.

Os outros cá de fôra eſtavam com medo d'elle. Eſtá
[28ᵛ] muito quieto diziam. Deve-se apertar a corda pelo outro
lado da arvore. Mas se fôr preso chega ao pé d'elle...
ora, ainda eſtá bem preso.

A victima eſtorcia ainda, cada vez mais com mais
força. E pesava ás vezes assim tambem.

Ainda tinha o pé livre.

E olhei a sorrir o seu pé ensanguentado.

———

— Ó Sñr. Pantaleão; ora certamente você teve graça nela.

— Tantas vezes, portuguez, não tem graça, não tem.
Maldito de quem vira a lêl-o.

---

469. ~~fugiu~~ desatou
470. ~~corr~~ ↑ ˡʰᵉ enrolava
471.   *~~Visão.~~*

~~Disse eu para o phantasma:~~

~~— A monarchia portugueza está desfeita, perguntei.~~

~~— É verdade, repetia elle, está feita em [c|C]acos com C grande.~~

Visão.

199

Visão. [471]

Na monarchia portugueza — disse eu ao phantasma ex-
tranho — há muito talento, o que é é que se acha escon-
dido. É modesto. Se ha [472] talento, ha □, ha sciencia, ha...
Ha caco.

Sim esta mistura [473] de modestia e de saber é o que   [29ʳ]
se pode, jovialmente, chamar um |*pedaço| de sciencia.

Ha uma caverna de caco. [474] Sciencia, não. Mas há
caco. Ah, não é força de |*palavra| é caverna de caco.

(Ler in versu)

Visão

Casa roubada, trancas na porta; disse eu, com originali-
dade, ao phantasma extranho.

— Não é assim, replicava elle; "casa roubada, fechadura
   nova" assim é que é...

— Então.

— E chave na mão dos politicos ladrões. [475]

---

472. — ~~expoz-me o~~ ↑ disse eu ao phantasma extranho — ~~é uma gruta~~
      há muito talento, o que é é que se acha escondido. É modesto.
      Ө ↑ Se ha

473. ~~amal~~ mistura

474. Ha uma caverna de caco. ↑ Sciencia, não. Mas há caco. Ah, não é força de
      |*palavra| é caverna de caco.

475. dos ‡ politicos ladrões / ↑ amigos dos outros \ .

— Chave? Chave †, chave †, chave □, chave □, chave falsa? qual d'estes artigos é □

    O quinto. (artigo.) [476]

Visão de Obras Monarchicas.

Tive a visão de varias [477] obras que achei bem ter o ar do outro mundo. É assim que em visão as vi:

"O Transformismo" por Fernando Martins de Carvalho [478]

? "A Immaculada" por José Luciano de Castro [479] (J.L. de C.).

? "Introdução á Sciencia da Linguagem." Por Oliveira Mattos.

"A Arte de Furtar" por xxx.

"O Manual do Prestidigitador" Por Manuel Affonso Espregueira. [480]

? "Só" por Sebastião de Souza Dantas Baracho. [481]

2? { "A Infância Abandonada" [482] pelo Sñr. José Lourenço de Mattos.

---

476. — ~~O que a chave dos ladrões~~? o O Quinto. (artigo.)
477. de que varias, *in the original.*
478. Fernando Martins do Carvalho /↑ F. M. do C.\
479. J[osé] L[uciano] de Castro
480. Aff[onso] Espregueira
481. ? "Só" ~~pelo~~ por S[ebastião] de S[ouza] Dantas Baracho.
482. ? { "~~Prole~~ ↑A Infância Abandonada"

"Os deveres do Sacerdote" pelo mesmo.

⸮ "A Arte *&* a Politica" por Manuel de Mattos, O Pintor.

⸮ "O Porto-Franco" (Vasconcellos Porto e João Franco)

[92X — 86]

Visão jornalística.

Lia distrahidamente o jornal — sonhei — *&*, enganando-me na columna, fiquei surpreso (pois estava lendo[483] uma secção politica) ao ver o seguinte:

Terriveis gatunos

hespanhoes

Sorrindo, vi que eram hespanhoes. Nos partidos rotativos não ha terriveis gatunos hespanhoes

Over

Persian flower, persian flower
Song with immortal life,

---

483. ~~lia~~ estava lendo

[86ᵛ]

Visão.

que *não é visão.*

Ouvi em sonho uma voz cantar no logar.

"Canto os cantos mal, sonhei."

Fallava ao cantar, do povo portuguez.

Era a voz da justiça.

Cessou. De repente reteve a sua canção. Extranhou-me. Não pareciam as mesmas palavras.

Era a voz da justiça era, fallava com † ao povo no canto portuguez. Mas parecia dizer:

"Canto aos ladrões, ladrões, ladrões."

Extranha hallucinação. [484]

———

[92X — 88–95]

Visão?

— Olha, pequeno, aquella ratazana.

— Tem graça, Sñr. Pantaleão, o feinho parecia [485] d'um gato.

———

484. ~~hall~~ hallucinação
485. ~~o ca~~ ↑ o feinho parecia

= Você não acha bem o costume de pôr nos centros [486] republicanos os nomes de grandes republicanos?

= Acho, com uma condição: que os grandes republicanos sejam grandes republicanos. [487]

[89ʳ]

Visão da Conferencia.

Sonhei que o Sr. Julio de Vilhena appareceu, para conferencia, em casa do Sñr. José Luciano. O Sñr. Júlio de Vilhena ia triste.

— Que tem? perguntou o Sñr. José [488] Luciano.

— Uma grande dôr de dentes, gemeu o Sñr. Julio de Vilhena.

— Não é nada, respondeu o outro; o mesmo tem muito gente boa.

---

486. —Parece sim, mas não é uma
    = Você não acha ~~bem que nos~~ ↑ᵇᵉᵐ ᵒ ᶜᵒˢᵗᵘᵐᵉ ᵈᵉ ᵖᵒ̂ʳ ⁿᵒˢ centros

487 ↓ —Você não acha indecente e vergonhoso as criticas do Padre Mattos aos republicanos?
    —Acho; e o mais indecente e vergonhoso, para mim, é que acertara com respeito a alguns republicanos.

488. ↑ᵒ ˢ̃ⁿʳ· José

O velho estava morrendo. Mal podia fallar.

"Com respeito aos meus partidários — disse elle, com voz enternecedora — é preciso entender [489] isto... Olhe, observe o Julio, o Júlio de..." E cahiu, □, para traz. Morrera. [490]

O medico assistente virou-se para o amigo que estava presente.

[89ᵛ]

— Que tal — hein? A gente faz de conta que se trata do Vilhena

— De que duvida se tinha se é d'elle? [491]

— Qual Villena, heim. Isto ha-de se crêr o Julio de Villena, como o Julio de Mattos.

— O Julio de Mattos?!

Sim; é entendido na materia. Até [492] foi elle quem traduziu para portuguez a "Criminologia" do Garofalo.

_____
_____

= O Julio de... bem podia escrever um livro sobre os politicos monarchicos; [493] elle é entendidissimo na materia.

---

489. c̶h̶a̶m̶e̶ ↑ é preciso entender

490. e̶ [m̶|M]orrera.

491. ⌐outra forma — O̶l̶h̶a̶r̶a̶m̶-̶s̶e̶;̶ ̶V̶i̶l̶h̶e̶r̶n̶a̶ ̶é̶ ̶o̶ ̶v̶u̶l̶t̶o̶ ̶†̶.
    — De que duvida se tinha se é d'elle?

492. Sim; ↑ é entendido na materia. Até

493. politicos p̶o̶r̶t̶u̶g̶u̶e̶z̶e̶s̶ ↑ monarchicos;

= O Julio [494] de Vilhena? N'isso é.

= Não é o Julio de Vilhena [495] — esse entende pouco do que se trata, |*baixo| esse ponto de vista. Referia-me ao Julio de Mattos.

= Bem pensado! Quer você então dizer que os politicos monarchicos devem ser tratados pelo Julio de Matos como alienista. [496]

= Não, não como alienista. [497] Rigorosamente, não. (É por outra causa.)

[90ʳ]

Visão do Zé da Zepha.

Appareceu deante de mim o Phantasma Extranho. "Conversêmos," disse.

"Você já notou," perguntei eu, "como os rotativos estão perdendo? Já notou você o desdém com que elles agora tratam os republicanos, o povo, a opinião publica? É unico. Só d'elles. Mas não apanharam nem susto. Por occasião do regicídio julgaram que alguem lhes fôsse á pelle. Depois viram que não & lá estão na insolencia, na impunidade, na □.

---

494. O ~~Vilhena~~ Julio
495. J[ulio] de Vilhena
496. tratados pelo J[ulio] de M[atos] como /↑ porque é \ alienista.
497. não como /↑ é porque é \ alienista.

"Certo!" replicou o Phantasma Extranho. "Mas o caso tem sua psychologia. Fez-me[498] lembrar — e como não o fazer, se os casos são analogos — o caso do Zé da Zepha."

"Queira contar."

[90ᵛ]

— "Vivia eu ainda na terra" começou com voz funda o | Extranho Phantasma |.[499] "Vivia eu ainda na terra e tinha amigos, uns rapazes alegres, com quem fazia muita partida, muita □. Iamos muito a um certo club — o nome não importa.

"O jardineiro do culb era um tal Zé da Zepha, typo bruto mas muito poltrão. Este sujeito tinha sido por varias vezes malcriado para com alguns de nós. Numa vez estávamos reunidos no club — eu e mais uns seis rapazes — decidimos metel-o na ordem com um susto de[500] partir dentes.

"Arranjámos cada um um revolver com carga de polvora apenas e puzemo-nos, um a um, na estrada[501] que ia para o club, a certa[502] distancia uns dos outros."

O Phantasma[503] Extranho suspirou com a revelação. Assoou-se e continuou.

---

498. ~~Fazem~~ ↑ ᶠᵉᶻ-me
499. eu ↑ ᵃⁱⁿᵈᵃ na terra" começou ~~lentamente~~ ↑ ᶜᵒᵐ voz funda o | Extra[nh]o Phantasma |.
500. ~~o~~ um sustoi ~~m~~ de
501. ↑ ᵘᵐ ᵃ ᵘᵐ, na estrada
502. ~~p~~ certa

[91ʳ]

— "D'ahi a pouco apparecia o Zé da Zepha. Ao passar pelo logar onde eſtava escondido o 1º de nós, eſte sahiu-lhe ao caminho e dizendo "vou-te pagar a tua malcriação" apontou para elle o revolver, e, indo elle já, correndo de mêdo, a fugir, diſparou. Iſto accounteceu com a vez de todos — com todos enfim. De maneira que a accomu-lação, por progressões geometricas,⁵⁰⁴ das sete mortes puzera o homem, que eſtava já chegando ás porta do club, mais morto do que vivo.

"Chegando ao edifício, o Zé da Zepha metteu-se a correr pelo⁵⁰⁵ corredor fôra para a retrete que era lá ao fundo, e para onde elle ia por duas razões — uma porque lá ficava escondido⁵⁰⁶ & melhor que em qualquer outra parte e mais seguro (pois havia uma porta e pela porta não se podia diſparar para o assento)... e também por-que as taes sete mortes tornaram absolutamente neces- [91ᵛ] saria a ida aquelle logar.

Os outros ficaram cá fôra, pois eſtavam unidos ás gar-galhadas — e uns, que as contiveram, approximaram-se sem ruído, da porta da retrete (que elle féchara segura-mente com |*a maior das forças| que tinha) para⁵⁰⁷ ouvir qualquer cousa.

503. "~~D'ahi~~ O Phantasma
504. geometricas ᐟ↑potenciais\ ,
505. ~~dirigiu-se~~ ↑metteu-se a correr pelo
506. ‡ escondido
507. ~~para ver~~ para

208

Certos ruídos indicavam[508] a força da sua pressão. Mas ouvi[509] antes successivos bater de dentes e umas tentativas de fallar, abortadas por completo. O bater dos dentes fazia vizivelmente notar[510] mêdo.

Antes de mais eu eſperei. Até que enfim se ouviu já[511] uma ou outra syllaba — cerrada certamente pelo barulho dos dentes[512] — mas já mais claramente.

Enfim ouvi uma voz[513] alienada (por causa da violencia), eſtremecendo e □ (por causa do mêdo), mais *auto-suggeſtivamente*, como d'um sujeito[514] que se quér persuadir que não tem medo, apesar de o eſtar sentindo — uma voz □ onvindo-se enfim lentamente, palpitante, mas lá vinha □

[92ʳ]

"Sim! O Zé da Zepha eſtava a persuadir-se que não tinha mêdo. † attentamente o ruido.

"E…e…e…e…e" só a voz toda tremendo.

"E…e…e…ê…ê…eu" disse elle afinal.

E enfim senti dois bater de dentes *&* dois suſpiros d'allivio, mais desempunhados d'eſte ruido.

"E.E. eu aqui a c.g.r[515] para elles!"

---

508. ruídos ~~de temor~~ indicavam
509. ~~Parecia que~~ Mas havia
510. vizivelmente ~~tal~~ notar
511. ~~melhor~~ já
512. certamente ~~pelo barulho dos~~ ↑ᵖᵉˡᵒ ᵇᵃʳᵘˡʰᵒ ᵈᵒˢ dentes
513. ~~ent~~ ouvi ~~umas syllabas~~ uma voz
514. ~~typo~~ sujeito

[93ʳ]

Visão.

— Os tolos, dizia-me o Phantasma Extranho, são sempre mediocres.[516]

— E depois?

— Tem você um exemplo e visivel.

— Qual é?[517]

— O da Maior-Besta-do-Mundo.

— O quê? Essa está sempre com sustos.

— Com sustos não direi. Mas (a Maior-Besta-do-Mundo) está sempre com apprehensões.

[93ᵛ]

Visão de um João da Sociedade.

Discurso do Sñr. F. do conselho em elogio aos assassinos de 5 d'Abril.

Sñr. Presidente. Eu levantei hoje a voz para uma ☐ que me é especialmente grata, mas á altura da qual não posso ☐ que esteja a minha parca retorica. Cabe-me como presidente d'esta sociedade, o elogio dos soldados[518]

---

515. ~~c.r.g~~ ↓ c.g.r

516. Ph[antasma] Extranho

517. — Qual é [?]

518. ~~gloriosos~~ soldados

da gloriosa jornada de 5 d'Abril. (No fim: uma voz do painel "Muito Bem!" Voltaram-se todos & viram subita a physiognomia reparada do Sñr. João Franco.)

Folga que fôra no meu consulado que aquelle acto de heroismo fôsse praticado, folga que fôra a minha voz que relatasse □ dos cadaveres inimigos da MONARCHIA que □

[94ʳ]

Fim da Visão do Crucificado.

Quando morreu houve feriado nas repartições do estado.

———————

[95ʳ]

Visão

Los Jornales Republicanos — dizia a um hespanhol o Phantasma Extranho [519] — simplifican siempre la ortografía. |Onde| los otros ponen dos letras, este disse, como lettras en doble [520] — ponen los republicanos una. Por ejemplo: los jornales republicanos [521] escriben *aplicar* y no *applicar, falar* y no *fallar.*

———————

519. P[hantasma] E[xtranho]
520. ~~dob~~ en doble
521. ↑ jornales rep[ublicano]s

— Comprendo.[522]

— Esto nos permite hacer juicios sobre la politica republicana y monarquica.

— Como hacer juicios?

— Así. Un republicano escribe *politico*.[523] Esta es la politica republicana. Ler v.

— Politica. (repudio[524] a una das letras).

— Y la politica monarchica, para ser coerente se escribe así: *Pollitica*. Ler v.

— *Pollitica*.

---

522. — Comprendo.
    —Assi, por ejemplo. Assi, por ejemplo un jounal republicano — escola politica.

523. Assi Assi. Un republicano escribe pol poll *politico*.

524. Politica Politica. (aun repudio

2.3 — A Nossa Administração Colonial

[92H— 22–26]

A Nossa Administraçao Colonial

(*Notas de um monarchico*).

. . . .

Não é outro o fim d'este trabalho senão bordar algumas leves considerações sobre o panno quasi desfiado da chamada questão colonial. É possivel que as nossas reflexões não tenham accentuado caracter de originalidade. Á conclusão a que chegâmos já outros tacitamente chegaram; os methodos que indicâmos já outros, sem pensadamente os reduzir a systema theorico, os puzeram em pratica.

Certo é, contudo, que nos inspiramos apenas em uma consideração □ posto que certa das condições da nossa administração colonial e do que, dentro do regimen monarchico (unico em Portugal compativel, como está bem provado, com a liberdade, com a honestidade e com a justiça) se pode fazer a favôr das [525] nossas possessões ultramarinas.

─────────────┤

525. a favôr das /↑ com relação ás\

[22ᵛ]

Alguma coisa já tem sido feita — forçoso é confessal-o; mas muito ainda ha a fazer sem sahir d'aquella linha de conducta, d'aquelle modo de proceder que sempre tem distinguido financeiramente os defensores e partidários, n'este paiz, do systema constitucional.

Os homens publicos da monarchia portugueza podem seguir estes conselhos nossos sem abandonar nem os seus processos, nem o seu caracter, sem serem necessariamente reaccionarios, sem serem — ah, decerto que não! — revolucionarios ou republicanos.

As reflexões que vamos fazer são poucas, &, n'ellas, não especializamos nem particularizamos methodos ou meios; é nosso intuito, simples e único, indicar as linhas geraes que devem seguir [526] os estadistas monarchicos na sua administração das nossas colonias, sem deixarem [23ʳ] um momento de mostrarem claramente o que são & o que teem sido, fieis aos seus processos e ás suas tradições.

. . . .

Não seguindo nós n'estas notas um methodo philosophico, mas sim discursivo, patenteando as nossas opiniões á medida que a associação de idéas nol-as traz, não se admire o leitor que appareçam separados assumptos que logicamente deveriam ser consecutivos. [527]

---

526. que devem seguir que devem seguir, *in the original.*
527. se deveriam ~~seguir~~ ser consecutivos.

[24^r]

A maneira como[528] até agora as colonias de Portugal teem sido administradas (de um modo geral) mostra bem a incapacidade administrativa do povo *portuguez* — do povo, que não dos seus dirigentes. Com effeito, em muitas mãos habeis tem[529] estado a administração das nossas colonias e quasi sempre, pelo desleixo e miseria dos colonos, pelo seu pouco zelo e espirito civico teem ficado as finanças envolvidas, o commercio sem desenvolvimento, mal administrado. A culpa é principalmente do povo d'essas colonias. Bastante attenção — ah, bastante! — tem sido prestada às finanças coloniaes por varios funcionarios.[530] O cuidado que na administração financeira das colonias tem sido empregado é *tal*, a attenção prestada ao delirio tem sido tanta, por parte[531] dos governadores como por parte dos outros funcionarios, que se pode affirmar que quasi todos[532] teem tomado conta das finanças das colonias como se o dinheiro fôsse seu.

[25^r]

Ninguém, crêmos, ousará desmentir esta asserção. Que propômos — então — n'este assumpto? A que conclusões chegamos?

---

528. [Ө|A] ~~modo~~ ↑maneira como
529. ~~encarecidas~~ ↑habeis ↓habilidosas tem
530. ~~governadores~~ ↑funcionarios.
531. ~~que todos~~ por parte
532. ~~todos~~ quasi todos

Quanto a conclusões — não[533] é evidente que o culpado da má administração financeira das colonias — é o povo d'ellas que não tem prestado ás finanças o mesmo cuidado, a mesma attenção que os funcionarios [do] estado, mais ainda, que não têm querido alliviar de tanto trabalho os mesmos governadores, dignando-se amigavelmente a distrahir um tanto a attenção das finanças das colónias, como a distrahir dos outros ramos da administração colonial.

Sim, é preciso dizer-se em abono e desculpa d'esses trabalhadores financeiros incansaveis:[534] concedendo que a questão financeira é a da primeira importancia, visto que pela dita é que tudo se faz, os funcionarios[535] a que nos vimos referindo teem desattendido tudo o que não seja o manejo do dinheiro sumido, nos cofres. Dizem inimigos politicos que não se tem[536] creado fontes de receita. Mas como queriam elles que houvesse tempo para [25ᵛ] tudo. O modo de repartir e applicar o dinheiro em cofres usurpa, tem usurpado a attenção de todos os funcionarios de que tratamos. Por isso a agricultura, o comercio, a instrução — tudo o resto — tem sido pouco tratado.

---

533. ~~só temos~~ não
534. trabalhadores ↑ financeiros incansaveis:
535. ~~fun~~ funcionários
536. não ↑ se tem

Demais a mais não arriscamos então dizer aos inimigos do regimen & da administração monarchica que os fins d'essa crença de fontes[537] de receita eram talvez beneficiais aos bolsos dos proprios funcionarios? Prezando de mais[538] a sua honra para a submetter á imminencia de taes appreciações, teem-se abstido — e quem os accusará? — os governadores & outros funcionarios de taes creações de receita de taes inutilidades e *puras creações*[539] *de despeza* como a fundação de escolas, etc., concentrando-se na administração puramente financeira,[540] □

O argumento especioso dos inimigos[541] da pátria que não se tem pago a fornecedores não colhe. Pois então o dinheiro pode ir para dois logares ao mesmo tempo? Pois queriam os *criticos* que os interesses *mais próximos* se desprezassem — pelos outros,[542] os dos taes fornecedores? Inutil argumentação! Inspira falta de seriedade na apreciação politica dos adversarios.

---

537. d'essa ↑ crença de fontes
538. ~~Só uma justa defeza talvez pela opinião publica tivesse~~ Prezando de mais
539. ~~er~~ *puras creações*
540. financeira, ~~de~~
541. ~~f~~ inimigos
542. ~~ini~~ *criticos* que os interesses *mais próximos* se desprezassem — pelos ~~⚊ dos~~ outros,

[26ʳ]

· · · · · · · ·

O que aconselhamos pois?

|Em essencia|, não aconselhamos divergencia alguma dos methodos que até agora teem caracterizado os funcionarios administrativos a que nos temos referido. Na administração financeira nada temos a aconselhar, confiando [543] nós absolutamente em que — enquanto houver a monarchia em Portugal — os seus homens publicos serão incapazes de substituir os processos que os [544] caracterizam e que merecido renome lhes teem obtido. E excusado |pois| que aconselhemos a persistencia n'esses methodos, pois seria muito pouco extranho que, dentro da monarchia, outros se puzessem em pratica; É mesmo hypothese que não admittimos.

543. ~~nad~~ confiando
544. os ~~seus~~ processos que ǂ os

3.0 — Jean Seul de Méluret

$$[48C - 4^r]$$

Jean Seul.

Full name supposed to be:
Jean Seul de Méluret.

Supposed to be born in 1885 on the 1ˢᵗ· of August, one year older than Charles Search and three older than Alexander.

———————

Task: Writing in French — poetry [545] *&* satire or scientific works with a satirical or moral purpose.

———————

1. "Des Cas d'Exhibitionnisme."
2. "La France en 1950" — Satire.
3. "Messieurs les Souteneurs." — Satire.

———————

545. poetry (?)

3.1 — Des Cas D'Exhibitionnisme

$$[15B^3 — 27–30]$$

Jean Seul.

Préface

[I]

Ici, à Lisbonne et absorbé dans des occupations qui nous éloigne nous avons lu il y a quelques mois ce fait, qui jusqu'à ce jour-là nous avait[546] resté ignoré: de ce qu'on exposait, dans des music-halls, □ — à Paris, des femmes nues. Cela sentait si fort la décadence — la grand, la profonde décadence — que la surprise m'a été plus que doloreuse. Mais il n'y avait pas là-dedans[547] — je réfléchis[548] — rien à s'étonner. Étant données les immenses forces de décadence — s'il[549] y a quelque chose que l'on puisse appeler une force de décadence — déchaînées depuis[550]

546. à Lisbonne ↑ et absorbé dans des occupations qui ~~n~~ nous éloigne ~~j'ai~~ ↑ nous avons lu il y a quelques mois ce fait, qui jusqu'~~e ta a~~ ↑ à ce jour-là nous avait

547. pas là ↑-dedans

548. Reflechis, *in the original.*

549. ~~si~~ s'il

550. ~~dans~~ depuis

[28ʳ]

longtemps dans la civilisation⁵⁵¹ moderne et, spécia-
lement, dans la France, qui la représente⁵⁵² plus que
|toute| autre nation, il n'était pas difficile à prévoir⁵⁵³
que l'on verrait dans peu de temps⁵⁵⁴ des formes plus
accentués — plus accentués je veux dire, pour la vision
— de dégénérescence⁵⁵⁵ sociale.

Et pourtant tout esprit naturellement, quoique mo-
destement, épris⁵⁵⁶ du bien de l'humanité s'endormait
volontairement, |en| voulant échapper en quelque ma-
nière à l'inévitable par l'ignorance. Mais ceci ne pouvait
durer. Ces "formes plus accentuées," plus visibles, "de
la décadence,"⁵⁵⁷ dont je viens de parler, devraient un
jour se présenter. Ce jour venu, le péril vu clairement,
complètement, il n'y avait⁵⁵⁸ pas d'excuse pour l'esprit
le plus modeste dans sa sincérité, soit pour rêver, soit
pour espérer, soit pour ignorer. Rêver, espérer passive-
ment, ignorer volontairement — ce serait lâcheté morale,
complicité, ou par analogie⁵⁵⁹ de nature.

---

551. civilization, *in the original.*
552. répresente, *in the original.*
553. à /↑ de\ prévoir
554. dans peu de temps /↑ dans peu de temps apparaîtraient\
555. dégenerescence, *in the original.*
556. ↑ quoique modestement, épris
557. ~~dege~~ décadence,"
558. ~~plus plu~~ ↑ complètement, il n'y avait /↑ aurait\
559. ↑ ce serait lâcheté morale, complicité, ou par ~~egalit e ↑ égu homo~~
analogie

Quand le bruit des [560] canons éclate, quand la fumée de la poudre s'élève — on ne peut ignorer que la bataille a commencé. S'abstenir d'y prendre part, refuser à défendre les siens, ce serait, ou une lâcheté pure ou une trahison. [29ʳ]

Or la guerre entre la décadence et la société [561] a éclaté; que les forts et les sains d'esþrit, les logiques, les cohérents, les penseurs, lès sincères viennent défendre l'humanité contre l'homme. [562]

II.

Le but de ce livre reste indiqué dans les lignes ci-haut. [563] Il n'est qu'une balle dans le combat. Mais étudions d'abord, dans quelques lignes, la forme qui doit prendre cette bataille. Si nous étions un grand et fort esþrit, instruit et pondéré, nous aborderions la question [564] de la dégénérescence de la civilisation [565] occidentale, et, surtout, de la France, dans toute son ampleur, |en| étudiant toutes ses formes, toutes ses tendances, toutes ces □, etc. Nous en étudieront [566] l'étiologie, les symptômes,

---

560. ~~des~~ des

561. ~~bataille~~ ↑guerre entre la décadence et la ~~socie~~ société

562. ↑les penseurs, lès sincères viennent défendre l'humanité contre /↑de\ l'homme.

563. ci-haut /↑dessus\.

564. ~~toute~~ la question

565. civilization, *in the original.*

566. ↑en étudieront

la thérapeutique; nous en ferrions le pronostic dans la mesure du possible. Ce livre-là, si l'on pourrait l'écrire, serait une belle œuvre, une œuvre vraiment utile. Mais l'entreprendre non seulement [567] pour nous, mais pour |de beaucoup| qui valent bien plus que nous, n'aboutirait qu'à une œuvre manquée.

[30ʳ]

Nous avons donc pris *un fait* seulement — le fait que nous |citons aux| premières lignes de |cette| préface — et de ce fait nous avons cherché à déduire [568] l'état de la conscience et du psychisme social dont il n'était qu'une manifestation.

Même ainsi, l'œuvre ne devient [569] pas facile. On a d'abord à prouver une chose que beaucoup de gens ne voudraient |pas| croire, si vrai qu'elle soit; ensuite, il faut faire sortir de ce fait, ainsi éclairé, la signification qu'il a comme symptôme. C'est déjà beaucoup.

Nous ne sommes cependant pas satisfaits, si notre livre appelle un peu l'attention non exclusivement ou spécialement sur ce fait |où il est basé|, mais sur l'état de l'esprit collectif que ce fait représente. [570]

Lisbonne, □

Jean Seul [571]

---

567. l'entreprendre ~~soit, po~~ non seulement

568. ~~remonter~~ déduire

569. l'~~ouvrage~~ ↑œuvre ne ~~reste~~ ↑devient

570. ~~Cep~~ Nous ne sommes cependant pas satisfaits, si notre livre ~~p~~ appelle un peu l'attention ~~sur cela~~↑ non exclusivement ou spécialement sur ce fait |où il est basé| / ↑qui l'a provoqué\, mais sur l'état ~~de~~ ↑de l'esprit collectif que ~~il~~ ↑ce fait représente.

[15B³ — 31–32]

Jean Seul

Chapitre Premier.[572]

Dire qu'il existe une perversion sexuelle appelée[573] *l'exhibitionnisme* n'est de nouveau pour personne. Aujourd'hui on lit beaucoup sur les perversions sexuelles, non parce qu'elles sont des maladies, mais (toute simplement) parce qu'elles sont des perversions[574] sexuelles. J'espère donc n'étonner que quelques jeunes personnes |de moins de 9 ans| avec cette déclaration initiale.

Dire, en continuant, que cette perversion consiste dans le besoin d'exposition des organes sexuelles (les organes génitaux à soit bien entendu)[575] c'est peu d'ajouté, car quoique soit qu'il existe une perversion sexuelle nommée *l'exhibitionnisme*,[576] ne peut manquer de savoir la signification de ce mot dans les dictionnaires de médicine. Pas même les jeunes gens |susdits|,[577] en entendant

---

571. J[ean] S[eul]

572.   *Chapitre Premier.*

⊞

573. séxuelle appellée, *in the original.*

574. perversions ^/↑ maladies\

575. ^/↑ en\ l'exposition le besoin d'exposition des organes sexuelles ^/↑ génitaux\ (les organes sexuels ↑ génitaux à soit ↑ bien entendu)

576. *l'exh*[*ibitionnisme*]

577. Pas a même les jeunes gens |susdites ^/↑ s\|,

la définition du mot, ne restent dans l'étonnement, car, si par hasard |ils| ignoraient le mot, ils ont certainement[578] l'expérience de la chose à laquelle il s'applique.

[32ʳ]

Or, il est plus que notre conviction profonde que les cas de nudités publiques dans les music-hall(s), de Paris, &, peut-être, d'ailleurs — car pour le cas c'est le fait qui importe et rien de plus — ne[579] sont que des cas d'exhibitionnisme inévident, |masqué|. Cette conviction paraît étrange, mais ce n'est que quand on n'a pas étudié la[580] maladie en question. Pour bien montrer que les faits dont nous parlons ne sont que des cas d'exhibitionisme[581] il faut creuser cette matière, il faut l'approfondir, il faut analyser dans toute son extension[582] cette perversion sexuelle.

C'est ce que nous allons faire.

———————

———————

578. le l'étonnement, car, s'il y si par hasard |ils| ignoraient le mot, ils en ont certainement / ↑certes \
579. les cafés music-hall(s), de Paris, et, peut-être, d'ailleurs — car ↑p pour le cas c'est le fait qui importe et non ↑rien de plus — n ne
580. Cette ↑Or conviction paraît étrange, mais e ↑ce n'est que quand on n'a pas étudié l'exh la
581. Pour ↑bien montrer la que les faits dont nous parlons ne sont que des cas d'exh[ibitionis]me
582. il faut que nous analyser, dans toute son extension,

[15B³ — 34–35]

1.

L'Exhibitionnisme.

I.

(Historique)

II.

La première difficulté que l'on trouve dans l'étude de cette perversion est la nécessité de distinguer [583] le vrai du faux exhibitionnisme. C'est une difficulté qui, cependant, n'est pas écrasante. Si l'on y réfléchit [584] un peu il devient évident que l'exhibitionnisme — dans le sens le plus large du mot — celui que nous l'avons donné dans les lignes introductoires de ce Chapitre — on trouve que l'on peu le considérer [585] sous □ aspects, que l'on peut trouver dans le fait d'exhibitionnisme progressivement : (1) une action folle, (2) une action folle de sexualité, (3) une action folle de sexualité consistant dans une action d'*exhiber.*

---

583. perversion est ~~de~~ la nécessité de ~~separer~~ distinguer

584. Refléchit, *in the original.*

585. celui ~~qui~~ ↑que nous l'avons donné dans les / ↑avec \ ~~premières~~ lignes ↑introductoires de ce Chapitre — on trouve ~~qu'il se divise naturellement en □ classes~~ que l'on peu le

    ~~(1) Exhibitionnisme pur~~ / ↑comme \ / ↑en tant \ ~~action folle.~~

    ~~(2) Exhibitionnisme comme sexualité~~ / ↑manifestation sexuelle \

considérer

Ces[586] considérations produisent la classification né-
[35ʳ] cessaire qui va nous |élucider| sur ce qui est le faux, le
vrai exhibitionnisme. Car naturellement □

(1) Cas où l'action exhibitionniste n'est qu'un acte fou
(c'est-à-dire, cas de folie, où l'exhibitionnisme[587]
est un épisode[588] ou une part de délire).[589]

(2) Cas où l'action exhibitionniste[590] est un acte fou
faisant partie d'une excitation sexuelle générale.

(3) Cas où l'acte exhibitionniste □

$$[15B^3 - 38\text{-}39]$$

Cas d'Exhibitionnisme[591]

I. □

II. □

III. Déductions sociales.

───────────────

586. ~~Cette~~ Ces
587. l'ex[hibitionnisme]
588. episode, *in the original.*
589. delire, *in the original.*
590. l'act[io]n exhibitio[nnis]te
591. *d'Exhib*[*itionnisme*]
592. ~~exhi~~ exhibitionnismes

I. Le public

1. Le fait suprêmement sérieux et important n'est pas
— on le voit bien — l|es| exhibitionnismes[592] des pau-
vres femmes dont il a été question. Ce qui |importe|,[593]
quoiqu'il n'étonne pas, c'est le fait de ce que ces exhibi-
tionnismes ont un public — non un public particulier,
limité, mais un vrai public, digne de tel[594] nom. En |eux|,
les cas d'exhibitionnisme que[595] nous avons étudiés ne
sont que des cas d'exhibitionnisme (quoique compli-
qués d'hystérisme) comme tant d'autres qui sont étudiés
dans les livres médicaux. Mais ceux-ci sont[596] particuliers
(pour ainsi dire), limités; les autres — ceux-|lá| dont
nous[597] avons traité — sont publics. S'ils persistent donc
— c'est que le public les approuve. Or ceci mérite une
considération (si légère qu'elle soit) de ce public & de
sa psychologie.[598]   [38ᵛ]

II.

On voit bien, dès le commencement, qu'on n'a pas affaire
à un public sain. Ceci ne comporte pas de contradiction
pour une personne saine. Mais il y en a des contradictions.

---

593. |importe| / ↑ frappe \,

594. de / ↑ d'un \ tel

595. ~~des~~ que

596. d'autres ↑ qui sont étudiés dans les livres médicaux. Mais ~~ces autres~~ ↑ ceux-ci sont

597. ~~il~~ nous

598. considération / ↑ observation \ (si légère qu'elle soit) de / ↑ sur \ ce public
& de / ↑ sur \ sa psychologie.

Il faut donc que[599] nous prouvions le point; ce qui est embarrassant, comme si l'on avait à prouver qu'un cercle n'est pas carré. Du moins[600] cette preuve aura un très grand avantage: c'est que nous y trouveront, en la cherchant, ou, pour mieux dire, en cherchant l'exprimer,[601] des détails psychologiques, des □ psychologiques qui auront une application dans la suite.

[39ʳ]

III.

Un phénomène[602] anormal ne peut être □ pour normal[603] que pour un homme anormal.

───────────

Aux deux espèces d'impuissance[604] qu'on registre[605] dans les livres de médecine on devrait joindre une troisième, au moins quand on ne considère pas la question de l'impuisance d'un point de vue exclusivement médical,

---

599. est̶ / ↑ faut \ donc un̶e̶ ↑ que
600. Du p̶a̶r̶ ̶u̶n̶e̶ ̶p̶r̶e̶u̶v̶e̶ ̶s̶p̶é̶c̶i̶a̶ moins
601. ↑ l̶a̶ cherchant ↑ l'exprimer,
602. phenomene, *in the original.*
603. être p̶o̶u̶r̶ □ pour / ↑ comme \ normal
604. d'i̶m̶p̶o̶t̶e̶n̶c̶e̶ ↑ impuissance
605. régistre, *in the original.*
606. ne considère ↑ pas la question de l'im̶p̶o̶t̶e̶n̶c̶e̶ ↑ puisance d'un point de vue exclusivement médical, mais bien d'un p̶

mais bien d'un[606] □ plus exclusivement psychologique. Outre l'*impotentia coeundi* & l'*impotentia generandi* il y a une *impotentia mentalis*, une impuissance mental,[607] qui consiste |dans la faiblesse d'excitation sexuelle normal|, dans la faiblesse de la partie mental (il n'y a ici rien[608] de platonique) du sentiment sexuel. Il y a une impuissance qui consiste dans la faiblesse de la sensibilité mentale sexuelle, manque de sensibilité aux conceptions sexuelles, aux représentations sexuelles. Cette espèce d'impuissance est souvent liée aux autres — |très souvent, sinon|[609] toujours, à l'*impotentia coeundi* par épuisement.   [39ᵛ]

$$[15B^3 — 33]$$

Fin.

Notre civilisation[610] meurt, surtout la civilisation[611] française. D'où viendra la civilisation[612] suivante ? |Sera-ci| une civilisation germanique, une civilisation orientale,[613] japonaise ? C'est que nous ne pouvons pas dire.

607. *impotence*↑*tia* *mentalis*, une ~~impotence~~ ↑ impuissance mental,
608. La ~~pa~~ partie mental (il n'y a↑ici rien
609. sinon /↑et\|
610. civilization, *in the orginal.*
611. civilization, *in the orginal.*
612. civilization, *in the orginal.*
613. civilization germanique, une civilization ~~amé jap~~ orientale,

En tous cas — nous le disons avec une sincérité absolue — si la race française est en décadence — qu'on l'écrase, et vite. Si c'est une civilisation[614] allemande qui doit venir — qu'elle vienne, même en nous terrassant. Nous n'aimons pas les allemands, mais nous ne voyons[615] pas qu'il y ait besoin de mentir ou parler obscurément,[616] parce que[617] nous ne les aimons pas. Lier l'Angleterre[618] a soi contre cet autre pays[619] serait — dans ce cas — un crime devant la nature et vers l'humanité[620] (si bien qu'il soit devant le droit); car si l'Allemagne est plus forte (& nous ne sommes pas un petit pays) elle[621] a le droit de nous écraser. Que le plus fort foule aux pieds le plus faible, rapidement,[622] insensiblement, pour que s'accomplisse l'éternelle loi de la nature. Prolonger par les sentiments la vie des peuples décadentes — c'est peu de service à l'humanité.

Les races animales épuisées, agoniques, incapables de sincérité, d'honneur & de |chasteté| n'ont plus le droit à l'existence.

---

614. civilization, *in the orginal.*
615. nous ~~ne avons~~ ↑ne ~~avons~~ voyons
616. Parler ~~de les~~ obscurément,
617. Parceque, *in the original.*
618. ~~Si lier An~~ ↑Lier
619. ↑autre pays
620. la nature ↑ et vers l'humanité
621. plus forte ↑ (et nous ne sommes pas un petit pays) elle
622. ~~pour que~~ rapidement,

[33ᵛ]

La France est elle — horreur ! — dans ce cas? Elle pa-
rait bien avancer a grands pas vers lui.[623] Qu'on l'arrête
dans cette route. Qu'on la retienne. |Ne peut-on pas| la
freiner? C'en est donc fini. Il faut, pour le bien général,
qu'elle périsse. Que fait, du reste, au monde une race sans
âme, une nation sans cœur? Rien. Si en effet la France
est en décadence (elle ou tout autre pays[624] qui sera
dans le même cas) — moi, homme de l'humanité, qui
comprends jusque là la nature, n'ai qu'une chose, triste
et amère, à désirer: c'est que le peuple qui lui succé-
dera vienne vite |pour| l'écraser.[625] Brutal? Sans doute.
Horrible? Très horrible. Triste, amer, □? C'est vrai.

Mais c'est[626] une loi de la nature...

——————

Quiconque veut exister — une[627] nation surtout — doit
avoir le droit de le faire. À plus forte raison un pays tel
que la France, ayant une influence énorme sur d'autres

———————

623. avancer l'être y a grands pas ↑ vers lui .
624. Si Si en effet la France est en décadence (elle ou quelque ↑ et ou
    ᵗᵒᵘᵗ autre pays
625. c'est que que le peuple vienne qui l'écrasera vienne bientôt ↑ lui
    succédera vienne vite |pour| l'écraser .
626. Mais est c'est
627. doit une

234

nations doit-il en [628] avoir la conscience, et la conscience de la responsabilité des nations civilisatrices.[629] Cette nation entre-t-elle en décadence; il importe qu'elle en sorte ou qu'elle soit écrasée.

---

628. doit-elle ↑il en
629. civilizatrices, *in the original.*

3.2 — La France en 1950: Satire

$$[50A^I — 14^v]$$

France en 1950.

La natalité est presque nulle — ce qui est très avantageux. La mortalité est si grand que M. □, chef de □, a très bien dit |que la plupart des vivants étaient des morts|.

———

Germany must conquer, or help to conquer some Slavic race. A country, as an organism, is not animated. All is struggle and conflict. The oddest is the weakest. So the weakest goes to the wall.

———

Nous autres — les autres nations — ayons soin de nous arranger de façon[630] à ne pas être entraînés dans leur chute.

———

630. de ~~ne pas~~ ↑ nous arranger de façon

[55E — 86]

= France en 1950 = [631]

On lave les assiettes avec le sang des petits enfants qu'on a violés *&* égorgés. On ne essuie[632] pas les assiettes après. C'est — m'a-ton dit — une volupté un peu veillée.

On a obtenu des éjaculations séminales en mangeant le corps d'un petit enfant.

Le sperme d'animal comme breuvage n'est pas déjà à[633] la mode.

[55E — 87]

France' en 1950.[634]

M. est accusé de n'avoir pas violé un enfant de 2 mois.

|C'est[635] extraordinaire qu'il y ait aujourd'hui un manque d'esprit gaulois.|

Il a répondu qu'il pensait ce qu'il ferait mieux que de violer[636] quand on l'avait attrapé. Il ne méditait aucune offense à la décence du comité socialiste.

---

631. F[rance]
632. On ~~laisse~~ ne essuie
633. ~~ne pe perd son~~ ↑n'est pas ↓déjà à
634. *F[rance]*

[87ᵛ]

Ce-gît la France

Merde

[138A — 2]

France' en 1950. [637]

Ici il n'y a pas de gens |normaux|, ce qu'il y a c'est des gens deux fois anormaux, des sexuels deux fois *invertis*, de façon qu'ils son en retour à la normalité. Je connais même un Monsieur qui à nous paraît être très normal, mais qui, à ce qu'on affirme, n'est que 4 fois anormal. Comme[638] 2 négatifs font un positif, tous ces gens □ . . . .

L'autre jour fut mis en |prison| un nommé M. Couche-dans-le-lit-de-4-femmes Giraud; son crime était de se refuser de commettre l'inceste. Il se □ très firement en disant que toute l'humanité étant sa sœur, toutes les femmes étaient ses sœurs et par conséquent couchant avec une femme quelconque, il couchait avec sa sœur.

635. H̶ C'est
636. ↑ᵈᵉ violer
637. *Fr*[ance]
638. E̶n̶ Comme

$$[2^v]$$

———————

Un homme nommé □ (qui est gérant de la Compagnie d'assurances "Volupté Surhumaine"[)], ayant l'autre jour perdu une partie de son testicule gauche, et ayant trouvé, par ce qu'auparavant on appellerait une perversité, cette perte plaisante, il a été[639] pendant quelque temps à la mode de perdre un □ de cette part du corps. Mais, à ce qu'on rapporte, c'est un[640] plaisir à ne pas être exagéré.

———————

On étudie[641] beaucoup aujourd'hui les grands hommes et de précieuses monographies dues aux distingués talents de plusieurs illustres littérateurs ont été écrites ces dernières années.[642] Tout en n'aillant pas de traiter la partie littéraire[643] de leur œuvre, on s'applique de plus en plus à déterminer[644] quelle serait la longueur de leur verge.

———————

639. a ~~était~~ été
640. ~~ce~~ c'est ~~une~~ un
641. ~~On a □ les statues des poètes~~
     On étudie
642. dernières ~~jours~~ années.
643. ~~de~~ a
644. determiner, *in the original.*

[138A — 3–4]
France en 1950 (in French)

Fetichists □ can all object "la femme d'un ministre meurt pour un □ et[645] le préfet de police |s'|est épris d'un pot de chambre."

Il n'y[646] a pas, |c'|est clair, de professions comme il y a 50 ans; aujourd'hui, il y en a quelques[647] grands groupes professionnels; ce sont les syphilitiques, les tabétiques, les spermatorretiques, □

Les noms des choses, les □ ont tous pris une allure amoureuse. Partout, il y a des images pornographiques. Les dames ont un voile au lieu de décolletage; le voile va jusqu'au genoux, □

Machine de couture "La Sensuelle," appareil à □ machine à écrire "Épuisence."

Chacun a un pseudonyme, car c'était là[648] l'usage *il y a* 50 ans chez les apaches, et tels autres.

Compagnie d'assurances "L'œuvre de Chair," □

Aux théâtres l'on ne représente que des □

---

645. ~~est~~ meurt pour un ~~?~~ et
646. Il ~~y~~ n'y
647. ~~les~~ quelques
648. car ~~c'est~~ ↑c'était là

[3ᵛ]

Les □

Il n'y a pas, — il n'est besoin de le dire — d'écoles techniques; il y a seulement "L'École de Masturbation," l'"École de Sadisme"[649] *&* quelques autres de même espèce.

Les[650] mères couchent avec leurs fils, les pères avec leurs filles. On s'ennuie déjà de ça. C'est trop commun. Pas danger d'être laid, car il y a beaucoup de personnes qui aiment le laid.

Tous écrivent des livres. Quelques uns de ceux-ci se limitent[651] à des planches de photographes d'après créatures avec les textes en bas.

Toute conversation est sexuelle.

Beaucoup de gens se sont faits prêtres, parce que[652] il là le charme du défendu.

---

649. y ~~en~~ en a seulement "L'É[cole] de Masturbation," l'"É[cole] de Sadisme"

650. ~~Les~~ Les

651. se limit[ent]

652. Parceque, *in the original.*

[4ʳ]

Il y a des temples à des hystériques et à des prostituées, parce que ce sont là les déesses du peuple français.

Les statues ont beaucoup d'amants.

Beaucoup de personnes sont très religieuses.

La science s'est changée en enquête sexuelle. Il y a des professeurs d'absortion & d'infanticide. On lit dans les journaux que[653] des enfants de 4 ans se sont suicidés parce qu'ils ou elles ont été abandonnés par leur *amantes ou amants*.

La plupart des gents sont photogéniques.

Aux théâtres[654] on fait des tableaux vivants.[655]

Rien de fort, rien de vrai, rien de sain — pourtant de la pourriture vivante.

On a trouvé des voluptés étranges, leur exemple: estropier les pauvres, les tordre les oreilles, □

Beaucoup de femmes d'esprit se[656] meurent à la vue des choses.

L'armée française n'existe pas. Il y a dans le pays un seul homme sain, et celui-là c'est muet, sourd et aveugle. Il est sain parce qu'il ne peut avoir de grand relation entre lui & le monde.

---

653. q[ue]
654. Théatres, *in the original.*
655. [sa|vi]vants
656. ~~meur~~ se

[4ᵛ]

Les modes sont très □ ; les dames ont des goûts exquis, qui sont, tout simplement, la continuation de ceux d'il y a 50 ans.[657] Il y a les chapeaux □ les toques pot-de-chambre.

Vendus par la "Maison à[658] l'œuvre de chair doré," au Palais □

Beaucoup de gens sont atteints d'un très grand nombre d'espèces de folies.

(Car dans cet[659] □ la France est depuis quelque temps une colonie de l'Allemagne.)

Les théories métaphysiques abondent, car chacun a une à soi; toutes sont compliquées, personnes ne peut les comprendre.[660]

Je dédie cet article aux Français modernes, aux "raffinés," aux "chercheurs de voluptés" aux "□." [661]

Les □ d'aliénés ne sont pas très pleins; mais c'est simple, c'est qui insistent[662] a n'enfermer que des gens sains, qui sont les anormaux.

---

657. de le ['] il y a 50 ans.
658. à au à
659. cette cet
660. ne les ↑ peut les comprendre.
661. "□ ["].
662. Les asyles d'aliénés ne sont pas très pleins; mais c'est simple, c'est qui dans insistent

$$[138A - 1]$$

$$[1^v]$$

Il n'y a pas de mot — on le prévoit — pour classifier la bassesse *&* la lâcheté de ces âmes ordurières et bourgeoises. Un écrivain écrit pour l'humanité, pour ses semblables (?), pour □. Celui qui fait de la corruption, de la *volupté* (c'est leur mot favori), de la pornographie □; celui qui jette au visage de l'humanité l'ordure de sa bassesse d'âme, □ est un irresponsable, c'est, □ un idiot moral à qui on devrait enveler le droit de voter, de prendre part aux choses publiques □, même de disposer de leur propre avoir.

Je haïs la prostitution des rues, mais je sais que pire est celle des |cerveaux|.[663]

La société veut faire □, le progrès, et c'est triste que les dégénérés viennent mettre □ à □

Honte à celui qui trouvera cette satire amusante. Honni qui en rira!

---

663. |cerveaux| / ↑ âmes \.

$$[1^r]$$

France en 1950 [664]

end

Il y aura peut-être quelqu'idiot qui pourra penser que cette satire est indécent et qu'elle est immorale. Ce serait le propre d'un idiot de penser ainsi; car les plus grands hommes de science ont aujourd'hui reconnu et constaté ce fait, que les idiots pensent bêtement, & qu'ils font de sottes choses.

Dans cette satire il y a de la grossièreté, très consciemment [665] voulue.

La littérature □ des onanistes moraux, des gens sans sens moral, des □ de la littérature augment. La loi du □ ne peut rien faire.

Over

❧

---

664. *F*[*rance*]
665. ~~très voulue~~ très consciemment

3.3 — Messieurs les Souteneurs : Satire

$\left[27^{22}\text{'}T^4 - 1\text{-}3\right]$

French Satire.

Dédicace. Au temps

Cher et estimé maître …

Je n'aime pas la France plus que j|e| |n'|aime quelqu'autre[666] pays; pour moi tous les pays sont la même chose. Ce que je n'aime pas, c'est la corruption et la décadence. Il |m'importe| peu quel système de société a n'importe quel peuple, ou quel est sa façon de penser; mais ce qui[667] ne plaise pas c'est que ce système soit celui des souteneurs et que cette façon de penser soit celle des idiots & des imbéciles.[668]

Du reste, MM. Du Saussay & Mmes Jane la Van-dère, … pourront continuer à écrire leurs romans (passe le mot), leurs poèmes en prose (où il n'y a ni poésie, ni prose digne du nom), leurs études de mœurs de tel ou tel pays, de n'importe quel époque, nous savons bien[669] qu'il n'y là que □

Ce n'est pas moi qui |peux| les empêcher ; □

---

666. quelqu'autre
667. mais ~~pour ça je ne hais~~ ce qui
668. soit ~~la folie pure~~ ↑celle des idiots et des imbéciles.
669. ~~bien~~ nous savons bien

[1ᵛ]

Ces Messieurs feront bien de mettre à la fin de leurs ouvrages les adresses respectifs, les indications pour trouver les compétentes maisons de filles.[670] Il n'est pas nécessaire d'y joindre l'importance de la commission qu'ils gagnent — ça peut[671] rester secret.

Pour faire leurs ouvrages plus intéressants, (car à présent elles sont très bêtes) ces messieurs peuvent entre-couper[672] le texte avec des annonces de pastilles contre l'impuissance, de □ pour la chaude-pisse et syphilis, de syringes vaginales etc.

Quant aux éditeurs *&* publieurs d'images nues (Étude Académique etc.) — de l'art, je crois qu'ils l'appellent — □

Cessez de vous |lamenter|! La décadence est venue! C'est le règne des souteneurs *&* des prostitués, car aujourd'hui même ces gens-là écrivent des livres.

Duel. Pas de mal avec des revolvers. "Vierge dans la nuit de noce" *&* avec des balles "Cupidon naissant." Le seul effet a été de plus la mortalité d'un des combattants qui n'on usé que l'□ "flirt," peu de chose.

---

670. de ~~putains~~ /↑ filles\.

671. ça /↑ cela\ peut

672. ils /↑ elles\ sont très bêtes) ~~ces~~ /↑ ces\ messieurs peuvent ~~le~~ entre-couper

[2^{r}]

À l'homme qui viole une fille on le met en |prison| ; à celui qui provoque dans les cerveaux malades le crime, dans les cerveaux jeunes l'esprit dont vient la masturbation, dans[673] les cerveaux faibles les perversions et □ — à celui qui ainsi se porte en souteneur doublé de □ on ne le fait rien, on l'admire quelquefois, quelquefois on l'appelle auteur, artiste même.

Que la loi soit juste pour tous. Si le peuple français trouve bien ces écrits, si ces romans, ces contes, ces □ sont agréables[674] à son caractère c'est un peuple perdu, un peuple malade. Les souteneurs ne sont admirés que |par| d'autres souteneurs.

Pauvre peuple qui fut un des plus grands sur la terre. Quand □

[2^{v}]

Âmes basses, âmes mesquines et sans □ qui ne pensent jamais au mal qu'ils peuvent faire, à l'effet de leurs œuvres sur l'humanité,[675] ou, au moins, sur cette part — qu'elle soit petite — de l'humanité qui les lit.

Écrire des choses qui peuvent nuire aux autres, qui peuvent leur faire du mal est un crime.

---

673. jeunes l'état d'esprit dont vient la masturbation, ~~aux~~ dans
674. ces □ ~~conf~~ agréables
675. ~~les~~ l'humanité,

Ces infortunés jetés par ironie dans la littérature, quand leur place eſt dans les *bordels*, ces pauvres âmes perdues de souteneurs intellectualisés qui trouvent à propos de provoquer le vice, de multiplier de toutes leurs forces la malheur... où le mot violent qui leur conviendra, où le nom qui ne soit trop faible pour la bassesse de leur exiſtence moins qu'inutile?[676]

$$[3^r]$$

Jusqu'|à| aujourd'hui on n'avait pas noté[677] qu'entre les nombreux |ornats| de caractère et d'intelligence qui généralement se nous montrent dans[678] l'eſprit des proſtituées et des souteneurs, on □ celui d'écrire[679] des livres! Que le public en prenne[680] note! C'eſt une nouvelle manifeſtation de talent souteneuriel. Il faut dire quelque chose. Les livres ne manquent pas. Ce sera à propos du premier venu. Le voilà, c'eſt le □. Non; ce ne sera pas |celui-ci.|

Ah, bien — très bien, ce sera ce livre pour cette semaine, "□"[681] — de M. Victorien de Saussay.

Commençons par le commencement. Le |capa| eſt un dessein, assez bien fait □

---

676. moins /↑plus\ qu'inutile?

677. pas ~~ch~~ noté

678. montrent /↑distinguent\ dans

679. on ~~ne comptaient pas le don~~ ↑celui d'écrire

680. Pren[~~de~~|ne]

681. "□['"]

Le 2ᵉ page nous présente quelque chose d'intéressant, c'eſt la liſte des ouvrages de M. de Saussay: La voici, □. Si les français étaient un peuple qui se reſpect une telle liſte suffirait a jeter l'auteur⁶⁸² des ouvrages mentionnées hors la société.

Ceci par la raison que ce n'eſt pas une habitude de □

[3ᵛ]

Ceci eſt-ce la France? Non, c'eſt un pauvre peuple.

L'épitaphe sera écrit sur son tombeau. La lapide sera fait des |capas| de ces livres et sur elle en lettres de merde par la main du temps sera à peu près comme ça: Ci gît le peuple français. A fin de se faire un peuple de souteneurs il n'a pas pu se soutenir.

Si MM. Du Saussay etc écrivent ces livres en artiſtes ou en littérateurs, ils sont fous. S'ils les écrivent pour de l'argent,⁶⁸³ ou même pour gagne-pain, il eſt, il faut leurs dire, de|s| façons de gagner le pain qui déshonorent. Si MM. du Saussay etc sont⁶⁸⁴ auteurs de ces livres pour de l'argent, s'il acceptent un sou que ce soit de gain de leur vente, ils sont, carrément, des souteneurs.

---

682. Si ↑L̶a̶ les français étaient / ↑ Chez \ un peuple qui se respect une telle liste suffirait a jeter s̶o̶n̶ l'auteur

683. g̶a̶g̶n̶e̶-̶p̶a̶i̶n̶ de l'argent,

684. du S[aussay] etc é̶c̶r̶i̶v̶ sont

[14³ — 86–96]

La Littérature [685] *des Souteneurs.*

Un livre qui peut être compris par le cerveau *&* par la moelle [686] épinière.

———

La forme de votre ſtatue eſt quelquefois belle [687] — je l'admets. Mais pourquoi tailler votre ſtatue en merde?

———

Les cœurs prient. Les âmes s'étalent, et elles sont pourries. La mort d'une société eſt plus horrible que la mort d'un organisme individuel. La société pourrit (se décompose) en vie.

[87ʳ]

———

Il ne suffit pas que dans la merde de notre exiſtence [688] nous nous trouvions toujours en face de l'ordure; non, MM. [689] les Souteneurs la ramassent *&* nous l'offrent confeƈtionnée [690] par eux. (Pour les sains, inutile: on sait qu'on ne mange pas ça).

———

685. *La Litt*[*érature*]
686. ~~méd~~ moelle
687. ↑ quelquefois belle

Vous connaissez sans doute cette hiſtoire du □ qui avait par habitude de dresser tous[691] les matins ses excréments par ordre de grosseur sur le parquet? C'eſt un cas véridique, et cependant je me demande si cet-homme-là n'avait dans la tête quelque idée de se faire symbole. Oui, j'y pense, car il eſt l'emblème[692] le plus frappant de l'œuvre MM les Souteneurs littéraires.

[87ᵛ]

La société[693] malade *&* ſtupide ramasse ses propres excréments, leur donne des formes artiſtiques et les dresse devant |soi|; les excréments (vous le comprenez bien) ce sont les passions basses et dégénérées de souteneurs *&* de proſtituées, les formes de boucle, etc., sont les formes littéraires, artiſtiques, dramatiques qu'on leur[694] donne. "Mais on donne les *Souteneurs?*" Oh, MM. les Souteneurs[695] — ce sont les inſtruments, ce sont par conséquent les *mains* de la société qui ainsi s'amuse.

---

688. n[otre] existence

689. ~~MM.~~ MM.

690. *&* ~~la~~ nous l'offrent ~~e~~ confectionnée

691. ~~l'~~ ↑cette histoire du □ qui avait par habitude de dresser / ↑faire en boucles\ tous

692. ~~Oui~~ Oui, j'y pense, car il est / ↑c'est \ l'emblème

693. ~~Ils ramassent~~
    La société

694. ~~les~~ ↑leur

695. ~~les souteneurs~~ ↑MM. les Souteneurs

"Oui; et le type qui ainsi s'amusait se |salissait| les mains, sans doute."

C'eſt bien cela et c'eſt pourquoi je dis □

La société intimement (comme le type en queſtion) eſt malade, mais se sont surtout les mains qui sont plus sales. C'eſt juſtement le symbole des mains ordurières que fait des MM Souteneurs littéraires[696] artiſtes viles.

[88ʳ]

Ce pamphlet eſt écrit en toute sincérité[697] & n'eſt pas fait pour rire. Il faut bien que dans la société il y ait des excréments, mais il n'eſt pas nécessaire[698] que l'on laisse à ces excréments le droit de parfumer tout. L'excrément, c'eſt la littérature qui[699] aujourd'hui abonde.

Si du reſte, le peuple français arrive a sentir de l'ordure □

Le tableau de la décadence d'un peuple eſt toujours pénible, & ce qui y eſt plus triſte eſt que le peuple qui dégénère ne s'en soucie guère[700] |jamais|.

Mater Natura, fiat Voluntas tua!

---

696. litt[éraires]

697. sincerité, *in the original.*

698. necessaire, *in the original.*

699. excrém[ents] le droit de parfumer tout. L'excrément, c'est la littérature ~~que~~ qui

700. & ~~le~~ ↑ ce qui y est plus ~~pénible~~ triste ~~en est~~ ↑ est que le peuple qui dégénère ~~na jamais~~ ↑ ne s'en soucie guère

[89ʳ]

C'eſt en socialiſte que j'écris contre eux, c'eſt en socia-
liſte que je proteſte contre l'invasion dans le milieu social,
dans l'humanité que nous voulons developper, de cette
infamie en livres, de cette ordurerie imprimée.[701] C'eſt
en |tant que| socialiſte que je dresse toutes les formes de
mon âme contre les dégénérés égoïſtes, □ incapables[702]
de pensée cohérente et de raisonnement vrai. L'humanité
— pour le moins notre civilisation[703] — eſt déjà malade;
il faut lutter durement, sincèrement avec toutes les forces
de ce qu'on appelle[704] l'âme pour en amoindrir le mal.[705]

Les offenses à la morale publique sont toujours très
graves, même où il n'y a pas de morale publique; elles
sont plus dangereuses que les offenses politiques.

[89ᵛ]

On peut comprendre d'ailleurs, comme chose à demi
raisonnable, le crime politique anarchiſte □. Par exem-
ple, rien de plus compréhensible que l'assassinat du roi
Carlos de Portugal. Mais il y a beaucoup de choses qui
l'excusent.

---

701. en ~~laude~~ ↑livres, de cette ~~merderie~~ ↑ordurerie imprimée.

702. ~~artistique~~ □ incapables

703. civilization, *in the original.*

704. apele, *in the original.*

705. en ~~dimi~~ amoindrir le mal. ~~C'est la seule dictature que je com-
prends: la dictature contre les offenses~~

Les attentes portées à la morale n'ont pas d'excuse possible; ce n'est pas l'esprit révolutionnaire (car on ne se révolte que[706] contre le mal), ce n'est pas □. C'est l'individualisme oppresseur.

Oui, c'est par cela que je combats toute manifestation de saleté[707] et d'érotisme dans[708] la littérature, dans le théatre[709] — tous partis. Oui, car autant que je haïs le dictateur,[710] le roi absolu, le tyran, autant que je haïs l'homme qui fait[711] mettre des autres dans une prison, qui fait tuer et déshonorer,[712] |tant|[713] je déteste la sensualité littéraire, l'homme qui met les autres dans la [90r] prison et la bassesse d'âme qui leur tue l'esprit d'élévation, qui les déshonore[714] par le contact avilissant de sa mentalité ordurière et stupide.

Je haïs le sensualisme littéraire parce que[715] c'est une attente à la liberté individuelle, et j'aime & je respecte plus que toute autre chose, la liberté due[716] à chacun.

Si l'homme était libre, ce serait bien; ne l'étant pas, l'érotisme littéraire est un crime grave.

706. q[ue]
707. sâleté, *in the original.*
708. ~~hors~~ dans
709. théâtre
710. haïs ~~l'homme qui~~ ↑le dictateur,
711. ~~met~~ fait
712. déhonnorer, *in the original.*
713. ~~au~~|tant|
714. déhonnore, *in the original.*

N'étant pas fou je ne demande pas aux Souteneurs de raisonner □

La liberté (comme je l'ai prouvé autre part) consiste |en| trois choses: 1° *étant né, continuer à vivre* — par laquelle raison on ne peut — même[717] sans doleur — tuer quelqu'un. 2° *vivant, vivre sans douleur* — par laquelle raison on ne peut faire[718] du mal, causer de la peine à quelqu'un. 3° *vivant, se développer au plus de'* □

Il y a eu des grands hommes sensuels? C'est vrai, mais ils n'étaient pas grands par leur sensualité mais[719] par leur grandeur. Shakespeare n'est pas □ que le viol de Lucrèce. (quote Pascal) — La vérité est que les petits esprits aiment toujours à voir qu'ils ressemblent aux grands par quelque endroit si ce ne soit que par le dérrière. [90ᵛ]

Il est facile, Pascal disait, d'être[720] sensuel comme il facile de tomber d'un précipice.[721] On n'a que ne pas tenir main en soi.[722]

---

715. parceque, *in the original.*

716. ‡ due

717. peut ~~pas~~ — même

718. peut /↑doit\ faire

719. mais ils n'ét[aient] pas grands par leur sen[sualité] mais

720. Il est facile[,] ↑Pascal disait [,] d'être

721. précipice ~~en bas~~.

722. ↑Les oppresseurs oppriment toujours ~~en~~ au nom de l'ordre;
     les Souteneures ↑artistes oppriment toujours au nom de l'art.

Qu'est-ce qui caractérise le crime d'oppression po-
litique? En quoi consiste-t-il? Dans l'épanchement de
la personnalité, dans l'imposition[723] anti-sociale de la
force psychique, dans le □

Ce cas ne diffère pas de celui-là. Un homme qui écrit
érotiquement suit son sentiment sensuel; un tyran suit
son sentiment de dominer. Tous les deux sont égoïstes,[724]
inégalement dangereux, selon les conditions et selon le
moyen où ils vivent. Mais ce n'est pas le dictateur ou
le roi absolu qui est *toujours* de plus dangereux.

[91ʳ]

On m'a dit qu'il y a des personnes qui ont des idées
socialistes *&* qui[725] □ écrivent des livres plus au moins
immoraux. Ce ne peu pas être. Des idées anarchistes ou
socialistes, je[726] le crois, car l'anarchisme est l'expression
égoïste[727] et individuelle du sentiment de révolte, ceci
dans le meilleur cas. — Socialiste est immoral? Non.
Fou, peut-être, ou imbécile, ou |pendard|. La démo-
cratie est[728] l'ordre, le socialisme est la glorification de

---

723. l'imposition / ↑usage \

724. egoistes, *in the original.*

725. On ↑m'a dit qu'il y a des personnes qui ont des idées socialistes
& qui ~~cependant~~

726. Des id[ées] anarchistes ↑ou socialistes, je

727. egoiste, *in the original.*

la loi, c'est la loi nouvelle, égalitaire et libérale dans la mesure du possible. Il[729] ne peut donc pas avoir un cerveau bien équilibré où se mêlent des idées si antagonistes que le socialisme & l'immoralité.

Le mieux qu'on peut en dire est qu'un homme peut être sincèrement socialiste, et, au même temps d'un tempérament sensuel. Bien. Qu'il soit sensuel chez lui et non dans les livres. Être[730] sensuel n'est pas un crime ; être immoral, c'est-à-dire écrire sensuellement, publiquement est un crime, d'autant plus grave que l'intelligence de l'écrivain est plus grande.

Over

[91ᵛ]

Mais tel est l'état des choses actuel que des imbéciles comme M. □, & des incurables idiots comme □ (pour ne pas citer quelques individus de l'autre sexe, à juger par les noms) — tel est l'état des choses que ces faibles[731] d'esprit ont une clientèle littéraire, un public à eux.

---

728. ou ~~criminel~~ |pendard|. L[e|a] ~~socialisme~~ ↑ démocratie est

729. la mesure / ↑ les limites \ du possible. ~~Car~~ Il

730. Etre, *in the original.*

731. quelques ~~dans~~ individus de l'autre sexe, à juger par les noms) — tel est l'état des choses que ces ~~idiots~~ faibles

[92ʳ]

Honneur à eux, pauvres souteneurs! Gloire à leurs eſprits!

La dégénérescence [732] croît et aucun homme ne le voit □

Le temps |futur| collectionne les pages de leurs livres pour en faire les pierres de leurs tombeaux, du grand tombeau de [733] leur pays; & sur ce tombeau l'Hiſtoire écrira en lettres de merde l'épitaphe qui leur conviendra. [734]

Mais cet épitaphe l'Hiſtoire le trouvera. Mais je ne puis le trouver. Il n'y a pas de mots, ni de combinaisons de mots qui puissent donner expression à toute la rage faite de dédain, de juſtice et d'aversion [735] profonde.

Honneur aux souteneurs! Paix aux □ Gloire à ceux [736] qui proſtituent leur eſpèce. Si quelqu'un tache de proſtituer [737] sa femme, sa fille, sa sœur □, que si quelqu'un tache de proſtituer l'humanité? Car l'humanité [738] eſt plus que femme, fille, sœur.

---

732. dégenerescence, *in the original.*

733. des ↑leurs tombeaux, ~~de~~ ↑du grand tombea[x|u] de

734. conviendra / ↑convient \ .

735. ~~de~~ d'aversion

736. ~~aux~~ à ceux

737. ↑tache de prostituer

738. l'h[umanité]

739. L[·|a] ~~imm~~ ↑mo ralité

740. pas ↑non plus ↑rien à

741. ~~Non~~ Non,

742. q[ue]

[92ᵛ]

Moi qui écris je suis fou □

|Sont ils des artistes? Non. L'art n'a rien à voir avec la moralité; par conséquent il n'a rien à voir avec le mal ni avec le bien, mais seulement avec la perfection. L'art ne doit être ni bonne ni mauvaise, car c'est encore une bêtise de ces souteneurs de dire que l'art n'a rien a voir avec la moralité,[739] tant en ne voyant pas qu'elle n'a pas non plus rien à[740] voir avec l'immoralité.|

Sont-ils des artistes? Non, je le répète, non.

Sont-ils des penseurs? Non,[741] |non son|. On sait aujourd'hui que[742] ce qui caractérise les penseurs c'est penser; ceux-ci ne pensent jamais.

[93ʳ]

Oui, le[743] caractère le plus répugnant de ces œuvres, c'est qu'elles sont terriblement bourgeoises. Un homme qui blasphème *est religieux*; l'irréligieux ne blasphème pas, il ne voit pas dans la religion[744] une valeur quelque, *&* pourtant ne l'attaque en blasphémant.[745] L'érotique perverti, l'hyperexcité sexuel sont très bourgeois, parce que le caractère de perverti et d'hyperexcité n'élimine

---

743. ↑Oui, le
744. religion, *in the original.*
745. blasphemant, *in the original.*

pas celui d'extérieur ou d'excitation sexuelle,[746] et l'on sait que le bourgeois est essentiellement érotique.

Épater le bourgeois? C'est le bourgeois qui s'épate à lui-même. Quel bon bourgeois que ce Théophile Gaultier!

Mais nous sommes jeunes, s'écrient ces grands auteurs, nous sommes jeunes excepté ceux qui ne[747] le sont pas. C'est la même chose que si je demandais à un vagabond qui jetait[748] de l'ordure sur les passants: "pourquoi faites-vous ça?" & il me répondait: "parce que[749] je suis jeune, je puis m'abaisser et par conséquent ramasser l'ordure, et, pourtant, la jeter sur les gens." C'est la même[750] chose, tout à fait. Personnellement, cependant, je préfère qu'on me jette l'ordure.

[93ᵛ]

La politique funeste (anarchisme & capitalisme), l'art des souteneurs (réalisme, naturalisme, □), la religion de □ attendent la pauvre humanité dans son chemin vers

---

746. parceque le caractère de perverti et d'hyperexcité n[e|'] retire / ↑ élimine pas \ celui d'extérieur ou de sexualité / ↑ d'excitation sexuelle \,

747. ces ~~nobles~~ grands auteurs, ↑ nous sommes jeunes excepté ceux qui ~~ont~~ ne

748. jettait, *in the original.*

749. parceque, *in the original.*

750. ~~Exactement~~ ↑ C'est la même

l'avenir. Grâce à eux, elle y arrivera très sale.[751] Car je me figure les trois dans la route, ramassant ce qui est sur les chemins, et criant, l'une "je vous jette de la liberté," l'autre, "voilà la beauté," l'autre "voici le bien."[752] Et c'est ce qui est sur les chemins qu'ils ramassent. Boue, au nom de l'homme! Ordure, au nom de la liberté! Au nom[753] de Dieu, merde!

L'art — ah, l'art *&* la beauté — ce sont 2 choses très belles; ce n'es pas au bourgeois de les connaître. Un bourgeois poète n'est qu'un bourgeois. C'est ne pas la ainsi un bourgeois, pour dire que l'on ne l'est pas, pour □. Par exemple, en bas d'une caricature d'un M. Josset, j'ai lu ceci: "le bourgeois □ par bonté □ pas." J'ai parcouru le plus grand nombre des caricatures de ce M. *&* en effet je trouve quelque chose d'analogue. Seulement je comprends pourquoi le dit Josset ne veut pas admettre que le bourgeois pense bien et c'est qu'il ne veut pas être bourgeois. Car ce serait intéressant de savoir où est manifeste le pire de Mr. Josset.

---

751. sâle, *in the original.*

752. et ~~criant j~~ criant, l'une "je vous jette de la liberté," l'autre, "voilà la beauté," l'autre "~~voila~~ ↑ voici le bien."

753. ~~Merde~~ Au nom

[94ʳ]

Le lecteur aura remarqué un peu⁷⁵⁴ scandalisé et □ que j'emplois incessamment des termes sales,⁷⁵⁵ tels qu'ordure, merde, etc. Qu'il en passe ces expression d'ailleurs⁷⁵⁶ inévitables. C'est une chose étrange que quand j'écris sur ces auteurs je ne pense qu'à ces saletés. Je ne puis⁷⁵⁷ penser à ces MM. sans penser à merde et à de l'ordure. Du moment que ma pensée se dirige⁷⁵⁸ sur ces MM elle □ trouve immédiatement de la merde, de l'ordure, de la saleté.⁷⁵⁹ C'est un phénomène d'association d'idées sur lequel⁷⁶⁰ j'appelle l'attention des personnes compétentes.

Ce n'est pas mon habitude de penser salement, ni □, mais l'association d'idées est si fort que je ne puis m'empêcher de penser de⁷⁶¹ cette manière.⁷⁶²

---

754. a̶v̶e̶c̶ un peu

755. sâles, *in the original.*

756. d̶u̶ r̶e̶ d'ailleurs

757. puis ⁄ ᵗ eux \

758. d̶i̶r̶i̶g̶e̶ dirige

759. Sâleté, *in the original.*

760. q̶u̶e̶ j̶e̶ f̶a̶i̶s̶ ᵗ devant sur lequel

761. sâlement, ni □, mais l'ass[ociation] d'idées est si fort que je ne puis m'empêcher de penser a̶i̶n̶s̶i̶ de

762. ─────────

    L̶a̶ N̶a̶t̶u̶r̶e̶,̶ l̶a̶ m̶è̶r̶e̶ N̶a̶t̶u̶r̶e̶,̶ g̶r̶a̶n̶d̶e̶ e̶t̶ s̶u̶b̶l̶i̶m̶e̶
    Noblemen w[ith] his strange habit.

763. si i̶l̶s̶ elles

[95ʳ]

Un □ nauséabond s'exhale de cette pourriture d'eſprits, de cette bassesse d'âmes. Les cabinets secrets ont une valvule avec de l'eau pour nettoyage; les sentines de ces cœurs n'ont ni même cela, ou, si elles[763] l'ont, il eſt long-temps cassé. Il y a des désinfectants qui *peuvent* faire propre les |canalisations, etc|; mais pour la *malpropreté* (filth) des ces âmes, il n'y a de désinfectant moral.[764]

———————

Du reſte, ceux d'entre les écrivains qui s'appellent modernes et qui sont plus grands, sont frappés de cette □. Rien eſt sain chez eux. Ils ont l'amour irritabilité.[765]

Leur socialisme n'eſt pas fait d'amour ni de pitié, mais si de révolte inconsciente, de l'eſprit de contradiction qui, loin d'être grand, eſt[766] petit chez les idiots.

[95ᵛ]

Leur anarchisme, ce qu'ils appellent leur eſprit de révolte ne naît pas □ mais seulement de l'irritabilité du dégénéré et de son désir faible de se singulariser *&* d'épater le normal.[767] C'eſt de la folie pure.

———————

764. n'y a u̶n̶ de désinfect[ant] moral
765. l̶e̶ l'amour irritabilité. I̶l̶s̶ ̶p̶a̶r̶l̶e̶n̶t̶
766. de'amour ni de pitié, mais si de révolte inconsciente, de l'esprit de contradiction qui, loin d'être grand, p̶ est
767. d̶e̶ d'épater le a̶u̶t̶r̶e̶ normal.

Autour de cette âme centrale de l'étrange composi-
tion de bassesse, d'étroiture d'esþrit, de superſtition sans
religion,[768] de radotage sans pensée, d'inſpiration sans
idées, les facultés individuels se groupent.[769]

Ils n'ont aucune religion;[770] je ne les blâme pas —
moi aussi, je n'en ai pas (de religion proprement dite).
Mais ils ont presque tous de la superſtition. Et s'ils sont
irréligieux gardez vous[771] bien de croire que c'eſt par
force de raison — non, aucun d'eux ne sait raisonner; ni
par indignation — aucun d'eux ne sait aimer, et quand ils
veulent être pleins de pitié ils étalent une pleurnicherie
exagérée,[772] même comme pleurnicherie — caraĉtéristi-
que[773] du │dégénéré inferieur│.

[96ʳ]

On a dit: "l'homme eſt la nature prenant conscience de
soi (même)." On peut appliquer ici le simile: ces auteurs,
cette société eſt │de│ l'ordure prenant conscience de soi.

---

768. réligion, *in the original.*
769. se ~~sentent~~ groupent.
770. réligion, *in the original.*
771. v[ous]
772. exagerée, *in the original.*
773. charactéristique, *in the original.*

La nature devenue consciente dit[774] "que moi nature suis grande." La merde devenue □ dit "que moi, artiste, que moi, homme de société, suis grand!"

La nature jouit de soi, de son existence dans l'homme, ignorant sa bassesse. L'ordure se joute, se complait.

Caligula, on le sait,

Cheval ou curial

Mais[775] il reste un pauvre, simple cheval.

[133F — 39]

Je m'abstient entierement de considérer les œuvres de Mme. Jeanne La Vaudère. (Je ne puis plus dire).

———

Fin.

On connait la définition de liberté que donna ce prêtre de je ne sais où: "Je ne veux pas qu'on m'emmerde." C'est ça que le peuple français devait dire au pluriel,[776] à moins qu'il ne soit déjà emmerdé. Mais c'est là bien le cri: "Je ne veux pas qu'on m'emmerde."

———

la merde de leur existence

———

774. ‡ dit
775. C' Mais
776. dire ↑ au pluriel,

[39ᵛ]

Penser, c'est difficile; rêver, aucunement. On rêve même en dormant.

———————

Reformer l'humanité c'est très difficile. La □ c'est très facile. Il est facile aussi, par exemple, de laisser pourrir les mets — on n'a qu'à[777] les laisser pourrir. Les conserver — voilà la difficulté.

Il n'est pas encore avéré que les mets se conservent davantage dans les latrines.

———————

On dit par exemple,[778] c'est de la méchanceté d'appeler M. Maeterlink un idiot. Ce n'est pas du tout une méchanceté. Car ce serait une mauvaise □ si il était possible que le dit Monsieur réussi à le croire et à en souffrir.[779] Mais, par la nature de la chose même, c'est impossible. Car si, par exemple, je disais à un âne: "Tu es un âne" jamais le dit âne ne le croirait.

Je ne veux pas approfondir la raison.

———————

777. qu[e̶|'à]
778. On dit /↑ peu dire\ par exemple,
779. C[ʼe̶s̶t̶|e] n'est pas du tout une /↑ de la\ méchanceté. Car ̶M̶.̶ ce serait une mauvaise □ si il /↑ c'\ était possible q[ue] le dit Monsieur réussi à le croire ↑ et à en souffrir.

[133F — 46]

À propos j'ai a vous conter une jolie historiette, qui peu être fable ou symbole. C'était dans [780] un village quelconque d'un pays quelconque; ni le pays ni le village n'ont rien a voir à l'affaire. [781] Un |bonhomme| de la localité avait |invité| pour quelques jours un ami de la ville. [782] Celui-ci arrivé, le matin le hôte lui demanda s'il avait bien |passé| la nuit.

"Non," répondit le voyageur, "je ne sais pas bien pourquoi, mais je n'ai dormit du tout."

L'hôte s'étonna; aucun des deux ne pu trouver [783] la raison d'être de cette insomnie.

Les deux matins suivants même question de la part de l'hôte, [784] même réponse de la part de l'invité; l'insomnie continuait.

Le cas fit penser le bonhomme de province; il mit à but de le résoudre. Il prit un large pot-de-chambre plein d'ordure et [785] le mit dans un coin de l'appartement.

---

780. ↑ C'était [Đ|d]ans
781. voir ~~dans~~ ↑ à l'affaire.
782. ↓ ~~const~~ ↑ et une chambre de ~~propre~~ propre lui fut.
783. pu ~~en~~ trouver
784. la part ~~du~~ ↑ de l'hôte,
785. plein ~~de~~ ↑ d'ordure et

[46ᵛ]

"Quelque chose de familier, de □ dans l'atmosphère, n'est-ce pas?"

"C'est ça, c'est ça. Je me crois à la ville."

Je demande au peuple français: [786]

Ce symbole que signifie-t-il?

Je demande aussi [787] au peuple français □

Le voyageur de cette histoire à quel peuple ressemble-t-il?

Si je pourrais frapper plus dur, je frapperais.

Fin.

---

786. ~~Le~~ Je demande au peuple français:
~~De quoi~~

787. J[e] d[emande] aussi

4.0 — Charles James Search: Fragments of Translations

$$[48C - 5^r]$$

Charles James Search.

in l.: Charles Search.

Supposed to be born in 1886 and therefore[788] to be two years older than Alexander. To be precise, born on the 18th April 1886.

Task: solely that of translation. May write the prefaces to his translations if these do not involve analysis, etc., when they will be written by Alexander.

---

788. ∴ [therefore]

Translations to be Undertaken:

1. Espronceda's "Student of Salamanca."

2. Anthero de Quental's "Complete Sonnets." [789]
    (together with pessimistic pieces – ? –).

3. Couto Guerreiro's "Epigrams."

4. Sonnets (chosen) of Camoens.

5. Guerra Junqueiro — Choice. [790]

6. Eça [791] de Queiroz's "The Mandarin."

7. "Some Sonnets from Portugal."
    (excluding those separately translated).

8. Henrique Rosa's Poems (some). [792]

9. Almeida Garret — Choice.

---

789. A [nthero]
790. G [uerra]
791. E [ça]
792. H[enrique]

4.1 — Anthero de Quental's "Complete Sonnets"

[74 − 24–55]

Soulful sight of Unknown things

(Translation [of] Anthero de Quental)[793]

[25ʳ]

Anthero de Quental — 4 — [794]

[Lament]

A flow of light □
Behold the day! the sun! the husband dear
Where over the whole earth is there a care
Not of the light that the world.[795]

———————————

Flower □[796]
Where is there being so forgot of God
For whom the sky has no peace and no |balm|.

A son I may be, but a |forlorn| child.[797]

---

793. *Soulful* sight of Unknown /(or nightly)\ things
    (Trans[lation] [of] A[nthero de] Q[uental])
794. *A[nthero de] Q[uental]* — 4 —
795. ~~That be not~~ ↑Not
796. Flower ~~had~~ □
797. A ~~child~~ ↑son I may be, but a |forlorn| child /↑son\.

[26ʳ]

Anthero de Quental 5. [798]

[To M.C.]

God laid upon thy hair □: [799]
He that doth fate the poet and the knight [800]
Turned his eyes upon thee □ [801]
□ | fair be then |. [802]

———————

But I… can I perchance □ merit thee?
God gave thee, woman, what | forbidden | is [803]
Angel! a world part the Lord did □ thee [804]

And unto me, whom he gave eyes to see
Thy beauty, no more powerful what | gave he |
A voice to sing thee *&* a soul to love thee!

———————
———————

798. A[nthero de] Q[uental] 5.
799. God laid upon ~~thy front his~~ ↑ upon thy hair / brow \ □:
800. the knight // ↑ soldier \ / warier \ and the bard \
801. eyes / ↑ glance \
802. | fair be then | / ↓ be fair \.
803. [God|The] Lord ↑ God gave ~~at~~ thee,
804. ~~The Lord gave thee~~ ↑ a world

[27ʳ]

Anthero de Quental 7. [805]

[Torment of the Ideal]

I knew the Loveliness that doth not die
And |I| became sad. As he who from the hill [806]
The highest there be, seeing beneath him |still| [807]
The earth, sea, sees all, the largest ship or □

———————————

□ like the cloud that □
At sunset that over the sea doth fly

———————————

The baptism of poets □
And seated □ amidst incomplete forms [808]
For ever I remained pale & sad

---

805. A[nthero de] Q[uental] 7.
806. from the ~~mount~~ /↑hill \ /mount \
807. ~~that~~ there
808. seated ~~among~~ □ amidst

$[28^r]$

Anthero de Quental 13.[809]

[To M.C.]

In heav'n, if there be heaven for them that weep
Heaven for the woes of them that suffer so
If there □ glow

In heaven, if a soul in that ſpace keeps
That hears our prayer and □
If there be a Father that o'er us doth throw
The cloak of pitying love that □

$[28^v]$

In Heaven, oh maiden! my sorrows □
I will be born again there, I that seem

---

809. A[*nthero de*] Q[*uental*] 13.

[29ʳ]

Anthero de Quental 31.[810]

[Idyll]

How many times, sudden thy voice doth fail![811]
I know not what light in thine eyes floats, □;[812]
I fell thy hand to tremble, thy front pale…

From wind and sea do unknown orisons |deep|[813]
And the poets & the poetry of thing doth pass[814]
Amorous and slowly into our hearts[815]
Slowly & amorously into our souls.[816]

Over

---

810. A[nthero de] Q[uental] 31.

811. |t̶h̶o̶u̶ ̶j̶u̶s̶t̶ ̶m̶u̶t̶e̶| ↑thy voice doth fail!

812. I know ↑not what light in thine eyes floats, s̶w̶e̶e̶p̶s̶;

813. A̶n̶d̶ ↑From wind and sea do unknown orisons |deep| /↑a deep orison starts\

814. And ↑a̶l̶l̶ ̶u̶n̶k̶n̶o̶w̶n̶ the poets and the poetry of thing doth pass /↑poesy of things d̶o̶t̶h̶ ̶c̶r̶e̶e̶p̶ glide\ /↓doth creep\

815. S̶l̶o̶w̶ ̶a̶n̶d̶ Amorous

816. souls /↑hearts\.

276

[29ᵛ]

So gather daisies and lilies in the dales [817]

Yet □ of the night dew. [818]

When hand in hand □ we two
To gather lilies, daises in the dales [819]
□ hills
Not unabandoned yet of the night dew:

Or □

Piled one over one □ far horizon [820]

---

817. dales / ↓hills \
818. Yet □ ~~of the~~ ↑ of the night
819. gather ~~in the vales~~ lilies,
820. one ~~in the~~ ↑ ~~the~~ far

[30ʳ]

Anthero de Quental — 32.[821]

[Nocturnal]

I □ to thee the dream that is one bearing
An instinct of light, the darkness tearing,[822]
Seeking, visions among, eternal Good.

And thou dost understand my nameless ill
The fever of Ideal □
Thou alone, Genius of night, *&* □

---

821. *A*[*nthero de*] *Q*[*uental*] — 32.
822. of ~~the~~ light,

[31ʳ]

Anthero de Quental 39 [823]

[In the Chapel]

In the chapel among the foliage lost
The Christ □
Oh how intimately □ did mate [824]
My sore with the sore of that □ [825]

Sons of love both, an equal □

Martyrs of fate, both □ conquered

We looked mute one at the other — equal woe — [826]
Nor could I say □ which of the two
More pale, more sorrowful, more wearied.

---

823. A[nthero de] Q[uental] 39
824. Oh how intimately ~~that pain~~ did mate
825. ~~Th~~ My
826. We ~~sh~~ looked

$[32^r]$

Anthero de Quental 42.[827]

[The Palace of Venture]

I dream I am a knight errant. Deserts through □
Through suns & through □
A paladin of love, □ I seek
The enchanted palace of □

————————————

With mighty |blows| I □ & □
I am the Wanderer, the Disinherited
Open, oh doors of gold, my moans |before|[828]

The doors of gold open with □ din[829]
□ I find within
Silence & darkness |there| — and nothing more

————————————

827. *A[nthero de] Q[uental]* 42.

828. ~~si~~ moans

829. gold ~~with ar~~ open

[33ʳ]

Anthero de Quental 46 [830]

[Despondency]

Let her go, — her the little bird whose nest [831]
And little sons and all pitilessly
Have been stolen, let the endless air □ [832]
There where her broken wings will bear her best [833]

———————

Let it go — it, the sail that the |tempest| [834]
Flung in the mighty darkness o'er the sea, [835]
When night arose out of immensity
And the winds of the South rise in its breast [836]

Let her go — her, the soul with □ breath
That has lost faith and peace □ did stop
To the still death, unto the silent death

[33ᵛ]

Let it go — it the last note of the strife
Of a last song… and the last hope
And life and love … ay let it go too, life.

———————
———————

———————

830. *A[nthero de] Q[uental] 46*
831. ↓ little bird
832. endless ~~of~~ ↑ air
833. ↑ There where her broken wings ~~do~~ will

[34ʳ]

Anthero de Quental 95 [837]

[Nirvana]

Beyond the luminous □ Universe
Full of forms, full of murmur & of Strife
Of forces, of desires and of life
Opened is like to a □ void. [838]

The wave of that tumultuous sea [839]

And when thought, thus □ buried
□ from that |vague| world dead
And looks upon natural things □,

By the fire light of life, infinite, [840]
It seeth with □ in all that hits the sight
The universal dream & emptiness.

834. that the |tempest| /↑ at the West \
835. Flung o'er in
836. rise /↓ woke \ in
837. A[nthero de] Q[uental] 95
838. Ought Opened
839. The ay wave
840. ampl infinite,

[35ʳ]

Anthero de Quental — 101.[841]

[Transcendentalism]

It quiets down after so much fight
It □ to peace — my heart
I found at laſt how 'tis a vain delusion
The good as from the world and fate would tear.

□ with brow not unwet □
Sanctuary of the temple of Illusion
I did but find, with pain and with confusion,
Darkness & duſt, cold & brute matter — there[842]

[35ᵛ]

'Tis not in the vaſt world — howe'er immense
It may seem to our youth's imaging crude — [843]
That the soul satiates its desire intense…

Over deserts, □ solitude □

---

841. A[*nthero de*] Q[*uental*] — 101.
842. ~~a~~ ↑cold and
843. to ~~your~~ our

[36ʳ]

Anthero de Quental — 102 [844]

[Evolution]

I was a rock once & was in the world old
In forest unknown branch or trunk — [845]
A wave I foamed breaking me □
Against granite, ancient foe and □ cold.

———————

I roared, a wild-beast haply, seeking hold
A lair i' th' [846]
Or, a primitive monster □

To-day I am a man □

That goes in spirals to immensity

[36ᵛ]

The infinite I question and I weep [847]
Sometimes, but □

—————

844. A[nthero de] Q[uental] — 102
845. In a̶ ̶u̶n̶k̶n̶ ↑forest unknown
846. lair i̶n̶ ̶t̶h̶e̶ ̶c̶a̶v̶e̶ ↑ I' th'
847. The ↑infinite I question

[37ʳ]

Anthero de Quental 104 [848]

[Praise of Death]

[II]

What myſtical desires madden me here
The abyss of Nirvâna do[es] appear
In mute immensity to mine eyes showeth

In this voyage across □ empty ſpace
I seek but to meet thee, but thy embrace
Death, the siſter of Love *&* of Truth! [849]

[37ᵛ]

In the foreſt of dreaming, day by day,
My aching thought □
In the regions of vague forgetfulness [850]

In the darkness I cross the □
Of a ſtrange world, □ peopled by the wind
And my plaintful and □ and undefined
In the visions of night □

---

848. *A[nthero de] Q[uental]* 104
849. ~~D~~ Death,
850. vague ~~of~~ forgetfulness

[38ʳ]

Anthero de Quental — 106 [851]

[IV]

An inward light showed me □ flame [852]
Daughter of the same father, I now know thy name [853]
Death, coeternal sister of my soul! [854]

I did not love thee then nor know thee [855]
My inert thought
(I know thee. My inert thought nothing read)
Over that mute front, austere and calm, □

---

851. A[nthero de] Q[uental] — 106
852. inward ↑ light showed *and* flame → (show)
853. father, I ↑ now know thy name → (know)
854. soul! → (extraordinary depth of expression)
855. nor know thee /nor did\

[39ʳ]

Anthero de Quental 107.[856]

[V]

What name, image austere, shall I thee give
That in an angle of the road □
When already my □

In thine eyes doth the crowd a □ perceive
And it covers its face and □ [857]
But I, veiled shadow, □
And that I □ thy language do believe ... [858]

856. A[nthero de] Q[uental] 107.

857. ↑ And it covers

858. And ~~thy~~ ↑ that I □ thy language do ~~perceive~~ ↑ believe ...

859. A[nthero de] Q[uental] 108

860. ~~w~~ where

[40ʳ]

Anthero de Quental 108 [859]

[VI]

He but that fears Not-Being doth distruſt
And from thy vaſt silence where Death ſtays [860]
Night without ending, solitary ſpace
Night of Death, □ *&* auguſt…

Not I: my ſpirit humble but robuſt
Enters with faith thy funerary place: [861]
For others thou art a vacuum [862]
To me thou smilſt *&* thy smile I truſt. [863]

Me doth charm th'ineffable and holy place,
Silence of the Inalterable, |peerless|
That endless love with endless woe □

[40ᵛ]

Perchance a sin it may be to seek for thee
But not to dream of thee, not to adore thee,
Not-Being, only Being Absolute.

---

861. Enters ↑ with faith thy funerary ~~hall~~ place:

862. a vacuum / ↑ a emptiness \

863. To me ~~a find~~ ↑ thou smilſt *&* thy smile I trust. / → face \ / race \ /embrace\ / grace.\ / trace \

[41ʳ]

p. 109 — Anthero de Quental 864

[Contemplation]

I dream with open eyes, walking among
Not forms now, nor among appearances 865
But Seeing the changes 866
Among ideas and spirits □ hung…

What is the world □ smoke-waves 867
Visions without being □
A nebula of errors, of impotencies 868
Over a □ vacuum trailed *&* |slung —|

[41ᵛ]

And from the mist □
Only a murmur reaches among all moans,
'Tis the complaint, the groan comes from the earth 869

Of things, that blindly seek *&* blindly strain 870
In their night with □ of pain
Another light, an end but □

―――――――――――
―――――――――――

―――――――――

864. A[*nthero de*] Q[*uental*]
865. Not ~~now~~ forms ↑now,

[42ʳ]
Anthero de Quental — 110 ⁸⁷¹
[Lacrimæ Rerum]

Night, oh sister of Reason *&* of Death

Confident and interpreter of Fate.

———————

12. All around me is mourning *&* doubt ⁸⁷²
And lost, in a dream immense, □ ⁸⁷³
I listen to the sight of darkened things. ⁸⁷⁴

———

866. ↑ But Seeing the changes / ↑ unchanging form of essences \
867. smoke-waves / ↓ wave-flung \
868. nebula / ↑ mist \ of
869. ↑This 'Tis
870. see blindly
871. A[nthero de] Q[uental] — 110
872. me is doubt woe ↑ mourning & doubt
873. dream immense, I listen to
874. darken / ↑ night \ things.

[43ʳ]

Anthero de Quental 120.[875]

[What death says]

Let them come to me, they whose toil is dare
Let them come to me, they who suffer |here|
And they who full *&* sorrowing look upon [876]
They own vain □ at which they sneer

In me the suffering that □ [877]
Passion and Doubt and Evil □
And the torrents of pain, that ever run [878]
As in a sea in me do disappear.

---

875. A[nthero de] Q[uental] 120.

876. full /↑ weary \ and

877. that ~~do not heal~~

878. And the torrents of pain, that ever run /↑ Pain's torrents that cease not to run \

879. My heart at last did rest /↑ could find its repose \

880. ~~Step by step~~ The ↑ narrow staircase

881. deepen /↓ laid down \

882. imperfect ~~form~~ ↑ ~~stripe~~ shape

[44ʳ]

111

[In the hand of God]

In the hand of God, in his right □
My heart at last did rest [879]
Of the enchanted palace □
The narrow staircase I did □ step by step [880]

Like |the| mortal flowers with which itself doth drape
Childish ignorance, a vain remnant of my own
Of Ideal and passion I did deepen [881]
The transitory and imperfect shape. [882]

Like a child on a journey □
That the mother bears warm against her breast [883]
And crosses, vaguely smiling, in |*sleepy| glee [884]

Plains, seas, desert sands □ … [885]
Sleep through thy deep oh □
Sleep in the hand of God eternally!

---

883. the mother ↑ bears ~~close~~ warm against her ~~caries cl~~ breast
884. And crosses, vaguely smiling, in |*sleepy| / ↑ sleepily \ glee
885. / ↑ Wild \ Plains,

[44ᵛ]

[Redemption]

[II]

112

Thou'lt see the Forms, daughter of what doth seem
Fall □ like an |empty| dream[886]

[To the Holy Virgin]

88

A mystic suffering, a happiness,
Made but of pardon, but of tenderness
And of □

Oh, vision, vision sad *&* □

---

886. |empty| ᐟ ↑ vain ᐠ dream

[45ʳ]

Anthero de Quental 121 [887]

[In the hand of God]

11. And crosses, smiling in □ vagueness, seas

12. And □ and desert sands…
    Sleep through thy sleep oh □ thus freed heart [888]
    Sleep in the hand of God eternally!

---

887. *A[nthero de] Q[uental]* 121
888. Sleep ↑ through thy

[46ʳ]

Anthero de Quental 47 [889]

[Das Unnennbare]

Oh |child of dream| that doſt pass by rocked in [890]
The wave of my □
And toucheſt with thy □ dresses |passing| me [891]
My pallid front and weariedly serene! [892]

The air of the calm night □
In vain I ask with eyes of anxiety
What name is it that happy ones give thee
In thy country □ [893]

---

889. A[nthero de] Q[uental] 47
890. Oh |child of dream| that ~~p~~ ↑ doſt pass ↑ by rocked in |→ airy|
891. And ↑ touchest with
892. ~~An~~ My ↑ pallid front and weariedly serene! |→ weary|
893. In thy country / ↑ own native land \ □ |→ fairy|

[47ʳ]

Anthero de Quental 75 [894]

[Homo]

No tone of ye for sure □
Ye stars of space, ye branches of the trees
Not one has guessed my secret
Not one has interpreted my prayer.

No one knows who I am … *&* more □

I am a monstrous thing born of the earth [895]
Of the primitive and dark humus a birth
Fatherless, motherless, a birth of chance [896]

[47ᵛ]

Unhappy □
I am Satan perchance; a bastard son [897]
Perchance of Jehovah, no one perchance.

─────────────

══════════⇒

894. A[nthero de] Q[uental] 75
895. thing ~~born~~ ↑ born of
896. ~~Cold,~~ ↑ Fatherless, motherless,
897. ~~perchance a son~~ ↑ a bastard son

296

[48ʳ]

Anthero de Quental p. 79.[898]

[Unconsciousness]

11 Spectre I love and hate with anguished bliss

14 But I myself know not what my name is.

[48ᵛ]

But once to question him □ did dare
"Who art thou (asked I with a □ fear)[899]

— — — — —

"Thy brothers (he replied) the vain mankind
Through ten thousand years he called me God

---

898. A[nthero de] Q[uental] p. 79.
899. art ↑ thou (asked I

[49^r]

Anthero de Quental 79 [900]

The familiar spectre that with me
Walks, though I ne'er its countenance could behold [901]
That sometimes I do face with □
And may watch and follow anxiously [902]

Is a mute spectre, grave, □
But seems □
Before that □ ascetic and cold [903]
A thousand times I open my mouth □

---

900. A[*nthero de*] Q[*uental*] 79
901. Walks, though I ~~never could~~ ↑ne'er ~~see~~ its countenance ~~see~~
        ↑ could behold
902. may /↑ often\ ~~others anxiously~~ ↑ watch and follow anxiously
903. B[e]f[ore]

[50ʳ]

Anthero de Quental — 83.⁹⁰⁴

[Divine Comedy]

☐ to the distant sky
And ☐ to the gods invisible

7. Pain, sin, illusion horrible fights fall⁹⁰⁵

Were it not better in the ☐ peace
Of nothingness and of what yet is not
To have remained asleep without cease.⁹⁰⁶

[50ᵛ]

Why unto pain did ye ☐ us?
But the gods yet sadder⁹⁰⁷
☐ "Man ☐ and why did ye create us?"⁹⁰⁸

---

904. A[nthero de] Q[uental] — 83.
905. horrible fights /↑ dreadful combats \ fall
906. asleep ~~and sleep seems~~ ↑ without cease.
907. gods ~~more~~ ↑ yet sadder
908. create us? ["]
909. A[nthero de] Q[uental] 86.
910. I also ~~took a place~~ in the
911. An impotent wish of /↑ ache for\ infinite things doth rage
 /↓| Comes of a wish of infinite aught ††|\
912. Like ↑ the others

[51ʳ]

Anthero de Quental 86.[909]
[The Converted]

Among the children of a cursed age
I also at the impious table sat [910]
When, 'neath the joying moans the sadness that
An impotent wish of infinite things doth rage [911]

Like the others a spit full of gall & rage [912]
Upon the altar I too spat [913]
But one day all my firmness □
And my remorseful heart □

Over

[51ᵛ]

|Arid| and full of □ & of spleen
Opening the barrier to my tears held-in [914]
My sad soul turned to God □

I shrouded in faith my thought & found [915]
Peace in forgetfulness and □ profound... [916]
One thing remains: to know if God exists!

---

913. Upon ~~I spit upon the~~ ↑the altar
914. barrier to my /↑dykes unto its\ tears
915. in ~~my~~ faith
916. in ~~the~~ forgetfulness

[52$^\text{v}$]

Anthero de Quental 91.[917]

[Quia Æternus]

Thou art not dead, however much to us
A proud and vain philosophy it may cry
Not with such ease, not so □ thus
The yoke of divine tyranny made fly[918]

They shout in vain, and that triumph luminous
With which Reason drunken doth lie[919]
Is but a new form, bitterer □[920]
Of thine eternal, tragic irony.

No thou art not dead, ſpectre! As before
Thought looks upon thy face, thou torture hoax
Of all who on books |fill their thoughts| & fail

[52$^\text{v}$]

And they who joy in the wild orgic sup
Alas!, how many times □ cup[921]
Stop and, took by shivering, grow pale.

Sadly ſtop and, shivering, grow pale!

---

917. A[*nthero de*] Q[*uental*] 91.

918. made fly ↓ of divine tyranny among / land by \

[53ʳ]

Anthero de Quental 92.⁹²²

[In the Whirlpool]

9. — Phantoms of mine own self and of my soul
That stare at me with calmness dread *&* |cold|
Borne on the □ wave that others fly ⁹²³

Who are ye, oh brothers and my hell?
Who are ye, visions □ and terrible?
Woe is me! Woe is me! And who am I?

———————————

[53ᵛ]

In my dream □ visions are unfurled
Spectres of mine own thoughts □
Like a □
Swept far away and in □ whirled.

———————————

In a spiral of strange contortions curled
□ loud
I see them pass in groups □ cloud
And now *&* then their features □

———————————

919. Reason — ~~poor Reason~~! — drunken

920. new ~~form~~ ↑ form,

921. ~~Alas~~ ↑Alas!,

922. *A*[*nthero de*] *Q*[*uental*] 92.

923. that others fly / ↓ passing by \

302

[54ʳ]

Anthero de Quental — 93.[924]

[Ignotus]

— Complain not, children of anxiety
I also, since □ eternity
Do seek myself — *&* have not found me yet.

924. A[nthero de] Q[uental] — 93.

[55ʳ]

Anthero de Quental 94. [925]

[In the Circus]

Far, very far from here, when I do not know
Nor when that world was there I then □
But so far □
That while in it, □ go [926]

Because everything air-like and slow [927]
Was there *&* brightest □
And I □ till on a day [928]
A wind did take me □

---

925. *A[nthero de] Q[uental] 94.*

926. in it ~~I went,~~

927. ∵ [Because] everything air-like and ~~slow~~ slow

928. I □ ~~til~~ till

4.2 — Sonnets (chosen) of Camoens

[74B — 74]

O gentle spirit mine that didst depart
So early of this life in discontent
Thy rest with heaven's eternity be blent
And I bear here on earth my restless heart. [929]

If in the ethereal seat where now thou art
|A| memory of this life God doth consent,
Forget not that pure passion eloquent [930]
Which in these eyes sad light had the best part. [931]

And if thou see aught worthy of thy light
In the great darkness that hath come on me
From thine irreparable loss's spite [932]

---

929. And [h|I] bear here on heart my restless / ↓ separate \ heart.
930. pure passion / ↑ [great|pure] |*heart self| \ eloquent
931. Which in these eyes / ↑ |*suffering| pure eyes \ sad light had best
/ ↓ got \ part.
932. And if thou see aught worthy of thy care light
In the ↑ great sorrow ↑ darkness that keeps his neam with ↑ hath come
[with|on] me
From the pain without cure thy loss did / ↓ From thine i loss
irreparable loss's spite

Ask thou of god, who cut thy years [933]
As from my mortal eyes he haſted thee
So soon to haſt me to thy reſtless sigh.

[74B — 87]

Oh gentle ſpirit mine that didſt depart
So early of this life in discontent
Eternally in heaven do thou reſt
And I live here on earth with broken-heart

If to the Holy Throne □ thou art
Memory of this our life God doth consent
Forget not that my love which eloquent
And pure within mine eyes |did start|.

And if thou see that to thee [934]
Aught □ doth mean [935]
The pain that ever with me did remain
Of the unavailing sorrow □ [936]

---

933. / ↑ Pray \ Ask thou of god, who cut thy years
~~That so early from here take~~ ↓ ~~doth~~ ~~me to thy sight~~
~~So Soon □ did □~~
~~As soon as he from mine eyes did take thee~~
/Ask / ↑ Pray \ God, who made thy years so short to be,\
934. to / ↑ in \ thee
935. ~~aught~~ doth
936. ~~sorrow~~ unavailing sorrow

Ask God that did thy years make short
So early □
So early from my eyes □

───────────

And if thou see that aught to thee is worth
The pain that ever with me □
Of th'unavailing sorrow of thy (│dearth│) [937]
Pray God that did □ thy years [938]

───────────

And if that aught to thee doth mean thou see
The pain that □
Of th'unavailing sorrow of loving thee,

Pray God that did □
So soon from this life to me to thee
As soon He from my eyes □
As early □ from mine eyes. [939]

───────────

937. (│dearth│ / ↓ thy years \ )
938. did ~~thine~~ ↑ th □ thy years
939. ~~from~~ □ from

[87ᵛ]

Oh gentle ſpirit mine that didſt depart
So early from this life □
In Heaven do thou reſt eternally
And live I on in earth with broken heart

If in the heavenly region where thou art
God doth allow of life the memory
Forget not that my love which thou didſt see
In mine eyes pure & ardently to ſtart.

[74B — 86]

Sonnet CXXXI — *p. 74.*

Everyone conceives me to be lost [940]
Seeing me thus so taken of my □ pain, [941]
So ever in my way away from men [942]
And of human relations all forgot.

But I that know the world doesn't have thought
And am almost doubled □
Also small and coarse *&* erring they [943]
Who with such woe as mine are not. [944]

Let others' time in land, in sea be spent [945]
Let others honors, riches seek
Conquering fire, sword, cold, □ control

That I for |your| love Lady am content [946]
Thy worth □ have eternally
|Your| lovely gesture graven in my soul. [947]

---

940. conceives /↑ the\ me to be lost /↑ sad my lost\
941. me ↑ thus so
942. away /↑ apart\ from
943. small /↑ mean\ and
944. ↑ Who Who with such woe as mine is not ↑ are not.
945. sea, in wind ↑ be spent
946. for ↑ |your| love
947. |Your / ↓ Thy\ | lovely

But to have graven eternally [948]
Your lovely gesture deep with my soul.

———————————
———————————

With bearing sculptured eternally
Your lovely gesture within my soul

948. to have /↑ bear\ / With bearing \ graven

[74B — 79]

p. 187.

Those lovely eyes that □ to weep
Woe muſt when I from them □ [949]
What will they do now? [950] Who can tell of me?
If happily they on me their thought do keep? [951]

If they have on their mind □
I saw me far □
Or if that happy day when I may see
Thou again are imagining in □ deep.

Are they [952]

Happily imagining on me I love [953]
That in this obscure, errors so sweet
Can put the sadness of my thought close. [954]

---

949. must ~~why~~ when
950. do now / ↑ now do \ / are doing now \ ?
951. If ~~they~~ happily they
952. Thou again are imagining in □ deep. / ↓ Again they imagine in their soul □ deep. \
~~If~~ Are they
953. Happily imagining on me I love / ↑ The happy fancies ~~of me~~ I □ \
954. Can put the sadness of my thought close. / ↑ Can cast upon the sadness of □ \

4.3 — Guerra Junqueiro: Choice

[74B — 36]

Guerra Junqueiro — *Morte de D. João* — *p. 44* — *end* [955]

> The sun in the east side at □ explosive
> The Muse floats in air. Tranquil □ ocean
> A good hymn of a joy immense did sing
> In the religious, blue, formless *&* |whitening|
> The full moon like a wandering dream did flee [956]
>
> . . . .
>
> I began then to write this epopee.

[36ᵛ]

p. 51

ll. 9–10

> Rotten as a rag lies swag in the road
> The man made belly and the soul made toad.

---

955. G[uerra] J[unqueiro] — *Morte de D. J*[oão]
956. ~~Let~~ The

[74B — 77]

"*Canção Perdida.*"

G. Junqueiro.

Lost Song.

Someone remembers me not
In ☐ beyond the sea;
If thou wouldst take him my life [957]
Oh Death I'd give it to thee

———————

3.

In mighty shapes of dream ecstatic mount with Moon [958]
Feeling a voice of tears the infinity languor thrills: [959]

Who moanth, oh nightingale
☐ sea
'Tis my love that in his yearn

4.

Oh sleep, oh my dear, oh sleep
In the thin sand of the sea
That ere the star of the dawn [960]
I will lye me down by thee

———————

957. my life → again
958. ecstatic / ↓ spell-boned \ mount with Moon / ↑ the granite hills \
959. languor ~~falls~~ ↑ thrills:
960. dawn → and again

$$[74B - 82]$$

Translation Luz Negra [961]

Guerra Junqueiro [962]

In my sad life of |agony *&* dread|
I had a great love that I disdain
I will now find another love, I said
And I sought for it, but I sought in vain.

———————————

slain

———————————

961. *Transl [ation] Luz Negra*
962. *G[uerra] J[unqueiro]*

II ADDENDA

1.0 — Biographical Texts Concerning Alexander Search

[20 — 1–7]

No soul more loving or tender than mine has ever exist-
ed, no soul so full of kindness, of pity, of all the things
of tenderness and of love. Yet no soul is so lonely as
mine — not lonely, be it noted, from exterior, but from
interior circumstances. I mean this: together with my
great tenderness & kindness an element of an entirely
opposite kind enters into my character, an element of
sadness, of self-centredness, of selfishness therefore,
whose effect is two-fold: to warp & hinder the develop-
ment & full *internal* play of those other qualities, and
to hinder, by affecting the will depressingly, their full
external play, their manifestation. One □

[2ʳ]

I shall analyse this, one day I shall examine better,
discriminate, the elements of my character, for my
curiosity of all things, linked to my curiosity for myself
and for my own character, leads to one attempt to
understand my personality.

It was on account of these characteristics that I wrote, describing myself, in the [963] "Winter Day":

> *One like Rousseau…*
> *A misanthropic lover of mankind.*

I have, as a matter of fact, many, too many affinities with Rousseau. In certain things our characters are [3ʳ] identical. The warm, intense, inexpressible love of mankind, and the portion of selfishness balancing it — this is a fundamental characteristic of his character and, as well, of mine.

My intense patriotic suffering, my intense desire of bettering the condition of Portugal provoke in me — how to express with what warmth, with what intensity, with what sincerity! — a thousand plans which, even if one man could realise them, he had to have one characteristic which in me is purely negative — the power [4ʳ] of will. But [964] I suffer — on the very brink of madness, I swear it — as if I *could* do all and was unable to do it, by deficiency of will. The suffering is horrible. It holds me constantly, I say, on the brink of madness.

963. "[T|t]he
964. ~~Linked to~~ But

And then unununderstood. No one suspects my patriotic love, intenser than that of everyone I meet, of everyone I know. I do not betray it; how do I then know they have it not? How can I tell their case is not such as mine. Because in some cases, in most, their temperament is entirely different; because, in the other cases, they speak in a way which reveals the non-existence at least of a warm patriotism.

[5ʳ]

The warmth, the intensity — tender, revolted & eager —, of mine I shall never express, so as not to be believed, if ever express at all.

Besides my patriotic projects — writing of "Portuguese Regicide"[965] — to provoke a revolution here, writing of Portuguese pamphlets, editing of older national literary works, creation of a magazine, of a scientific review, etc. — other plans, consuming me with the necessity of being soon carried out — Jean Seul projects, critique of Binet-Sanglé, etc. — combine to produce an excess of impulse that paralyses my will. The suffering that this produces I know not if it can be described as on this side of insanity.

---

965. "P[ortuguese] Reg[icide]"

[6ʳ]   Add to all this other reasons still for suffering, some physical, others mental, the susceptibility to every small thing that can cause pain (or even[966] that to a normal man could not cause any pain), add this to other things still, complications, money difficulties — join this all to my fundamentally[967] unbalanced temperament & you may be able to *suspect* what my *suffering is.*

Alexander Search.[968]

— 30–10–08 —

= One of my mental complications — horrible beyond words — is a fear of insanity, which itself is insanity. I am partly in that state betrayed as his by Rollinat in the opening poem (I think) of his "Névroses." Impulses,

[7ʳ]   criminal some, insane others, reaching, amid my agony, a horrible tendency to action, a terrible *muscularity,* felt in the muscles, I mean — these are common with me and the horror of them and of their intensity — greater than ever now both in number & in intensity — cannot be described.

966. cause ↑ pain (or even
967. ~~natu~~ fundamentally
968. *A[lexander] Search*

$$[20-9]$$

$$[9^v]$$

Alexander Search's

Life-bond.

$$[9^r]$$

Bond entered into by Alexander Search, of Hell, No-
where, with Jacob Satan, master, though not king, of
the same place:

1. Never to fall off or shrink from the purpose of
   doing good to mankind.
2. Never to write things, sensual or otherwise evil,
   which may be to the detriment and harm of
   those that read.
3. Never to forget, when attacking religion in the
   name of truth, that religion can ill be substi-
   tuted *&* that poor man is weeping in the dark.
4. Never to forget men's suffering and men's ill.

October 2nd. 1907.

Alexander *Search* [969]

+ *Satan.*

his mark.

———

969. ~~Alexan~~ Alexander

[20 − 10]

The earliest literary food of my childhood was in the[970] numerous novels of mystery and of horrible adventure. Those books, which are called boy's books and deal with exciting experiences I cared little for. With a healthy & natural life I was out of sympathy. My craving was not for the probable, but for the incredible, not even for the impossible by the degree, but for the impossible by nature.

Alexander Search[971]

My childhood was quiet, □; my education was good. But since I have consciousness of myself, I have[972] perceived in myself an inborn tendency to mystification, to artistic lying. Add to this a great love of the spiritual, of the mysterious, of the obscure, which, after all, was but a form and a variation of that other characteristic of mine, and my personality is, to intuition, complete.

---

970. was ↑ in the

971. *At the end of the page the signature "Alexander Search" is repeated several times, written in several different directions.*

972. ~~know~~ have

[48C — 18]

Ultimus Joculatorum.

Persons:

Caesar Seek (= Alexander Search) whose character is without laughter, moving from deep thought [973] & torturing to bitterness (bitterly joking sometimes ???)

Dr. Nabos: whose character [974] goes from bitterness to open mirth

Ferdinand Sumwan (= Fernando Pessoa, since Sumwan = Some one = Person = Pessoa) A normal, useless, lazy, [975] careless, weak, individual.

[18ᵛ]

Jacob Satan: (A Spirit of ill, the master & real conqueror there). (Bad part)

□ [976] (a woman) strain of tenderness, different [977] from high philanthropy of □

Erasmus? Dare? (Philanthropist) a *great friend* of Seek's.

Place of meeting:
Moment House.

---

973. w̶o̶ thought
974. ch[aracter]
975. l̶a̶z̶y̶ ↑ lazy
976. M̶a̶g̶d̶a̶l̶e̶n̶a̶
977. diff[eren]t

1.1 — Further Fragments Concerning the Insanity of Jesus

[26A — 53ʳ]

1. Jesus ⁹⁷⁸ was either God, or man, or both God & man.

2. Being man, Jesus was an ⁹⁷⁹ abnormal man.

3. Being an abnormal man, he was either a genius, or a madman, or a criminal. ⁹⁸⁰

4. He was not a genius, nor a criminal.

5. Therefore he ⁹⁸¹ was a madman.

[26B — 21]

But Jesus is claimed to be something more than abnormal; he is claimed to be *supernormal* — by his wreaking of miracles and of wonders — proofs ⁹⁸² these of his being the Son of God & of Divine Revelation in him.

---

978. J[esus]
979. J[esus] was ~~either~~ an
980. a criminal. ~~(or a combination of these).~~?
981. ∴ [Therefore] he
982. *supernormal* — ~~and here~~ by his wreaking of miracles and ↑ of wonders — proofs

Now in the gospels the narration links the abnormal and the supernormal Jesus. The abnormal one may[983] be explained by psychiatric science — and classed into this or that species of madness. But the supernormal one[984] — What of him? Science can do nothing with him and if we deny the authenticity of the supernormal element in the gospel narrations, we[985] in fact pronounce a verdict of inauthenticity on those narra-

[21ᵛ] tions altogether, rendering them incapable of becoming proper objects for scientific & historical investigation.

[26B — 23]

Now the abnormality of Jesus in the gospels may have another explanation — this ... For suppose we should hit upon forging an account of a □
    etc.

    Rebuking the mind etc. are "says Dr. Binet-Sanglé[986] common ideas in insanity." Unfortunately they are also common mythical creations to show the power of the Redeemer or[987] Miracle-maker over Nature; easy to imagine & invent.

---

983. abnormal ↑ one may

984. one ?

985. we deny ~~all authenticity to~~ ↑ the authenticity of the supernormal element in the gospel narrations, ~~in the~~ we

986. B[inet]-S[anglé]

987. ~~Redemption~~ ↑ eemer ~~and~~ or

This would be spurious, yet would lend itself excellently to that purpose.

———————

When we join to the ease there is in discovering stigmata of degeneration, the fact that an abnormal or "superhuman" figure, mythical or otherwise, would tend to appear insane, an account of its non-normality, several reasons are suggested to hinder us from being so forward in enhancing the whole doctrine set forth by Dr. Binet-Sanglé.[988]

[23ᵛ]

A third circumstance, connected with the 1ˢᵗ of these points, may be added: the mistakes into which may be led the man,[989] or the scientist, who has only *one'* point of view. Now Dr. Binet-Sanglé[990] has really only one manner of seeing: that of an alienist. This is dangerous. Nordau slipped several times in the □ road of his "Degeneration," a book — written — admirably written, we admit — in the same spirit as the "Folie de Jesus," and from the same exclusivist standpoint. The observations made on Nordau by an anonymous critic of his are here worth quoting, because to the purpose: □ *"Quote"*

————————

988. B[inet]-Sanglé.
989. the ~~scien~~ man,
990. B[inet]-S[angl]é

[26B — 95]

Character of Christ.

Stigmas of Degeneration: Impulsiveness, Asexuality.
(Repugnance of Life);[991] hatred of material things; pre-
vision (such as in hysteria);[992] in this person a certain
latter sureness of death. (Lombroso's case) ill-spectation
women.

Violence and indignant anger — to the[993] extent of
personal violence, in a sort, by overturning the benches
of those who[994] traded in the temple.

Comparison with the character of Shelley: liknesses
& differences.

Origin, morbid origin of the character of Christ.

Any facts from heredity.

Comparison with Indian fakirs and people of the
kind. V. Jacolliot and such volumes. Renan, Strauss for
study of surroundings and of influences[995] on Christ.

Christ's theories. Examination of them.

---

991. Life[)];
992. hysteria[)];
993. anger — ~~the~~ to the
994. those ~~sales~~ who
995. ~~origins~~ influences

$$[26C - 37]$$

Note. Christ: what was the nature of his abnormality?

Antecedents: [996]

Family, character of:

Personal |Stigmas|: *appearance*: Tall (?) Never laughed.

Wept often. *In rages.* Impulsive temperament. Opinions coherent in the character, theories vague (?), & incoherent (?). Asexuality (Side study of Kant, W. Pitt, Newton, virgins) (Study of virgin sentiment. D. Henrique etc. in Portuguese history).

Cases of solitary genetic (as regards Virgin Birth). (Character of women in whom this occurs. Is it anything special.) [997]

---

996. ~~Antecedents~~ *Antecedents*:
997. anything special.)
~~as regard to clust~~

1.2 — Projects and Lists of Poems Concerning "Delirium"

[48C — 15–17]

"DELIRIUM"

The Prison.
On a Hand.
Insomnia.
Soul-symbols.
Analogies.
A Winter Day.
Obsession (clown)
Heart-Music. Copied.
The Chocolate Box.
Comedy. Copied.
Epigram (I love my Dreams). Copied.
Mystery (open sea).
Woman in Black.
Doubt (who dreams most). Copied.
Night on the City.
Mania of Doubt.
An Epitaph. Copied.
The Sleeper.
Laughter (grave).

A Glance (haunt appearances).[998] Copied.

Nirvanâ. Copied.

The Land of Dreams.

One Impure.

Thou asked in perplexity.

To a Prostitute.

I know not whether my mind is broken.

Finite mysticism.

To one playing (spirit stress).

Pain.

On the Death of A…

Who would make the spirit's real…[999]

I have built my temple… Copied.

The Unnatural and the Strange.

A curtain hides the mystery.

….. (Exclusion from Mankind). Copied.[1000]

Song of Dirt. Copied.

Giantess.

I feel a rage… Copied.[1001]

Feast of Life.

Feast of Emptiness.

I pass before the window lit…

Suddenly in the middle of life…

---

998. appear[a]nces).

999. spi[ɛ|r]it's

1000. fr[om]

1001. ..[.]

[16ʳ]

DELIRIUM.

E. ~~The Prison (egotism). x July 1907~~

D. ~~On a Hand.~~ x January 1906

D. ~~Insomnia.~~ x

~~Soul-Symbols.~~ x

~~Analogies.~~

E. D. P. ~~A Winter Day.~~ All styles

D. ~~Obsession (Clown).~~ x

D. ~~Heart-Music. Copied.~~ x

~~The Chocolate Box.~~

~~Comedy. Copied.~~ x

~~Epigram (I love my dreams). Copied~~

~~Mystery (open sea).~~ x

~~Woman in Black.~~ x

~~. Doubt (who dreams most?). Copied. x June 19 — 1907.~~

~~Night on the City.~~

~~Mania of Doubt.~~ x

E. ~~An Epitaph.~~ Copied. x Julho 1907.

⸮ Oh, to be a child.

~~The Sleeper. x~~ x

~~Laughter (grave).~~ x

D. ~~A Glance (haunt appearances). Copied.~~ x

P. Nirvâna. Copied. x

D. The Land of Dreams. x

   One Impure.

   Thou askest in prepelexity.

   To a Prostitute.

   I know not whether my mind is broken… x

   Finite Mysticism. x

? To (Tr. sense). x

   To one playing. (spirit stress).

   Pain.

   On the death of A…

   Who would make the spirit's real…

D. I have built my temple. Copied. x August 1907

   The Unnatural and the Strange. Copied.

? Requiescat. (Pain, hope). Copied. — Agosto 26–1907[1002]

   A curtain hides the mystery. Copied

   …… (Exlusion from mankind). Copied. October 16–1907.[1003]

   Song of Dirt. Copied. 4 Dec. 1907

   Giantess.

? Build me a cottage. Copied — 20 Dez. 1907.

   I feel a rage… Copied. Dez 3 (seek 4) 1907.

1002. Ag[osto]

1003. Oct[ober]

$$[17^r]$$

(x or √) *see next S. + S. (songs)*

DELIRIUM — 2.

⸮ Apollo unto Neptune. Copied √ — 8 Dz. 1907.

~~Feast of Life.~~ x

~~Feast of Emptiness.~~ x

~~I pass before the windows lit … x~~

~~Suddenly in the middle of life.~~ x

~~Horror. Copied. x — Oct. 17. 1907~~

~~Into the night.~~

~~All things are symbols.~~ x

~~When I ponder on the world.…~~

~~As the soft gleam of the moon~~

~~The Circle~~ x

~~A stranger in the hall.~~ x

Aspiration.

⸮ Farewells, departures…. Copied √ – 27 Dezembro 1907.[1004]

Weep for the last things. √

1004. D[e]z[embro]

⸮ The Cup. √

~~The man w. one lip. Copied~~ √

⸮ The Maiden of Dreams. Copied √ December 29–1907 [1005]

The Fairy Queen. √

Burn me that book, hangman. Copied x

Let us play a game little boy.... Copied √

~~The Portrait. Copied x Agosto 1907~~

~~A vision (poor at all doors). x~~

1005. Dec[ember]

[48B — 93]

DELIRIUM — 3.

√ I Remember the good. -- -07.

√ What matter if the time…? -- -07.

√ Morning (dewness) -- -07.

√ I saw the dew upon the flower -- -07.

x who would make the ſp's real -- -0.

√ Scientific Truth -- -0.

√ In a gold casket lock -- -0.

√ He who hath seen beautiful -- -0.

x I've built temple (Space) -- -0.

√ One Dead (peace at laſt) −8−07.

x The unnatural and the ſtrange -- -0.

x Feaſt of Life 16−8−07.

x The Crown 16−8−07.

x Requiescat (pain, hope) 26−8−07.

x The banquet of Emptiness 2−9−07.

[78B — 63–64]

Notes regarding the publication of poems.

————————

1. The first book of poems to be published is the trans-
   lation of Espronceda.

2. After this an original book of poems; this is to be
   formed of the poems in parts 2 and 3 of "Delirium"
   (as called on the sheets), namely those called "Mean-
   ing" & "Delirium" proper. [1006]

3. Then a book composed of poems in the first part
   of "Delirium" (sheets) and called there "Oddities."

4. After this a book made up of the poems in the 5th.
   part of "Delirium" (sheets) — "Agony."

5. Subsequently a book composed of the poems in
   part 4 of "Delirium" (sheets).

6. After this a book of Songs, more lyrical, from the
   sheet-cover called "Lyrical Poems."

7. About this time a book of poems called "Nonsense";
   see cover so named.

8. After all these, the "Death of God." [1007]

9. After "Death of God" a book containing earlier
   poems, "Old Castle," etc., etc.

10. Then a book containing other longer poems, such
    as "Vincenzo," "Voyage," etc.

11. Another volume: "Sonnets in Many Moods." (When
    to publish?)

Over

[63ᵛ]

Other Notes

Names of books:

2. "~~Delirium~~" = "3" ⎫
3. "~~Oddities~~."   ⎬ Only one — "Delirium"
            ⎭

4. "Agony."

5. "Dreams."

6. "~~Better~~."

7. "Nonsense." =

8. "Death of God." =

9. "The Old Castle and other Poems."

10. Sonnets in Many Moods.

———————

(4.) Contains "Winter Day" and "Woman in Black."

(9) Contains "Gahu."

(11) In chronological order; no sonnets in any other order.

—————

1006. *On the left side of the document — written in the vertical column —, covering numbers "2." & "3.," is the indication*: One Volume.

1007. After ↑ᵃˡˡ these,

[64ʳ]

Prieſt and Hangman (Here or Death of God?)¹⁰⁰⁸

Delirium.

= Preface. =

The Prison. (July 1907.)

√ Beginning (March 1905). 26.

√ Nirvâna. (1906). 28.

√ The Unnatural and the ſtrange. (1906) 24.¹⁰⁰⁹

√ The Curtain (26–8–07) 14.¹⁰¹⁰

√ … (Exclusion from mankind). (16–10–07) 25¹⁰¹¹

√ Rage. (3–12–07) 23.¹⁰¹²

√ Song of Dirt. (4–12–07) 18.

Giantess.

√ The Temple (Auguſt 1907). 9.¹⁰¹³

√ A glance (haunt apps). December 05 7.¹⁰¹⁴

√ Doubt (who doubts moſt). 19/6/07 12¹⁰¹⁵

1008. D[eath] of G[od]

1009. Unnat[ural] and the ſtrange. (1906) 24.

1010. A~~ curtain hides~~. ↑ The Curtain (26–8–07) 14.

1011. fr[om] mankind). (16–10–07) 25

1012. (4↑3–12–07) 23.

1013. Aug[uſt] 1907). 9.

1014. Dec[ember] 05 7.

1015. d[oubt]s moſt). 19/6/07 12

√ Heart-music. December '05 18. [1016]
√ Epigram (I love my dreams). (1906.) 6.
√ Comedy. (January. '06) 24.
√ Horror (October 17–1907). 49. [1017]
√ The Lip. (2/1/08) 18
√ The Picture (August 1907). 10. [1018]
   Feast of Life.
   Feast of Emptiness.
√ In the street (I pass before windows) (12–11–07) 140. [1019]
   A moment (suddenly middle of life a change)
   Into the Night.
√ The Giant's Reply (7–1–08) 8.
√ Regret (ag. a child) — (29–5–07) 32.
   All things are symbols.
   When I ponder on the world.
   Soft gleam of the moon.
√ The Circle (30–7–1907). 18.
   The Stranger.
   On a Hand.
   Insomnia.
√ Soul — symbols (February 1906). 40 [1020]

1016. Dec[ember] '05 18.
1017. Oct[ober] 17–1907). 49.
1018. ~~Portrait~~ ↑ Picture (August 1907). 10.
1019. ~~From~~ ↑ In the street (I pass b[e]f[ore] windows) (12–11–07) 140.
1020. Feb[ruar]y 1906). 40

Analogies (?).

Obsession (Clown).

The Chocolate Box.

Mystery (open sea).

Mania of doubt.

The sleeper

Laughter (grave).

One Impure

Thou askest in perplexity [1021]

To a Prostitute.

I know not whether my mind is broken... [1022]

√ To one playing (spirit stress). December '05/12. [1023]

Pain.

Aboulie (Who w. make the spirit's real...).

Winter Day.

Woman in Black. [1024]

Night on the City.

√ My life. (9–1–08). 128

[64ᵛ] √ An Epitaph. July 07 54.

The Land of Dreams.

1021. perpl[exity]

1022. wh[ethe]r

1023. Dec[ember] '05/12.

1024. W[oman]

A Vision (poor at all doors).

√ Prayer (That go mad!) (18–1–08) 73 [1025]

√ *Sonnets*: The apostle.

√ Death in Life.

√ Woe supreme.

√ Adorned.

√ *Blind Eagle*.

√ Justice.

√ Solomon Waste.

Jemmy Jones.

Dirty Day.

√ The Leper. (25–10–07) 66.

√ The world offended (10–1–08) 19.

√ A Question (wife and poems) (10–1–08) 18.

√ A Crime (being born) 19 (?)

Epigrams:

He asked me.

Heart's a pump.

(Die *&* know oneself dead) (10–1–08) 12.

1025. [(] That

$$[144V — 14^r]$$

Alexander Search: *Delirium.*

Poems to be included: —

---

1. ☐

2. ☐

3. ☐

4. ☐

5. ☐

6. ☐

7. ☐

8. ☐

9. ☐

10. ☐

1.2.1 — Fragments and Other Poems Related to "Delirium"

[49A¹ — 19]

July or March 1906.

Fragment of Delirium.

I know not whether my mind is broken
Nor do I know if my mind is ill;
I know not if love is but the laſt token
Of God to me, or a word unspoken
  In a chaos of will.

My thoughts are such as the mad muſt have
  And |dead| things know my soul
Grotesque *&* odd are the shapes that roll
  In my brain as worms in a grave…

[79 − 1]

Delirium[1026]

The young maiden
She thinks of me at eyes and lips
The dreams of me at □ *&* heart's end... her arm
So she |*dreaming-lurked| must not overflow.

1026. *D[elirium]*

1.3 — A List Concerning "Agony"

[144V — 17ʳ]

Alexander Search: *Agony*

Poems to be included: —

1. Soul-Symbols.

2. ☐

3. ☐

4. ☐

5. ☐

6. ☐

7. ☐

8. ☐

9. ☐

10. ☐

1.4 — Note from a Diary

$$[144\,\text{T} - 2]$$

Sunday — August 4, 1907.

Fine day, though rather warm. Spent part of the day, up to 4. P.M., in putting my papers in order. Preparing verses for "Delirium."

2.0 — Biographical Texts Concerning Pantaleão

$$[27^3H — 2^r]$$

Cartas de Pantaleão

Não tenho, meu caro Smith, vida ou sentimento infeliz; tenho um caracter infeliz.

Sobreloja

$$[27^3H — 3]$$

Pantaleão.

Quem não quizer soffer que se isole. Feche as portas da sua alma quanto possivel á luz do convivio.

Sou um sybarita de espirito; sou-o tanto que mesmo a petala de rosa da sensualidade incommoda[1027] a minha alma reunir gente.

1027. que ↑ mesmo a ~~minha alma não~~ petala de rosa da sensualidade ~~não d~~ incommoda

[27³H — 4-5]

Pantaleão

Eu sou, meu caro Sñr. Smith, um d'aquelles que choram em si o desuso do methodo interpretativo em psychologia. Brilhava-me, nos tempos mais suaves de outora, tirar do meu espirito, lenta-, curta-, analyzadamente um tratado de psychologia humana. Que trabalho difficil *&* meigo ao meu ser — esse de, fechado a olhar |extrospetivo|,[1028] seguir o encadeamento |lucido| das sensações, dos pensamentos, das correntes de desejos e |acções|! Ao menos, escripta a obra, ficaria[1029] um documento de auto-observação de algum modo util e conciso.

Lembro-me ainda, não sem certa tristeza sombreada de angustia, como eu uma vez[1030] estudei a constituição da minha memoria. O meu amigo, a quem as ostento, são lucidas,[1031] decerto desculpando-me eu, na falta de melhor materia, accordando saudades, transmitirlhe um exemplo de auto-observação.

[4ᵛ]

Sou um visual. O que na memoria trago, trago-o visualmente, se susceptivel é de ser assim trazido. Mesmo ao querer evocar em mim uma qualquer voz,[1032] um

---

1028. olhar ~~d~~ |extrospetivo|,
1029. ficar-~~me-hia~~ ↑ia
1030. como ~~um~~ ↑eu uma ~~dia~~ vez
1031. amigo ~~nas suas~~, ↑a quem as ostento, são lucidas,

perfume qualquer, não evito que antes que ella ou elle me vislumbre no horizonte[1033] do espirito, me appareça á visão |rememorativa| a pessôa que falla, a cousa d'onde o perfume partiu. Não dou isto por absolutamente certo; pode ser que, radicada em mim de vez a persuasão de que sou um visual, no logar final do sophisma que é a escuridão interior[1034] do ser me fosse desde então impossível evitar que a idéa de que sou um visual[1035] não levantasse immediatamente uma imagem falsamente inspiradora. Seja como fôr, o menos que sou, é um visual predominante. Vejo, e vendo, vivo.

Tento lembrar-me de um poema de um trecho de um verso ou prosa e penso, espiando-me a alma, de que no[1036] recordar-me, |raia| como muito atraz no meu sêr mental a visão dessas palavras escriptas. Mesmo o que de modo apressado se me vizualiza obscuramente no espirito ao |repetil-o|. Creio; não sei. A verdadeira memoria é[1037] inconsciente; e eu, analizando-me, conciencializo-me. Ainda assim, o facto de que, tornando-me consciente, me percebo[1038] visual é sufficiente como prova.

[5ʳ]

1032. Mesmo ao ↑querer evocar em mim uma ↑qualquer voz,

1033. na e̶s̶t̶r̶a̶d̶a̶ ↑no horizonte

1034. sophisma /↑erro\ que é a i̶n̶t̶i̶m̶a̶ ̶d̶o̶ ̶e̶s̶c̶u̶r̶o̶ escuridão interior

1035. sou ↑um visual

1036. que p̶a̶r̶a̶ no

1037. A verdadeira memoria /↑memoria em si\ é

1038. C̶h̶a̶m̶o̶ Ainda assim, o facto de que, tornando-me consciente, me v̶e̶j̶o̶ ↑percebo

[27³H — 13–14]

(Pantaleão)

O Boato.

. . .

E para mim, idealiſta integral, o proprio mundo, o universo inteiro, não é senão um boato e um boato falso. Todos os seus sêres, tempos, logares *&* □ são boatos, rumores, e galgos, que o desapparecer e passar d'elles continuamente desencanto. Parece-me haver [1039] *&* ter realidade tal sêr, tal cousa, mas seu haver, no devaneio do ser e do se moſtrar, nos indica que falsamente era e sem realidade [1040] parecia ser. Não temos modo de ter outra. A vida, toda a vida, é o eterno boato, e a morte, toda a morte, o eterno desmentido. Eſperança, amôr, illusão, a crença associada ao futuro, a confiança tremula no presente, tudo iſto cessa nos seus objeſtos e em si. Passar é desmentir-se. Não ha mais para isso do que a superficie das cousas *&* essa superficie finge-se-nos realidade. [1041]

1039. ~~A ha~~ Parece-me haver

1040. ↑nos indica |↑aponta| que falsamente era e ~~sem~~ ↑sem realidade

1041. mais ↑para isso do que a superficie das cousas *&* essa superficie finge-se-↑nos realidade.

[13ᵛ]

Da propria ponderação de um boato alegre nasce eſta
triſteza de o sentir symbolo do universo.[1042] É que como
"qualquér eſtrada, mesmo eſta eſtrada de Entepfuhl,
nos leva ao fim da terra," todo o objeƈto, mesmo eſte de
boatos, nos[1043] leva ao myſterio do mundo. Cada cousa,
porque é, resume e representa o universo, porque é
tambem: e cada cousa porque passa, representa e escon-
de o universo, porque tambem elle deixa-de-ser. — De
sorte que, para quem verdadeiramente tem alma e cons-
ciencia para a vida, toda a vida tem alma para elle, em
o pouco de cada cousa, o nada de cada hora, nem mais,
nem menos, do que a como-que-infinidade das cousas,
a similieternidade do tempo. A divisibilidade[1044] é, para
o eſpirito, infinita, tanto para dentro como para fora;
porque o pequeno, como o grande são infinitamente
divisiveis, e tanto n'um como n'outro a eſpirito sonha
perder-se. De modo que, para ter horror ao universo
como ser tanto nos baſta ser aſtronomos de imaginação,
como athomiſtas de phantasia. Todos os caminhos do
pensamento levam áquella Roma da dôr cujo supremo
pontificie não dá audiencias ao raciocinio, nem bullas
ao sentimento.

1042. do ~~mundo~~ ↑ universo.
1043. objeƈto ╱↑ assumpto╲, mesmo eſte de ╱↑ do╲ boatos ╱↑ o╲, nos
1044. ~~Baſta que, pensando, se veja que não só a raiz tudo se e~~
A divisibilidade

[14ʳ]

Pantaleão.

A mim é-me familiar o que a outros, e a raros outros, apenas em horrorosos accasos é de algum modo vagamente experiencia — o sentimento do myſterio e do horror intelleċtual do mundo. É minha do meu[1045] sangue e na minha alma quotidiana a sensação ôca de que o universo é[1046] uma pavorosa illusão. Passou[1047] já o tempo em que eſte mêdo me era occasional e, como um relampago, uma cousa de um horroroso inſtante. Hoje consubſtancia-se com a minha vida eſpiritual ao ponto de me parecer extranha & não de mim a hora do eſpirito em que[1048] de algum modo me desenvencilho da consciencia do myſterio do mundo. Prisioneiro, como todos, no carcere d'eſta vida, é me dado o |horror| conſtante de me ter desacoſtumado de me não pensar prisioneiro mas tomar por liberdade não muito pensada a limitada liberdade minha.

1045. do / ↑ como que no \ meu
1046. o ~~mundo~~ / ↑ universo \ é
1047. ~~Não~~ Passou
1048. extranha ↑ e não de mim a hora ↑ ~~nefaſta~~ do eſpirito em que

$[27^3H — 15]$

Torquato Mendes Fonseca da Cunha Rey

A. M. † Cabral

(□ d'um monarchico).

(publicado por "Pantaleão" — das visões.)[1049]

———————

Não sei o valor que terá este escripto; os entendidos que o digam. O meu unico fim foi □ a ultima vontade do meu querido e chorado amigo.[1050] Nada mais.

"Pantaleão"

———————

1049. visões. [)]

1050. a ↑ultima vontade do meu querido e chorado / ↑ malogrado \ amigo.

2.1 — Projects Concerning "As Visões do Sñr. Pantaleão."

[48A — 44–47]

Visões Politicas do Sñr. Pantaleão

Prefacio.

  I. Visão Primeira.
 II. □
III. □
 IV. □
  V. Visão dos Canalhas.
 VI. Visão jornalistica.
VII. Visão da camisaria.
VIII. Visão da planicie.
 IX. Visão da conversa.
  X. Visão das cobras.
 XI. Visão do proverbio.
XII. Visão da pergunta.
XIII. Visão da chave.
XIV. Visão de futuras contas.

XV. Visão da monarchia.[1051]

XVI. Visão do Velhinho.

XVII. Visão da Taboleta.

XVIII. Primeira Visão do Crucificado.

XIX. Visão do casaco do conselheiro.

XX Visão do desenho.

XXI Visão extranha.

XXII Visão de um museu monarchico.

XXIII □

XXIV □

XXV □

[45^{r}]

XXVI □

XXVII □

XXVIII □

XXIX □

XXX □

XXXI □

XXXII □

1051. monarchia. /(|*chica|).\

XXXIII ☐

XXXIV ☐

XXXV ☐

XXXVI ☐

XXXVII ☐

XXXVIII ☐

XXXIX ☐

XL ☐

XLI ☐

XLII ☐

XLIII ☐

XLIV ☐

XLV ☐

XLVI ☐

XLVII ☐

XLVIII ☐

XLVIX ☐

L ☐

[46^r]

LI □

LII □

LIII □

LIV □

LV □

LVI □

LVII □

LVIII □

LIX □

LX □

LXI □

LXII □

LXIII □

LXIV □

LXV □

LXVI □

LXVII □

LXVIII □

LXIX □

LXX □

LXXI □

LXXII □

LXXIII □

LXXIV □

LXXV □ [1052]

$[47^r]$

LXXVI □

LXXVII □

LXXVIII □

LXXIX □

LXXX □

LXXXI □

LXXXII □

LXXXIII □

LXXXIV □

LXXXV □

1052. $[46^v]$

"As Visões do Sñr. Pantaleão," ~~incluindo~~
~~Seguidas de um estudo feito pelo mesmo snr., sobre uma nova~~
~~especie nosso phychose.~~
                    — Sem vocabulário —

LXXXVI □

LXXXVII □

LXXXVIII □

LXXXIX □

XC □ [1053]

XCI □

XCII □

XCIII □

XCIV □

XCV □

XCVI □

XCVII □

XCVIII □

XCIX □

C □ [1054]

1053. ~~LXXX~~ XC
1054. ~~X~~ C

[48A — 5]

Visões do Sñr. Pantaleão.
Visão Final.
Visão da queda do corpo.
Visão do crucificado (1ª).

2.2 — Further Writings Concerning
"A Nossa Administração Colonial"

A nossa administração colonial (a †)

Irony; if 'tis bothered it will give more money to steel for ministers friends, & for ministers.

————————

O Sñr. D. Manuel ainda é novo, mas é de crer que a acção dos annos, e o amadurecer que vem de preencher [21ᵛ] o seu alto cargo lhe trazem maiores necessidades financeiras. Vantajoso será pois crear receitas para isto ☐

Ora como as nossas colonias fôram adquiridas pelos nossos[1055] navegadores quando eram da monarchia absoluta, é claro que as colonias pertencem *de jure* á monarchia e não aos povos, tendo o povo usufruto d'ellas, que [21aʳ] |*expele governabilidade| dos nossos reis. Nada mais natural pois[1056] — e bem pouco nos parece — que os rendimentos das colonias do occidente (exceptuando talvez

——————————

1055. n[ossos]
1056. Nada mais natural pois / ↑ É pois absolutamente natural \

—, e o anterior[1057] governo da monarchia leva a crer que assim se passa — o povo de Angola).

Não há porisso necessidade de chorar o acto sem
[21aᵛ] moral do paiz † e simples |*reino|. Continuado no sábio methodo dos illustres ministros que ultimamente teem passado pelos conselhos da coroa, isto é, de pôr o dinheiro & entregar a el-rei sob outros títulos como por exemplo; † para o †: 240.000$000 reis.

1057. ant[erior]

3.0 — Biographical Texts Concerning Jean Seul de Méluret

$$[144Z - 23^v - 26^r]$$

J'ai été anarchiste, aux 17 ans, et je sais bien quelle[1058] est dans son essence la théorie de l'amour libre, c'est celle de ce qu'on peut aimer aujourd'hui une femme, demain une autre, si l'on veut. On peut aussi, si l'on veut, aimer une femme toute sa vie, tout à fait comme[1059] dans le mariage.

$$[24^r]$$

L'anarchisme est le |faisant théorie| l'impulsion maladive et non sujette au |contrôle| de la volonté consciente et raisonnée. En général l'état intellectuel du dégénéré supérieur (meneur) et du dégénéré inférieur (mené)[1060] est l'intellectualisation de l'impulsion et de l'obsession. Les théories anarchistes en sont un bon, sinon, le meilleur[1061] exemple. Elles incluent toutes la suppression du pouvoir, l'élimination du mariage, par exemple □.

1058. sais ↑ bien quelle

1059. ↑ tout à fait comme

1060. supérieur ↑ (meneur) et du d[égénéré] inf[érieur] (~~serviteur~~ ↑ mené)

1061. sont ↑ un bon, sinon, le meilleur

Tant une chose que l'autre sont absolument contraires à la science; seuls les idiots *&* les dégénérés peuvent penser le contraire. Le but de l'évolution n'eſt autre chose que la |concrétisation| de l'ordre, son affirmation (ſtrengthening). Le mariage eſt le moyen par lequel la nature dans la société [1062] fait la sélection du plus pur. Mais, me dit-on, le mariage actuellement n'eſt pas ainsi; il eſt fait en vue de l'argent, de la position. Vous argumentez donc, non contre le mariage en soi, mais contre son état actuel, contre les imperfections qu'une *société dégénérée* [1063] (sentez-le bien) lui impose. Vous êtes donc avec [1064] moi; nous sommes d'accord.

[24ᵛ]   Mais, me dîtes [1065] vous, croyez vous donc que la cérémonie [1066] □ the cerimonial can make the love, that the fact of being called *Mrs.* can make a woman purer? No, if I thought that I □ je serais [1067] sot ou fou. Personne ne le croit. Mais le mariage n'eſt pas une cérémonie, ni □; ces [1068] choses-là ne sont que des conventions. *Le mariage' eſt l'amour conſtant et fidèle d'un homme pour une femme;* il n'eſt plus que ça. Un homme qui s'unit à une femme sans rien de cérémonie; c'eſt-à-dire qui vit toute sa vie

1062. la nature ~~à travers~~ ↑dans la société

1063. *dégé*[*nérée*]

1064. êtes ↑donc avec

1065. Mais, ~~vous me~~ me dîtes

1066. *céré*[*monie*]

1067. that I ~~would be~~ je serais

1068. ~~ce~~ ces

en concubinage (comme l'on dit) avec *cette* femme-là, est marié.

Mais, donc, répondez vous, vous donnez dans notre théorie. Je me permets |de| répondre que je ne comprends pas comment. Ou bien vous êtes contre le mariage en soi, ou bien vous êtes contre *le cérémoniel*,[1069] le □ du mariage, si vous vous |tenez| seulement à ce dernier, pourquoi ne le dîtes vous pas?

[25ʳ]

La vérité est que votre "amour libre"[1070] n'est pas une chose dont vous ayez une idée quelconque. C'est purement une impulsion qui se transforme en idée mi-consciente et que vous croyez tout naturellement avoir produit par votre raison, par votre[1071] raisonnement (même le vôtre).[1072] En tant que phénomène psychologique cela suffit à ce que je comprenne votre théorie:[1073] c'est une impulsion dégénérée.

En avez une idée claire? Eh, bien que veulent dire ces mots "amour libre"? De deux choses possibles ils font

---

1069. [la|le] *cérémoniel*,

1070. "amour li[v|b]re"

1071. v[ous] croyez tout naturellement avoir produit par v[otre] raison, par v[otre]

1072. Même par

1073. que théorie phénomène psychologique cela suffit à ce que je comprenne v[otre] théorie:

qu'ils signifient l'un ou l'autre: un "amour libre" [1074] veut dire pouvoir [1075] d'aimer indistinctement, cette femme aujourd'hui, celle-là demain, l'après demain cette autre etc.; ou, différemment, "amour libre" [1076] signifie se lier avec une femme pour la vie mais sans cérémonie extérieur, sans changement de Mlle en Madame, sans régistre, sans fête etc. Dans le 2nd cas, vous ataquez les imperfections du mariage.

Mais enfin — me dîtes-vous — vous donnez encore dans notre théorie. Car en faisant le mariage non-*cérémonial*, non-extérieur, en donnant à l'homme et à la femme le libre droit de se séparer vous [1077] dîtes la même chose que nous. Pas tout à fait la même chose, je l'aurais dit si j'eusse fini, mais j'ai encore quelque chose à ajouter.

[25^v]

Actuellement le mariage conventionnel est la forme de sélection et le faiseur de respectabilité. Mais [1078] la société moderne, tout en admettant le mariage, ne le respect pas trop; c'est vrai, c'est la dégénérescence, c'est la décadence

---

1074. possibles ~~ils veulen~~ ils font qu'ils signifient l'un ou l'autre: un "am[our] l[ibre]"

1075. ~~p~~ pouvoir

1076. "am[our] l[ibre]"

1077. se ~~révolter~~ ^séparer vous

1078. ~~Si~~ Mais

de cette même société. Si argumenter contre les défauts d'une chose était argumenter contre elle ce serait terrible. Par example, si je vous prouve que la religion catholique est mauvaise je ne me vois plus à l' Inquisition car ce serai l'attaquer par le coté le [1079] plus noir.

Mais peut-on répondre, ce qui produit, ce qui devient mauvais est en soi pas bien. Si par conséquent [1080] le mariage venait à être comme il est, il avait en soi la possibilité de le devenir, il était imparfait.

Oui, c'est vrai, mais il y a certes une grande réponse: ce n'est pas seulement le mariage, mais la fin que dégénérait, c'est *tout*, c'est une loi général de l'évolution.

[26ʳ]

Ce qu'il faut déterminer est si le mariage avec toute sa possibilité de devenir mauvais est inférieur à l'état d'amour libre. Dans l'amour libre évidemment on ne peut dégénérer ni être immoral.

La réponse à cela frappe de mort la théorie entière.

La perfection [1081] étant impossible dans le monde, le seul état dont on ne peut dégénérer, le seul □, est *la dégénérescence' en soi*. L'amour libre est dans la dégénérescence pure.

1079. coté ~~ma~~ le
1080. conséq[uent]
1081. ←Note!! La perfection

(Degeneration[1082] is actual state; pure love is pure atavism. Is it so?)

On ne peut pas être anarchiste sans être malade ou inconscient.[1083]

Sentimental triade against anarchism[1084] at end.

Reason hence as degeneration.[1085] Next page.

(Logical basis of anarchism: pessimism which is linked to and is true, which anarchism is only taking pessimism out of its sphere).

1082. Deg[eneratio]n
1083. anarch[iste] sans être malade ~~et~~ ↑ou inconscient. ~~On~~
1084. anarch[ism]
1085. deg[eneratio]n.

[133A — 9]

Jean Seul

Dans la place Octave Mirabeau, dans le quartier entre |la| Rue Félicien Champsaur & |la| Rue Lacenaire,[1086] □ pas de l'□

Institut Marquis de Sade pour l'□ des jeunes filles.

□ les mangeurs d'ordures, que l'on appelle ici des[1087] |anthropophages|.

[9ᵛ]

Un jeune[1088] libertin ayant trouvé un nouveau plaisir en □ les yeux de sa grand-mère, il est devenu □ de l'imiter; l'opposition à ce raffinement n'ayant |eu| d'opposition que chez quelques vieilles dames, |vieillies|[1089] pour le |plaisir|.

1086. Mirabeau, ~~pres de~~ ↑ dans le quartier entre |la| Rue Félicien Champsaur & |la| Rue ~~Émile Zola~~ Lacenaire,

1087. ~~en quelque sort~~ ↑ que l'on appelle ici des

1088. Un ~~cher~~ jeune

1089. ~~vie~~ |vieillies|

3.1 — Further Fragments Concerning Exhibitionism

[15B³— 36]

Cas d'Exhibitionnisme.

As to Maud Allan.
  Evolution of Dancing,
  (_ □
  criticize her style of dancing *&* find if it is atavic or
degenerative.

[15B³— 37]

Exhibitionnisme[1090]

Or le fait c'est que l'exhibitionnisme présente tous les
caractéristiques[1091] d'une impulsion hystérique. Consi-
dérez[1092] bien la nature de cette perversion et vous le
verrez |aisément|. C'est, d'abord, un *exhibitionnisme*;
or on sait bien que l'amour de l'exhibition, de □, de

1090. *Exhib*[*itionnisme*]
1091. caracteristiques, *in the original.*
1092. considerez, *in the original.*

l'originalité est un caractéristique[1093] — c'est même le caractéristique[1094] le plus frappant — de l'état mental hystérique. Nous verrons que *l'exhibitionnisme théâtral*[1095] n'en est qu'une forme, ou, plutôt, une intensification (une forme plus complexe).

Quelles sont les bases psychologiques de l'exhibitionnisme? Quelle est la psychologie de l'impulsion qu'y mène? C'est ce que nous allons étudier.

[15B³ — 40]

Il est évident[1096] que les vêtements, |par soi|,[1097] ne pouvaient *originer* le sentiment de la pudeur. Ils pouvaient cependant le maintenir[1098] et le développer.[1099] C'est qu'ils on fait. Aucune |extériorité|[1100] ne peut faire naître un sentiment quelconque; les sentiments naissent d'autre façon; ce que toute |extériorité| peut faire, (*&* ce qu'elle effectivement fait), c'est □

1093. caracteristique, *in the original.*
1094. caracteristique, *in the original.*
1095. théatral, *in the original.*
1096. evident, *in the original.*
1097. |par soi| / ↑ eux? \
1098. le ~~développer~~ maintenir
1099. developper, *in the original.*
1100. exteriorité, *in the original.*

Voici la psychologie du vêtement

1º On n'emploie d'abord le vêtement qu'en tant que |couverture| pour les parties sexuelles.

2º On emploie couleurs,[1101] de la |parure| (use des vêtements) pour s'emblir.

3º Les vêtements, étant donnés (ou trouvés) pour la honte des parties sexuelles, d'un côté, les vêtements étant ainsi donnés,[1102] et, d'autre côté, le goût[1103] de la parure étant donné; la conjonction de ces |instincts ou tendances| a donné lieu à la conception *du vêtement comme parure.* C'est-à-dire, l'amour de la parure[1104] (de l'ornement) trouve un moyen, un excellent moyen de se manifester dans le vêtement, originellement simple, expression de pudeur sexuelle.   [40ᵛ]

3º L'usage des vêtements en a produit la nécessité absolue par rapport |au chaleur *&* au| froid. (aux exchanges atmosphériques)[1105] (Peut-être dans le Nord a-t-on □)[1106]

Examinons maintenant la psychologie □

1101. d̶e̶s̶ couleurs,

1102. honte ↑des parties sexuelles, d'un côte, ↑ les vêtements étant ainsi donnés,

1103. côte, le gout, *in the original.*

1104. l̶a̶ ↑l'amour de la parure

1105. atmospheriques), *in the original.*

1106. Nord a-t-on □ [)]

[15B³ — 41]

La question du use, trait(é) du point de vue psychologique, n'est d'abord que[1107] la question de la psychologie des vêtements.

Je ne demanderai pas |encore| la cause ou la signification du sentiment |de honte| qui est attaché dès la plus légère[1108] □ vers la civilisation,[1109] aux parties sexuelles. Je commencerai par étudier quel a été le rôle du vêtement dans la psychologie humaine, et dans son évolution.[1110]

On a |d'abord| à constater que dans la nature de grandes et |d'|importantes modifications sont produites par des causes apparemment insignifiantes, par des extériorités auxquelles on n'attacherait pas □ une signification d'importance.[1111]

Il semble d'abord qu'on peut[1112] considérer[1113] les vêtements et leur rôle sous trois points de vue distinctes: 1° en tant que |défense| contre le climat — contre le froid naturellement,[1114] car la chaleur ne □; 2°en tant

[41ᵛ]

<hr />

1107. n'est ↑ d'abord que

1108. Legère, *in the original.*

1109. civilization, *in the original.*

1110. evolution, *in the original.*

1111. on ~~n'at~~ n'attacherait pas □ une signification ~~quel~~ ↑ d'importance.

1112. ↑ (Il semble ~~que~~ d'abord qu') On peut ↑ ~~uis~~

1113. considerer, *in the original.*

1114. sous ~~deux~~ ↑ trois points de vue ~~tre~~ distinctes: 1° en tant que |défense| contre ~~la les~~ le climat — ~~chaud~~ ↑ contre le froid ~~n~~ naturellement, que productions de la pudeur; 3° en tant que parure.

Examinons plus *attentivement* cette matière.

On a remarqué beaucoup de fois que la véritable *&* primitive raison d'être psychologique ou naturelle des vêtements n'a pas été ni[1115] la décence,[1116] ni le |confort|, mais seulement la parure, l'ostentation. C'est ainsi que (quote from the beginning of Spencer's "Education") dit: □ (Quote[1117] others if possible.)

$$[15B^3 - 42]$$

Nous distinguerons:

Les exhibitionnismes à impulsion pure

Les exhibitionnismes à impulsion sexuelle

Les exhibitionnismes à impulsion vraiment exhibitionniste[1118]

p. 38–39 (Salome)

Here exhibitionism is an episode of the insanity[1119]

1115. On a ~~be~~ remarqué /↑ fait remarquer \ beaucoup de fois que la véritable et primitive raison d'être ↑ psychologique ou naturelle des vêtements n'a pas été ~~leur~~ ni

1116. decence, *in the original.*

1117. ~~Quote~~ ↑ Quote

1118. Les exhib[itionnisme]s à impulsion pure
   Les exhib[itionnisme]s à imp[ulsion] sexuelle
   Les exhib[itionnisme]s à imp[ulsion] vraiment exhibitionniste

1119. Here exh[ibitionis]m is an ep[isode] of the insanity

[15B³ — 43]
Exhibitionnisme Vrai [1120]

1. C'est une impulsion sexuelle.

2. C'est une impulsion d'exhiber.

3. C'est une impulsion consciente, théâtrale. [1121]

Définition. [1122] L'exhibitionnisme vrai est une impulsion sexuelle & consciente & perverse à exhiber théâtralement des organes [1123] génitaux. Il est caractérisé par un sentiment [1124] de plaisir dans cet *étalage.*

Notez bien l'étalage.

Regressivité de cette perversion — par contraste à l'inversion [1125] sexuelle, par exemple.

On pense que la pudeur domine (que l'on voit en grand nombre de gens).

L'explication: "C'est pour l'art" est déjà connue par ceux [1126] qui l'ont inventée: hystérisme.

1120. *Ex*[*hibitionnisme*] *Vrai*

1121. théatrale.

1122. *Déf*[*inition*].

1123. impulsion ~~conse~~ ↑ sexuelle & consciente ↑ † ↓ & perverse / ↑ ∴ [cependant] † social N.\ à exhiber ↑ théâtralement [l|d]es organes

1124. Sent[iment]

1125. àse ~~le~~ l'inversion

1126. par ~~les~~ ceux

Gagne pain? C'est l'excuse des souteneurs, mais elle ne l'ennoblit pas son métier.

Il y a dans l'exhibitionnisme tendance au statuesque.[1127]

[43ᵛ]

Formes

(1) antérieur

(2) postérieur

(3) seins. (femmes)

———————

(1) À un individu.

(2) Publiquement[1128]

(3) Avec éclat (exhibitionnisme social).[1129]

———————

Si par hasard il y |a| quelque homme dont l'exhibition-nisme[1130] |soit| la seul manie, et ceci sans sexualité — ce ne sera qu'un délirant.

———————

———————

1127. l'exhib[itionnisme] tendance au ‡ ↑ statuesque.

1128. À Publiquement

1129. exhibitionnisme social)

1130. l'exh[ibitionis]me

L'exhibitionnisme[1131] vrai a une base consciente et sexuelle.

———————

Le plus il pense à la perversion, le plus il se sent porté à elle.

$$[15B^3 - 44^r]$$

Pensons *au social*, par exemple, la pédérastie.[1132] Comment l'excuserait-on? Aisément: en disant que le corps masculin est plus parfait que le féminin,[1133] ou de quelque façon analogue.

On finit par croire cette explication.

———————

Soc^s: le sadisme. Dans ce cas on trouverait aussi une excuse.

———————

Cette idée sotte que l'exhibitionnisme c'est l'art est basée sur le fait de ce que c'est un étalage, et, en plus, sur la[1134] simulation.

On dit qu'il est décent. On proclame souvent: c'est indécent et voilà pourquoi nous l'aimons.

———————

1131. L'exh[ibitionnis]me

1132. péderastie, *in the original.*

1133. feminin, *in the original.*

1134. Cette /↑ sotte d' \ idée sotte que ↑ l'exhibitionnisme c'est l'art est basée sur le fait de ce que c'est un étalage, et, en plus, sur ~~ce~~ la

[15B³ — 45]

Que c'eſt ce, essentiellement, une tendance *à exhibition*.
Puisque c'eſt dans un théâtre ou hall — ceci se prouve[1135]
par soi-même. En effet, de toutes les perversions sexuelles,
l'éxhibitionnisme[1136] était naturellement indiquée com-
me la plus *scénique*. Le théâtral[1137] eſt sa nature même.

———————

Regressive

L'art eſt une idéalisation.[1138] Car le réel en soi n'eſt
pas une idéalisation. Donc ces exhibitions ne sont pas
l'*eſthétique*.

    C'eſt ainsi qu'une photographie peut être belle, mais
ce n'eſt pas de la peinture.[1139]

[45ᵛ]

1. Il n'eſt pas nécessaire de noter que dans les cas en
   queſtion il y a exhibition génitale. Passons au second
   point.

———————

1135. c'est dans une ↑un théatre ou hall — ceci se se prouve
1136. l'éxh[ibitionnisme]
1137. théatral, *in the original.*
1138. idéalization, *in the original.*
1139. de l['art|a] peinture.

2. *Il y a impulsion* (impulsion[1140] morbide, bien entendu). Admettons qu'il n'y a pas. Qu'est-ce qui pourrait produire cette action?[1141] Gagne-pain?

3. *Que cette impulsion[1142] est sexuelle.* Étant donnée l'impulsion, elle ne peut être que sexuelle.

4. *Que cette impulsion est consciente.*

5. Que cette impulsion est perverse.[1143]

$$[15B^3 - 46]$$

Si l'exhibitionnisme[1144] est esthétique, cette description d'une chambre est admirable de réalisme artistique:

Dimension 7^m x 4^m x 5^m

Plafond en blanc.

Papier bleu *&* blanc.

Un lit

Un □ [1145]

Un vase de nuit dans le □ susdit

Voilà de l'art.[1146]

─────────────

1140. imp[ulsion]

1141. n'y a / ↑ en ait \ pas. Qu'est-ce qui pourrait produire cette ~~exhibitionnisme~~ action?

1142. *imp[ulsio]n*

1143. 4. *Que c[ette] i[mpulsion] est consciente.*
   5. Que c[ette] i[mpulsion] est perverse

1144. l'exh[ibitionnisme]

Nous aurons bientôt d'idiots qui mettront des photographies dans les romans au lieu des descriptions. Il y en aura peut-être qui ne sait composer que des photographies. Le meilleur serait de ne pas[1147] illustrer ce volume-là.

[15B³ — 47]

Il y a 2 choses dans l'exhibitionnisme; un *étalage* & une *perversion consciente*. (Tous 2 hystériques).

On a conscience de la perversion de cet étalage en tant que perversion.

[15B³ — 48]

Cas d'Exhibitionnisme[1148]

Aimer à voir une action, un état d'être,[1149] c'est le point initial d'aimer à la faire. Car aimer à voir, c'est trouver agréable et trouver agréable c'est trouver bon à faire.

1145. Papier ~~bleu~~ ↑ bleu & blanc.
~~Une~~ ↑Deux ~~table~~ Un lit
~~Quatre chaises~~ Un □

1146. Voilà / ↑ oici \ de l'art.

1147. peut-être ↑qui ne sait composer que des photographies. ~~Le p~~
Le meilleur serait de / ↑ 'avenir voudrait \ ne pas

1148. d'Exhib[itionnis]me

1149. état / ↑ façon \ d'être,

L'homme qui aime à voir des cruatés est cruel, quelle que soit[1150] l'exteriorité de son caractère. L'homme qui aime à voir faire le bien est instinctivement bon.

Il est donc claire que l'homme qui aime à voir l'exhibitionnisme sexuel est mentalement un exhibitionniste.

[15B³ — 49]

Cette dégénérescence[1151] hypocrite, car elle n'est pas franche dans son vice, mais[1152] cherche des arguments pour l'appeler vertu.

Des Cas d'Exhibitionnisme.

———

Ce n'est qu'une sexualisation[1153] de l'art, mettant l'instinct sexuel au lieu de l'instinct esthétique — pourtant, réversion de l'art, *dégénérescence.*[1154]

———

1150. que ~~en~~ ↑soit
1151. degenerescence, *in the original.*
1152. ~~et~~ mais
1153. sexualization, *in the original.*
1154. *Degenerescence, in the original.*

3.2 — Further Fragments Concerning "La France en 1950"

[133F — 38]

J'ai été l'autre jour à voir une école de demoiselles. Le nom de l'école est "Institut Sans Hymen." Il a été fondé, me dit-on, par une bénémérite qui avait eu 14 mille amants & qui est morte, à ce qu'il paraît de son dévouement.

Les jeunes filles dans ce pensionnat sont très bien élevées. Elles apprennent le plus des vices possible, et il est vraiment charmant de voir avec quelle facilité les chères petites dindes les apprennent!

Les punitions — il est vrai — ne sont pas très légè-res;[1155] par exemple, une petite fille qui a un peu crié parce que[1156] une autre l'a employée pour quelque acte de sa-disme a été condamnée[1157] par un conseil de professeurs à n'avoir que 3 amants et[1158] 6 amantes et à mettre un vête-ment de façon à ne laisser voir que[1159] la partie supérieure du corps! C'est horrible!

Une autre a été punie □

Ces punitions ont soulevé beaucoup d'indignation publique et il y a eu une grève des employés des postes.

———

1155. pas ~~trop~~ très legères;
1156. a ↑un peu crié parceque
1157. a été ~~punie avec a~~ condamnée
1158. e[t]
1159. voir /↑entrevoir\ que

[38ᵛ]

Mme. Jérébite[1160] Jaudasamier a été mise en prison parce que,[1161] à ce que l'on dit, elle a commis le crime de pudeur, ayant, dit-on, rougie légèrement[1162] à cause d'un homme & 5 femmes qui étaient couchés sur le pavé. Elle a nié son crime.

Mlle □ a été condamnée à 4 jours de[1163] chasteté pour s'avoir refuser, dit-on, à se livrer à ses fils en même temps.

M. □ a été □ devant le tribunal parce que[1164] sa fille, ayant déjà 2 jours, il ne l'a pas encore violée.

M & Mme[1165] □ ont été condamnés à ne se donner que des baisers pendant une heure et demie pour avoir commis la perversité de faire l'acte sexuel à l'ancienne façon. À leur sorties du tribunal de peuple s'est manifesté très violent et on a entendu dire sur eux des[1166] mots tels que "gens vertueux" &[1167] même, on a honte de l'écrire, "pudiques."

Le crime, suivant ce que l'on dit, a beaucoup |diminué|; on ne constate un crime qu'en cas d'attentat à l'indécence.

1160. ~~Mlle~~ ↑ Mme Jérébite
1161. parceque, *in the original.*
1162. legèrement, *in the original.*
1163. à [5|4] ~~ans~~ ↑ 4 jours de
1164. parceque, *in the original.*
1165. M & ~~Mme~~ Mme
1166. dire ↑ sur eux des
1167. ~~dans~~ ↑ &

[133F — 47]

Ministère

École □ pénalités

Le garçon qui parle pendant la leçon est défendu de se masturber plus de 2 fois par jour.

Attentat à l'indécence

―――――――――――

2nd letter.

No such country there □

There is actually a country here in the old place, but it is no longer called France and it is a province of another country: the people like sex enough. Statues have been raised to □

[47^v]

Maudit celui qui en rira !

Honni soit qui en rira !

Malheur à celui qui [1168] en rira ! [1169]

―――――――――――

Le Lear

―――――――――――

1168. q[ui]

1169. ↓ ~~This prophecy Merlin shall make for I have before time~~

394

3.3 — Further Fragments Concerning "Messieurs les Souteneurs"

$$[14^3 - 84]$$

J'ai entendu conter il y a peu de temps l'anecdote qu'une sage-femme[1170] ayant par négligence mis un enfant au lit la tête en bas et ceux que venaient n'en ayant vu que le derrière, ceux-ci[1171] se seraient retirés pleins d' horreur de la monstruosité qui venait d'être mise au monde. Comme on le voit, l'anecdote est très probable mais dans ce cas-ci elle est superlativement instructive.

Car je conviens qu'autant que le derrière de l'enfant susdit était sa figure, le cerveau de Paris est digne du nom de cerveau de l'Europe. La belle □![1172]

1170. qu[e|'] lune ~~nourrice~~ ↑‡ sage-femme

1171. et ~~les~~ ceux que venaient n'en ayant vu que le ~~cul~~ ↑derrière, ceux-ci

1172. qu'autant ↑que le ~~cul~~ ↑derrière de l'enfant susdit était sa figure, le cerveau /↑la ville\ de Paris est digne du nom de /↑le\ cerveau de l'Europe. La belle □!

   ~~C'est donc le propre du cerveau de contenir de la merde?~~

[84ᵛ]

Je vois où tend le monde littéraire tout entier: à faire le roman sur le De modo Cacandi de Tartaretus.

Answer to them: Consider self not great, but, certainly, greater than them all. Moral and social respect. Pity them universally and undoubtedly. My own case *&* my own tendencies.

J'avais lu ces livres et, sentant [1173] ce qu'ils faisaient en moi, flairant en moi le commencement de la corruption, je me suis révolté, indigné, d'abord contre moi-même, puis contre ces écrivains.

Je le confesse, sans pénitence aucune, je suis entièrement un révolté, je ne me révolte que contre [1174] le mal. C'est pour cette raison que je m'appelle révolté; si j'étais comme la plus grande partie des révoltés ☐

1173. ~~sentait~~ sentant
1174. je ↑ne me révolte ↑que contre

[14³ — 85]

Statuts de la Compagnie de Pornographie, de Sottise & de Merderie.

Société Anonyme de Responsabilité très limitèe.

Conseil d'Administration: [1175]
MM. Anatole France (and others of name)
par-devant le notaire du monde M.
□ année
La responsabilité [1176] □ (et même de tous concernés) est extrêmement limitée.

[133F — 40]

Le titre réel de cette société sera "Société Pornographie, Merde & Sottise." Mais on emploiera comme [1177] firme "Compagnie pour l'embellissement du Monde."

Directeur [1178]
Secrétaire: M. V. de Saussay

Relatoire (aussi).

1175. ~~Directeurs:~~
     ~~MM. Anato~~
     Conseil
1176. resp[onsabilité]
1177. titre ~~officiel~~ réel de cette société sera "S[ociété]. Por[nographie], Merde & Soutise." Mais on ~~pe~~ emploiera ~~la~~ comme
1178. D[irecteur]

Il est à supposer que les nombreux attentats contre la pudeur, □ sont dus à la bénéfique influence de la Compagnie. On[1179] doit très spécialement noter les viols d'enfants, indication indubitable du progrès: la Compagnie espère qu'elle n'aurait[1180] été sans influence dans ces évènements. On peut toutefois constater que le nombre des délits sexuels (ainsi on les appelle quelque fois) est[1181] encore très petit, étant, à ce que l'on croit, inférieur au nombre des morts (décès). C'est une chose à laquelle il faudra penser.[1182]

1179. ~~On Les~~ On

1180. la Comp[agnie] espère qu'elle ~~ne ser~~ n'aurait

1181. sexuels ↑ (ainsi on les appelle quelque fois) est

1182. faudra / ↓ faut \ penser.

4.1 — Fragments of "The Student of Salamanca" Signed by Alexander Search

[74A — 64–66a]

The Student of
Salamanca.

Part I.

Espronceda

translated by

Alexander *Search*.

[65ʳ]

The Student of Salamanca.
Part the first.

> His titles his courage
> His parchments his own will.
> Don Quixote — Part I.

'Twas more than the hour of midnight,
As is told by ancient stories,
When all in sleep and in silence
Enwrapped is earth and gloomy,
When the living seem but dead men
And the dead their graves relinquish.
It was that hour when perchance
Terror-hushed voices formless
Sound, and trembling ears may listen
To still and hollow foot falls,
And when mute and dreadful phantoms
In the |ill-penetrable| darkness
Wander vaguely, and the watch-dogs
Mark with fearful howls their passing:
When haply the bell unswinging
Within some ruined church-belfry
Yieldeth full mysterious soundings

[66ʳ]

|Of curse and of malediction,|
That on |Saturdays| doth summon
The witches to their dread feast.
The sky was unfair and gloomed,
And not a star woke its shrouding,
The wind howled drearily
|And yonder in air like phantoms| ¹¹⁸³
Blackly in the night upjutted
Solemnly lovely church-towers,
And of the ancient Gothic castle
The highly-built battlements,
Where haply singeth or prayeth
In his cumbrous fear the sentry.
|In fire, at the hour of midnight|
All rested, and of its living
Lock'd in their slumber was a tomb, that
Ancient city by whose walls
Rolleth Tormès, fruitful river
In poetic love remembered,
Widely-famed Salamanca,
Renowned in arm and in letters,
Mother of illustrious men,
Of sciences noble storehouse.
Suddenly of swords the dashing

1183. air ᐟ ↑ in the mute ?! air \ like

[67ʳ]

[E-1-3]

Soundeth, and a moan is heard;
A moan of death-toil, a moan
That pierceth unto the heart,
That unto the marrow chilleth
And makes tremble him that heard it,
The moan of one that is giving
To the world his laſt farewell.

The sound,
Is done,
A man
Pass'd on
Cloak'd full,
And his hat
Careful
Drew his eyes
Upon.
He glideth
Close-press'd
'gainſt the wall
Of a church,
And in shadow
Is gone.

[68ʳ]

A narrow street and high-stretching,
La Calle del Ataud,[1184]
As if of black crape the blackest
A gloomy eternal hood
Covered it, always in darkness
And at night not lighted move
Than by the lamp that |illumines|
Of Jesus an image mall,
The masked wanderer doth traverse
Holding yet in hand his sword
Which threw back a sudden lightning
In passing before the cross.

As hiding the moon when a cloud all of blackness
With luring of silver's embroidered |around|,
And when the wind stirs it 'tis torn into darkness
And lo! to white vapour in air 'tis unbound:

E'en so, a vague phantom of dark *&* of lightness,
A doubtful and airy, weird vision doth gleam
A moment, then hide it the clouds in their rightness
Too like a sweet hope or a joy that did seem;

The street all in darkness, the night come already,
The lamplet with sadness whose flame is now spent,

1184. /←Lit. *Coffin Street* \. *La Calle del Ataud,*

[69ʳ]

[E-I-5]

At times that upplanning the image lights ſteady,
Than shrinketh and hideth the night to augment.

The nightly, vague phantom awhile that appeareth,
And then with rapid dread footſtep comes on,
And then in the darkness awhile disappeareth
Like the piercing shadow of one who is gone|,|

The ſpirit the boldeſt of ſteel to withſtand it
Had shrunk into caution, had ſtricken with fear;
The fierceſt, moſt cursing and blaſphemous bandit
Had felt with its terror his lips find a prayer.

But not to the masked one, whose sword though yet dripping
Hot blood, did the phantom inſpire fear and dread,
But the weapon in hand with a ſtrong firmness gripping,
With boldness to meet it and slow did he tread.

Don Juan Tenorio the second,
A proud and insolent ſpirit,
Impious, in courage his merit,
Quarrelsome in deed and word,
Always insult in his glances,
His lips e'er irony bearing,
Fearing nought, all things referring

[69a^r]

[E-I-6]

To his valour & his sword.

A corrupted soul that sneereth
At me he courts, as if prizing,
He leaveth, to-day deſpising,
Her who was his yeſterday.
Never a fear for the future,
Nor fear the paſt ever sadden'd
By thoughts of her he abandoned
Nor of money loſt at |play|. [1185]

Ne'er in dreams he saw the phantom
Of him in duel his victim,
Nor fearful care to afflict him
His fearlessness never woke.
Always in gambles, in |*loves|,
Always in bacchical orgies,
An impious ſpeaking he merges [1186]
A blaſphemy in a joke.

Famous in all Salamanca
For his beauty and life imprudent,
As the bold, the fearless ſtudent
Among a thousand he's known;
To all his boldness entitles,

1185. By thoughts of her / ↑woman\ he abandoned
　　　Nor / ↓or\ of money lost at |play| / ↑ gambled away\.
1186. An impious speaking / ↑ impiously speaking\ he

[68aʳ]

[E-I-7]

And for all his wealth, his nature
Of noble, generous feature,
And manly beauty atone.

Thou whom in arrogance and vices
And bearing noble and knightly,
Courage and grace none so brightly[1187]
Can shine or equal by far:
For in his crimes very blackest,
Haughtiness and impious candour
Yet doth set a seal of grandeur
Don Felix de Montemar.

Beautiful, purer than the sky's pure blue
With sweet and languid eyes tenderly bright
Where haply love hath share the soft veil through
Of modesty that hides their soul's delight,
A timid star doth reflect unto
The earth brilliant and doubtful rays of light,
Love's angel pure, love to inspire unsated
Such was Elvira innocent, ill-fated.

Elvira, that was once the student's love,
Happy & proud in her love's tender glows,
Where first her heart did hope, when love did move,[1188]

1187. so /↑mere\ brightly

[67aʳ]

[E-I-8]

As to the sun's warm ray the timely use,
Of the false lover who such sweetness wove
She the false honey pain his lips that flows
Gulps in her ardent thirſt, her breaſt unthinking
That poison hid in honey she is drinking.

Not more serenely in its mother's arms
The tender infant doth its reſt receive
Than she in the false net and full of charms
Her knowing lover cunningly doth weave
Caresses sweet, embraces, soft alarms,
Pleasures — alas! — which but a moment live
Elvira thinks eternally will shine
In her illusion childlike and divine.

The virgin soul a pleasure did caress
With a sweet dream within its purity
Wreathes all about with truth & holiness,
Thinketh in all virtue & charm to be.
In the blue sky's immense and ſpangled dress,
In the sun's deathless wealth she more doth see
And deep in air and fields & flowers sweet-scented
Their ſplendour, colour, life she sees augmented.

All in Don Felix lays the unhappy maid

1188. did ~~hope~~ ↑ [h]ope, when

[68aʳ]

[E-I-9]

Her happiness in love unquestioning
Unto her eyes his eyes that love betrayed
Are stars of glory, life's translated spring.
And when his lips unto her lips are laid
When she to his voice wrapt is listening,
Soul-drunken of the god her heart that moves
She eyes him sweetly and ecstatic loves.

BIBLIOGRAPHY

Paulo Borges, Nuno Ribeiro, Cláudia Souza (eds), *Nietzsche, Pessoa e Freud* (Lisbon: Centro de Filosofia da Universidade de Lisboa, 2013).

António de Pina Coelho, *Os Fundamentos Filosóficos da Obra de Fernando Pessoa, Vols I e II* (Lisbon: Editorial Verbo, 1971).

Luísa Freire, *Fernando Pessoa Entre Vozes, Entre Línguas* (Lisbon: Assírio & Alvim, 2004).

Aníbal Frias, "Pessoa à Coimbra et Coimbra dans Pessoa," *Biblos, VII* (Coimbra: Faculdade de Letras da Universidade de Coimbra, 2009) 363–387.

Kenneth Krabbenhoft, *Fernando Pessoa e as Doenças do fim de Século* (Lisbon: Imprensa Nacional-Casa da Moeda, 2011).

Teresa Rita Lopes (org.), *Pessoa Inédito* (Lisbon: Livros Horizonte, 1993).

———, *Pessoa por Conhecer, Vols I e II* (Lisbon: Editorial Estampa, 1990).

Pablo Javier Pérez Lopez, *Poesía, Ontología y Tragedia en Fernando Pessoa* (Madrid: Editorial Manuscritos, 2012).

Fernando Cabral Martins (org.), *Dicionário de Fernando Pessoa e do Modernismo Português* (Lisbon: Editorial Caminho, 2008).

José Paulo Cavalcanti Filho, *Fernando Pessoa: uma quase autobiografia* (Rio de Janeiro/ São Paulo: Ediora Record, 2011).

George Monteiro, *The Presence of Pessoa: English, American, Southern African Responses* (Kentucky: University Press of Kentucky, 1998).

Fernando Pessoa, *Cadernos — Tomo I*, ed. by Jerónimo Pizarro (Lisbon: Imprensa Nacional-Casa da Moeda, 2009).

———, *Escritos Autobiográficos, Automáticos e de Reflexão Pessoal*, ed. by Richard Zenith (Lisbon: Assírio & Alvim, 2003).

———, *Escritos sobre Génio e Loucura, Vols I e II*, ed. by Jerónimo Pizarro (Lisbon: Imprensa Nacional-Casa da Moeda, 2006).

———, *Eu sou uma antologia: 136 autores fictícios*, ed. by Jeronimo Pizarro and Patricio Ferrari (Lisbon: Tinta da China, 2013).

———, *Moral, Regras de Vida, Condições de Iniciação*, ed. by Pedro Teixeira da Mota (Lisbon: Edições Manuel Lencastre, 1988).

———, *O Marinheiro*, ed. by Cláudia Souza (Lisbon: Ática, 2010).

———, *Obra Poética e em Prosa, Vols I, II, & III*, org. by António Quadros (Porto: Lello & Irmãos, 1986).

———, *Obras de Jean Seul de Méluret*, ed. by Rita Patrício and Jerónimo Pizarro (Lisbon: Imprensa Nacional-Casa da Moeda, 2006).

———, *Páginas Íntimas e de Auto-Interpretação*, ed. and with a preface by Georg Rudolf Lind & Jacinto do Prado Coelho (Lisbon: Ática, 1966).

———, *Páginas de Estética e de Teoria e Crítica Literárias*, ed. by Georg Rudolf Lind and Jacinto do Prado Coelho (Lisbon: Ática, 1994).

———, *Philosophical Essays: A Critical Edition*, ed. by Nuno Ribeiro (New York: Contra Mundum Press, 2012).

———, *Poemas Ingleses — Antinous, Inscriptions, Epithalamium, 35 Sonnets. Tomo I. Vol. V*, ed. by João Dionísio (Lisbon: Imprensa Nacional-Casa da Moeda, 1993).

———, *Poemas Ingleses — Poemas de Alexander Search, Tomo II, Vol. V*, ed. by João Dionísio (Lisbon: Imprensa Nacional-Casa da Moeda, 1997).

——— (Alexander Search), *Poesia*, ed. & tr. by Luísa Freire (Lisbon: Assírio & Alvim, 2000).

———, *Poesia Inglesa I*, ed. and tr. by Luísa Freire (Lisbon: Assírio & Alvim, 2000).

———, *Poesia Inglesa II*, ed. and tr. by Luísa Freire (Lisbon: Assírio & Alvim, 2000).

——, *Poesia Íntima e de Autoconhecimento*, ed. by Richard Zenith (Lisbon: Assírio & Alvim, 2007).

——, *Selected Prose of Fernando Pessoa*, ed. and tr. by Richard Zenith (New York: Grove Press, 2001).

——, "Tábua Bibliográfica," *Presença* Nº 17 (1928).

——, *Teoria da Heteronímia*, ed. by Richard Zenith & Fernando Cabral Martins (Lisbon: Assírio & Alvim, 2013).

——, *Textos Filosóficos de Fernando Pessoa*, ed. and with a preface by António Pina Coelho, Vols I e II (Lisbon: Ática, 1968).

Jerónimo Pizarro, *Fernando Pessoa: entre génio e loucura* (Lisbon: Imprensa-Nacional Casa da Moeda, 2007).

Antero de Quental, *Os sonetos Completos de Antero de Quental*, ed. by Patricio Ferrari (Lisboa: Guimarães, 2010).

Nuno Ribeiro, Cláudia Souza, "Charles Robert Anon & Alexander Search: Filosofia e Psiquiatria," *Revista Filosófica de Coimbra*, Vol. 21, Nº 42 (Coimbra: Instituto de Estudos Filosóficos da Faculdade de Letras da Universidade de Coimbra, 2012) 541–556.

Nuno Ribeiro, *Fernando Pessoa e Nietzsche: O pensamento da pluralidade* (Lisbon: Verbo Editora, 2011).

——, "Heteronímia e Perspectivismo. 'Espaço literário' e multiplicidade de estilos nos pensamentos de Nietzsche e Pessoa," *Cadernos Nietzsche* Nº 26 (São Paulo: Grupo de Estudos Nietzsche, 2010) 155–176.

———, "O Corpo Político e a Política do Corpo em Nietzsche e Pessoa," in Paulo Borges (org.), *Olhares Europeus sobre Pessoa* (Lisbon: Centro de Filosofia da Universidade de Lisboa, 2010) 231–238.

———, "Os Livros Filosóficos Inacabados de Pessoa — Problemas e Critérios para a Publicação dos Escritos Filosóficos de Pessoa," *Philosophica* Nº 38 (Lisbon: Edições Colibri, 2011) 165–174.

———, "Pessoa, filósofo," *Revista do Centro de Estudos Portugueses*, Vol. 32, Nº 48 (Belo Horizonte: Faculdade de Letras da UFMG, 2012) 127–152.

———, "Tive em mim milhares de Filosofias" — questões para a edição dos escritos filosóficos inéditos de Pessoa," *cultura ENTRE culturas*, Nº 3 (Lisbon: Âncora Editora, 2011) 192–200.

———, *Tradição e Pluralismo nos Escritos Filosóficos de Fernando Pessoa / Escritos Filosóficos de Fernando Pessoa* (Lisbon: Faculdade de Ciências Sociais e Humanas da Universidade Nova de Lisboa, 2012).

Arnaldo Saraiva, *Fernando Pessoa Poeta Tradutor de Poetas* (Porto: Lello Editores, 1996).

João Rui de Sousa, *Fernando Pessoa — Empregado de Escritório* (Lisbon: Assírio & Alvim, 2010).

Cláudia Souza, "A estética do desassossego: Fernando Pessoa e o Romantismo alemão," *Literatura, Vazio e Danação*, org. by Osmar Pereira Oliva (Montes Claros: Editora Unimontes, 2013) 101–112.

———, *Ciências do Psiquismo Humano, Política e Criação Literária no espólio de Fernando Pessoa (1905–1914)* (Belo Horizonte, PUC: Minas Gerais, 2011).

———, "Inconsciente e Arte: um encontro entre Fernando Pessoa e Freud," *A Cultura Portuguesa no Divã*, org. by Isabel Gil and Adriana Martins (Lisbon: Universidade Católica Editora, 2011) 113–123.

———, *"Marcos Alves*, de Fernando Pessoa: entre a psiquiatria e o desassossego" *Revista do Centro de Estudos Portugueses*, Vol. 32, Nº 48 (Belo Horizonte: Faculdade de Letras da UFMG, 2012) 111–125.

Nuno Venturinha, *Lógica, Ética e Gramática — Wittgenstein e o Método da Filosofia* (Lisbon: Imprensa Nacional-Casa da Moeda, 2010).

COLOPHON

THE TRANSFORMATION BOOK
was typeset in InDesign.
The text and page numbers are set in *Adobe Jenson Pro*.
The titles are set in *Legacy Sans*.

Book design & typesetting: Alessandro Segalini

Cover design: Contra Mundum Press

Cover image: Giuseppe Arcimboldo, *Bibliotekarien*, ca. 1566.
Oil on canvas, 91 x 71 cm. Skoklosters Slott, Bålsta, Sweden.

THE TRANSFORMATION BOOK
is published by Contra Mundum Press
and printed by Lightning Source, which has received Chain of
Custody certification from: The Forest Stewardship Council,
The Programme for the Endorsement of Forest Certification,
and The Sustainable Forestry Initiative.

Contra Mundum Press   New York · Berlin

CONTRA MUNDUM PRESS

Contra Mundum Press is dedicated to the value & the
indispensable importance of the individual voice.

Contra Mundum Press will be publishing titles from all the
fields in which the genius of the age traditionally produces
the most challenging and innovative work: poetry, novels,
theatre, philosophy — including philosophy of science &
of mathematics — criticism, and essays.

Upcoming volumes include Mallarmé's *The Book*,
Oğuz Atay's *While Waiting for Fear*, &
Robert Musil's *Short Prose*.

For the complete list of forthcoming publications, please visit
our website. To be added to our mailing list, send your name
and email address to: info@contramundum.net

Contra Mundum Press
P.O. Box 1326
New York, NY 10276
USA
info@contramundum.net